SHARED
INNOCENCE

STEVE BRADSHAW

I0608453

SHARED INNOCENCE©

1st Edition 2020

FORENSIC MYSTERY/THRILLER

ISBN: 978-1-948059-59-6

Library of Congress Cataloging-in-Publication Data

SHARED INNOCENCE/Steve Bradshaw

Printed in USA

BOOKS BY STEVE BRADSHAW

The Bell Trilogy
Bluff City Butcher
The Skies Roared
Blood Lions

Evil Like Me

Serial Intent

Terminal Breach

"There are truths we have to grow into."

Orson Welles

SHARED INNOCENCE

Bullitt, Moe	**Tampa PD Homicide Detective**
Burcher, David	Jack's younger brother (Real Estate)
Burcher, Emily	Jack's grandmother
Burcher, Jack, MD	**Hillsborough County Medical Examiner**
Burcher, Leonard	Jack's uncle
Burcher, Melissa	Jack's younger sister (Ornithologist)
Burcher, Patricia	Jack's ex-wife
Burcher, Ronan, MD	Jack's father (retired ME)
Burcher, Rose	Jack's mother
Deron, (Frank) Francis	**Tampa PD Chief of Police**
Janice, William, MD	Psychiatrist, Forensic Psychologist
Mesmer, Eric, MD	Hypnotist, Psychotherapist
Novak, Hugo	Forensic Investigator
Penland, Buford	Burcher estate groundskeeper
Quin, Deborah, MD	Assistant Medical Examiner
Sato, Mamaru	Landscaper
Shuck, Paul	**Central Florida Director of the FBI**
Webster, Kayda	**Court Stenographer**
Worthington, Tate	Private Investigator

ONE

Tampa, Florida – July 14, 1970

"Stay in bed tonight," Rose whispered as she tucked in Jack. Her ten-year-old had become quite the night explorer. "Your brother and sister are sound asleep and your father's out of town just one night, young man."

A gentle breeze left Hillsborough Bay, stirred the wildflower fields on Ballast Point, lifted the window sheers, and filled the bedroom with honeysuckle and sage. She moved hair from his eyes and kissed his forehead. "I don't need any surprises tonight, my young man. I love you." She closed his door, checked on the others, and went downstairs for some quiet time.

Two hours passed. The empty bottle of Lafite Rothschild sat next to the half-empty wine glass. Beneath a jumbled pile of newspaper, Rose had sunk deep into her chair. She did not hear the phone ring the first three times. On the fourth, she reached under the only lighted lamp in the house. With her eyes still closed she breathed, "Hello."

"Hi. It's me. Sorry for the lateness." Sitting on the edge of his king bed at the Boston Downtown Marriott, Ronan kicked off his shoes and loosened his tie. He squinted at his watch for the first time all night. "Damn. I didn't realize it's after midnight, honey."

"It's okay." With one eye open she reached for her wine glass. "I'm awake, now."

"Today's sessions were excellent," he bubbled. "Damn board-of-governors dinner went way over again—happens every damn year. I just got to my room. Tinsley Swanson could not stop talkin', the egotistical boob. I don't know why I keep comin' to this conference—"

"—because it's a once a year thing and medical examiners love to talk about their most hideous cases. It's one of those— *mine's bigger than yours*—things," she teased.

"Yeah. Well, I've grown out of it then. I swear this is my last time, Rose."

"It's okay. I enjoy my quiet time. It's a beautiful night, on Ballast Point. Kids are in bed and the smell of fresh wildflowers fills the house. I'm sipping my favorite blended Cab-Merlot and enjoying the *Tampa Bay Sentinel*. You know I never get to read it without interruptions. I used to love slowly digesting the newspaper. Very medicinal." She lit a cigarette. "And if Jack stays in bed all night, everything is just perfect."

"Jack's a typical ten-year-old boy. He's curious. That's all. It's a stage."

"Well, he could fall and hurt himself climbing on that old trellis. He could break his neck. If he fell, how would I know? Every little sound gets me up to check on him—"

"—you gotta stop, Rose. Stop worrying. I had the trellis fixed last week. He can't pull it off the side of the house. I had Buford Penland personally cut back the ivy so Jack would not get his foot tangled. You know he's been the family gardener since I was a kid. He loves our family. And Jack can climb just fine. I didn't have a safe trellis when I grew up. And Otto never worried about me. There's somethin' magical about that field on summer nights. It draws a kid."

"It's not just the trellis. Our family has a lot of money, Ronan. Someone could be watching us. Someone could be waiting for an opportunity to—"

"—take one of our kids? I know, and I really don't want to go there tonight."

"Our family has two-billion dollars in assets. People know. It's in the news all the time. We're targets, Ronan. I am not at all pleased with your idea of security around here. We do not live in some middle-class neighborhood. We live on a twenty acre estate, on the bay, in an old house you refuse to update. We need more protection than a crumbling rock wall and old iron gates left open all the time. We don't have anyone watching out for us, Ronan. We don't even have a dog. At the very minimum we should not encourage Jack—"

"—to explore at night. I agree. I do not encourage him. I'm watching out for him, Rose. And I'm letting him grow up like a normal kid." Ronan looked out the hotel window at the towering brick wall. "The real world closes in on us soon enough," he muttered. "So, what if our boy sits in a field in the middle of the night with his dreams. The only thing he's gotta worry about out there are the mosquitos."

"I understand the *exploring-boy* thing. I'm a mother. I'm saying I worry about Jack out there alone, in the middle of the night exposed to unknowns. How can you be so smart and not see this? We need security. I should feel safe, in my own home. I felt eyes on me all week. I'm not imagining it. Someone's watching our family. They probably know you're out of town. It was in the newspaper—your big conference in Boston. Billionaires have security, Ronan. Add to that you're a medical examiner handling homicides every day. Evil people take kids—"

"—and when I get home, I will fix it." Ronan lit a cigarette and looked at his briefcase stuffed with presentations. "One session dealt with the new exposures medical examiners and their families face today. Pretty bad things, Rose. No. Tonight you did not need to say anything about our security. My eyes have been opened. It's the '70s. The world's changing. I realized today I cannot keep our home like it was when I was a kid. I'm sorry it took this for me to get it."

"You see terrible things every day, Ronan. Your word is final. It changes people's lives. To most it's for the good. But to some it's for the bad. As Hillsborough County Chief Medical Examiner, you are revered by most living in this city. I worry about the bad people out there that despise you, Ronan. They know where you live. They know you have a family. They know you have a lot of money. If just one of those bad people decides they want to hurt you, then God only knows what they are capable of doing if given the chance."

"We're in agreement, Rose. Can we please change the subject before we say goodnight? We need to slow down our heart rates. Tell me what you read in the *Sentinel* today."

She scanned the jumbled pile and grabbed a section. "Actually, not much happened around here. The Atlantic Bank's under investigation for fraud. Circus animals paraded down Main Street and backed up traffic—one of the elephants got loose. Sears is expanding. And the Park Tower building downtown got some architectural-design award."

"Sounds exciting," he teased. "What about my area of interest?"

"No homicides, dear. And no accidental deaths. Nothing in the county. I guess you picked a good day to play hooky. Didn't miss one juicy forensic mystery."

"Well that's good to know. I guess my job is safe."

Rose flipped a few pages and took another sip of wine. "There's a whole page dedicated to Lieutenant General Leslie Richard Groves, Jr. The man died. Says he was one of the bigwigs that oversaw the construction of the Pentagon in Washington DC."

"Must have been a really slow news day. One way to get a page dedicated to you."

She ran a finger down the article. "Says he directed the Manhattan Project."

"That's newsworthy. Now I remember Leslie Groves. He was one of the brains assigned to that top-secret project during World War II—development of the atomic bomb. It's a shame he died. He will be missed. A very smart man, and an American hero."

"I don't think bringing the *atomic bomb* into the world makes one an American hero?"

"There are good people on both sides of that debate, Rose. World War II was terrible for everyone. The bomb did bring a bad thing to an end."

She leaned closer to the newspaper. "Says he died on July 13; a heart attack caused by chronic cal-ci-fi-ca-tion of the aortic valve. He was 73."

"Aortic stenosis," Ronan said. "It's an associated condition to one of the most common degenerative disease— atherosclerosis. It's the one that gets most of us, in the end."

"Lieutenant General Groves was taken to Walter Reed where he died yesterday. Says he'll be buried in Arlington Cemetery." A door whined. Rose turned an ear to the dark hall to the back staircase off the kitchen. "Better go," she whispered. "I think our son's on the move. He may be sneaking out the kitchen door."

Ronan chuckled. "Probably hasn't discovered the fixed

trellis. See. He is a smart kid. After you get him back to bed, I want *you* to go to bed too. Know that your worry-days are over. I'll be home tomorrow afternoon. We'll take care of the family security. I promise."

"Thank you. Okay. I love you. I'll see you tomorrow." Rose placed the handset on the cradle. A second whine floated into the room. This time it came from one of the many warped floorboards, but Jack knew them all. *You're off your game tonight, son,* she thought.

"Jack. Is that you? Are you out of your bed?" She called out.

Nothing...

"It will be better for you to speak up now, young man."

Nothing...

She downed her last inch of wine and tossed the newspaper onto the sofa. *I gotta leave the comfort of my chair and only light burning in the house...* Her bare feet inched along the cold wood floor to the edge of the hall. She leaned into the dark abyss. "Jackson Ronan Burcher, show yourself this minute," she called out. "I mean it. I am not pleased. I told you to—"

—maybe you're already outside. She blindly fingered the wall for the light switch.

An arm fell from the dark. It wrapped around her. Like a python it squeezed the air from her lungs, and then lifted her off the floor. A hand covered her mouth and nose, and forced her head back, and exposed her throat. Rose kicked and twisted and squealed, but before she could grasp the terror, a crushing blow to the head ended everything.

Curtains lifted and floorboards whined. A blood trail crossed the wood slats and kitchen tiles and front porch steps. Like a bent rolled rug her lifeless body hung over the shoulder of a monster. They moved in the night fog toward the open gates and a long, gray tube with fins. It growled and hovered inches above the ground.

The unusual sound caught the interest of the ten-year-old boy lying in the wildflowers a hundred feet away. He had used the trellis Buford fixed the day before. His father said he could go out at night, but he had to be quiet—so as not to worry his mother. Most nights he sat in his matted nest and stared at the stars—*how could life be restricted to just one tiny dot in the vast, unending universe?* Jack's ten-year-old imagination, and his insatiable curiosity, often made it hard to separate fantasy from reality. On the night his mother disappeared, the growling sound broke from the cicada screams. It had to be real, an unexpected visitor to Ballast Point.

He had seen it before, in the movies. But this time he saw it with his own eyes a hundred feet away. He never thought it would happen on Ballast Point, but it did. There it was. The flying saucer emerged from the fog in a flash of white light—a long, gray tube with big fins and black windows on the top. It floated in the night fog on the other side of the opened gates.

From his secret nest he watched it float a long time. He would not get closer—he did not want to be abducted by aliens. He watched as it started to move. It sunk back into the fog. After another flash of white light, the UFO vanished. Jack ran to the spot where it had hovered seconds before. Standing there, the swirling leaves fell like confetti and settled to the ground around him.

When the police came, they told Jack his mother had been taken. Jack tried to tell them about the visitor at the gates, but Detective Francis Deron would not listen to the ramblings of a traumatized ten-year-old boy—especially one known for his wild imagination. Deron told Jack a UFO did not land on Ballast Point, in the early morning hours of July 14, 1970, and aliens did not abduct his mother.

The night she disappeared Jack was confined to his bedroom and the Tampa PD and Central-Florida branch of the FBI launched a five-county search for the kidnapped billionaire heiress. They set up the call-tracking center in the Burcher's kitchen. A small army watched the phone. They waited for a ransom call that would never come.

On the next night—July 15, 1970—Jack left his room his way. He climbed down the trellis and returned to his place in the field by the house. This time he did not look at the stars and dream the dreams of a boy. This time he struggled with a new kind of pain and confusion and terror. *Who took my mother and why? Did the aliens come for her? Why didn't I do something to save her? What kind of person am I...?*

Struggling with new burdens, Jack sat in the field of wildflowers. And then he heard the rolling growl and saw the flash of white light. *Am I* asleep, he wondered? *Am I dreaming? I gotta grow up. I gotta do something to find my mother.*

"Mom," he whispered. With his head low, he parted the wildflowers and saw the long, gray tube. It hovered in the same place. *How long have you been here? Should I tell someone?*

There were two shadows. They stood on the edge of the driveway under the trees. One held a box. *Where did you come from? Are you going to or coming from my house? Why can't I see? Why am I confused.* Jack sank back into the weeds. He slapped his face and pinched his arm. *Wake up. Wake up. Pay attention.* He rubbed his eyes and spit on his hands. *Think! It's gotta make sense. Police are in the kitchen. You gotta be with them. But what about the growling thing outside the gates? The police weren't here last night, and you were. Did you take—?*

His hands trembled. He buried his head in his hands. *Please God. I don't want to be taken by aliens, but I do want you to make them give back my mother.* He took a deep breath and parted the wildflowers again. He looked past the opened gates at the gray tube. *There are still two of you. What are you doing? Why are you walking back and forth at the end of the driveway? Why are you moving a box around, to different places?*

Jack sank back down. *I gotta talk to them. I gotta ask 'em to give me my mom.* Minutes passed as he searched for the courage. He stuck his head out one more time. *Why do you have a shovel? Is he holding a potted plant, a bush?* Jack sank again. *I gotta do this.* More time passed. Then the rumbling growl got louder. He saw the flash of light—gone.

On the second night, Jack told the police about the box. He also told them about the two aliens and UFO. Detective Deron only smiled. He had no questions. They did not tell Jack what they had found inside the box delivered to the end of the Burcher's driveway. On that night, the search for Rose Burcher changed. The TPD and FBI took the box with them. They removed the phone-tracking equipment and left the Burcher estate. On that night, they put a needle in Ronan Burcher's arm and took him away by ambulance. Even after Jack's father returned home, Jack would be alone. The rest of his life. Except for the ten-year-old boy that now lived inside him—the boy who saw everything the night his mother was abducted by aliens.

THIRTY-THREE YEARS LATER

TWO

Sun Bay Nursing Care Center – September 9, 2003 – 19:00

"Are you going in?" asked the pushy nurse with the cluttered food tray.

Jack stood outside his father's room, his nose to the small window. He did not turn from his private moment. "When I'm ready," he said steaming the glass. *Pop's not going anywhere*, he mused. With a huff, the nurse pivoted and rattled her tray down the hall.

Family visitations trumped everything at the Sun Bay Nursing Care & Rehabilitation Center, one of the most advanced convalescent facilities in Florida. But, Ronan Burcher, Sr. would not benefit from any of the state-of-the-art treatment protocols. His decline left no options. He had been admitted eight years earlier. The family wanted their patriarch nearby, comfortable, and in a secured facility. Money was no object.

The well-dressed businessman in his mid-thirties eased up behind Jack Burcher and peered over his shoulder into the small window. "Heard the old man had a bad day."

Still not turning Jack said, "So you got the call, too?"

"Mel was a bit more agitated than usual. She's convinced something new is going on with Pop. I suppose it's possible."

"Maybe we can help sort things out."

"You're the doctor. I'm just a real estate guy."

Jack turned to his younger brother. "I'm a forensic pathologist, David. Everyone I deal with is dead."

"Okay. Point taken. But you do understand all that medical mumbo-jumbo. I don't have a clue about any of it." He loosened his tie and leaned closer. "Pop seems even more distant just standing there like that. Something's bothering him. You think it's possible to communicate some with him tonight? You know, the Parkinson's and all—"

"Yes. I do," Jack sighed. "We should be able to for a while longer, but stage-3 dementia does complicate things. It's been eight years." *A very slow process for all of us.* "We're losing him physically and mentally. He'll have fewer moments of clarity each day."

"You mean those rare, lucid swings into the real world?"

Jack rubbed his chin half listening. "Yeah, swings." He leaned closer. "It's disturbing he's not moved from the window since I arrived. Been almost ten minutes. He's fixated."

"You can see most of the Hillsborough Bay from there. Even now. After sundown."

What are you looking at, Jack wondered, as he stared at the man he was losing?

"Melissa said he started talkin' about mother again, and Uncle Leonard. This time he said their deaths are connected. I don't know how Uncle Leonard dying in a car wreck in 1948 ties to mother's abduction in 1970. One's an accident and the other's—"

"—an unsolved mystery." Jack rubbed the back of his neck and studied his father like one of his forensic puzzles. "We don't know much about Leonard's accident. And we'll forever be haunted by mother's disappearance and, you know. Anyway, the two events may be Pop's most painful memories— loss of an only brother and a wife. It's possible the two have merged in his private world. Now they are one terrible nightmare."

"That could explain why he hasn't thrown in Aunt Caroline—her suicide in '75—and Uncle Harold's bizarre death in '78."

"Caroline and Harold Lawton are not his blood," Jack muttered. "They're mother's."

"Still doesn't explain the other things he was saying, according to Mel. He thinks he's next on the list. Pop said someone's comin' for 'em."

"Really? That is new." Jack stood on his toes to see the crumpled newspaper hanging from Ronan's trembling fist. "Did Mel bring Pop a paper today?"

"Yeah. She brings him one every time she comes. He seems to have an interest in the news. Puts on his glasses and fans through the paper like he's lookin' for somethin'. I think he's just goin' through one of his routines, life before Parkinson's."

"Before it robbed him," Jack huffed. "I've been so busy I did not even know my dying father got some degree of pleasure from a newspaper."

"Whoa, Dr. Jackson R. Burcher. Do not go there. Do not start with the blame game again. You're a busy man. The Hillsborough County Chief Medical Examiner cannot just drop things whenever he wants. Unlike me and Melissa, you have real deadlines. Families, cops, and courts are waiting on you, Jack. They expect answers when people die. It's no different from when Pop was the Chief M.E. around here. Back then he lived the same kind of life you live now. Don't fight me on this, my brother. You know that is a damn fact."

"No. I do not. In his prime, Ronan had way better control."

"Not true. Nothing more than you do now. Pop was forced to step down in '94 because of Parkinson's. You took things over in '95 because Hillsborough County wouldn't take *no* for an answer. You caved and we were glad you did. The job's right for you, Jack. You made Pop proud. I think it allowed him to face his inner demons, especially blaming himself for the loss of mother. He never forgave himself for not protecting her. The damn house unsecure and all."

"It's not that."

"You can't keep beating yourself up." David turned Jack from the door window. "When mother was taken that God-awful night in 1970, you were ten. You couldn't stop a thing. If you had tried, you would have been taken too, Jack. You wouldn't be standin' here today. Mel and I and Pop would have lost both of you that night."

"I hear you. I just don't know how to let it go," Jack sighed.

"You're a great M.E. Tampa's lucky to have you. But that damn title does not make you responsible for all of life's tragedies around here. You gotta stop with the self-flagellation, and the drinking. Both are gonna make you really sick someday."

"I know you're right but—"

"Hey, don't forget I was two and Melissa five, when they took mom. We were there too, Jack. And we didn't do a damn thing either," he poked. "We found a way to move on."

They embraced as Jack looked down the hall. The redhead nurse with the food tray leaned a grimace around the corner.

"Okay baby brother, I just got the stink eye. We best go inside before the nurse-Nazi starts throwin' knives."

The spacious, well-appointed room with the enormous picture window smelled like old urine and fresh flowers. The two rounded the bed to where Ronan stood like a statue. His eyes were locked on something outside the window.

Jack squinted at the horizon. "Looks like a fire on Bird Island. Must be a big one. I can see flames." He put his hand on his father's shoulder and squeezed gently. "Pop. The fire. Is that what's upsetting you today?"

"I bet it's been smoking all day," David said. "Sun's down. Now the flames are visible."

The east side of the ten-story Sun Bay tower gave a view of Hillsborough Bay to downtown Tampa, the main shipping lanes, and south to the Alafia River Channel. Beyond the shipping lanes Spoil Islands 2D and 3D sit on the horizon. Between them Bird Island and Sunken Island sit lower.

"The local chapter of the National Audubon Society's gonna be pretty unhappy about the fire," David scoffed. He and Jack flanked their father ready to catch him if he fell. "I think those people are way overprotective of all the bird sanctuaries around here. You'd think they'd give it a rest once in a while. It's not like the damn birds are more important than people."

"I hope Melissa's not out there with her friends," Jack breathed.

"Ornithologists are not called upon to fight fires, even on Bird Island, Jack."

"Really David," he shot back. "Our sister has official clearances to camp on those islands to do her research. Please call. I want to make sure she's safe."

"It's ringing," David had the phone to his ear."

Jack knelt and looked up into his father's hanging face. Jack saw lines of angst and twitching eyes. *You're not looking at Bird*

*Island. Or even the bay. You're looking down at the grounds of
Sun Bay from your fifth-floor observation nest.*

"Mel. David. Where are you?" he barked into his phone.
Then his tone changed. "Right. No ma'am. I understand, and
yes, I do remember. Right! Okay, Mel. Damn it. Jack just
wanted to know if— Fine then! Yes, I will tell him. We just
wanted to make sure you were— What? We are with the old
man right now. Yes, I hear you. I was gonna say somethin' but—
Okay Melissa. Goodbye." He pocketed his phone and stared
out the window.

"That went well." Jack got to his feet and studied the view
below.

"Well, I managed to piss her off. She's so bossy. A guy can't
even get a word in—"

"—edge wise." He chuckled. "You think?"

"Mel knows about the fire on Bird Island. She said it's
arson. And no, she is not there. She's on Sunken Island with a
covey of tree-huggin' bird scientists. I can't pronounce the name
of the friggin' bird they're so concerned about today. All I know
it's probably been on the planet for a million years. I do not
understand why they need our help to hatch their eggs in 2003.
Natural selection may be at work, Jack. Could be their number
is up and we are in the way."

"Right. Now focus, David. What was Melissa upset
about?"

"I forgot to tell you somethin'. She told me the old man told
her there would be a fire on Bird Island today."

"Are you serious?" Jack said. "You think maybe that
information should have been shared with me when I told you I
saw a fire on Bird Island?"

"Probably. I mean, yes. Now I do. She also said he went on
about Uncle Leonard and mother. She could not shut him up.
That's when he dropped the *firebomb*. She ignored it at the

time, but later felt she should tell us about it. Boom—there's a fire on Bird Island. Now she's freakin' out. She's convinced somethin' bad's gonna happen, and Pop knows all about it."

They turned back to Ronan. He had not moved since they arrived. A crumpled newspaper hung from his white-knuckled fist, and a fat string of saliva hung from his mouth. Jack wiped his chin. "Pop, what's going on with you today? Why're you upset? Is it the fire, or somethin' else? Talk to us, Pop. We're here to help."

"He doesn't hear you." David fiddled with the small vase of fresh flowers on the windowsill. He looked around for the *obligatory card*. "The old man's MIA today," he muttered. "What do you think? Has he lost more marbles?"

"Pop. Talk to me," Jack pushed. "Tell me what's bothering you?"

Ronan's lips started to form a word. He lifted his head. His eyes widened. He turned to Jack and shouted, "It—is—star—ting. It—is—time—ah—gain." Ronan's legs quivered. They buckled and he collapsed. On his way down, David and Jack caught him by his armpits and backed him to the edge of the bed. He sat. He hung his head like a ragdoll.

"What is *starting*?" Jack asked. "What do you mean *it is time again*, Pop?"

"I don't think he knows," David said.

Ronan lifted his head. His bloodshot eyes bulged from their sockets. He looked at the window and then at the crumpled newspaper. He started to gasp for air. His face turned beet red. A fat vessel ran down his forehead.

"He—killed—my—brother," Ronan spewed. "Made—it —look—"

"Go ahead, Pop," Jack said. "Made it look—?"

Ronan grunted, "He—took—Rose. Now—he—back—for—me. The fire. It—tells—you. It is a—sign."

"Who is 'he', Pop? Why is he coming for you?" David asked.

"My—turn—to—sac—" Ronan crashed a fist on the bed and sobbed. Then he sat up straight, as if someone put a hot knife in his back.

"You're okay, Pop," Jack whispered as he rubbed his back. "You're safe. No one can hurt you here. Tell us, who is coming. Tell us about the fire. A sign for what, Pop?"

With a surge of frightening strength, Ronan jumped to his feet. He broke free from the tight grips of his boys and pushed Jack away. David fell back on his own—cornered and on the floor, he hid behind his hands like a child at a scary movie.

Ronan changed before their eyes. He took a rigid stance and transformed into the man of thirty years ago. The steely, scrutinizing eyes. The enraged brow. The chin out. David and Jack blinked back into their childhood—the imperious Dr. Ronan Burcher now owned the room. He demanded respect and total compliance. The 2003 weakling had left the hospital room.

"I am a dead man," he bellowed. He reached for the heavens with a trembling hand. "I ask for nothing—" Ronan raised the fist with the crumpled newspaper and shook it above his head. "—for I will die like each before." His eyes froze. Then they rolled into his head. The white balls bulged from their sockets as his hard face melted like wax in the hot sun.

David and Jack watched Ronan return to his feeble state. The Parkinson's and dementia and age resumed their undeniable death grip. Ronan whimpered, squealed, and then stopped breathing. Like a dead tree in the forest, he fell backward onto his bed and didn't move.

"Holy Mother of God," David gasped. "Did the old man just croak right in front of us? I've never seen anybody—"

Jack rushed to him. He checked Ronan's pulse and listened

to his chest as David crawled to the side of the bed and got to his feet. Jack opened each lid and passed his hand over each eye. In deathly silence, he lifted Ronan's dead legs onto the bed and slid a pillow under Ronan's limp head. Jack pulled up the covers. He stopped at the neck and tucked in the old man.

"He's asleep—exhausted. He said all he's going to say tonight."

"Asleep? Jesus, Jack. What in the hell was that? The old man turned into the friggin' monster we feared as kids. And what was he ranting about? He had the fear of God in his eyes. Scared the living shi—"

The relentless nurse with the food tray pushed open the door without knocking. Jack spun around and pounced. "Ronan Burcher will not eat tonight. So, take the tray away. He is sleeping and cannot be disturbed. He needs sleep more than the food you're determined to unload. Please, leave the room. Do you understand me?

"Yes," she said, her head down. Her red hair covered most of her face.

"Return in the morning—a late breakfast," Jack ordered. "If my father is sleeping, let him sleep." *You're new*, Jack thought. *I've not seen you before.* "If anyone has questions, they can call me—Dr. Jack Burcher, the Chief Medical Examiner. Have I been clear, Miss—?"

She did not fill in the blank. She nodded and backed from the room as Jack watched the door muffle closed behind her. *I guess I wouldn't give my name either,* he fumed. He turned back to his brother. "I didn't mean to bark, but what was that all about?" he muttered.

"Forget about that. What's this all about?" David scratched his head. "The old man said he's dead, Jack. Said the one that killed Uncle Leonard took mother. And now that person is comin' for him. Pop asks for nothing—what the hell does that mean? And Bird Island. The fire is some kind of a sign? For what? How the hell did Pop even know about a fire—"

"Stop, David. It's all bizarre right now. We don't know what's going on in his head. I'm sure it can all be explained. He's in an irrational state. All of this could be as simple as a problem with his meds. A reaction. I need to check his chart and see what changed."

"Fine. But how'd he know there was gonna be a fire on Bird Island before it happened?"

"I don't know. Maybe saw smoke. You said it had probably been smoking all day. Maybe that's why he said something to Melissa. He said smoke and she heard fire. He looks out this window all day. It's all he does now. I'm sure he could pick up on the slightest change in the haze over those islands. I'll bet Melissa didn't even look out there after he said it. There're many plausible explanations for all of this. I can tell you one thing for sure. Pop did not predict a fire before it happened. That would be impossible."

"You don't know."

"Seriously. That's where you're going with this?"

"Okay. Then what about the fire being a sign?"

"I don't know what it means, David," Jack snapped.

He took a deep breath and turned to his brother. "Look, I'm sorry. We're both tired. This has been a long and strange day. I need time to review the medical aspects—where's Pop in his disease process?" Jack attempted a smile. "Let's talk tomorrow night. I've got cases stacking up. Another crazy day coming." He touched Ronan's arm. "Pop should sleep all night and most of tomorrow. I doubt he'll have the energy to get out of bed for a few days. He's very weak. When he does wake up, he won't remember any of this."

He folded Ronan's crumpled newspaper and slid it under

his arm. He glanced at the flowers on the windowsill. "Did you order the oleanders?"

Standing where he had found Ronan, Jack looked out the window and down at the busy hospital grounds—the changing of the guards. Medical staff flowed in and out of buildings to and from waiting cars. Then he saw his redhead pass under a light. *I couldn't miss that hair,* he thought. She looked back at the building. *Are you Asian? Wonderful. I bet you were just trying to do your job—a nurse's aide.* He squinted. *Maybe not fluent in the language. Probably didn't understand my subtle directives—but got my ire. The universal language. Just great. Well, still, you need to learn sometimes a nurse's agenda's not the only thing, especially in a place where the patients are on their last lap...*

"I didn't order flowers," David said as he held open the door into the hallway.

Jack perused the Sun Bay grounds from Ronan's bird nest. They moved in all directions like ants on a mound. "Okay," he muttered. "Did you find the note so we can thank whoever gave those flowers to Pop?" His eyes moved on a line from the redhead to a car parked under a giant oak tree on a side road. Jack leaned closer. He made out the old gray Cadillac with big fins and black tinted windows. His heart skipped a beat. He grabbed the windowsill to steady himself. Blood drained from his head.

"You okay?" David asked, his head leaning back into the room.

"I don't know what—" Jack took a deep breath and tried to focus on his feet. "I think I'm okay—"

"Good. If you didn't hear me, I said no note. Now, can we stop with the questions, forensic man? Let's go home. The old man's sleepin' like a kitten."

Jack swallowed hard. He patted the folded newspaper

under his arm and forced himself to look out the window one last time. "Okay," he muttered. "You're right. We should go."

I guess the flowers are from Mel, Jack thought. *She's the bird and flower person in the family.* His eyes climbed the sidewalk to the side road and the oak tree. The old Cadillac and the redhead were gone.

THREE

FBI Southeast Regional Office – September 10, 2003 – 07:00

"I'm pulling all the files and taking another look." Paul Shuck had been with the FBI twenty years, and on the Rose Burcher cold case seventeen.

"What brought this on?" Crabtree asked as he pushed over clutter and sat on the worn leather sofa. His baby face and backwards baseball cap made him look more like a high school PE teacher than FBI agent.

"I don't know, Milton." Shuck glanced at his watch—7:02 AM.

"You haven't found a thing *new* for years. It's not cold. It's a block of ice. Why now?"

"I woke up this morning with a feeling about this. I don't know why, but it has been cold long enough. Now I've got some more time. I'm gonna poke around."

"Poke around? You close the Preston Case and have

nothing to do. You don't know how to relax—Paul Shuck, the committed bachelor." Crabtree lit a cigarette. "Why don't you take a break? You're a good lookin' guy. Go meet a nice girl. Have some fun for a change."

"The Preston Case was a slam dunk. I don't need or want a break. I'm happy knowing Scott Trent Preston will spend the rest of his life behind bars with thugs."

"Thugs he screwed one way or another. I never liked him either. Back to the Rose Burcher Case. Did you ever rule out the money angle? The family's loaded."

"No. Still in the equation. The *money* lines of investigation. A pile of spaghetti."

"What kind of wealth are we talkin' about?" Crabtree asked.

"Two billion give or take a few hundred million." Shuck flipped through the file tabs in the bottom drawer of a long row of government-secured black, metal cabinets.

"Never would know by lookin' at the old mansion on the Burcher estate."

"At one time the family owned the whole Interbay Peninsula—everything above water between the Old Tampa Bay and Hillsborough Bay."

"Now they own a tiny sliver of Ballast Point on the west side of that peninsula."

"Actually, they own all of Ballast Point. They lease 90% of it."

"Lease?"

Shuck moved a stack of files to his desk and squinted at Crabtree. "They control Ballast Point with long-term lease agreements they can cancel without cause or notice. The standard terms of a Burcher lease."

"Who in their right mind would sign a deal like that?"

"People that like a lease at a cost of one dollar a year."

"Okay. Tenants accept the bizarre conditions and take the risk," Crabtree said.

"A very low risk. Burchers have never cancelled a lease."

"How'd they get their hands on so much prime real estate, in the first place."

"Many deals over many generations, Milton."

"Give me the short story."

Shuck leaned back in his swivel chair. "The Burcher family started a cigar manufacturing business in the late 1800s after the Spanish-American War. Horace Burcher was the first family patriarch in the states. He came from Poland. Organized Florida state militias that helped free Cuba, when Spain ceded to U.S. colonies in Guam, Puerto Rico, and the Philippines. The world was a very different place back then. A lot of big deals were made. A lot of—you scratch my back and I scratch yours—going on. Lifelong deals and partners.

"Horace was in the right place at the right time with the right idea. He was one of the few people that knew Cuban tobacco was *perfecto mundo*, and he did something about it— locked up a bunch of tobacco growers. The Burcher Cuban Cigar Company took off. Cuban tobacco made them billionaires."

"A Polack comes to America in the 1800s and starts a tobacco company. You can't make this stuff up. Why'd he leave his homeland in the first place?"

"It was a time of political and cultural repression in Poland. There were a lot of uprisings, deadly revolts. I can see people wanting to leave if they could find a way."

"What was it about the Cuban tobacco that made him into a billionaire?"

"Like I said. He locked up his suppliers. Horace made all his deals with the Cuban tobacco farmers. They became close friends. Got wealthy together. Horace brought in Otto Burcher, 1930. Otto took care of the company. Found new places to park money. Land has always been a limited commodity. A good investment. The value only goes up."

"So, Otto bought a lot of land in Florida with Horace's money."

"Florida and other places around the world. Land was cheap back then. Soon the family owned the Interbay Peninsula. Their only real competition was the U.S. Government. The Fed claimed land all over the country. They would grab it up as soon as they found it and could process the paper. The Feds got hold of the tip of the Interbay Peninsula before the Burchers."

"Now the Burchers own Ballast Point. What happened to all the rest of the peninsula?

Shuck slid files into his briefcase. "Over the last hundred years they traded land for other things—banking, technology, energy, commodities, and political connections. Their fortune continues to grow today with little effort."

"And the huddled masses only see the Burcher family as the beloved philanthropists of Tampa, the gracious helpers of society with their financial gifts. They are so wonderful because they give back to us, the little people."

"A bit of socialist negativity there, but yes. Something like that."

Milton blew a smoke ring across the room. "With all their connections and power, there had to be losers. The poor bastards on the bad side of the deals. The people who hate their guts. Any one of them could have kidnapped and butchered Rose Burcher in 1970."

"Clearly the Burcher family benefited from the failures of others. There are always gonna be winners and losers, Milton."

"Winners cultivate their own enemies. The question is whose been hurt enough to kill."

Paul Shuck walked over to his picture window on the 42nd floor of the Bank of America Plaza building, in downtown Tampa. He squinted at the sun above Harbour Island. Hillsborough Bay sparkled. Then he found the coastline of the Interbay Peninsula and the Ballast Point pier.

Shuck pushed his hair from his forehead and rubbed his neck. "That's why this is a difficult case. Today the Burcher family is nothin' like they were in the days of cutthroat wealth-creation. Finding and tracking a killer on a cold trail is next to impossible. It's easy to get lost on one of these bunny trails. There are a lot of losers." *Who would kill over it?* Shuck wondered.

"I don't understand. What do you mean, the family's different now?"

"They're not aggressive, self-focused elitists building an empire. Most of the family is dead. Dr. Jack Burcher is the Hillsborough County Medical Examiner. The city loves the guy. His father—Ronan—is in a nursing home with Parkinson's. The city loved him, too. He was the first medical examiner in the Tampa Bay area. Caught a lot of bad guys over a thirty-year tenure. Both Burchers helped thousands of families, who lost their loved ones."

"What about Jack's wife and his siblings?"

"His younger brother David manages the family leases and real estate on the Interbay Peninsula. He's a playboy with zero goals. Melissa is an ornithologist. She spends her life in a tent with binoculars watching birds. Neither one gives a hoot about money or power."

"Any living relatives?"

Shuck opened a file on the windowsill and flipped pages.

"Otto Burcher was born in Poland in 1907. He married Emily Monroe in 1929, and Otto came here to work with Horace. Otto and Emily had two boys, Leonard and Ronan. Leonard died in 1948, a bizarre car accident in California. And you know Ronan's story.

"He married Rose Lawton in 1959. They had Jack, Melissa, and David. Rose Lawton Burcher was abducted in 1970. Her heart was delivered to the house the very next night, in a box at the end of the driveway. Jack saw everything. He was ten. It changed his life."

"I can imagine. What about Rose's side of the family? Anything to look at there?"

"Rose's parents died of natural causes, although records are not good. Rose had a sister. Caroline—she committed suicide in 1975. That was five years after Rose's abduction. Rose had a brother, Harold Lawton. He died in '78. I recently discovered his cause of death was classified as undetermined. Don't know how I missed it? Will need to take a look. Could be something."

Crabtree joined Shuck at the window and followed his gaze. "I think someone wanted a big payday and never got it," he muttered. "You can see Ballast Point over there."

"No kidding, Sherlock. I've just been looking at it for seventeen years. I guess I hoped it would somehow magically help me solve the Rose Burcher cold case."

"I don't know, Paul. Looks like this mystery started with Rose's abduction and ended with the delivery of her heart to the end of their driveway. No smokin' guns, my friend."

"Money never changed hands, Mr. Crabtree. What's the motive?"

"Does it matter after thirty-three years?"

"I think it does, but—"

"—but what?" Crabtree prodded.

"I'm missing somethin', Milton." Biting his lip, Shuck closed the Rose file and squinted at Ballast Point twinkling in the distance.

"What's your gut say?"

"This thing's not over..."

FOUR

Hillsborough County Morgue – September 10, 2003 – 07:00

Every morning Jack Burcher leaves his house at 06:00, the only house he's ever known. The small, neglected estate on the coast of Ballast Point is 18.2 miles from the Hillsborough County Medical Examiner's Office. By 06:40 he has finished his second coffee and first review of the day's case files. By 06:55 he is in surgical scrubs at the lightboxes studying first x-rays. Jack's scalpel always touches cold skin at 07:00, but not this time.

Above the swinging metal doors, the gold plaque says, "In this room the dead speak, and we listen." Before entering, each member of staff touches it—their daily reminder. They put on their disposable gloves, hats, and masks, and go to their designated workstation. Unlike a hospital operating room designed to protect the patient from the medical staff, the autopsy room is designed to protect the medical staff from the dead.

At the giant stainless-steel bed under the tight cluster of halogen lamps, deaners (cutters) wait for their first naked body. They are surrounded by sparkling counters stocked with bone-cutting saws, knives, chisels, and hammers. Nearby, histologists and toxicologists prepare to aseptically process human tissue and fluids. The medical photographer waits at the edge of darkness with his stepladder-on-wheels and table-on-wheels with a wide assortment of cameras and lenses. Only the morgue clerks are missing. They are with the bodies inside the county walk-in refrigerator. There they match toe tags with orders-of-transport on frosted clipboards. The morgue clerks move the dead from the cold depths into the autopsy room as directed by the medical examiner—the day's game plan.

On the morning of September 10, 2003, Dr. Jack Burcher and his #1 forensic investigator stood at the lightbox at 07:05—the events at the Sun Bay Rehab Center the night before had had an impact. Jack stared at his first x-ray but did not see. His mind replayed his father's odd behavior and cryptic declarations. Jack's angst only grew after he saw the thirteen dead souls on gurneys waiting for his undivided attention. This time, the family nightmare tortured him more than before. He knew in a few hours he would know more about thirteen dead strangers than he knew about his missing mother and dying father—the contradiction tore him apart inside.

"Dr. Burcher. Are you alright, sir?" Novak asked as he tapped the face of his Rolex—if correct they were behind schedule for the first time.

Hugo Novak met Jack Burcher at a forensic conference in London three years earlier. The precocious English forensic investigator and the veracious American forensic pathologist had broken meeting protocol—they dared to challenge claims of a presenter in the main hall. Protocol forbade debate from the floor in the general session. Neither Novak nor Burcher could allow such gross misrepresentations of facts to stand even a moment unabated. In the end, they had made their point. Both were escorted out. The two spent the rest of the day in an old English pub. Within hours they had resolved most of the problems of the free world, and by the end of dinner Novak's employment package had been finalized. Jack Burcher had always wanted a top-notch forensic investigator. Novak wanted a change.

"Yes. We are ready, Mr. Novak." Jack cleared his head. The x-ray came into focus.

A tweed suit and red bow tie in September was out of place everywhere, except possibly London. The attire was especially abhorrent in balmy Florida. However, a chance of adjustment in the Englishman's attire did not exist. Novak touched his bow tie like a precious gem as he put his nose into his small, dog-eared leather notebook. He saw the unbridled onslaught of questions from the M.E. as an exhilarating exercise of great minds. Only in the beginning would Novak hold any advantage. Burcher's superpowers of observation and deductive reasoning skills would vanquish the forensic investigator's dreams of superiority well before the scalpel touched skin. Novak played for minutes. His record was twelve.

"What do we have today?" Burcher asked as he touched the x-ray and leaned in.

With a history of 2,000 traumatic deaths successfully adjudicated to his name, Novak had new needs. American forensics could expose him to more. A change in venue would be daring, and the move to Tampa, Florida made perfect sense after his untidy divorce.

"Thirteen, sir. At this juncture I have eight who faced horrific ends and five snuffed out like candles in the bloody wind." He always spoke with British color, and he lacked any sense of humor. Novak's stodgy demeanor left people cold but authenticated his diligent search for truth.

"Yes. Thirteen."

In the beginning, manner-of-death is a presumptive label given by the Field Agent. It is based on a cursory death-scene investigation, often a few hours old. On this morning, Novak would provide answers to the medical examiner's questions for five natural deaths, three suicides, three accidental deaths, and one homicide—according to him. Regardless of the presumptive descriptor each case would be handled as a homicide to insure nothing is missed. Killers have always attempted to hide their malevolent work. Today they are more creative.

Jack spread his fingers and popped on his latex gloves. "Tell me about Mr. Brule'."

"Michael Brule' is a 32-year-old white male and dock worker employed by Ports of America. He is the unfortunate victim of a nasty encounter with an unnamed Eastern Asian male, as described by eyewitnesses."

"There was a disagreement that led to a friendly scuffle around 02:00 in the alley behind the Calypso Sports Bar on Channelside Drive. Michael Brule' and a childhood friend— Tom Shandling—were drinking bourbon for several hours."

"Do we have an alcohol level?"

"In the works." Novak returned to his notes. "They had an argument over a pool bet and took it outside to settle. Three unrelated witnesses observed the fracas. They say the matter was resolved after a few shoves followed by what you call a *bro-hug*, sir."

"A bro-hug?" Jack smiled. "Is that a British aphorism?" he said, tongue in cheek, as he studied the x-ray.

"Certainly not," Novak muddled. "It is American, sir."

"I see. Please continue."

"The two were quite ready to return to their bourbons and Coke when an Eastern Asian male in his mid-fifties stepped out of the alley shadows."

Jack held a ruler to the x-ray. "Eastern Asian is a broad descriptor, don't you think?" he challenged. "Stepped out of alley shadows. Do you mean like a Samurai or Bushido warrior?"

"I use words presented by the witnesses. Their words, not mine. Open for interpretation, sir."

"Please. Continue, Mr. Novak."

"It is unclear if words passed prior to the Eastern Asian male's challenge of Mr. Brule', the one who pulled a billhook from his belt first. The Eastern Asian fellow countered with a rather large Bowie knife. Seconds later Mr. Brule' lost his left hand—holding the billhook—and the Bowie was implanted in—"

"—his head." The ME leaned to his ruler and slid it down the x-ray. "One could say our Eastern Asian man is talented." Jack squeaked numbers onto a grease board.

Novak flipped a page. "Quite, sir. There were no defense wounds." Novak glanced up at the x-ray. "I assume Mr. Brule' died instantly. A plunging force and ideal positioning to—"

"—penetrate the skull at the coronal and sagittal suture intersect. How tall is Mr. Brule'?"

"Six feet two inches."

"And our Eastern Asian male, do we have an estimate?"

"Witnesses say short. By measure of landmarks, I estimate five feet five inches."

Jack made more measurements. "The average male skull thickness is 6.5 millimeters." He ran a finger down the edge of the white image dominating the cranial x-ray. "The seven-inch Bowie knife entered here—the precentral sulcus—and passed through the cerebral cortex, corpus callosum, fornix and thalamus. The blade exited the cerebral peduncle. When we get inside, we will find wholesale lacerations to the carotid vessels and severe structural damage.

"The downward thrust shattered the skull and pithed the brain. Mr. Brule's large motor muscles shut down instantly. His hips and knees buckled and released. To witnesses, he appeared to sit down in a controlled fashion. Fact was, he died instantly. His body did not know it for maybe four or five minutes. Do we have a time for the fight?"

"I would put it at 02:05," Novak said with his nose in his notebook.

"I will put adjusted time of death at 02:10."

Novak nodded. "Mr. Shandling had no blood splatter. However, he did have bloody markings on his face."

"Bloody as used by the Brits, or bloody as a descriptor of the nature of the markings?"

"The latter, sir—descriptor of said markings. A bloody half-circle drawn on his forehead and two parallel lines from the open area drawn down each side of his nose." Novak passed a photograph. "This was taken at the death scene prior to loading Mr. Shandling on the ambulance after paramedics confirmed no injuries. Mr. Shandling is unconscious. He fainted."

"I'm sure he was in shock after witnessing his friend's death and the killer turning to him." Jack studied the photograph. "The markings are a primitive finger painting—maybe a symbol or sign with an Asian meaning."

"There was no other blood on Mr. Shandling."

Jack looked up from the photograph. "I need more, Hugo."

"Witnesses say after the Eastern Asian man dropped Mr. Brule', he knelt over the dying man and dragged a finger across the head wound. He touched his bloody finger to his tongue and smiled. He then walked over to Mr. Shandling. He drew the sign. He then climbed the wall on the other side of the alley and vanished. I doubt we'll learn much more from Mr. Shandling."

"Did he say anything to Mr. Shandling?"

"A witness heard, 'nee-fer fag-got.'"

"Or maybe, 'never forget'," Jack said. "This is an old and expensive knife—a Legacy Arms Musso Bowie. They cost upwards of $500. Not the typical leave-behind."

"I will pass that information to Homicide Detective Bullitt?"

"The TPD will be pleased to know the Legacy Bowie knife is a restricted weapon. The owner had to register it at time of purchase. Federal law.

"I'll get the serial number off the blade when I pull it out of his head at autopsy. It may help. I don't know. Our Eastern Asian male is definitely a cutlery connoisseur. I doubt he would leave an easy trail for us. Then again..."

What did Michael Brule' do to you, Eastern Asian man? Jack wondered. *Was he just in the wrong place when you were looking for a fight? Have you been a person of interest before?*

"We need to get FBI on this early. I want to know what the half circle and two lines mean. Maybe they've seen it before. It was important to the executioner."

The swinging metal doors popped open. The morgue clerk rolled in the body of Michael Brule'. A hush fell over the autopsy room as all eyes found the knife handle protruding from the top of the dead man's head. That sight was not terribly unusual for most members of Jack's team. The severed hand holding the billhook was a rarity. Cradled between the legs of the cadaver, the dismemberment still gripped the bloody weapon.

Burcher and Novak watched Brule' roll to a stop under the steaming halogens. There the ME would conduct the external inspection. The deceased would be undressed, and all physical evidence would be collected, bagged, and labeled. The naked body would then be placed on the autopsy table for the postmortem dissection procedure.

When Jack stepped up to begin the examination, the swinging metal doors exploded open a second time. Heads turned to Dr. Deborah Quin—Assistant Medical Examiner—as she walked a line to Dr. Burcher. They stepped away from staff. "Something terrible has happened at the Sun Bay Rehab Center," she whispered.

"Ronan? Did something happen to my father?"

"They would not say, Jack. Chief of Police Francis Deron is there. He wants you to come, now. Go. I will take over here."

Jack's eyes found Novak. The forensic investigator's antenna went up. He nodded. Without a word, Jack left the autopsy room pulling off gloves and mask.

FIVE

Sun Bay Nursing Care Center –September 10, 2003 – 08:00

Jack turned off Bayshore Boulevard onto Hawthorne Point and into a police blockade. He could see Sun Bay Towers behind the trees. Without a word they waved the medical examiner through. Like most crime scenes, squad cars with flashing lights were everywhere. Unlike most crime scenes, police on foot with dogs moved in all directions. *I thought this was about my father.* He thought. *Maybe not. Maybe I went there too soon—Pop's been on my mind. This looks like a major crime scene. Multiple fatalities. Someone on the run.*

Unmarked cars, with blue lights flashing behind tinted windshields, were in a tight line behind three ambulances and two fire trucks in front of Ronan's building. An ambulance pulled out with lights and siren as Jack pulled up behind one black suburban with government plates.

Someone has a chance, Jack thought. *And someone should have told Dr. Quin about this. My office must never be in the dark on these catastrophes. The sooner we know the better. If there's a lot of fatalities, we need to prepare. You can't tie our hands. Best add this topic to the next board-of-aldermen's agenda—*

He got out of the car. *—or maybe it's because Pop's here. Maybe Francis wanted to keep a lid on things so I could make arrangements. A professional courtesy.*

The TPD Chief exited the sliding glass doors and waved. Jack froze. *Wait a minute. That is not a happy-to-see-you wave. That's a hurry-up-and-get-here wave.* Jack hurried his gait. Two guards backed away with hands on holstered guns and eyes on him.

"It's not good, Jack," the Chief huffed checking his watch.

"What's going on? Why the dogs? Why no information on the—?"

In 1970, Francis Deron was the detective when Rose Burcher was abducted. Now, he is the Chief of Police for a city of 400,000 and a friend of the Burcher family. Francis worked with Ronan back when Ronan was the County Chief Medical Examiner. Francis Deron was one of the few permitted to visit anytime the Burcher patriarch at Sun Bay.

"Ronan's gone, Jack."

"I'm not surprised. He had a very bad day. When did he pass?"

"No, Jack. Ronan is missing."

"Missing? What do you mean, missing?"

Francis walked Jack to the far edge of the sidewalk away from the hectic flow and ears of guards trained to observe and act on everything.

"The floor nursing staff went into Ronan's room at six this morning to check on him. Their standard procedure is to check patients every two hours, day and night. A note at the nurses' station said you left orders—Ronan was not to be disturbed until morning. The routine night checks were canceled, Jack."

"Okay. I did leave those orders. Go on." Jack scanned the area and listened.

"At six they discovered he was not in his bed. They spent the next thirty minutes looking for him—a room to room search. Nothing. They called the Tampa PD. We sent a squad car. Our people checked Ronan's room. We found something disturbing."

"What did you find, for God's sake, Francis?"

"We found a severed ear." He gripped Jack's shoulder. "We think someone took Ronan in the early morning hours. They got him out of the building and off the property. Sometime later they returned. Someone placed a bloody ear on the windowsill in Ronan's room. We found it next to the flowers." Francis hung his head.

"My God!" Jack cringed holding his gut. "How could anyone—" He gasped. He ran a hand through his hair and swallowed hard.

"He's gotta be here," Jack barked. "He's gotta be here. It's incompetence or someone's playing a game. That's it. Payback. And I think I know who."

"What're you talking about?"

"A nurse. I was not nice. She wouldn't leave us alone with the food tray. Ronan had us on edge—acting very strange. Saying things. He was getting very agitated, risking a medical event. The nurse kept putting his damn food tray in our face. I guess she came in at the wrong time. I jumped on her. My bad. She was not happy with me. Looking back, I don't blame her. This could be some payback that got out of hand."

"So, you were here last night."

"Yes. David and I got here around seven. Stayed about an hour. Melissa had come earlier in the day. You'll need to get her details from her. She asked us to visit our father. Said he was having a bad day thinking about Rose and his brother—both gone. Ronan collapsed last night. Exhaustion. I didn't want him awakened. He needed sleep. His Parkinson's and dementia were really ganging up on him."

The Chief waved off a cluster of police officers coming his way. "I don't think Ronan's here, Jack. We have the dogs. They tracked him from his room down the hall and back stairs to the loading dock. That is where we lose him."

"He couldn't walk there. I don't know why he would—"

"I asked my people to take the dogs over every square-inch of this property, but they won't find anything, Jack. We know Ronan was taken off campus in a vehicle."

"Why would anyone take a dying old man?" Jack muttered.

"I don't know," Deron looked away.

"Cameras! Video surveillance! Francis, they're all over this place. This is a high-security facility. One if the main reasons we put Ronan here."

"We're looking at all that. They've not gotten back to me yet, but it's early."

"The ear. I want to see it. How do you know it wasn't cut off here?"

"No blood up there, Jack. I think it was removed somewhere else and brought back."

"That makes no sense. Lord! How sick is that? And why? I still want to see it. I want to see Ronan's room."

"CSI is up there now. I can't let you go up until they're done. I know you understand."

Jack nodded and rubbed his red eyes. "I want you to find that nurse. She is short—maybe five two. A hundred pounds. Long red hair. I didn't get a good look at her face. A glimpse. Maybe Asian. Maybe in her late forties." Jack rubbed his neck.

"Gait. I remember she had a slight limp. Could be leg length—an asymmetry. Club foot or injury or planter fasciitis."

"You forensic guys don't miss much," Deron said.

"I've been coming here for eight years, Francis. I've never seen this nurse before."

"Sun Bay's a big place—350 patients, 200 staff members. A dozen or more people die here every week. They're replaced. There's a long waiting list. And staff comes and goes. Maybe this nurse has been here, but never worked on the fifth floor in Building A. There are four buildings. Ronan's been in the same one for eight years."

"Still seems odd," Jack muttered.

"We'll look into it. We'll find her. Here comes your brother."

David ran up from behind. "What the hell happened? Is the old man okay? I got a call. They said get to Sun Bay. Find your brother. I was not expecting this."

"Who called you, David?" asked Chief Deron.

"I don't know. They didn't identify themselves. I just—"

"Jack, fill him in. I'm going to check on the nurse and the progress." Deron turned to David. "No one was told to call you, David." Deron left into the building.

"They think someone has taken Pop," Jack said.

"Taken!"

"He's not in his room. He's not in the building. The dogs tracked him to a loading dock. There are surveillance cameras everywhere. We'll find out more. It's still early."

"Maybe he just wandered off," David mumbled. "Maybe he had one of those lucid moments and the strength we saw last night. He could have left here on his own."

David turned to the building and looked up at the fifth floor. "He was acting very strange last night. He did not want to be here. I would not be surprised if he just left or got a friend to come get him. He was rattled last night, Jack."

"Pop was taken, David."

"You don't know. Just because you're a medical—"

"Stop. Ronan was taken. It's a fact. I haven't told you everything."

"What are you not telling me?"

"I don't want to upset you more. It's too early to—"

"—tell me what you know because I'm your little brother. Stop, Jack. We're grown men. What makes you so sure someone's taken the old man?"

Jack pinched the bridge of his nose and swallowed the sick taste. When he looked into David's eyes, he saw fear. *You're right. You should know what I know.* "They found Pop's ear, David. Someone cut off his ear and put it on his windowsill next to the flowers, the Oleanders."

"My God! Cut off his ear. Who does that sh—?"

"Monsters." *I see it every day,* Jack mused. *There are evil people out there.*

"That's what he was tryin' to tell us last night. We didn't listen. He was lookin' out the window at something. He said someone was comin' for him, Jack. It was his turn. The one who killed his brother and our mother was comin' for—"

"Don't do this to yourself, David. This is why I hold back. You go all over the place."

"He was scared. He shook the newspaper at you. He keeled over. We didn't want to understand him. We even put off talking about it. We convinced ourselves he was nuts."

"We listened, David. We just didn't understand. We still don't."

"Pop knows more than we give him credit for. He's been trying to tell us for years, but we kept explaining it away. I think he knows who killed our mother. I think he may even know why. I don't know how he could possibly know someone was comin' for him."

"I don't know either, David."

* * *

They entered room 523. CSI had completed their sweep. They left with the physical evidence—including the ear. But, prior to removal, Jack inspected the ragged, bloody specimen through the walls of the plastic sterile container.

Not many people would recognize an ear detached from one of their family members, but Jack knew immediately it was Ronan's left ear. He recognized the crescent scar on the antihelical fold. His father had been bitten by a squirrel as a child. Years later most of the scar had blended. That did not keep Ronan from talking about his near-death experience. If they had cut off his right ear, a visual ID would be impossible. Jack would have had to wait for the results of the DNA test. But they cut off Ronan's left ear. *You know my father's story*, he thought. *That's why you left me his left ear. What are you doing? Do you think you can terrorize me?*

Jack stood at the window looking around the room for something that mattered. David stayed at the door looking for a hole to crawl into. Deron nudged David the rest of the way in and closed the door. "I've got some disturbing information."

"They do not have a nurse fitting my description," Jack said.

"They do have Asians on staff. They do not have a redheaded Asian."

"I was here," David huffed. "I saw her, too. She's real."

"No one doubts that," Deron said. "She is an imposter. Your family has a major lawsuit. This place promotes it's level-one security rating. Sun Bay's home for a lot of elder statesmen, U.S

Senators, generals, and wealthy patriarchs and matriarchs. People pay a lot of money for the protection this place claims to provide.

"They allowed a complete stranger access to the entire operation. That put every patient at risk. Sun Bay's guaranteed-protection policy has been woefully breached. We now know this redheaded imposter is complicit in Ronan's abduction. We have her on video."

"Ronan was taken like our mother," Jack fumed. "I'm not interested in any lawsuit, Francis. We need to find my father. I want to know more about the surveillance around here?"

"For now, I prefer to tell you as opposed to show you. We have a chain of evidence to protect. Some people will litigate. I don't need anything thrown out for—"

"That's fine." Jack waved him off. David joined them at the window.

"Your father was removed from this room on a gurney," Deron said. "At three in the morning. The mystery nurse rolled him from his bed onto the gurney. She did it alone."

"Pop allowed that?" David asked.

"She gave him a shot before. We think a sedative. He went limp. No resistance."

"But still alive?" David asked.

"Yes. He moved his arms and head under the straps."

"Continue Francis," Jack prodded.

"The nurse pushed him down the hall to the back staircase. She met someone. He carried Ronan down five flights. Went out the doors onto the dock. Loaded him into a car."

"Jesus," Jack sighed. "No alarms or anything."

"We have the car. It left the property at 3:32 am, lights off. An old Cadillac."

"What about the ear? How did it get up here?" Jack asked.

"Someone met the nurse two hours later, in the shadows off

the dock. She returned to Ronan's room at 05:00. We believe that's when she placed the ear on the windowsill. The room camera is on the bed, not the surroundings. We can't be 100% sure about the windowsill."

"And then the nurse vanished?" Jack muttered. Deron turned away. He looked out the window. The sun reflected off Hillsborough Bay. "What are you not telling us, Francis?"

"I had hoped you would have talked to Mr. Novak before now."

"What does my forensic investigator have to do—?"

A knock came at the door. Deron rushed to open it. Hugo Novak entered. "You're very late," Deron whispered.

"Complications." His eyes found the boss. "Dr. Burcher, I'm sorry about your—"

"Start talkin', Hugo."

"Yes sir. We found a female. She fits the description you provided Chief Deron."

"If you're involved, she's dead. Stop beating around the bush, Hugo."

Novak stumbled into the room and gathered himself. "The nurse is deceased, sir. We found her in a dumpster behind this building, the body hidden beneath a sizeable mountain of discarded food and human waste. Clearly a dastardly attempt to—"

"—hide a body from a K9 squad," Deron puffed. "We found the imposter's discarded uniform in this room. The dogs got a good sniff and took a beeline to the dumpster."

"Hugo, give me the forensics," Jack said like an order in his autopsy room.

"Aggressive strangulation, sir. Severe bruises about the neck. The hyoid bone shattered and pushed deep into the tracheal canal."

"Someone wanted her very dead," Jack muttered. "Do we have video of this, Francis?"

"We should. They're going through it now. It will take time. We have many hours of video to look at on eighty-four cameras. I want a closer look at the car."

"Is the redheaded nurse in the morgue, Hugo?" Jack asked.

"On her way, sir."

"I want Dr. Quin to start the process. I want this nurse identified fast."

Deron nodded. "I'll send Detective Moe Bullitt to get things moving on our end."

Jack looked into his brother's wet eyes—the one silent since Novak arrived. "Maybe we will get lucky with the DNA. If she's not in CODIS we'll go the ancestral-marker route. This is big, David. This could put us on Pop's trail."

"Do you really believe he's alive?" David asked with all the air he had left.

Jack turned to the window and Ballast Point on the horizon. "Why take a dying old man from a convalescent home? Why return with his ear? If they wanted Ronan dead, they had the needle in his arm. No. This time someone wants money. And unlike mother, Ronan cannot identify his captors. For once his medical conditions could extend his life instead of shorten it."

"I agree," Deron said. "They kidnapped your father for money. I think we can expect ransom demands. The FBI is on this now. You remember Paul Shuck, the SE Regional Director. He wants to talk to you about last night. He will want to go over every minute. You know the drill. Please cooperate. Jack, you know the most valuable time is now."

"I don't have great confidence in the FBI," Jack muttered.

"Still, they have a job to do," Deron said. "And we need all the help we can get."

"I'm sorry, but I agree with Jack," David chimed in. "It's been more than thirty damn years since mother was taken out of our home. The FBI was on that one fast, too. What do we have to show for it? We've got diddly."

On David's last word, Ronan's door opened. A short, blonde girl entered. Dressed in combat boots, holey jeans, and a camouflage windbreaker. Enormous binoculars swung from her petite neck. Her big, green eyes moved around the room like a puma hunting for perfect food. First Novak, then Deron, and then David. When her eyes found Jack, they stopped. "I told you somethin' bad was gonna happen. So. Where's Pop?"

SIX

Somewhere in Hillsborough County – September 10, 2003 – 22:00

Inside a dark place a shadow moves. A light grows. It flashes and flickers and sizzles and pops. Then it dies. Like a beast in the woods it waits for its next meal. When it eats, black smoke leaves the rock chimney beneath the sliver moon. The plume is filled with infinite sparks that melt away and horrid tales that linger forever. The column of death rises above the live oak trees and fireflies and cicada screams and is forever lost over Hillsborough Bay.

Beneath a dusty lightbulb death waits. A rusted spike pins a bloody ankle to the gnarled wood. The other leg is already gone. A large spike pins a neck. Blood encrusted ropes hang on a nail—they are no longer needed to bind raw wrists and broken bones.

The scalpel sinks deep into the right sideburn. The depth of the cut is maintained as the scalpel moves on a line above the right ear around to the back of the head, and then to the left ear and left temple. A small spatula digs beneath the meaty flap and separates the scalp from the boney skull. Then the scalp is pulled forward, torn from the skull, from the back of the head to the front. The hair and the face are turned inside-out like a rubber mask.

The skull is circumferentially sawed. A skull cap—like a salad bowl—is pried off the top of the head revealing the brain. Beneath the dusty lightbulb the pearly-white, mushroom-like mass is detached and lifted out. Held in wretched hands, it drips into a pail. It is rinsed and patted dry like a delicate newborn. The brain is set down on a table next to an empty cardboard box. A knife blade sinks into the top of the pristine organ. A pouch is carved. A medallion is slid inside, and the pouch is sealed with glue.

A dripping hand with a knife returns to the big table. Another arm drops from another shoulder. It is taken to the furnace. The iron door opens. Smoldering embers wait. Then the beast eats and a new column of death reaches for the sliver moon over Hillsborough Bay.

SEVEN

Burcher Estate – September 10, 2003 – 23:00

The Burcher estate, twenty acres of prime real estate, hugs the Hillsborough Bay on Ballast Point. Behind majestic iron gates and rock walls the white clapboard mansion with fat pillars and sweeping porches hides in a cluster of live oaks. Grandpa Otto and Grandma Emily built the house in 1930. In 1960 Ronan and Rose added the boathouse and dock. After Rose's abduction ten years later, everything started to change. David and Melissa moved out after college. In '96 Jack placed Ronan in Sun Bay. By 2001 Patricia—Jack's estranged wife—had relocated to Boston. Jack stayed in the old house alone because someone had to.

The ME would not be the first to arrive at his house on the second most miserable day of his life. The Ronan mystery lingered. The cars matched personalities. The shiny black SUV with government plates parked at the front of the line on the edge of the gravel driveway. Then Chief Deron's old Lincoln Continental. Then David's red convertible Mercedes. And then Melissa's Jeep Wrangler. Jack parked his dirty and dented Ford Taurus next to Detective Bullitt's dirty and dented unmarked Crown Victoria.

Deron, Bullitt, and Shuck drank from water bottles. Jack, David, and Melissa drank from the well-stocked bar in the den. Empty pizza boxes cluttered kitchen counters with the bank of telephones and recording devices. Everything had been set up an hour after Ronan's abduction. Everyone expected a ransom call this time.

"Is Patricia on her way back?" David asked as he poured a bourbon.

"No," Jack said. "She'll stay in Boston with her family. There's no reason to expose her to all this. It's a safer place to be."

"She's still your wife," Melissa sniped. "She should be—"

"—let it go, please," Jack said. *She hasn't been my wife for many years.*

"Well then. I think that's enough on Patricia Burcher's travel plans," Deron said.

"Melissa. Let's go back over your statement," Shuck said. He leaned on the mantle with a fistful of papers. "The part when your father—"

"—said he saw smoke. I guess my brain heard fire," she huffed. "And no, I did not look out the window to see what he was talkin' about. Really. How many times are you going to ask me that question? Why would I make it up?"

"Is it possible to see smoke on Bird Island from Ronan's window?"

"Yes," Jack said. "I'm certain Ronan saw smoke. He looks out the window every day. It's his world. He noticed a change and said something, that simple."

"What I don't get is the connection he made between the

Bird Island fire and the deaths of his brother and wife. He said it was a clue. What am I missing?"

"Mr. Shuck, the smoke is a standalone," Melissa said. "After five minutes of silence Pop started to talk about Uncle Leonard and Rose."

"Did your father say the person that killed Leonard was the same that kidnapped and killed your mother?"

"Yes. Those words."

"And he said the same person was coming for him?"

"Yes," Jack said. "We've been over this enough, Paul. It's late. We're all tired, and we're getting nowhere."

Deron cleared his throat. Heads turned. "I agree with Jack. But we are looking for a small aberration in testimony— something we could be missing. I'm sure you know *redundant reviews* are often necessary to get to the bottom of—"

"I don't need an education from you, Francis. I'm well aware of the merits of repetitive questioning techniques. It is my life, remember? That said, it is my professional opinion we will learn nothing more tonight by going over the same ground anymore. The police are not dealing with reluctant, oblivious, or combative witnesses. We want the answers more than you do."

Bullitt raised a hand. "What Moe?" Deron snapped.

"I agree with Dr. Burcher. We've been over last night's discussions between Ronan and family a half-dozen times now. We need to move on. I suggest we shift focus from the existence and accuracy of information to the significance of the information."

"Everyone's right," Shuck said. "Let's move to *most likely scenarios* to explain Ronan's comments and abduction. There are several to consider. Each will need to be investigated."

"Agreed," Deron said.

"Agreed," Jack said. Melissa and David nodded and rolled their eyes.

With his stack of files, Shuck sat by the dead fireplace. "Category one—enemies of Ronan and/or Jack Burcher. Two county medical examiners that determine the fate of many."

"Exactly," Deron said. "Who has Ronan and/or Jack angered based on their rulings and court testimony. Both Hillsborough County Medical Examiners are admired by the vast majority of citizens. And they are despised by some. We need to identify and investigate each."

Jack lowered his glass. "We covered Ronan-haters in 1970 after my mother's abduction. I'm sure you remember, Francis. At the time you were Detective Deron."

"That is correct," Deron muttered. "Ronan-haters up to 1970 turned up nothing."

"Same with the FBI," Shuck said.

"We now need to look at Ronan-haters from '71 to '96 retirement."

"Someone in that group could seek retribution," Bullitt muttered.

"Why wait seven years after a man's retirement?" David asked.

"The Ronan-hater could have been in prison. Recently released. Or they could have been too young to act on their anger. Seven years later they are older and even more toxic."

"Or they could have been waiting for the perfect storm," Jack said.

"We will put a team on this," Deron said. "We'll need guidance from your office, Jack. I'm sure you know the types of cases that expose medical examiners to the wrath of criminals and/or disgruntled family members."

"Of course."

"And I will send Agent Crabtree. FBI oversight," Shuck said.

"What else?"

Shuck flipped a page. "We need to look at Jack's history, too. It's possible he has a disgruntled stalker. One who went after Ronan to get to him."

"That is possible," Jack said. "I have seven years to look at." He poured another scotch. "I could be blind on this topic. I'll involve Dr. Quin. She will have a more critical eye."

"Good."

"What else?" Deron asked.

"The Burcher family is wealthy. You own Ballast Point and possess vast amounts of real estate in the state and around the world." Shuck opened another file. "I was reviewing this earlier today. Actually, before I got the call from Frank."

"Why? You haven't had anything to do with us for three years," David snapped.

"David. Enough," Jack scolded.

"No. He's right. I have not talked to your family for three years. But David, that does not mean I have set aside your mother's case. It is the one I struggle with. Nothing makes sense. No logical reason for such a brutal mystery. Your mother had no enemies. Her life was about you as children, Ronan, and the community. No ransom. Just the horrid box." His head dropped.

"Thanks for nothing, FBI," David said.

"Lighten up," Jack scolded. "You don't understand a lot, David. There are bad people in the world. Many homicides are complex. I know. I've had my share. What you need to grasp is lack of resolution is not a lack of effort or caring. Don't make that mistake."

Shuck cleared his throat and continued. "The Burcher family owns a lot of land and manages a lot of leases. We need to take a closer look at these family assets. We need to investigate the people squeezed out, denied, and/or ruined by Burcher family transactions."

"The real estate piece is mine," David said.

"Good. I will meet you at your office. The morning. You can help on this line of the investigation."

"I suggest you prioritize a review of my father's transactions just prior to Sun Bay."

"I agree, Jack." Shuck closed his file. "Now. Let's move to another investigatory track. Most of the world knows the Burcher family's net worth exceeds $2 billion. That attracts bad people. They want your money. The removal of an old, billionaire patriarch from a nursing home could be a well-thought-out tactical step."

"In a sinister mission," Deron said.

Shuck nodded. "Kidnapping for ransom is our most-likely category. At any moment we could receive demands. Cooperation will be contingent upon Ronan's safe return."

"Ergo our people and all the technology in your kitchen," Deron said.

"We have not had one phone call since Pop's abduction," David said.

"It's still early," Deron said.

Jack walked his scotch to the window. He parted the sheers and looked out over the moonlit fields of wildflowers. Like thirty-three years ago, he could see fireflies flashing under the live oaks, and he could hear the cicadas. His eyes moved to the place where he sat that night—the place from where he watched his mother's abduction.

Shuck recognized Jack's frozen stance. He knew Jack knew. "What if this is—"

"—connected to Rose's abduction?" Jack said as he dropped the sheer and turned.

"That is ridiculous," Melissa scoffed. "Mom and Dad's abductions connected! It's been thirty years since we lost mother."

"Time is irrelevant," Bullitt mumbled.

"Someone could be stalking our family," Jack said. "They could be on a mission."

"Why? Because of something someone did a long time ago?" David said.

"Jack. You gotta stop with all the forensic murder-mystery stuff," Melissa said. "We can't always get lost in your world. I'm sorry, not everything in life is diabolical."

"If we listen to Pop's words last night, this is connected," Jack said. "Pop said he who killed my brother killed my wife and is coming to kill me."

"That is a possibility," Deron said. "Somewhere in the Burcher family history some action or event could have launched a mission to kill your family."

"We must consider the possibility," Shuck said.

"You're all nuts." David slammed his glass to the bar. "I'm not stayin' around for anymore of this creative crap. I'm scared enough for the old man. I don't need to add me, Jack, and Melissa to the kill list."

"Leonard Burcher died in a car accident in 1948," Shuck said. "Rose was kidnapped and killed in 1970. Rose's sister, Caroline Lawton, committed suicide in 1975. Her brother Harold died in 1978. His death is unresolved. Four traumatic, unexplained deaths in your family."

"I was eighteen when Uncle Harold fell from a scaffold," Jack said. "Fell twelve stories. He was a window washer in Boston. A terrible accident. Not a homicide, Paul."

"The M.E. ruled it undetermined," Shuck said.

"You sure about that?"

"Yes. Looked into it today. Boston M.E. could not settle on

manner of death. Not clear cut. At the time of the tragic incident, your uncle had lost two sisters in five years. He kept a journal. In it he spoke of joining them. M.E. could not rule out suicide."

"Okay, an accident or suicide. Neither support your crazy theory someone is knocking off our family," David scoffed.

"Homicide was not ruled out," Shuck said.

"I don't know about that," Jack said.

"Two witnesses claim someone pushed Harold Lawton. The unidentified man fled into the building. Was never found. Mr. Lawton is still a cold case today."

"The M.E. could not rule out foul play," Jack muttered.

"Why the hell was Uncle Harold washing windows anyway?" David barked. "We're rich. Why didn't we give him money or help him find a decent job?"

"He rejected our help," Jack said. "A proud man. That's why I rejected the suicide theory. But I thought it was ruled an accident. Now it could be a homicide."

"I've requested police reports and the M.E. files. You can take a look for yourself. It is definitely suspicious now."

"Why did it get by me?" Jack muttered as he swirled his glass.

"You were in college. Harvard. You left Florida," Melissa said. "Remember, you didn't want anything to do with the family."

"Congratulations, FBI man," David puffed. "You got my genius brother to support your insane theory. Go ahead, Jack. Make the point you've been dying to make all night."

"What're you talking about, David?"

Paul held up a hand. "We cannot ignore—"

"No. We cannot invent a friggin' conspiracy theory," David said.

"David's never dealt with the dark side, Paul," Jack said.

"David. I'm sorry it upsets you, but relevant history cannot be ignored."

"For Christ sake. You guys are doing it again. You're putting everything on the table. Therefore, we get nowhere. I'm done here. I'm going home." David stormed out.

Melissa started after him. Jack wrapped an arm around her and pulled her back. "Honey," he whispered. "Let him go. He's tired. He'll be okay, in the morning."

Deron peered through the kitchen blinds as David's corvette spit gravel all the way to the gates. "Officer Dowlan, I want you here until 07:00. Officer Treadwell will relieve. Remember, only Jack answers the house phone. You know the drill."

"Yes, sir." Dowlan lit a cigarette, checked his watch, and opened a paperback.

"David's departed in haste, people. Hopefully, the flying-gravel damage is minimal."

"We're all on edge," Bullitt muttered as he pocketed his tattered notebook.

"And we still have a lot to think about," Shuck said.

"Let's all get some rest. We can get back into this tomorrow. Maybe there will be some good news." Deron pointed the way out. "Thanks, everybody."

Melissa kissed Jack's cheek and forced a smile. "Goodnight big brother."

"Are you sure you don't want to stay here tonight? I worry about you, Mel."

"Now, that's not scientific, Dr. Burcher." She wrapped her arm around his waist and pulled him close. "Really, Jack. You don't need to worry about everyone all the time, especially me. I watch my back, and I'm carrying."

"Okay then. Look. Do me a favor. Take your flowers, the

oleanders you gave Pop. I didn't want to leave them at Sun Bay. You should enjoy them."

She stared at them. "I didn't give father flowers. I haven't done flowers for many years. He always tossed them the second I left." She hugged Jack. "Just maybe Pop had a secret admirer. Put that concept in your forensic pipe and smoke it."

He watched the line of red taillights crawl down the driveway and disappear at the rock wall. Jack downed the rest of his scotch as he eyed the potted plant—another unsolved mystery. *Oleanders.* He thought. *Where did you come from...?*

Dropping a fistful of cubes into his glass he grabbed a new bottle, broke the seal, and went outside. The flagstone terrace and plush lawn furniture would be his bedroom this night. Instead of staring at walls and old paintings he would look at the stars and smell Hillsborough Bay and wildflowers. Maybe then he could fall asleep.

Standing next to his future bed, he took another big swallow of scotch and digested the spray of stars merged with the bay. For a brief moment time meant nothing. He forgot about his mother and father and that night. Then a gentle breeze lifted his hair and the cicadas stopped. In the eerie silence, he slid back into his life of relentless tragedy.

It had consumed him from the moment Quinn said go to Sun Bay. It did not let up until Deron's taillights disappeared behind the rock wall. For the first time in seventeen hours Jack could do what he does best alone—FOCUS. Someone intended to bury him in information and swimming in alcohol for the first twenty-four hours. Why?

The cicadas returned. The trees swayed. *Why are you killing my family?*

EIGHT

Burcher Estate – September 11, 2003 – 03:00

The night after Ronan's abduction, Jack fell asleep on the terrace next to an empty bottle and full ashtray. Physical exhaustion and alcohol content were no match for his recurring nightmare—the horror story of 1970. Each time Jack went back to the two hideous nights in July, he danced with his demons and moved closer to death.

This night was no different—it always begins the same way. His hands tremble as severe spasms ripple through his rigid body with excruciating pain. His face contorts and twitches and transforms into an unrecognizable ghoul. His heart beats in his ears and his wet eyes dilate and dart beneath tight lids. Then it all stops. Everything goes silent and still, except the cicadas and the wind. Jack opens his eyes and only sees a summer night in 1970. He is ten. He is sitting in the field outside his bedroom window. Jack is engulfed in stars and fireflies and wildflowers. But his childhood wonder and awe would only last seconds. Then came the darkness.

His father is out of town. His mother is asleep on the sofa. Jack is alone in the field. It is July 14, just after midnight. He watches his mother's abduction. Jack tries to explain it to police, but they cannot hear him—Jack has no mouth. Then it is July 15, just after midnight. They return with a cardboard box. They position it at the end of the driveway. Jack opens the box but cannot see—he has no eyes. Again, he tries to tell the police everything. They laugh and turn away—Jack is invisible.

You are back. God! I can see you; Jack dreamed as he struggled for air and tossed and turned on the terrace lounge.

I see you slidin' out of the fog and growlin' in the gloom. I see your dull gray body and black eyes and black smile and those big fins. What are you? Why did you take my mother? You must bring her back to me.

Nobody believes me. The police. Fantasies of a ten-year-old. But I am here. I see. But I don't know what is real and what is my imagination. I just don't know if I am seeing—

God. I don't have a mouth! It's skin. No lips. My eyes, they're white, milky marbles. Am I going blind? Someone's makin' me forget. Numbing my brain. Am I invisible?

Stop. There you are. I see you! Wait. This time you're leaving somethin' on the driveway. Good. Now the police will believe me. I have a mouth again. They will see everything with their eyes. Then they will bring my mother home.

Now I'm sittin' in the field again. Why are the police standing at the end of the driveway with their flashlights and guns, and their radios talkin' and cracklin'? They're closing in on the box, like it's a bomb. Now, they're lookin' inside.

They're jumping back. They're falling down. One is puking. One is running away. He's scared. One is looking away. Why? They are leaving me without my mother.

Now I'm over the box. I don't need the police. I don't need anybody. I'm gonna find my mother myself. I'm gonna find the monster myself. But first I gotta look in the box. I gotta open the flaps. God, no—

Shirt soaked, Jack sat up and blinked his way back into the real world. His nightmare ended the same way each time. He had witnessed his mother's abduction on the first night, and he had witnessed the delivery of a box on the second night.

"APPARENTLY THERE'S NOT ENOUGH SCOTCH ON THE PENINSULA TO STOP MY MISERY," he yelled at the swirling bay waters. "Must I be HAUNTED the rest of my life?"

Jack lit a cigarette. He tossed the smoking match onto the wet grass and peeked in the kitchen window. Officer Dowlan had buried his head in his arms next to the phones. Jack went to the edge of the terrace and watched the water slap the rocks. A quarter mile out slow lights climbed the main channel. Jack's eyes filled with tears. *There are three tankers headed for Tampa harbors, and Pop's not coming home...*

It was late. He poured another and flopped down on a chair. *This goes back farther than mother,* he thought as he took another drag off his cigarette. *I need to look closer at Leonard's death. He was only eighteen. The car accident was in 1948. It will be difficult to find out much, but I must try. If it's suspicious in any way, I will need to go back even further. I must find where this nightmare begins—*

His cellphone vibrated. "—Paul. What're you doin' up?"

"The FBI never sleeps."

"Good to know. Nice commercial. What are you selling?"

"I thought you might be up."

"Of course, you did. Your clandestine satellite surveillance assets are at work 24/7," Jack poked as he pinched the filter and sucked his cigarette to the filter.

"Don't worry. I won't tell anybody about the satellites."

"I wish we did have some. Would make my life a lot easier."

"I get by with four hours a night. Always been that way. It's how I got through med school. Now, I don't know if it's an asset or liability." *Only got two hours tonight. But, no need to share my nightmare with the Feds.*

Jack unscrewed the cap from his beloved bottle and held it to the sky for Shuck's imaginary satellite. "Can you see my Dalmore 1964 Trinitas?"

"Of course. Turn it so I can read the label," Paul poked back. "Yeah. There you go. That is one fine blended Scotch whisky for the ultimate connoisseur. But maybe you should save it for another night." Paul held a paper to the only light burning in his office and the building.

"So, tell me, what's got you stirred up enough to call now?"

"Look, I know you had a rough 24 hours."

"Even though my father's at the end of his natural life, this is an abomination. It's like taking a child from a nursery."

"I know. But I gotta think if they wanted to kill him, they had plenty of opportunity to do it in his room, Jack. Why risk taking him off campus? Why return to—"

"—drop off a bloody ear? We both know this is not your typical abduction."

"Macabre, to say the least," Paul muttered.

"So, what's on your mind?"

"Today we identified several tracks for investigation. The abduction of Ronan with a predicate makes this very different from Rose's case."

"The predicate being the abduction and murder of my mother," Jack said.

"I did not say much about what I was thinking earlier. The group was tired and too—"

"—emotional," Jack said.

"I was gonna say *diverse* to handle the emerging and bizarre aspects of this case." Paul looked out his fifth-floor window at

Ballast Point. "You're an experienced forensic pathologist trained to handle sensitive matters. You've handled thousands of cases, hundreds of horrific homicides. You've seen it all, Jack. And I know you are somewhat gifted to boot, capable of simultaneously navigating a number of complex routes in a search for truth."

"What do you want to ask me, Paul?"

"I need to know. Can you disassociate yourself from this case enough to be effective? Ronan is your father. We both know he is not coming home. That chilling reality destroys family members. In this case, it also reopens painful wounds."

"You want to know, as the jurisdictional medical examiner, will I recuse myself?"

"Yes. Will you?"

"No. I can handle this. I want to handle this. There's no way I will step away from it."

"I thought as much," Paul muttered.

"Good. That's out of the way. Is that all?"

"There is only one way I will allow you to be involved in this case, Jack."

"You think you have that authority, Paul? You think you can take the Hillsborough County Chief Medical Examiner out, on your own?"

"You talking about Rose's Law?" Paul asked.

After the abduction of Rose Burcher and delivery of her heart to the gates of the Burcher estate, Ronan spent a lot of money on a lot of lawyers to keep him on the inside of his wife's investigation and anything related. The "Special Considerations" amendment to the Florida State Constitution happened after they got Rose's Law on the ballot. It was all about affording elected professionals the right to employ their rare knowledge and unique skills without prejudice in their designated jurisdictions notwithstanding personal or political relationships and real or perceived interests, when approved by the state on a case-by-case basis. Ronan Burcher M.D. was allowed to work on any and all death cases—autopsies and all—in Hillsborough County regardless of connection to the Burcher family as long as defendant's rights were not infringed.

"I'm not talking about victim rights. There's no question I have the same clearances as my father. They were granted by the state in 1996, or I would not be the Medical Examiner. No. I'm talking about my emotional connection."

"You know I can have you fishing for the next six months if you get in my way."

Jack lit another cigarette. Paul does have that power. The FBI can leverage many things to get their way in a state. Jack was a bit surprised it had not been brought up long ago. Ronan's abduction put a lot of the decisions in the Fed's hands. Now there were related homicides across state lines. Now, the FBI pretty much owned the Burcher family nightmare.

"What do you want from me?"

"I want a promise. You include me in everything."

"I don't understand. I think I do."

"You have blind spots, Jack. When you go it alone you risk missing something that could get you or someone else killed. Or you could miss something that could blow this thing wide open. Right now, we don't know who or what we are dealing with. There are things your heart may not let your head see. You know that's true. I need to be with you every step of the way."

"I see."

"You've been drinking. I don't know if you can fully appreciate—"

"I have been drinking. I may be physically impaired, but my head's right."

"I'll accept that, to a point."

"Look. I'll make this easy for you. I agree with everything."

"That's too easy."

"Yes, it is. Paul, it's been thirty-three years since my mother's abduction and execution. I still don't know who did it or why. We still haven't found her body. All I have is a heart buried in a $10,000 casket at Rose Hill Cemetery.

"Since I lost my mother, I've not found one thing new on my own. God knows I've tried. I think about it all the time. Maybe too damn much. I have theories and dead ends. I am sure I have blind spots, too. This family nightmare's killing me slowly. I can be hard on everybody. But my objective is simple. Solve this before I die. I will try not to get in the way."

"Then we're good for now, Jack. We share the same frustrations and objectives."

Jack stared into the bay and flashed back to the night he will never forget. "When my mother was taken, the Tampa Police and County Sheriff's Office thought they were dealing with a *singular event*, Paul. They launched a countywide search. They looked for a kidnapper while they waited for a ransom call. A call that never came. When the monster delivered my mother's heart to the house in a cardboard box, the police abruptly changed tactics. Now they were convinced they were dealing with a psychopath. They put all their assets to work looking for a sick serial killer. Ronan's abduction has changed tactics again."

"I agree. We must keep adjusting to accommodate the accumulated effect of facts."

"The new foundation is a matriarch and patriarch of a wealthy family taken. The two are connected by name, wealth, methodology, and body parts returned to the family."

"A heart is very different from an ear, Jack."

"Removing a heart is a diabolical act with a message we do not understand. It can either point to a sick person and random targets or a calculated killer with specific targets for a reason.

"Leaving an ear behind is tantamount to leaving a calling card, Paul. On its own, it says I want you to know I exist. Coupled with the heart, it says I am back—"

"—fear me! I am not new to the Burcher family."

"That spells *family vendetta* to me. One with roots."

"Roots back to 1970—"

"—or before. We have unexplained, traumatic deaths on both sides of our family. Only after we construct an *accurate victim list* can we even begin to close in on motive. And motive can lead to the killer or killers."

"We have a lot to do while we look for your father," Paul said.

"Before you called, I was thinking about Leonard's accident. It may be hard to investigate a fifty-year-old—"

"—car accident." Paul pulled a file from his stack. "I looked into it a few years ago." He flipped through papers. "He died on September 6, 1948, outside Pasadena, California."

"I remember the date. My father talked about his brother missing the Davis Cup finals. Leonard was 18, a big tennis fan. He died the day the U.S. beat Australia."

"I have more information coming—people running down more pieces for me."

"You have a commitment from me. Now I want one from you."

"What do you need, Jack?"

"David and Melissa cannot be dragged through all the theories—especially the *family vendetta* one. These multiple investigation tracks complicate their worlds. They have nothing to give us, Paul. I don't want to take them down what could be another rabbit hole."

"I agree. I will try at my end, but I cannot prevent others from exposing them. A word from you to Frank Deron could go a long way."

"I will talk to Francis." Jack lowered his phone. Growling mixed with the cicadas. It came from the front of the house. *I've heard that before,* he thought, as he stepped off the patio and started toward the side of the house.

"Paul. I gotta go. It's been a long night. I will see you tomorrow." Jack navigated along the edge of the junipers. He struggled to walk a straight line. The scotch and moving night shadows were a challenge. He pocketed his phone.

"Jack?" Paul yelled into his phone. He went to his window and looked across the bay at Ballast Point, a fifteen minute trip down the peninsula. "Jack, are you there?" *I can hear you breathing. Are you running? Are you okay? Or did you just forget to turn off your phone?*

"Jack, what's going on?"

No response. The phone went dead. Paul grabbed his keys and flew out the door.

NINE

Burcher Estate – September 11, 2003 – 04:00

I'm drunk...
  Every few steps he fell to the wet turf, each time his mission less clear. The simple act of walking had become a herculean task. He crabbed along the side of the house in the shadows and night fog. His stupor only confounded his meager effort to navigate the property he had grown up on. He battled booze, grief, and time. Determined to see what produced the strange but familiar sound, Jack stayed the course.

  The steady growl grew when he reached the front of the house. It came from the other side of the rock wall, Crescent Drive. Jack moved forward with eyes on the gated entry. He could see something—it floated in the fog above the road. *What are you?* Then a shadow appeared, a man holding a box. Jack inched forward and tripped on an edge of the porch step. He fell face-first into a massive mud puddle. Lying on his stomach he wiped eyes and refocused. The rather long object started to slide away. It sunk into the fog. White light flashed. It was gone.

I know you, he thought as he got to his feet. *You've been here before. Or did I imagine you. Am I drunk? Did any of this happen?* Wiping his eyes, he sat down on the step. *I think I remember you from before. Everything's the same. The sound. The gray tube with the black windows. The big fins. And I remember the flash of light.*

"Snap out of it," he huffed. "Are you gone? Were you even here?" he whispered. Then the square shadow on the driveway came into focus. *You left a box like last time. I'm not imagining this.* He stared at it like he did in 1970. "No." Jack yelled as he pulled himself up. He blinked three times and started toward the box at the end of the driveway.

"No... no... no..."

When the black Suburban turned down Crescent Drive, the lights found Jack Burcher standing in the middle of the cul de sac. His hands hung at his sides, his head down. Paul Shuck slowed the car and approached the open gates. His lights found the cardboard box at the end of the Burcher's driveway.

"Oh my God," he breathed. Paul had studied all the pictures of Rose Burcher's case. *Not again,* he thought. He spun the wheel tight. His SUV blocked the end of Crescent and kept lights on the box and the broken medical examiner.

Jack dropped to his knees and rolled onto his back. Shuck approached as more spinning lights and sirens turned onto Crescent—the Tampa PD, Hillsborough Sheriff's office, Tampa Ambulance and Fire, and Chief Deron.

"Did you look inside?" Shuck asked as he lifted Jack from the asphalt.

"I'm sorry," Jack sighed. "How'd you know to come?"

"I knew."

The others approached. Shuck turned to Deron. "Frank, we don't need EMTs or Fire. Jack's alright. Alcohol kept him from going into shock. He's confused, disoriented. We need the city's CSI to wait on this box. FBI CSI people are on the way."

Deron nodded and waved everyone back to their cars. Moe Bullitt slid to a stop and joined Deron out of earshot. They talked and stared at the box on the driveway.

"Someone get me some coffee for this man," Shuck yelled. He walked Jack to the black Suburban. In a daze, he sat on the seat with his legs hanging out the passenger door.

"We're all here now. We got this, Jack. I want you to focus on getting your heart rate down. Don't talk. Just gather yourself. We've got plenty of time to talk. We're waiting for CSI and my people anyway. No one can do a thing until they get here."

"I looked inside, Paul."

"I know. Stop talking. Remember—heart rate. Focus, Dr. Burcher."

Jack looked up Crescent and whispered, "It happened again. Everything the same—the growling at the end of the driveway. Like thirty years ago. I heard it, Paul. I had to see. All these years. What were fantasies and was real."

Paul put a steaming Styrofoam cup in Jack's face. "Don't talk. Heart rate. Drink this, Jack. You've had way too much Scotch tonight. It's messin' with you. Drink a lot of coffee and then we talk. No clocks on us."

The red and blue spinning lights washed over Crescent Drive, the live oak trees, and the rock wall around the Burcher estate. Radio chatter flowed from cars and handhelds. Jack sipped coffee and sucked in the cooler night air now sweeping off the bay. "You hear that, Paul?"

"Actually, I don't hear anything, Jack."

"My point. The cicadas, they're quiet. That is rare."

Paul shook his head in Deron's direction. The Chief leaned on the back of the SUV and returned a knowing smile.

"The things I heard and saw as a boy, the night my mother was taken, it all happened again." Jack stared at the box. "I'm not drunk. I'm not imagining things. You need to listen to me." *Back then nobody listened. They said because I was ten. Now drinking's their excuse.*

"Jack, you're drunk," Deron said like a father scolding a teenage boy. "You don't know what you saw or heard. Just like last time, you're talkin' crazy."

Deron leaned to Shuck and whispered, "Possible this is an elaborate prank. *Tampa Tribune* ran a story on Ronan's abduction. They did a spread on Rose, pictures and all."

"This family has its enemies," Paul said.

"Someone put the box there to mess with us?" Deron said. "Maybe worse. A bomb."

"It's possible but—"

"That's not what happened," Jack snapped. "I can hear you guys. My ears work just fine. I'm not drunk, Francis. And this is no prank."

"How can you be so sure, Jack?" Deron snapped back.

Paul held up a hand. "Stop. Both of you. Jack, you need to slow down. You're a doctor. You know what alcohol, grief, and lack of sleep can do to a person. You're human. You need to be able to separate things you saw from an overactive imagination. Until you consume more caffeine, we're going to probably get nowhere."

The white FBI CSI van crawled onto Crescent. It skirted the roadblock and rolled to a stop fifty feet from the gates and next to the Tampa CSI van. Lights off, both sat.

"What are they waiting for?" Jack asked. "FBI and Tampa CSI are here."

"We're waiting for the bomb squad," Deron said.

"No, Francis."

"Nothing you say will change standard operating procedure, Jack. This is a suspicious container with unknown contents. It's not Christmas morning. We gain nothing from risking a life to open the box without taking the appropriate precautions."

"Francis, I know what's in the box. I looked inside. The first thing I said to Paul, when he got here. I looked inside the box."

"So, you are admitting to tampering with evidence? Is that true. Did he, Paul?"

"Yes, he told me he looked inside. That was all."

"I suggest you two stop treating me like a random, intoxicated drifter in your damn city. I am the Chief Medical Examiner for this county. By law this is my death scene. I order the city to forego the bomb squad and send in CSI now. FBI can join if they want. Francis, if you don't do as I directed, I will order you and your people to leave this death scene. You got it?"

"Oh, I'm sorry, Jack," Deron said. "But I don't see a body anywhere. That makes this a *crime scene*, not a *death scene*. By law, the Tampa Police Department is in control here."

"Jack's right, Frank," Shuck said as Moe Bullitt approached the threesome. "This is a death scene. He is in control, inebriated or not. It is the law."

"Oh yeah? Is there a body stuffed inside that little box, Paul?" Deron scoffed. "I think not. Or maybe Jack contaminated that evidence as well. Dragged it off somewhere for safe keeping."

"Bomb squad's here," Moe Bullitt injected. "They're waiting for orders."

Jack ignored Bullitt. "The contents of the box confirm this is a *death scene*, Francis."

"What about the bomb squad, Chief?" Bullitt pushed. "You want to send 'em in or not?"

Jack chuckled. "Only if you're afraid a brain will explode." He lowered his coffee cup and turned to three pairs of wide eyes. "Oops, guess the cat's out the bag. Yes. There is a brain inside that box, gentlemen. Now you know what I know. Let's stop wasting time. Get CSI in there and let the bomb squad go home so they can faithfully serve another day."

"My God," Deron grumbled with a hand over his mouth.

"The brain must be transported to the county morgue."

"Bullitt, send the bomb squad home." Deron waved in the CSI team.

"I'm going in with 'em." Shuck pulled on rubber gloves and departed.

From the front of the SUV Jack, Francis, and Moe watched the circle of flashlights close in on the box. They heard Shuck dish-out process instructions. "A portion of this cardboard box has been contaminated—top flaps. All other aspects are of evidentiary value. Treat accordingly."

They watched the flaps open from afar but could not see the light fall onto the crown of the gray, glistening organ in its burlap nest. Jack walked up behind the cluster of professionals huddled around the box. "I want this aseptically transported to the county morgue. No detours." He turned to Shuck. "Once I remove the brain, the box belongs to the FBI."

Deron and Shuck nodded. The three stepped back and watched CSI do their job.

"It's my father's brain," Jack muttered. A cold silence hung in the air. "I have his DNA on record. I will confirm by noon. I must go prepare. Time is never on our side."

Deron grabbed his shoulder. "There's a chance this is not Ronan's—ah—brain. It could belong to another person, Jack. It could be someone is messing with us."

"How's that even remotely possible, Francis?" Jack said.

"Some sick person determined to inject themselves into the high-profile Burcher case, that's how. We cannot jump to any conclusions before we have the facts. I know you know that. I'm just talking to Jack now, not the county medical examiner."

"I appreciate that, but I'm not the ten-year-old boy you didn't listen to 33 years ago, Francis. I am the Chief Medical Examiner you must listen to. And let me assure you, I never reach conclusions without facts."

Shuck stepped between Jack and Deron. "This is not necessary."

"Right, Paul. I will not jump to the assumption the ghoul that cut out my mother's heart also carved my father's brain from his skull. But as the M.E. with that experience, I do recognize the rare kind of evil that suggests the monster has returned."

"And I say again we do not have enough facts to go there," Deron muttered.

"You want some facts, Francis? Allow me to give you some. A very small circle of people know the details about the positioning of my mother's box by the gates. To this day that information has been held confidential. Since you have not committed that information to memory like me, allow me to refresh your memory.

"The positioning of this box is a perfect replication of the positioning of my mother's box, Francis. Both boxes are precisely twelve feet six inches from the north gate pillar, and nine feet nine inches from the south gate pillar. My mother's box was off center for a reason, Francis. It is so our monster can return and reveal their authenticity by replication."

"It is still not enough, and you know it, Jack. We need to—"

"The cardboard boxes are identical dimensions, Francis."

"It's a standard size box, easily available."

"I saw the logo on the inside flap. This box was manufactured by the Belford Box Company. They produced my mother's box, too."

"I don't recall the name," Deron said looking away. He could not compete with Jack's photographic memory.

"Trust me. I'm right. I looked for the Belford Box Company and discovered they went out of business in 1985; fifteen years after their box was used for my mother's heart. Don't you think it odd tonight's box is a Belford—"

"—my God," Shuck sighed.

"More facts for you, Francis. Both boxes were positioned three feet four inches west of a line connecting the north and south gate pillars. And both boxes were turned forty-five degree to the south." Jack pulled a tape measure from his pocket. "I've been carrying this in my pocket ever since I learned the measurements of Rose's box." He slammed it into Deron's hand.

"For Christ's sake, Jack," Deron moaned.

"When CSI completes their investigation and records their findings—their measurements and precise details—and when they issue their report a week from now in the format you need Francis, you will have allowed another hot trail to go cold."

"That's not necessary," said Paul Shuck.

"No. I'm afraid it is necessary. It is an accurate observation. I am making a point to Francis." He spun from Paul to Deron. "You were here in 1970 with the Tampa Police Department. You were the homicide detective in charge. You failed to recognize and process important information from a ten-year-old boy because the information was not in a format you could allow. Never mind it was true.

"I was that ten-year-old boy, Francis. You did not listen to me then. You failed, Francis. Now I am the Chief Medical

Examiner. I will not allow anyone to dismiss or drag their feet on important information because they are uncomfortable with the way it is presented, or because it suggests incomprehensible possibilities that scare the hell out of your city."

"You feel better now?" Deron sighed. Jack stood up straight nose to nose.

"I'm sorry you've carried all that for so long," Deron said. "You still look at this nightmare through the eyes of a child. Grow up, Jack. People do bad things and get away with it all the time. It does not mean we screwed up."

Jack had argued *for* Deron's point with David just hours before. An uncomfortable silence passed. "This is as good a time as any," Shuck said. "Jack and I discussed something last night. I called him around three with some thoughts gnawing at me. It was right before—"

"—all this happened?" Deron said.

"Yes. We believe mounting evidence points to a *family vendetta,* one that has been going on since 1970 or possibly 1948. Tonight's events further support our theory. We think someone has something against the Burcher family."

"I see." Deron watched the CSI team place the cardboard box into a secured transport container. "And when were you going to share this with the rest of us?"

"Today, Frank. Then this happened."

"I need to go," Jack said. "I need to take a shower and get to the morgue."

"We're not done here," Paul said.

"The sooner I get a look at that brain the better. If it does not belong to my father, you are right and I am wrong, Francis. We will have a new homicide on the books and all our theories on the Burcher family killings stay on the table."

"And if it is Ronan?" Deron asked.

"My father is homicide #72 in the great city of Tampa in 2003. Our family-vendetta theory moves to the top of the list and gets our complete focus."

"I see," Deron said.

"I want David and Melissa moved to an undisclosed location, now."

"We will do that. What about you?"

"You know better. This is what I do. I'll be fine."

"I'm assigning security. That's what I do."

"I need to go," Jack huffed.

"After your little lecture, don't you think it important you stay and tell us what you witnessed?" Deron said.

"No. Actually you were right. I should gather my thoughts, drink coffee, and take a hot shower. I will examine the brain in the morning. We will have answers by afternoon. At one o'clock we can sit down. At that time, I will go through my experience in detail. I remember everything."

On Jack's last word, a stiff cool wind slid off the bay and raked the trees. A tight whirlwind grew above the hot pavement of Crescent Drive. The spiral of leaves and debris took shape and moved toward the CSI team. They put the sealed transport container into the van and turned backs to nature's inconvenient nuisance.

Up and down Crescent jackets flapped, trees churned, and hands covered squinted eyes. Once again, an unknown force of nature had intervened. It dashed the fragile hopes of a forensic team. The small twister swept across the crime scene, in some's eyes like a white rhino in a crystal museum.

When the last swirling devil touched down, Jack turned his back. As he waited for it to subside, he perused the dark stand of trees between Crescent and Interbay Boulevard. His eyes found the small gap of light in the darkness. For an instant a portal through the bending branches appeared. He could see Interbay boulevard thirty yards away. Then the old gray Cadillac with the sweeping fins passed beneath a streetlight. In a blink it was gone, the same car Jack saw at Sun Bay the night Ronan disappeared.

TEN

Hillsborough County Morgue – September 12, 2003 – 7:30

B eneath the hot halogens they stood silent around the long, stainless-steel autopsy table.

Centered on the green sterile towel, the plump human brain glistened—more than 100 billion neurons with a storage capacity of 2,000 terabytes. The biological marvel defines the human mystery in an endless universe. The three pound organ processes and integrates and coordinates everything human. It makes infinite decisions in milliseconds and orchestrates life with impossible perfection. All eyes locked onto the majestic, pearly-gray mass of tissue sitting on the medical examiner's table. How could anything so perfect be dead?

"Hard to believe that's where it all happens," Crabtree whispered in the cold room.

Away from the table Jack Burcher studied an x-ray on his lightbox. After the comment he had second thoughts about Paul's alternate—Milton Crabtree. An FBI Agent. An unknown. Jack had enough unknowns in his autopsy room. He did not like inviting more. Shuck had convinced him. He had some loose ends to attend to before their one o'clock meeting.

"Aristotle believed the heart was the seat of intelligence," Jack said as he squeaked a number onto the grease board next to the lightbox. He took another measurement with his back to his medical team and visitors—Deron, Bullitt, Crabtree, and CSI Gompers. "Aristotle believed the brain was a biological cooling mechanism for blood."

"Like an air conditioner for the body?" Crabtree asked.

"In a way. He reasoned humans were more rational than animals because we had larger brains to cool our hot-bloodedness." Jack chuckled as he wrote another number.

"Hippocrates got it right," Gompers said. "He believed the brain was the seat of intelligence. That was an aggressive position to take back then."

Jack approached the table wearing his mask and hiding his pain. The circle opened and backed away. He snapped on surgical gloves, pulled out a ruler, and patted his father's brain like a newborn. "True Raymond. Good to see CSI reads." The room still felt awkward.

Jack leaned over the pristine organ and gently squeezed. *Still pliable,* he thought. "Every time we recall a memory, or have a new thought, we create another connection in the brain —" His words trailed off as he pressed the cerebrum with two extended fingers at several sites and assessed the elasticity. "—an incredible organ, indeed," he breathed.

"Can you tell me time of death," Deron asked.

Jack blinked back into the crowd at his table. His eyes found the Chief of Police. "It takes ten seconds to lose consciousness after the brain loses its blood supply. Deprivation of oxygen for four to six minutes starts brain death. Without access to the whole body, I am unable to assess most of the key determining parameters—rigor mortis, liver mortis, stomach contents, various vascular markers, changes in body and individual organ temps. Francis, without the body we lose most of the things that allow precision in the determination of time of death."

"I see." Deron huffed.

"However, a ballpark TOD is possible." Jack studied the posterior aspect of the brain. "This organ has not been chemically compromised—not preserved. No signs of refrigeration. No freeze-thaw sequence. Tissue resiliency is good. Water retention is good. That is important because the brain is 75% water. Shrinkage is a prime indicator of elapsed time...

"I do see early signs of desiccation—loss of water. But it's not significant. Happens the moment it's outside the body. Temperature at the end of my driveway at three in the morning —time of delivery—was 78.8°F. Average body temp is 98.6°F. Based on temperature of this brain, and in consideration of all known conditions, I put time of death at two. One hour before I saw it at my gates. Assuming immediate removal of the brain upon death, I give the procedure twenty minutes. Therefore, the execution of my father, and the ensuing operation, happened somewhere within a forty-minute radius of my place by car."

Bullitt leaned into the light. His nose flared. "Killed an hour before delivered—"

Jack scraped tissue from the cerebrum and dropped it into a sterile tissue-collection tube. He snap-sealed the cap and scribbled on the label. With eyes back on the brain, he held up the tube. "Jessica. DNA. STAT." The histologist swept by the ME—like a falcon on a field mouse—and disappeared through the swinging doors with the tube.

Jack slipped on his headset and nodded instructions to his

medical team. Each stepped up to the autopsy table and took their predesignated position. Visitors were escorted to the ceramic-tiled observation deck. Although located in the darkest shadows of the room, the elevation did provide an ideal view.

The Assistant Medical Examiner—Dr. Deborah Quin—pushed through the metal doors like a fighter entering the ring. She snapped on surgical gloves, tied her mask, and slid on her headset without missing a step. The medical team parted. Quin took the center of the table opposite Jack. Their eyes met. The two smiled under masks. Only they knew of the forensic bombshell soon to be revealed. But first the process—the gross, external examination of the organ would be done by the book. Every move mattered. One mistake could send the inquest down the wrong road and decimate a day in court. Only Quin knew Jack's internal struggle.

"Let's begin." Jack turned on his mic. "Date: September 12, 2003. Time: 07:42. Case: #47-589-003. The brain of JOHN/JANE DOE #24 is presented outside the body. Weight: 1175 grams. Temp: 27.33°C. Normal structures present—the cerebrum, cerebellum, and brainstem are intact and without signs of external trauma. Left and right cerebral hemispheres are normal with trace distortion of gray matter along longitudinal fissures on the posterior aspect of the cerebral mantle."

Jack gently flipped over the brain. "Examination of the hippocampus and entorhinal cortex—extreme shrinkage of the cerebral cortex noted." He squeezed the brain between open palms. "I am certain we will find severe enlargement of ventricles with dissection." His eyes found Quin. "Anatomic anomalies are indicators for advanced stage dementia and Parkinson's Disease." His voice cracked. He cleared his throat and pushed forward.

Heads dropped. Visitors whispered. They knew Ronan

Burcher suffered from dementia and Parkinson's. Jack knew long ago he was holding his father in his hands.

The sectioning examination would wait. Something more important had to happen first. "I ask the medical team to move to the ends of the autopsy table. Dr. Quin, please join me on this side. Visitors come forward. Stand across from me." They approached. "You are now official witnesses. Please pay close attention. You may be asked to testify in court."

Deron, Bullitt, Gompers, and Crabtree stood at the metal table; sweaty hands clasped tight behind their backs. Eyes moved from the ME to the brain. Jack held it at the anterior and posterior ends. He lowered his surgical loupes and leaned inches above the superior aspect (top) of the brain and tapped his head mic. "The anterior longitudinal fissure near the central sulcus and parietal lobe marks the site of the postmortem insertion of a metallic disc discovered on x-ray."

"Someone put something inside this brain?" Crabtree muttered.

"My God," Deron said. Heads turned to the lightbox to see what they had missed. The x-ray still hung in place. This time they saw the round white area in the center of the brain.

Jack used tweezers. "I am inspecting the interhemispheric fissure at the suspect entry site." Quin adjusted the overhead light. "I can see a five-centimeter incision line produced by a razor, scalpel, or knife. I can see incision has been rejoined. Not sutures. Not staples. By a liquid adhesive agent. Because there are only three small adhesion sites at the superior edge of the incision, I am confident they used a cyanoacrylate adhesive— CA glue."

His scalpel broke the adhered sites. The surgical wound opened. With tweezers Jack widened the pocket and Quin aimed a light inside. "I am introducing a measuring probe to size the pre-formed pocket in the cerebrum." He lowered the probe past the metal object and moved the width of the wound. "The pocket is nine centimeters deep and five centimeters wide.

"I am removing the metallic object." The medical photographer moved closer snapping shots. His strobe buzzed and recycled after each. After Jack removed the metal object, he placed it on his open palm and held it under the halogens for all to inspect. More pictures were taken. More flashes filled the room. "This is someone's mistake."

"What the hell is it?" Deron asked.

"A Presidential Medal of Freedom," Bullitt said. "I've seen one before."

"It's not real. It's a fake. A souvenir," Crabtree said.

Jack turned it over. More pictures were taken. He dropped it into a sterile bag. "This has trace blood to analyze. There could be a partial fingerprint. There could be DNA."

"Why put that thing in a brain?" Deron scoffed. Jack ignored the comment and tone from the Chief of Police. He turned his attentions to the pocket in the brain. Jack injected sterile saline until it was full. He inserted a sterile syringe, removed the fluid, and passed it to Dr. Quin. "We will evaluate this fluid and telltale debris. It very well could be—"

"—someone's playing a sick game. This is silly," Deron said. "A waste of our time to mess with. Just give me that thing. I'll take it. Doesn't need to distract from real evidence."

"You know better, Francis," Jack said as he bagged the medallion and leaned back into the shadows to a staff member. He turned back to the bright lights, picked up a large knife, and fileted the brain in seconds. He carved perfect, quarter-inch-thick sections. The brain was gone. Now a dozen petite steaks were evenly fanned-out for histological examination.

As his hands moved the delicate tissue slices onto slides, Jack eyed Deron. He had moved into the shadows. Jack watched him edge up to the controlled stack of evidence trays. And then Novak intervened. The two engaged in a brisk but muffled discussion. A battle ensued, but Jack did not need to hear words. He knew Deron would use position and power to brow-beat Novak into submission. And he knew Novak would not yield. The forensic investigator had a nickname in England —Beartrap. Nobody messed with Novak's chain of evidence. Not the Prime Minister. Not the POTUS. And not the Chief of Police.

Jack smiled when Deron stormed from the autopsy room empty-handed. CSI agents, Moe Bullitt, and Milton Crabtree followed. When the metal doors stopped swinging, Quinn passed the evidence bag with the Presidential Medal of Freedom and Jack left the table. Dr. Quinn and Novak would finish up.

"How does he do that?" Novak breathed. "Our fearless leader processed his father's brain by the book. Flawless. Without hesitations. And without emotions. Nothing. It was his father's brain, for God's sake. The man needs to take time for himself. He must—"

"—embrace his loss," Quin whispered as they both watched Jack push through the metal doors and disappear. "He has, Mr. Novak. It took a lot for him to do this, this morning. He felt he had to do it. He can't live much longer without answers to his family nightmare."

"Still. He was cutting up his father's brain. You can't just ignore that reality. The man's father was butchered seven hours ago. My God. He needs time with all that."

"Jack stayed with his father all night, Hugo. Like he was protecting him. I had to get him to bring the brain in here. Yes. He was his father's son from the moment he had that brain. And he was the Chief Medical Examiner all morning. Jack is not capable showing his pain."

ELEVEN

FBI Tampa Bay Regional Office – September 12, 2003 – 10:00

"I'm looking at it now, the Pasadena article on Leonard Burcher. Died in '48. Tell me you got more." With the phone pressed to his ear, Shuck squinted at his pitiful photostat.

The Pasadena Independent

10¢ or $1 a month delivered

Teen Dies in Car Crash

HOLLYWOOD – September 10, 1948 – Caltech freshman Leonard Burcher was found dead in a car off Highway 41 to Salinas. Pasadena Police reports the Burcher vehicle lost control on the shoulder of Highway 41. The 1940 Oldsmobile traveled into Savoy Canyon and dropped more than 100 feet landing upside down. According to the police, the car was found by hikers several days after the accident. Leonard Burcher was reported missing on September 6, when he did not return home as expected. The Los Angeles County Coroner ruled death occurred in the evening hours of September 6. Cause of death appears to be a broken neck. An autopsy is scheduled. Burcher is survived by a brother Ronan and parents Otto and Emily. Funeral arrangements are pending at this time. Those with information about this car accident are asked to contact the Pasadena Police Department.

"Believe it or not, I got my hands on the police report. It's not something I can fax you. If I scan the thing you would not be able to read much. The ink's fading. It's worse than the newspaper article I sent. Anyway, Pasadena PD allowed me to

"How's that even remotely possible, Francis?" Jack said.

"Some sick person determined to inject themselves into the high-profile Burcher case, that's how. We cannot jump to any conclusions before we have the facts. I know you know that. I'm just talking to Jack now, not the county medical examiner."

"I appreciate that, but I'm not the ten-year-old boy you didn't listen to 33 years ago, Francis. I am the Chief Medical Examiner you must listen to. And let me assure you, I never reach conclusions without facts."

Shuck stepped between Jack and Deron. "This is not necessary."

"Right, Paul. I will not jump to the assumption the ghoul that cut out my mother's heart also carved my father's brain from his skull. But as the M.E. with that experience, I do recognize the rare kind of evil that suggests the monster has returned."

"And I say again we do not have enough facts to go there," Deron muttered.

"You want some facts, Francis? Allow me to give you some. A very small circle of people know the details about the positioning of my mother's box by the gates. To this day that information has been held confidential. Since you have not committed that information to memory like me, allow me to refresh your memory.

"The positioning of this box is a perfect replication of the positioning of my mother's box, Francis. Both boxes are precisely twelve feet six inches from the north gate pillar, and nine feet nine inches from the south gate pillar. My mother's box was off center for a reason, Francis. It is so our monster can return and reveal their authenticity by replication."

"It is still not enough, and you know it, Jack. We need to—"

"The cardboard boxes are identical dimensions, Francis."

"It's a standard size box, easily available."

"I saw the logo on the inside flap. This box was manufactured by the Belford Box Company. They produced my mother's box, too."

"I don't recall the name," Deron said looking away. He could not compete with Jack's photographic memory.

"Trust me. I'm right. I looked for the Belford Box Company and discovered they went out of business in 1985; fifteen years after their box was used for my mother's heart. Don't you think it odd tonight's box is a Belford—"

"—my God," Shuck sighed.

"More facts for you, Francis. Both boxes were positioned three feet four inches west of a line connecting the north and south gate pillars. And both boxes were turned forty-five degree to the south." Jack pulled a tape measure from his pocket. "I've been carrying this in my pocket ever since I learned the measurements of Rose's box." He slammed it into Deron's hand.

"For Christ's sake, Jack," Deron moaned.

"When CSI completes their investigation and records their findings—their measurements and precise details—and when they issue their report a week from now in the format you need Francis, you will have allowed another hot trail to go cold."

"That's not necessary," said Paul Shuck.

"No. I'm afraid it is necessary. It is an accurate observation. I am making a point to Francis." He spun from Paul to Deron. "You were here in 1970 with the Tampa Police Department. You were the homicide detective in charge. You failed to recognize and process important information from a ten-year-old boy because the information was not in a format you could allow. Never mind it was true.

"I was that ten-year-old boy, Francis. You did not listen to me then. You failed, Francis. Now I am the Chief Medical borrow the original for a few days. I'm not allowed to take it out of the city."

"Come on, Worley. You can do better than that."

He flipped pages. "I gotta work with these people, Paul. You can always come here... Wait. I think I found something. Well, this is interesting."

"What? Talk to me." Shuck breathed into the phone.

"Leonard Burcher reported a traffic incident to police. He was being followed from campus. Smart kid. Went to Caltech. World-renowned science and engineering college. Not an easy place to get in—"

"Get on with it, Bob."

"Right. Burcher reported to police a car came very close to running into him. Left him on the side of the road. Guess it scared him enough to report it the same day. It happened three days before the fatal accident on Highway 41."

"Jesus. This is relevant. I need more."

"There's not a lot here. Wait! I found another notation to the file referencing—"

"Referencing what?"

"Here we go. Found it. This is worse. On September 5th at 3:20 pm a green Chevrolet ran Leonard off the road. This makes two. Happened on South Fair Oaks at East Walnut Street near Caltech. This time there were witnesses. Leonard was forced off the road. Fortunately, he found a vacant lot. No one got hurt—

"Says here the green Chevy backed up and driver yelled at Burcher before leaving the scene. A witness—Stella Pembroke, seventeen—described the driver. An Asian man in his 50s. There was an old Asian woman in the backseat holding a baby. No license plate number."

"What did the guy say to Leonard?"

"He said, 'you will pay. You *all* will pay.'"

You all will pay, Shuck thought. "And the Pasadena Police didn't find this a relevant connection to the unwitnessed fatal accident one day later?" he scoffed.

"Policing back then was not like today, Paul."

"This is not sub-par policing. This is an abomination. No sense in trying to run down Pembroke. She's probably married or dead or long gone from Pasadena."

"She'd be seventy-two. It's a long shot. Is it worth a look?"

"Not yet. Is there any chance they did an autopsy on Leonard?"

"They did. I sent it to you in July. Sent it with the Michaelson dossier. Remember, you wanted some backup dirt for the Preston case."

"I never needed Michaelson. Put Preston away without it. Never saw that postmortem."

"Maybe Mrs. Bertrand has it in one of your piles."

"I need you to do me one more favor. Take a look at the news stories on and around September 6, 1948, the Pasadena area. Maybe something will jump out that can help."

"That's a stretch, but I'll check and get back to you today." Worley hung up.

"Mrs. Bertrand," Shuck yelled into the reception area.

The plump administrative assistant with the silver bun entered. Peering over her candy-red eyeglasses with the swinging beaded chains, she braked at the front of his desk and held out a thin stack of papers. "It sat on my desk long enough to find the bottom of a—"

"—thank you, Mrs. Bertrand." Paul snatched the document and turned to the window flipping the cover page. After twenty years of dead bodies he had experience reading autopsy reports. A 1948 postmortem would be a forensic walk in the park.

"Let's see what we have here," Shuck whispered as he

flipped pages. *An eighteen-year-old white male,* he read, *presents in normal healthy condition.* "Really," *but for excessive trauma to the head and neck and upper torso. The transverse processes of* C1 *and* C2 *are crushed and dislocated tearing the ligamentum nuchea and severing the spinous processes.*

"Okay. We have a broken neck." He reads on. *The superior aspect of the parietal, frontal, nasal, and malar bones are fractured and intact. Deep bruising and extensive contusions present in the superior aspect of the frontal and parietal lobes, and the inferior aspect of the cerebellum.* "Okay, I guess that happened when the car landed upside down on the canyon floor. I need pictures. What else?" *Upper torso damage. Both clavicles snapped. Sternum crushed. Four ribs snapped. Both arms, humerus fractured. One radius and one ulna snapped. Both femurs crushed. Nothing to the pelvis, tibia, or feet...*

Shuck lit a cigarette and flipped through the anatomical diagrams. "What else? So far, I got a dead guy in a car at the bottom of a canyon, but something smells."

Conclusions. Summary. "I like conclusions and summaries." Shuck scanned and flipped pages. *Okay, okay, okay. Not helping, not helping, nothing, nothing. Here we go. What's this? Atypical or lack of bleeding at multiple secondary trauma sites presupposes that clinical death followed blunt force trauma to the head and neck. Absent to minimal evidence of hemorrhage at all other trauma sites indicates sufficient time elapse between primary trauma (head and neck) and secondary trauma (upper torso and femurs). Unable to reconstruct accident scene. Cause of death trauma to head and neck. Manner of death, accidental.*

"What the hell? There's no way the head and neck injuries happened at or near the same time as the other injuries," Shuck muttered as he stared at the glistening bay.

The phone rang. "Miss me," Worley teased.

"What do you want?"

"Whoa, all business. You found something in less than twenty minutes. Tell me."

"Leonard was dead before he reached the bottom of the canyon."

"How do you know that, Sherlock?"

"In '48 the police were not lookin' for homicides like we do today. Back then homicides found them. Too many of those guys processed death scenes without a critical eye. Not like today. Every death is first scrutinized as a homicide—must be ruled out. Fifty years ago, traumatic deaths were handled like they looked: nasty accident or a sad suicide. You know we see a lot of homicides made to look like suicides, accidents, and even natural deaths...

"Dead people don't bleed like live people, Bob. Someone hit Leonard over the head hard enough to shatter his skull and break his neck. That killed him damn near instantly. A body takes a few minutes to realize death. When it does, everything stops including the heart pumping blood through the veins and arteries. Leonard did not bleed at any of his other injury sites. That can only mean he had been dead long before he hit the floor of that canyon. I suspect the killer expected a fire would seal his tomb. Instead, inept cops did it for 'em."

"You'd have trouble getting anywhere with a 50-year-old theory in a courtroom."

"My assessment would not stand up in court. A forensic pathologist reviewing this postmortem would reach the same conclusion. Textbook. That would stand up in court."

"Why does Leonard's death matter to you?"

"It impacts two active investigations—the 33-year-old Rose Burcher cold case and the one day old Ronan Burcher case. Both are abductions and homicides. A theory on the table is we are dealing with a family vendetta with roots. Leonard takes this thing back to 1948."

"Multi-generational capers are rare and difficult to—"

"—get a handle on. I agree. Why'd you call back?"

"I did some checkin' on the news around his death day. Nothing stood out. As a matter of fact, there was only one story dominating the news around then. Richard C. Tolman died in Pasadena September 5th, 1948. He was a world-renowned professor of natural chemistry and mathematical physics. He taught at Caltech."

"Where Leonard matriculated," Paul muttered.

"It's possible he knew Tolman. I don't know if it's relevant—"

"—why was Tolman a big story? College professors die all the time."

"This one was big. He was one of the guys running the Manhattan Project during World War II. They developed the friggin' atomic bomb, Paul. Tolman stayed involved in that stuff up until his death. When he died, he was the chief advisor to the U.S. representative to the UN Atomic Energy Commission."

"Still, the Caltech connection's thin," Shuck said as he checked his watch. "Thanks for looking. Let me know if you find anything else. I gotta go. Have a date with a brain at the county morgue."

"Sounds wonderful..."

TWELVE

Hillsborough County Morgue – September 12, 2003 – 7:30

J ack agreed to a one o'clock meeting. He had another crazy morning after another crazy night. With more cases waiting, the conference room at the Hillsborough County Institute of Forensic Science would have to suffice—he had no time to travel to the TPD or FBI offices.

The long, polished-oak table seated twenty-four, the typical crowd for an inquest or press conference. When the doors closed this time, eighteen seats were empty. At the end sat Jack Burcher. On his left were Paul Shuck and Dr. Quin. On his right were Francis Deron and Moe Bullitt. With a *Diamante*™ keyboard on a tripod, a court stenographer sat catty-corner to Jack.

Although the meeting had nothing to do with a binding deposition or other official court business, a stenographer had been engaged by the FBI. Jack made it clear he would go over the early morning events at the Burcher estate once. The FBI needed the narrative on the record, and they wanted to keep Jack Burcher engaged, in a positive way. They would make all necessary accommodations.

The Burcher family mystery had escalated. More agents were being assigned. The FBI had to bring everyone up to speed, on all aspects of the case, fast. After 33 years, Jack was done jumping through FBI hoops. He rejected the use of recording devices because he learned the spoken word can often be manipulated to bite him in the ass. He agreed to a stenographer—the resulting written narrative then subject to his prior review and approval.

"Jack let's start at the time of our phone call," Paul Shuck said. "A quick recap. I called you at 2:57 am earlier this morning." He pulled a file and dog-eared yellow pad from his worn satchel. "We were winding up our conversation at 3:07 am.

"At the end of our call I sensed you were distracted. Your comments were short, dismissive. Then you said goodbye and were gone, but you did not disconnect your phone. For thirty seconds I listened to explosive breathing—panting. I imagined you were on the move, going somewhere or being chased. I heard the trampling of brush—maybe pushing through bushes or tall grass, or wildflowers. Your phone disconnected. Later you told me you had slipped it into your pocket. It was programed to shut off after thirty seconds of inactivity on your part."

"Sounds about right," Jack said as he watched the stenographer's fingers dance over the small keyboard at lightning speed. Then, with a soft smile, her eyes found his.

Kayda Webster was not new. She had been called to his office before—depositions, inquests, and other legal procedures.

She had always been accompanied by a covey of over-demanding lawyers on a clock.

Jack did not notice many women, but he did notice this alluring Asian beauty with jet-black hair, crystal-green eyes, and professional demeanor. When Jack separated from Patricia in 2002, he ran into Kayda at a political function at the Aloft Tampa Downtown. Many drinks and conversations later they shared a long dinner. It turned into a night of wild, athletic sex. After the most memorable night, they discretely saw each other or talked every day. Their budding love affair came to an abrupt halt, when the Burcher family attorneys orchestrated a business end to Jack's marital separation from Patricia. Billionaires do not divorce fast. Jack's *marriage of record* had nothing to do with love and everything to do with managing enormous family assets. The legal instrument restored the marriage on paper for the temporary management of assets and spawned a difficult end to Jack's torrid love affair.

"Jack...?" Shuck said. "Jack? Please go ahead. I'm done. You have the stage."

"Right." He rubbed his face as if he had just gotten out of bed. "It's been a long day."

"Give Jack a bottle of water, someone," Shuck ordered. "I know. You were up all night, and then busy this morning in the autopsy room—"

"—with my father's brain," Jack said glaring at Chief Deron. His eyes found Paul. "As you said in your opening comments, we were talking around three in the morning. Our conversation concluded. I heard something, the front of the house. For those wondering where I could have possibly been at three in the morning to hear something in the front of my house, I had fallen asleep on the back patio. It had been another long day. Paul's call awakened me from a deep sleep. One I desperately needed."

"Sorry about that, Jack. Tell us about what you heard in front of your house."

"A steady growling sound. Low pitched. Rolling. Continuous."

"Like an animal?" Shuck asked.

"More mechanical."

"Like a car engine?"

"Yeah, but not like today's cars," Jack said.

"An old car? Or perhaps something else, like a motor powering a craft of some kind?"

"Let's not get hung up on the *unknown* making the sound. The important thing is the sound got my attention for three reasons. It was unique. It was in the middle of the night. And, it was not the first time I had heard it."

"When did you hear it before, Jack?" Paul asked.

"33 years ago. I was ten. I heard it twice."

Deron shook his head.

"Back then I was sitting in the field outside my bedroom window, something I did most nights in the summer. I heard that growling sound first the night my mother was taken."

"You said you heard it twice."

"I heard it again the next night. The night the box was delivered to the house. Put at the end of our driveway. The one with my mother's heart inside."

The stenographer shrieked. "Ah... I'm so sorry."

"No. I'm sorry, Miss Webster. I should have been more delicate—"

"It is possible you're imagining this, too. Isn't that right Jack?" Deron said.

"Chief, please do not do that," Paul said. "You're my guest. The Burcher case is FBI jurisdiction. This is an FBI inquiry. Next time, you will be escorted out."

Deron's eyes narrowed on Jack. He nodded.

Jack's eyes stayed on Deron. "No. It is not possible I imagined it. I am as certain today as I was 33 years ago, when the Tampa police failed to listen to their only eyewitness. I know you remember this, Chief Deron. I was ten. You were the homicide detective in charge. You and your people blew it. If you had listened, maybe Ronan would still be sitting on his bed at Sun Bay and my mother's executioner would be in prison."

"Please delete the last paragraph, Miss Webster," Paul whispered. "Jack. Please. I want us to focus on the recent events. Let's go back to this early morning experience. You were saying you heard a mechanical growling sound. You went to investigate. What happened next? You left—"

"—the back patio. I was curious. I wanted to find the source of that sound. I had trouble walking. I had had too much to drink. I worked my way up the side of the house. You probably heard me rubbing up against the junipers along the side of the house. When I got to the front, I saw—"

"Go ahead, Jack."

"—this thing on Crescent at the end of the driveway. It floated outside the gates. They're always open." He swallowed hard and closed his eyes. "It hovered a foot off the ground. The morning fog is always thick on Ballast Point this time of year. The fog hugs the ground."

"Can you describe the thing floating, the source of the growling sound?"

"It was long. A dull gray tube with shiny black glass around the top. It had fins. I did not see lights. It floated above the ground and growled."

"Do you think it could have been a UFO, Jack?"

"I don't know. That is one possibility. An unidentified *floating* object. I don't necessarily want to put it in the Sci-Fi category. I do know it is real. Like the iron gates and rock wall are real. Exactly what it is, I don't know. I just stood there and watched it for several minutes. Fifty yards away. That's only a hundred-fifty feet."

"How much of it was the scotch talkin'," Deron muttered. Shuck held up a hand.

"A shadow appeared. Could have been a man or a woman. The shadow was short and thin. Moved at a determined pace. Approached the gates holding a box with both hands. Held it out front at the waist.

"Then I fell. Tripped on a front porch step. Fell face down in a puddle. Laid there. Disoriented. By the time I wiped the mud from my eyes, the shadow was gone, and the gray tube started to growl louder. It slid into a wall of fog. There was a flash of light. That was it."

"When did you see the box sitting on the driveway, Jack?"

"After the flash of light. I stood there processing."

"Processing all that you had just witnessed," Paul said.

"Yes. I did not want to go to the box but knew I would."

The stenographer's face revealed growing angst as Jack told his story. Her fingers moved over the keys robotically. Chief Deron and Detective Bullitt were masters at hiding emotions, but this time Bullitt revealed his greatest areas of interest. Each time he scribbled in his notebook and bit his lip. Dr. Quin was silent. She watched Jack like a student in love with her professor.

"Then what did you do, Jack?" Paul asked.

"I walked to the box. It seemed to take me forever. Thoughts were all over the place. I remembered all of it." He turned to Paul with burning eyes. "You are back. You killed my mother and now you are back to kill my father?" He turned to the window. "Who are you? What do you want with us? Why are you doing—?"

"—Jack. Jack. Let's take a minute. Someone give Jack more water."

He stared out the window as he drank water. In his head, his eyes stayed on the gates and the box. "I gotta get to the box, but I cannot disrupt a crime scene. There may be something important. A clue we desperately need."

He blinked back into the room and turned back to the table. "It never dawned on me to call anyone. I was alone in the moment. It was just me and the box."

Jack got to his feet and walked to the window shaking his arms. He stopped next to Kayda Webster. Her fingers stopped. He smelled her perfume. He turned to the table. "I stood there, a few feet away. I looked around, all directions. I was alone. I smelled something. It was bitter, caustic. A mixture of burnt oil, steam, wet gravel, and dead leaves."

"The smell of carbon monoxide mixed with the smells of wet asphalt and dead leaves?"

"Maybe. Maybe something else. Not sure." He rubbed his neck. His eyes found Webster's. Her fingers stopped again. Her face revealed nothing. *You feel distant,* he thought. *Do you hate me, now? No. It's my family nightmare. You think I'm crazy. I'm scaring you—*

"—Jack," Paul said. "What happened next? Do you need a break?"

His eyes left Webster. "No. I'm fine." He looked out the window. "Put on my gloves. Always have latex gloves. It's a habit," he snickered. No one laughed. "And my penlight. I pulled it out and turned it on. Held it in my mouth, shining on the box. I opened the flaps.

"The flaps were left loose. The box was not sealed on top. Whoever did this, knew I would not break a seal." He rubbed his neck. "They wanted me to look inside the box. Be the first. Do it alone. They wanted that. I know that now."

"You opened the flaps and—"

"—I looked inside. I see the top of a brain. It had been cleaned and rinsed. I knew it had to be my father's. They killed my father like they killed my mother. They want to hurt—"

"—but at the time you did not know," Paul said. "Is that right, Jack?"

He pivoted around to Paul with authority. "I'm a doctor. You know nothing about human anatomy. I'm not living in your world, sir. I know human anatomy. I saw the excessive shrinkage of the cerebral cortex and hippocampus. I medically assessed the enlarged ventricles. I know what that means, Mr. Shuck—dementia and Parkinson's.

"No! I could not select my father's brain from other similarly diseased brains. No one could. But my initial conclusion was the most reasonable one. It was not my final one."

"I understand. I'm sorry. I just wanted it on the record. At the time of discovery, you did not know for certain the brain belonged to you father. Let's move on. What happened next?"

"I did measurements. Yes. I always have a tape measure in my pocket, too. I'm a forensic person. I analyze. I study. After several measurements, I wandered onto Crescent Drive, the cul da sac. I was overwhelmed. I knew the monster had returned and wanted me to know."

"What happened next, Jack?"

"The lights coming toward me. I stood there. I was next. It was my turn. Then the lights stopped. I collapsed. I don't remember anything after that."

"Do you remember me taking you to my SUV?"

"No. I remember sitting in your SUV. People swarming. I remember coffee."

"Good. I have enough. I think we're done." Paul signaled

the stenographer. She dropped her hands to her lap. "Thank you, Jack. This has been very helpful."

Everyone got to their feet and stood behind their chairs awaiting instructions. Director Shuck approached the stenographer and whispered, "Did you get everything, Miss Webster?"

"I did."

"Good. Let me remind you of our agreement. The transcript of this meeting is the sole property of the FBI. As we previously agreed the FBI will take possession of your *Diamante*™ steno-machine. We will extract our property and scrub the device to our satisfaction and return it to you tomorrow morning."

"I understand," she said with eyes locked on Shuck's.

"Everything you heard in this room is privileged information. It is to be held confidential and proprietary. Under no circumstances are you authorized to disclose any part of it to anybody. That is under penalty of law. Do you understand this, Miss Webster?"

"Yes sir. I do." She got to her feet and straightened her dress. She smiled at Shuck and nodded at Jack. "I can find my way out."

The door closed behind the stenographer escorted by Dr. Quin. Shuck, Bullitt, Deron, and Burcher took their chairs. "I am ready to talk about the brain, gentlemen," Jack said.

His eyes leveled on Francis Deron. "The DNA confirms we have Ronan's brain."

"I'm sorry, Jack," Paul whispered.

"I'm not surprised," Bullitt said. "We expected—"

"I'm okay with you being right, Jack. I hope you know that," Deron said.

Jack stared without emotion. *You dropped the ball 33 years ago,* he thought. *I won't let you drop the ball again.*

"Before I continue, tell us about CSI findings with the box."

"We confirmed the manufacturer is the Belford Box Company," Deron said. "As you pointed out earlier, they are the same company that manufactured Rose's box. It is troubling this box appears to be new, never used. Belford no longer exists. Again, you were correct. They closed their doors in 1985"

"The killer planned ahead," Jack seethed. "I wonder how many more boxes he has."

"CSI recovered a plethora of particulate debris—soil, sand, silt, pollen, algae, and plant. It appears to be debris common to the Hillsborough region. All of it is surface debris, meaning it was not yet absorbed into the cardboard except for trace blood from the brain inside the box. This evidence could narrow down our search radius."

"What about fingerprints?" Paul asked.

"No prints. Also swabbed for DNA. No report yet."

"Send the box to Quantico. This case is priority."

Jack slid a plastic bag to Paul. "You missed this today. We found it on x-ray. A medallion inside a pocket in the cerebrum."

"Crabtree mentioned this to me." Paul studied the medallion. "An imitation Presidential Medal of Freedom. Something you can find in souvenir stores at every national museum around the country. They're not unique. I suspect they pound out thousands every year.

"I see a lot number," Paul muttered. "We can have our people look into it. May be able to find where this one came from. If we're lucky, there'll have video. We may see who bought it. Says it was made in 2003. This year. We're in September. Nine months to look at."

"Why put a Presidential Medal of Freedom in Ronan's brain?" Jack muttered. "What does it mean? Kill a sick old man, take out his brain, and give him a medal."

"It's a symbol," Bullitt said. "Means somethin' to the killer. Maybe some game."

"What are your thoughts, Jack?" Shuck asked.

"I don't believe this killer plays games. Everything means something. This killer is on a mission. My family has done something. I do not know what a President's Medal of Freedom means, yet. The cardboard box and the positioning connect the kills. The killer wanted to reveal authenticity. Wants me to know it's on. The organ selection means something, too."

"A heart first. Now a brain," Paul muttered.

Jack nodded. "Pieces to a grisly puzzle and—"

"And what, Jack?"

"The medallion. We missed something. Before. He wants us to go back for it."

"Missed what? Go back for what?" Shuck barked.

"You did not x-ray your mother's heart," Deron sighed.

"They just buried it," Jack said.

"In 1997, I established a new standard operating procedure. All bodies and organs that enter the county medical examiner's system must be x-rayed. Up until '97 it was a random procedure. Primarily done when we were looking for bullets or assessing skeletal trauma.

"Our killer knew we would x-ray the brain this time," Jack muttered. "He knew we would find the medallion. He wanted us to go find his little surprise inside my mother's heart. We must exhume."

"Killer knows your internal operation," Shuck said as he studied the medallion.

"He's closer to you than we thought, Dr. Burcher," Bullitt said. "Could be among us." Jack saw a hint of discomfort in Deron's eyes.

"What's this?" Paul held up the medallion. Looks like

something pressed onto the back. A capital "C" on its side with an equal sign beneath it."

Jack examined the image. "It has been stamped into the medallion. It's not part of the manufacturing process. The letter "C" disrupts the line of stars along the perimeter."

"Another piece to the puzzle," Bullitt muttered as he wrote in his pocket notebook.

"You're chasing ghosts. What else," Deron said. "I've got to be somewhere."

"I did not attend the autopsy this morning because I had a follow-up meeting with one of our agents in Pasadena," Shuck said. "He's looking into Leonard Burcher's death."

"He died fifty years ago in a car accident," Deron scoffed as he got out of his chair. "We looked at it in 1970. Nothing there. Lost control. Drove into a canyon at night. It happens."

Paul passed a stapled document to Jack. "Leonard's postmortem. Ruling was accidental death. Like Frank said, car left the road. Found at the bottom of a canyon. No witnesses."

"You're overthinking this one, Mr. Shuck." Deron pushed his chair to the table.

"Maybe. But something's not right. A few days before the fatal accident Leonard filed a report with the Pasadena police. Leonard said he was being followed. On two occasions, he reported being run off the road. Then we have the fatal accident. With that information, do you think the next day he suddenly ran his car off a cliff, Frank?"

"He was a teen. They do stupid things. Some pay the ultimate price."

"Leonard was eighteen. A freshman at Caltech. You could say he was into drugs and owed someone money or was a member of a fraternity drunk one night, or a member of a gang and was on the run. You can hypothesize anything you want.

Still falls short if you want facts." Paul watched Jack flip pages and devour the postmortem.

"I'm saying it's old. It's another distraction like the silly medallion," Deron said.

"A witness reported an Asian man in a green Chevy ran Leonard off the road into a vacant lot," Shuck said. "The Asian man backed up and yelled at Leonard—you will pay, you all will pay. There was an Asian lady in the backseat holding a baby. The man driving was in his fifties. And there was no license plate on the green Chevy."

"It's all relevant," Jack said.

"You don't seriously believe Leonard Burcher's death is connected to any of this?" Deron huffed. "The man died in a car accident. He died like most people who find the bottom of a canyon. People get mad in cars all the time. Road rage's been around a long time."

Jack looked up from the report. "Leonard was dead before his car found the bottom of the canyon, Francis." He slid the report back to Paul.

"What're you talkin' about? There's no way you could know."

"There's no question about it." Jack leaned closer. "Zero, Francis. The forensics are solid. I will take this postmortem report into any courtroom and change the ruling from accidental death to homicide. The pathology shows without a doubt Leonard Burcher was dead long before he and his car found the bottom of that canyon."

"Then why didn't the Pasadena Medical Examiner find that, Jack?" Deron pressed.

"Fair question," Paul said.

"In '48, coroners were not all doctors, and medical examiners were pathologists or GPs. They were not forensic pathologist. They missed a lot obvious today. All you need to know is *dead men don't bleed.* The 1948 postmortem on Leonard Burcher reported multiple and severe traumatic injuries: head, neck, arms, legs, and upper torso. Only the head hemorrhaged. Leonard was dead hours before his body was exposed to further trauma."

"Paul said the kid could have been into drugs or a member of a gang," Deron said. "He could have gotten himself into trouble. I don't see a connection to Rose or Ronan."

"Correction, Frank. I said possibly," Paul said. "By all accounts Leonard Burcher was described as a quiet, introverted boy. No police record. Played tennis and read books. The kid was a 1948 nerd. He loved chemistry and mathematics. He was on the dean's list all through high school. He got accepted to Caltech. That's where *genius nerds* go, Frank. I doubt seriously Leonard was a bad kid. It's more likely he was a good kid and important to his family."

"I wonder why he was being followed," Bullitt said. "Who runs a good kid off the road? Leonard did go to the police. You don't do that if you're up to no good."

"We need to pay attention to this," Jack said. "Ronan's only brother is the third family homicide we know about. We must look into all Burcher deaths to find out what it means."

"You're getting too scattered" Deron scoffed. "Everything can't be important. You gotta focus. All this other stuff takes us off the Ronan case."

"If this is some kind of family vendetta, we need to find out why."

"And if it goes back fifty years, we're probably dealing with more than one killer."

"An eighty-year-old person did not take and kill Ronan," Bullitt said.

Paul held up the plastic bag with medallion. "Someone is leaving us clues—"

The bag with the medallion exploded from Shuck's hand and flew across the room. Eyes turned to the window. A crack climbed the glass. Then another pelt and another crack. "Down," Bullitt yelled. "We've got us a shooter—"

Jack slid off his chair. He saw another flash in the trees. Jack dropped to the floor as Paul dove for the medallion. Bullitt reached for his gun. Deron got up from his chair last. Two more pelts came. The window exploded. Glass rained down. Blood sprayed the conference table.

THIRTEEN

Hillsborough County Morgue – September 12, 2003 – 14:05

At 13:30 Paul Shuck called the Tampa PD, Burcher attended to Deron, and Bullitt jumped out the window, in pursuit of the shooter. At 13:37 SWAT cordoned-off the medical examiner's building on North 46th and the ambulances pulled up surrounded by men with rifles.

At 13:50, twenty minutes after the shooting, the Hillsborough Sheriff had established a one-mile perimeter: roadblocks, choppers in the air, and deputies with dogs on foot. They would scour the cordoned area. The forensic staff had been moved to the secured basement of the county morgue for protection and vetting. The nature and extent of the assault was unknown.

Only four knew what really had happened, and they had no intention of sharing the details. The active FBI investigation could not be compromised. Jack and Paul kept a low profile as Moe ran with the herd and Francis fought for his life on an operating room table. The police had put Jack and Paul behind locked doors in the forensic library away from windows and staff for their own safety. As police hunted the shooter and secured the building, Jack and Paul sat alone. They scrutinized the medallion shot from Paul's hand—another piece to the puzzle.

"We can't bring more local law enforcement into this," Paul said. "The deal was only Deron, Bullitt, Quinn, and Novak. They got history." He shook the plastic bag with the damaged medallion. "And now, we cannot tell anyone else about what just happened here, this medallion shot out of my hand. We gotta get through this event without talking about this thing."

"Relax. It won't be hard to keep a lid on it." Jack ran a finger over a line of books on a shelf as if he was hunting for something special. "We process hundreds of homicides here every year. We send a lot of bad people to jail, and we send some real monsters to death row. It's too bad these psychopaths have someone that loves them so much they can't see the evil. They convince themselves the big bad world is picking on their loved one. Thank God only a sliver of these lost souls actually seek some form of retribution."

"That's another category for us to think about," Paul muttered as he looked at Jack through the hole in the medallion. "Our shooter obliterated the big star on this thing. He does possess some unique and disturbing skills. Probably could have put a bullet in my eye."

"I don't think that's what this was about. He patiently waited for you to hold the bag just right so he could hit the medallion. You'd be dead if he wanted you dead, Paul. I bet he could have killed anyone of us if he wanted. He didn't. Maybe he's telling us something about this medallion is important. It's like they want us to solve this mystery, but we gotta earn it."

"He took down Chief Deron." Paul said. "Is that another message?"

"I do not know. Maybe collateral damage. The medal is supposed to tell us something."

A knock at the door rolled through the small library. Paul stuffed the bagged medallion into his pocket. Jack cleared his throat and said, "Who's there?"

"Sergeant Mack Sutton. SWAT. We need to talk."

The sinewy officer made the door look small. He entered. His large hands loosened Velcro straps on his Kevlar vest as he slid a Glock into his hip holster. The black shoulder mic scratched and popped with jumbled transmissions—coordinating SWAT. It softened when he pinched the black knob. Jack tried not to stare at the saber tattoo on Sutton's neck. But the tip of the blade inched out his collar as he scanned the room looking for something to kill.

"How are my people?" Jack asked. "I guess maybe I should talk to them soon."

"They're good. Don't worry about it. They're in the basement with the dead bodies." He finished eyeing the room and turned his full attention to Burcher. "They're safe. And they're not going anywhere until we finish our sweep and vetting."

"When you find out what's going on, please let us know," Shuck said.

"You have trouble with any of your people, Doc?" Sutton asked.

"No. Thirty-eight professionals. Most have been here longer than me."

"Good." He checked his watch and turned a face dial three clicks. SWAT had a timeline for everything. "Chief's at Memorial. Bullet missed the heart, clipped the spine. He's in surgery. Probably live. May not walk again." Sutton spoke void of emotion as if itemizing the pros and cons of buying a used car.

As for Jack, he had gathered all the information he needed on Deron, when he kept the man alive on the conference room floor doing his doctor thing. Jack examined the entrance and exit wounds. He knew the path of the well-placed bullet and organs at risk and consequences. Even then, sitting in a puddle of blood holding the dying man, Jack did not care. He blamed Francis Deron for perpetuating his family's nightmare through gross incompetence. He believed the man had mishandled his mother's abduction from the start, had made zero progress over thirty-three years, and had now put Jack's father's head on the chopping block.

"Thanks for the update. How long do we need to stay here?"

"Do you know who shot him, Doc?"

"What kind of question is that?" he barked.

"Relax, Jack." Paul approached Sutton. "The Sergeant's only doing his job."

"Answer my question." His strong eyes locked onto the smaller, angry medical examiner.

"No. I will not answer such a ridiculous—"

"Sergeant, we were just shot at," Shuck said. "Chief Deron sat next to me. He took a bullet. I did not. Jack kept the man alive. Your Chief of Police is struggling to live while all hell broke out here. We are all invested professionals here. I think you can cut us some slack. This is not your typical situation. I doubt there's ever been a shooting here."

"Actually, there has been," Jack blurted. "1996. The Selmon Expressway Sniper. Killed eleven people with a Browning 30-06. He was quite proud of his perfect head shots in moving vehicles. He shot into our windows one day. I believe he was upset with me because I would not discuss his marksman skills with the news media. I ignored his threats. Pissed him off."

"I remember." Paul dropped down into his chair. "Another awful cold case."

"Who did he target?" Sutton asked.

Jack looked away. "Me and Deron," he muttered.

"Did we catch the guy?"

"Nope," Shuck said.

"Let me be sure I got this right. The Selmon Expressway Sniper shot into this building at the Medical Examiner and Chief Deron seven years ago and is still out there somewhere."

"Yes. You have it right."

Sutton stepped up to Burcher, their faces inches apart. "So, the answer to my *ridiculous* question is, 'maybe the Selmon Sniper shot Deron with a Browning 30-06.'"

"I don't think that's necessary, Sergeant—"

Sutton did not move. "—I bet when you're doin' an autopsy and your Forensic Investigator walks into the room you expect all of your questions to be answered. I bet you don't want them answered because you're a pompous, arrogant, egotistical asshole. No! I bet you want them answered because you are responsible for that dead person lying on your table. Your life is all about representing the poor bastard that had his life taken from him. I bet you don't take that responsibility lightly, Dr. Burcher."

Sutton continued, "Well sir, it is my responsibility to keep as many of you alive as I can and keep my men alive for the next four hours. It's what we call our *closing window of blood.* You know why we are okay with blood, a lot of blood? Because dead man don't bleed, Dr. Jackson Burcher. We don't want any dead men. I expected you—of all people—to get that. I expected you—of all people—to understand the importance of helping me help you so I can keep everyone important to me and you alive today."

Jack froze. Shuck looked at his shoes. Sutton spun around and reached for the door. Jack yelled, "Wait." Sutton stopped. "You're right." Sutton turned to Jack.

Don't do it, Jack, Paul tried to say with his glaring eyes.

"We think the person that killed my father is the one who shot through the window."

"What makes you believe that?" Sutton asked.

Paul pulled the plastic bag from his pocket and held it up. The medallion with the bullet hole hung in Sutton's face.

"We took that out of my father's brain this morning. It was put there by the killer," Jack said. "It has some meaning, I'm sure. We don't know what. A twisted clue."

"And the hole in the center?" Sutton snarled.

Paul cleared his throat. "When I held it up in our meeting, the shooter put the first bullet through the center. After a few more shots, the chief got hit."

Sutton's face hardened and eyes narrowed. His temples undulated as he turned the knob on his two-way and touched taut lips to the shoulder mic. "Big Boot coming—over," he said. "All ears on now—over." All chatter stopped. "New intel. Our shooter is an expert marksman. Likely military-sniper trained. From this point on employ *extreme-caution* protocol. I want my outside perimeter fixed ears, scopes locked. I want my nucleus to advance to my perimeter one sector at a time; shields up and audio check-off before new sector engagement. If shooter is still in target zone, we got time. Use it. Over and out—"

The two-way hissed and crackled. "B 2 4 here. Potomac quadrant. Big Boot clarify shooter range/accuracy capabilities. Counter-tactical adjustments and new exposure-risk profile resets necessary. Over—"

Sutton eyed the medallion and tilted his head to the mic.

"Big Boot—Range 0.3 klicks min, 2.0 klicks max. Accuracy—centered on moving silver-dollar target. Big Boot—out."

Paul pocketed the medallion with a knowing look. "You did not see this, Big Boot."

"See what, FBI man—"

Sutton and Burcher exchanged nods. Sutton left the room.

Jack looked at his watch. "It's been thirty-four minutes since the shooting. I don't know when they got their perimeter up, but if we're lucky *our guy* made his first mistake."

"You think he cut it too close, broad daylight, and attack on a government facility?"

"Yep," Jack said. "Maybe he boxed himself in this time. He can't hide in the night fog."

Shuck stared at the medallion as if it was about to give him all the answers. "Unless we can't find him before night." The hole in the center took his breathe away. *Perfect. Like everything you do... so far.* "I wouldn't get my hopes up, Jack."

Fourteen minutes and thirty-seven seconds earlier, the classic 1960 Cadillac Coup Deville—with a 30.06 Browning on the back seat—turned onto the 13,000 block of Lettuce Lake Parkway. The old gray sedan smoked into the shadows of the slash pines and live oaks as a line of spinning blues and crying sirens shot down East Fletcher Avenue. The police raced to set up their last checkpoint to complete their one-mile perimeter—they had to contain a sniper at the Hillsborough County Morgue.

Tampa Bay Sentinel

Tuesday, September 13, 2003   94°F Partly Cloudy

Sniper fire into County Morgue – Tampa Police Chief Deron in Critical Condition

Tampa – September 13, 2003 – At 1:30 PM September 12, sniper-fire rained in the Hillsborough County Medical Examiner's Office, on North 46th Street. Only one reported injured. Tampa Chief of Police Francis Deron was taken to the Memorial Hospital in critical condition, single gunshot wound to the back.

Hillsborough County Sheriff responded to the shooting immediately. "It took twenty minutes to set up a one-mile containment perimeter around the county morgue. We launched an air and ground search effort for the shooter," said Sheriff Janell Babcock. "It appears we were not fast enough. We believe the shooter left the area minutes before our perimeter got set." TPD deployed a SWAT unit to secure the county morgue and assist in the search effort. Chief Medical Examiner Dr. Jack Burcher was present when Deron was shot. "We were meeting in the conference room when the bullets shattered the picture window. We dropped to the floor to get out of the line of fire. Chief Deron was hit on his way down. We are thankful no one else was hurt and hope Francis is back on his feet soon."

The Sentinel confirmed another shooting had occurred at the county morgue in 1996. Police hunted the Selmon Expressway Sniper (shooter named in eleven deaths on Tampa Highways). The Selmon Exp. Sniper claimed responsibility for shooting out the windows at the county morgue. Police speculate he was angered because the ME refused to discuss the sniper victim's wounds that would reveal accomplished marksman skills. The Selmon Exp. Sniper has not been apprehended. When asked, Tampa police had no comments on similarities to the latest shooting.

FOURTEEN

Burcher Estate – October 4, 2003 – 22:00

Twenty-three days since the delivery of Ronan's brain, and twenty-two days since a sniper's bullet put Chief Francis Deron in ICU, there had been nothing new. Jack Burcher settled in for another night alone with more unresolved mysteries. A lamp glowed next to dying embers and an empty scotch bottle. An intruder clung to the shadows of the sprawling estate.

The first October cold front lingered on Ballast Point long enough to quiet the vestige of screaming cicadas destined to live the rest of their days alone. Now, almost blind, the persistent few crawled the cold bark and dead leaves as they prepared for something they could not begin to understand—their end.

Like all living creatures lost in a life experience, Jack hunkered down in the basement beneath the cobwebs and dust-laden lightbulbs with more questions than answers. In the bowels of the hundred-year-old house, he sat among the stacks of old boxes and a few bay rats. He savored the end of his scotch and sucked a cigarette while wallowing in the family nightmare. *Maybe after a lifetime of pain and confusion and investigations I know just enough to recognize that one key that unlocks this whole damn mystery,* he thought. *Maybe tonight I can open that one dusty box and find that one discolored file with that one faded piece of paper that points to—*

His cell phone buzzed and yanked him out of his melancholy place. He answered more out of habit than desire. "Can't you guys leave me alone one night?" he breathed into the phone.

"We got approval, Doc." Moe Bullitt made the announcement like a kid telling his mom no cavities. "We can exhume your mom's heart."

Bullitt's poorly chosen words echoed in Jack's head. He cringed with the painful memory and fell back against the cellar steps. With a smoldering cigarette in his lips, he stared at endless boxes. Family archives reached into the darkest depths of the creepy cellar he did not know.

"Dr. Burcher. Did you hear me? Benatar finally gave us the green light. I gotta tell ya, Paul Shuck made it happen. He was like a bird with a bug. Sheriff Janell weighed-in, too. I think Benatar had too much history. Didn't want to add to the wear-and-tear on your family.

"Doc. You there? Hello? You hear me—"

"I'm here," Jack muttered. *She never should have done that to me. I signed off on it.*

"So, what do you think?"

"I think it took three weeks and should have taken a day. Judy Benatar knows better. She knows to separate business from personal." *Then again, I can't do it. She's probably right. This exhumation will hurt Melissa and David. They want to move on with their lives. It's all my idea. But I know there's something in her heart. Some clue that may—*

"Did you hear Chief Deron is conscious?"

"I did not. When?"

"This afternoon. We called your office. They said you took the day off. Dr. Quin called me back. I guess I assumed she passed it on. I got sucked into this thing. Without Chief Deron, I had to take care of the paperwork with Shuck. Lots of butts to kiss in this town to get anything done. I'm not a political guy."

"I want it exhumed first thing in the morning. Can you do that?"

"Already scheduled. We'll have the backhoe out there at six. You gonna join us?"

"No. I need to get things ready. I'll look for you at the county morgue. Do me a favor. Make sure they do not damage the burial container. It is hermetically sealed to keep the moisture out. Moisture is a big driver of the decomposition process. If we're lucky the heart will be in relatively good condition. Things start to change fast when the seal's broken."

"Even after thirty-three years?"

A floorboard squeaked overhead. Jack looked up as he pulled out his penlight. "Yes," he whispered. "Don't get me wrong. It will be decomposed to a degree—mummified. But if the seal has been maintained we'll have a good chance of looking at an intact organ."

"Probably like beef jerky. But we're interested in what the guy put inside it?"

"I am too. But I also want to know where it's positioned. Anatomical location could mean something. This killer has a reason for everything. Understanding is how we find him."

Another floorboard squeaked. This time Jack turned off the basement lights and shined his penlight toward the sound. Dust sprinkled from the floorboards in the living room. He turned off his penlight and stepped on his cigarette. *The basement door's open,* he thought.

"Someone's here," he whispered into his phone. "There shouldn't be—"

"Where are you, Doc?"

"I'm home. The doors are locked. Nobody should be in here, especially this time of night. Someone's here."

"Lay low, Doc. I'm sending cars now. You got a gun?"

Jack moved under the steps. "Not on me, for God's sake." He reached through the open staircase and retrieved his almost empty glass of scotch. "I'm getting off the phone now. Get someone out here."

Jack downed the end of his scotch and pocketed his cell. Four miles away the nearest squad car got the call—nothing much happened on Ballast Point except for the occasional Burcher abduction and homicide. They all know Crescent Drive.

Did you decide to come for me, Jack wondered as he set the wet empty glass on the floor? *I thought things might have gotten a little too tame for you these last few weeks. You were on a roll—took Ronan out of Sun Bay and killed your accomplice, delivered Ronan's brain, shot the medallion out of Shuck's hand, and crippled the Chief of Police. Somehow, in broad daylight, you managed to escape every cop in the county. I guess you've gotten used to more risk lately. Maybe you've been bored. Maybe you just need to hurt another Burcher—*

A table leg scooted across the floor. *You bumped into the end table by the leather sofa. The one I hit every time I go that way.* Jack blinked at the whisper of light reaching down the stairs into the dark basement. *I should have planted guns everywhere. Been ready for—*

Another board whined. This time closer to the kitchen. Jack rotated his head like an owl on a branch. He would not move his body or use his penlight again. The intruder was too close to the pantry—inside was the open cellar door. The silence grew deafening. The police had to be minutes away. Jack trembled. Would they get to the house in time?

Why'd you come inside tonight? Did you plan this, or did something stir you up? Maybe you think I'd be easy because I'm drunk? Jack checked his watch. *It's too early for you. You do your best work in the wee hours, you sneaky, sick—*

The soft light falling down the cellar stairs changed. *You're standing up there.*

Jack had the dog-eared files from the box dated 1907 sitting on his lap most of the night. The FBI would not be able to help. They could not separate family history from mystery. Melissa and David would never get involved, and Patricia did not care much about the family after the separation and cold-blooded legal resolution. Only Jack could wade through the archives. Only he could examine property deeds, transfer agreements, investments, receipts, tax filings, and all the legal documents on deals around the world—the underpinning of the Burcher Empire. Jack had decided to take up the cause when he was ten. Now, if the family deaths are linked, he had to take the *vendetta theory* all the way to the end. He figured weeks ago that he had to go back far enough to find and get on the trail his family killer slithered down.

You've been watching the house tonight. You've been waiting for your opportunity. You know I'm alone. You saw me by the fire, lost in a bottle and going through a new pile of family files. Jack peered through the steps at the mountain of boxes. The light reached ten feet into the cellar. He stared at the endcap boxes of the three rows down the east wall. He counted them a week ago—each row of twenty-five and each box had five more on top. There were 450.

I could not believe we had family archives in this cellar going back to 1907, the year Grandpa Otto Burcher was born in Poland. The cellar door creaked. *There you are.* Jack stiffened and held his breath. *You found the cellar. I suppose it's only logical I'd be down here. You checked the house and couldn't find me. And no one leaves their cellar door open on Ballast Point. Not now. Not when the bay rats are lookin' for a winter home.*

Did you stop? Are you waiting? You don't know if I have a gun, do you? Jack felt for a weapon (anything) on the shelves behind him. He touched paint cans and rags and piles of stiff brushes. He moved his fingers to the next shelf. *I can't make a noise. You are right above me.* Jack's fingers found shears. He pulled. They did not move. He tugged. They did not move. He wiggled them as a bead of sweat hung on the tip of his nose. Three inches of the rusted clippers was pinned under a gallon paint can. *And you could be stuck to the shelf—*

The cellar door whined open further. The cellar lights popped on—the pantry switch lit six bulbs, but only a third of the cellar. Under the staircase Jack shrunk into a shadow between the bookcase and wall and stared at the shears he left. *You got to come down and go under these stairs to see me. I'm invisible even through the steps. I grab the shears. Shit. My empty glass is sweating. Will he see the circle on the floor? And the flattened cigarette butt... What are you waiting for up there? You've probably been watching me the last three weeks, maybe wondering why I'm here alone every night.* The top step creaked. *If you've been close you had to see the files I've been going through. If you watched through the window behind my chair, you could see everything over the back of my chair.*

The next step creaked. *That's it. You're not prepared tonight. This is not planned. If it was, you'd be down here fast. Something made you come in the house tonight. Was I looking at something you don't want me to see?* Jack closed his eyes battling the fog of another binge. *What file was I reading last? Otto's file—his birth records and early days in Poland.*

Sirens cried in the distance. There were many. They got louder. The cellar lights popped off. The door slammed closed. "You left," Jack gasped as he wiped sweat from his brow. Cars slid on gravel. Roaring engines surrounded the house. Car doors slammed in the front and on each side. There was pounding. Glass shattered onto the floor. The front and back doors were kicked open. The police were inside the house. Someone called out, "Dr. Burcher, POLICE. Where are you, Dr. Jack Burcher?"

Feet pounded the floors moving into each room. Furniture moved. Lamps fell. Lights went on and poured through the floorboards into the dark cellar. *He got away. I'm gonna be okay,* Jack thought. He eased out of his hiding place, moved to the front of the cellar stairs, and reached for the light switch. Looking up he saw a shadow move in the shadows at the top of the stairs. More feet pounded floors as the police called his name. They poured into the kitchen. Jack felt in the dark. He could not find the switch. He yelled, "Help—"

The colliding force came from above. The two exploded into the boxes. Jack's back slammed onto the concrete floor. They skidded ten feet to a stop. Jack screamed, "Don't." A hand covered his mouth. An arm crushed his chest. Then the razor-sharp pain. "God no," he breathed. And then something wet. And then nothing.

Tampa Bay Sentinel

Saturday, October 4, 2003   91°F

Dr. Ronan Burcher Still Missing

Tampa – Saturday, October 4, 2003 – Twenty-four days after the abduction of retired medical examiner Dr. Ronan Burcher, still little is known and the FBI and TPD are not talking.

In the early morning hours of September 10, Ronan Burcher was taken from his room at the Sun Bay Nursing & Rehabilitation Center on Ballast Point. Reliable sources say surveillance cameras at Sun Bay show a nurse transporting a sleeping Burcher on a hospital gurney to a loading dock around three in the morning.

Police were called to Sun Bay at 9:00 AM, when Burcher was discovered missing. Later that morning, an unidentified woman was found dead in a trash bin at Sun Bay. Tampa Homicide Detective Moe Bullitt said, "We are following all leads. I cannot comment on an active investigation." Because Dr. Ronan Burcher's abduction is presumed a kidnapping, the FBI has taken lead in the case.

Dr. Ronan Burcher served as the Hillsborough County Medical Examiner from 1965 until he stepped down in 1996 due to an undisclosed medical condition. Shortly after leaving his position, Dr. Ronan Burcher entered Sun Bay where he has been ever since.

Abductions are not new to the billionaire Burcher family. In 1970 Rose Burcher, wife of Ronan, was taken from the family home on Crescent Drive. One day later her heart was delivered to the estate in a cardboard box. The macabre development ended the five-state search for a kidnapped victim thought to be alive. To date, Rose Burcher and the perpetrator(s) have not been found. Sources close to the Ronan Burcher investigation say the FBI believes there could be a connection to the 33-year-old cold case. The regional FBI director Paul Shuck was not available for comment. A reliable source told the Sentinel, due to the escalation of the Burcher family misfortunes, new eyes could help. Engagement of a specialist is under consideration by the FBI. If the cases are connected, those responsible for Rose and Ronan Burchers' disappearances need to be brought to justice. An unnamed source said, "A fresh look at all the evidence could help."

The Tampa Police, Hillsborough County Sheriff's Office, and FBI are coordinating the ongoing search for Dr. Ronan Burcher. Dr. Jack Burcher, son of Ronan and the acting Chief Medical Examiner for the county, told the Sentinel his family is offering a $100,000 reward for information leading to his father's safe return.

FIFTEEN

Burcher Estate – Saturday, October 4, 2003 – 23:00

F lashlights and dogs combed the Burcher estate and Ballast Point for the unknown intruder. This time roadblocks went up minutes after Moe Bullitt sent cars to check on Jack Burcher. All main arteries—Selmon Expressway, South Dale Maybry Highway, and Gandy Boulevard—were set up with armed roadblocks. Squad cars were in place at all crossroads on West Swann Avenue, the east-west line of demarcation at the neck of the Interbay Peninsula. Leaving by water would be the only other viable option. Hillsborough Bay, Old Tampa Bay, and Tampa Bay benefitted from the beefed-up patrolling by the TPD Bay Authority and Coast Guard.

"Jack. Wake up." Moe nudged the medical examiner. They moved him to the living room after he had regained consciousness and paramedics treated the facial wound. Jack had dozed off again. "Jack." Moe prodded. "Sit up my friend. You're okay. They bandaged you up." He turned to the empty bottle and flow of police. "Make coffee, someone." *Again,* he thought.

The bandage taped to his face ran from under his left eye to the corner of his mouth. The cut was deep. He would need stitches. Jack was cognizant enough to refuse an ambulance. He would go in for stitches after he knew what was going on in his house.

David Burcher arrived with Paul Shuck. The two sat across from Moe and Jack as Dr. Quin pulled up in the driveway. Paul stared at the bandage and then looked over at today's Sentinel next to a stack of old files. "Jack," David said. "What happened?"

"I'm trying to piece things together. Give me a minute."

An officer leaned his head in the room. "Detective Bullitt, the house is empty; searched from cellar to attic. Looks like the intruder left through a cellar window, north side of the house. Probably hid in the bushes until our people moved—gave 'em an exit before the dogs."

"Anybody look in the boathouse?" Jack asked rubbing the back of his head. "And the boats; check the cabin of the sailboat. There's a rowboat out there, too." Jack looked around the room as he gathered his senses. Dr. Deborah Quin walked in with a smile and coffee—she knew how the ME liked it. Jack took the steaming Styrofoam cup with a confused smile.

"We have a good chance of catchin' him this time," Paul said. "Not a lot of ways off a peninsula. The main arteries have roadblocks up, thanks to Moe. Nothing will get across Swann. And we have a lot of eyes on the water." He looked at the pile of dirty files, and then back at the bandage on Jack's cheek. "You need to get that thing fixed. You really shouldn't wait too long. We can handle this, Jack."

"Thanks for your professional medical opinion, Dr. Shuck,"

Jack poked. "It's not like you to be so attentive. You think we have a chance to catch him this time?"

"Not really. Just wanted to cheer you up. Did you see him?"

"Nope," Jack muttered. "I heard him, and I smelled him. Smelled like Sushi. Last thing I remember, I reached for the cellar light switch at the bottom of the stairs. In the dark, I saw slight movement at the top of the stairs. I think he came down boots first. Knocked the wind out of me. My back slammed to the floor, him on top of me. We slid into the boxes. Next thing I know he had a hand on my mouth and elbow in my chest. I was already woozy. Then my face stung and felt wet. I pretty much blacked out after that."

"You're lucky it wasn't worse," David said. "I told you not to stay in this damn house alone. You're too vulnerable."

"I wonder why?" Moe muttered. "I wonder why he didn't—"

"—kill me. I don't know." Jack sipped his coffee. "Maybe he likes me."

"Cutting you was enough this time," Shuck said.

"I really don't think he planned this. It's not like him."

"What do you mean?"

"Maybe I was looking at something he didn't want me to see."

"Or he heard you talkin' to me," Moe said. "Exhumation of the heart?"

"No. He didn't know I was in the cellar. I heard him bumping into furniture. Looked for me up there before the cellar. Something else motivated him. He had to think before he decided to act tonight. It had to be big enough to make him step outside his routine. That includes letting me live. Tells me he's not done with me, yet."

"Shooting the medallion out of my hand in the middle of

the day was outside his routine. His kills have been stealth and early morning. Or, could be he's stepping up things. Throwing out more clues. Getting ready for something big."

"What were you doing tonight?" Moe asked.

"What I've been doing every night for three weeks, going through endless boxes of family archives. I've been looking for something to shine some light on this nightmare."

"The boxes in the cellar?"

"Yes. I open a box, grab a handful of files, take 'em upstairs and read them in the den. I've been through twenty-seven boxes so far."

"You're going through all that crap?" David scoffed. "Hell, there's gotta be a hundred boxes of old shit down there. I can only imagine the fun you're having with all those investment documents, tax returns, and family love letters. Better you than I."

"There are 450 boxes to be exact. They date back to 1907, Grandpa Otto's birth in Poland and the 1930s—the early days building this house on Ballast Point.

"I did something different tonight," Jack said as if he it had just hit him. "I spent the last few weeks looking at the most recent archives and going backward. Tonight, I changed things up. I decided to focus on the earliest history of the family and moving forward. I thought if we are dealing with a *multi-generational vendetta*, the trail has gotta start in our past."

"And to pick up that trail you needed to start at the beginning," Moe added.

Quin opened the top of the gauze bandage and examined Jack's three-inch knife wound. "It's a clean cut. Steri-strips will do for a while. I'll call Dr. Kelton. He can meet us at Memorial. Finish your coffee and we'll go. No debate." She left the room. He would do what she said.

"Kelton a plastic surgeon?" Paul asked. He picked up the folded Sentinel.

"Yeah. I best let him fix me up or you'll be looking at Frankenstein," Jack teased.

"Back to the family archives," Moe said. "What specifically were you looking at tonight, and where were you looking at it?"

"I was sitting in that chair by the window."

"Someone could watch through the window. It's close enough for them to read over your shoulder. What were you reading, Jack?"

"I was looking at some of the oldest family records. They touched on Horace Burcher in the 1800s and his Cuban cigar manufacturing business. Then they jumped to Otto Burcher's birth in Poland. I suspect Otto's parents or grandparents were related to Horace. Maybe they funded the cigar operation. It's not clear what brought Horace to Tampa or exactly when. The early records are sparse and cryptic. I do know they were all wealthy. Otto married Emily Monroe in 1929. They built this place on Ballast Point a year later. Then Leonard was born. Ronan was born five years later, 1935."

"We should ask Emily about the early days," David said perusing the newspaper. "Maybe she can fill in some blanks. Help with your sleuthin'." Jack rolled his eyes and sipped his coffee.

"Is Emily Burcher still alive?" Moe asked.

"Yes," Jack said. "Grandma Em is at Sun Bay. Another building. She's in her nineties. Very fragile. Has her good days and bad. Always been one not to talk much. I guess it's a good idea. I'll try. Maybe she will give me something I can't find in the boxes in the cellar."

Sergeant Mack Sutton entered in SWAT gear. "Nothing to report," he said with eyes on Bullitt. "We'll stay on the peninsula all night. He could be hiding. Doc, your rowboat's missing. Found it a few hundred yards south of your dock. We have dogs up and down the banks now. Unless he tries to swim Hillsborough Bay, we got him."

"Dr. Kelton can meet us at Memorial in an hour," Quin interrupted. "Since it's not an emergency, he wanted to shower to wake up, so he can do a good job on you."

"Paul. What paper are you looking at?" Jack asked.

Paul flipped it over. "The Sentinel. This is an old one."

"What's the date?"

"September 10, 2003. Why?"

Jack stared at the back of the newspaper. "That's the paper Ronan was holding the night he was taken from Sun Bay. He held it in his fist. Was waving it around when he was ranting about someone coming for him."

"You brought it home?" Paul asked.

"I did. Was gonna look at it. See what had 'em so upset. Never got to it. Please, give it to me, Paul."

Moe leaned in. David walked behind the sofa and looked over Jack's shoulder. "I'll be," David whispered. "That's—"

"—Otto," Jack said as he leaned closer and scanned the article.

"Are you sayin' there's a picture of your grandfather in the September 10 newspaper?" Moe asked. "That would be extremely odd, don't you think? What'd he do?"

"It's not him. Otto died in 1955, cancer," Jack said. "He didn't make the paper."

"It's not Otto?" Paul said. "I read the article. It's about a guy named Teller. He died on September 9. Teller was one of those theoretical physicists like Albert Einstein. A genius scientist. The picture is one of the other guys with Teller. The Manhattan Project."

"What the hell's the Manhattan Project?" David grunted.

"Damn, young generation doesn't know history," Shuck

scoffed. "Those guys developed the atomic bomb, David. Not too big a deal. Just ended World War II. Saved millions of lives."

Jack set down the paper. "Moe, the photo album next to you, pass it to me."

"I thought the atom bomb killed millions of people," David said.

Jack flipped pages in the album. He stopped and looked at the last picture of Otto before the cancer changed him. "This is uncanny. If I didn't know better, I would have thought the picture in the Sentinel was Otto at age 47. It was before the cancer took him."

Paul and Moe leaned over Jack's shoulder. They compared the picture in the Sentinel to the picture in the family album. "Take away the mustache and give him hair—"

"Twins," David blurted out. "But you can say that about a lot of people."

"The guy in the paper is Hans Bethe," Jack said. "He's a German-American nuclear physicist. Astrophysics and quantum electrodynamics." *Why do you look like so much like Otto?*

"Is Hans dead, too?" Moe asked.

"No. He lives up north," Jack said. "This is about Edward Teller. He died September 9th this year. The newspaper talks about his life contributions. The pictures are the other elite members of the Manhattan Project team. The people who created the atomic bomb."

"This is all very neat stuff but another waste of time. It's midnight," David said. "Go to the hospital *Scarface*. Get stitched up." Jack dropped the newspaper onto the sofa. Quin helped him to his feet. They all went out the front door.

It never crossed their minds *the intruder* could have cut loose the rowboat and opened the cellar window before entering the Burcher house. Outside, flashlights danced, and blood hounds barked, and spinning lights lined Crescent Drive as the police searched Ballast Point.

Inside the Burcher mansion, a monster curled up in its cocoon—a pile of oily towels, turpentine rags, and moldy tarps in the darkest corner of the cellar. The oil and turpentine stopped the dogs.

The monster would wait until they tired of the hunt. He often waited. Then he would go where they never looked—his secret place.

Tampa Bay Sentinel

Edward Teller father of H-bomb Dies

Stanford, CA – September 9, 2003 – Edward Teller, an elite member of the Manhattan Project team, and father of the Hydrogen Bomb, dies at his home in Stanford at the age of 95 following a long illness and multiple strokes. The recipient of the *Presidential Medal of Freedom* from GW Bush earlier this year, Teller will be missed. The Hungarian-American physicist will be remembered as a key member of an elite team of scientists, who ended World War II. The *Manhattan Project* is a code name for the American secret initiative to develop the atomic bomb. The first nuclear weapon was detonated at White Sands, New Mexico. These five men are credited with the profound achievement – Hans Bethe, Edward Teller, James Conant—

SIXTEEN

Hillsborough County Morgue – Sunday, October 5, 2003 – 07:00

Six halogen lamps burned over the MOPEC stainless-steel autopsy table. At its center, a human heart sat on a folded sterile surgical sheet like a miniature *Jabba the Hutt*. Instead of blood, a dark amber fluid with black-sepia flakes drained from one end of the bulging leathery sac. The organ had been preserved in an airtight burial capsule for 33 years. The seal slowed but did not halt the normal decomposition process. When the seal was broken, the heart began to shrivel like a prune in the sun.

Toxic gases from the embalming fluid escaped. Noses stung and eyes watered. Soon the putrid smell of decayed human flesh took over the room like a dead skunk takes over a neighborhood. Some observers had to leave. Burcher and Quin stayed. They had hundreds of autopsies and decomposed bodies under their belts. They also conducted dozens of exhumations. For them, a single decayed organ would not be much of an olfactory challenge.

On a stepladder above Jack's head, the medical photographer hovered. Three cameras hung from his neck. Bullitt and Shuck stood at one end of the autopsy table, with gauze plugs in their noses and goggled eyes. Hugo Novak and Thomas Purdy were opposite Burcher and Quin. They had learned long ago when to breathe through their mouth.

Jack tapped the button on his headset and gently gripped the mummified heart. With gloved fingers he held it like a baby about to get a shot.

"On October 5, 2003, at 07:19, Dr. Deborah Quin and Dr. Jack Burcher examine an exhumed heart. These remains are believed to belong to Hillsborough County Case #14-24-1970, the deceased Rose Lawton Burcher, born February 12, 1935, died July 14, 1970. COD—undetermined. MOD—homicide.

"At 06:50, burial capsule #4738AH70 arrived at the Hillsborough decomposition room. With the assistance of the Tampa Fire Department, the hermetically sealed capsule was opened. At no time did a tool or instrument contact contents of the capsule. At 07:04, I aseptically removed one organ from the capsule and transported it to this autopsy room in a sterile container for x-ray and postmortem examination.

"Witnesses to the removal of this heart from the burial capsule included Central Florida Regional FBI Director Paul Shuck, Tampa Police Homicide Detective Moe Bullitt, Forensic Investigator Hugo Novak, Senior Forensic Scientist Thomas Purdy, and Senior Medical Photographer, Chris Lemont."

Jack adjusted the overhead light. "The heart weighs 5.63 ounces. This is a 30% reduction from the 8.12 ounces recorded on July 15, 1970. The loss in weight is unremarkable and due to a slowed decomposition process in the controlled environment created by a sealed burial capsule." He pointed to parts of the heart as he spoke. "The pulmonary artery, pulmonary veins, superior vena cava, and inferior vena cava vessels are missing due to the natural decomposition process. All related orifices are present, intact, and deformed due to natural postmortem atrophy.

"The outer walls of the left atrium and left ventricle are present and rigid in texture as expected. The right atrium and right ventricle walls are missing. This too is expected because this organ rested on its posterior side in the capsule. The walls of the heart made contact with the inner surface of the burial capsule—the most aggressive decomposition occurred on the weight-bearing surfaces. There are no signs of tissue alterations or physical trauma other than the severing of the vessels."

Jack reached for a scalpel and pointed to the aorta. "X-ray examination of this heart revealed the presence of three metallic objects positioned in the left aorta interface with the left ventricle. I will now make a one-inch incision sagittal to the midline on the superior aspect of the left ventricle chamber."

An assistant wheeled up an *Olympus* video-endoscopy system. He turned on the monitor and passed the fiber-optic scope to Burcher. Jack waited for the thumbs up. Soon the system hummed alive. Jack fed the fiber optic tip into the left atrium and moved toward the orifice of the left aorta. The small light on the tip of the scope moved inside the heart chamber and projected its journey on the monitor screen. Like entering a dark cave, the endoscope tip neared the aortic valve. The screen whited out. "Mr. Munson, what's happening?" Jack asked.

Adjusting the equipment, the white faded. "It's a reflection," Munson said. "The scope light is reflecting off a mirrored surface. I've adjusted contrast. It should help."

A sharp silvery diamond tip filled the screen. "What the—"

"I suggest you pull back, Doctor," Munson said. "You are too close to the—"

Jack pulled the scope back. The diamond image shrunk in size. Then there were five tips pointing in five directions. The room stared at the monitor.

"Is that a star?" Shuck asked.

The silver image got smaller as Jack retracted the probe a few more millimeters. "I think it is a star," Bullitt muttered.

"Quiet, people." Jack turned on his headset. Quin held the tip of the endoscope in position. Jack reached for a pair of long-neck, needle-nose surgical plyers. He inserted the tip into the incision and navigated the chamber watching the monitor. The tip of the plyers appeared on the screen and moved to the star. Jack clamped on and removed it from behind the aortic valve. When it broke free, he held it in front of the camera lens and dictated. "At the proximal edge of the left aortic orifice there is no mechanical damage to the valve. Inside the vessel at the proximal end I have located a silver star. At this time, it appears to have been introduced into the aortic vessel from the severed distal end and pushed to the aortic valve."

Jack removed the star from the heart. He placed it on the surgical towel under the lights and went back in search for more. "This time I will reach deeper into the aorta from the proximal end. Dr. Quin, please follow me with the scope." They watched the monitor close in on a second silver star slightly deeper in the aortic vessel.

"I have located a second star." Jack removed it and placed it next to the first. He repeated the process. "After probing even deeper into the vessel, I have located a third and final star. There are no other metallic objects in this organ. We will confirm the endoscopic findings with the dissection of the heart."

He placed the third star with the other two and took over

the endoscope. "I will now examine the aortic vessel for signs of trauma or disease," Jack said into his headset. He moved the scope around. "All internal anatomical structures are present and do not present signs of trauma." *What's this?* He thought as he stopped on the valve. *Severe calcification of the aortic valve?*

Dr. Quin held out a scalpel. Jack turned from the monitor. "Time to dissect, Doctor," Quin said, with eyes on the obvious —and unexpected—medical condition. Jack's mother died at the age of forty. She would not have such an advanced degenerative heart condition. The extent of the calcification of the aortic valve is severe enough to be a cause of death.

Jack opened the heart with his scalpel and dissected each chamber and vessel. The room remained quiet as he dictated medical structures and pathology. Jack then sectioned the chambers and cardiac vessels independently. He placed tissue samples of each in formalin for histological examination.

The postmortem on the exhumed heart was completed. Tissue samples were sent to histology. The *heart remains* were collected and returned to the burial capsule. This time it would not be hermetically sealed.

Jack and Paul leaned over the green surgical towel staring at the three stars. Moe and Hugo stood at each end of the table. "Why put three silver stars in a heart?" Paul muttered.

"I think the first question is what do these three stars mean?" Jack said. "Then we can think about why they were put in someone's heart."

The autopsy room door swung open. A laboratory assistant approached Dr. Burcher and handed him a piece of paper. Jack read and nodded. The lab assistant left with the paper.

"SOMEONE'S heart, Jack?" Paul said. "You mean YOUR MOTHER'S heart."

"This is not Rose Burcher's heart," Novak said. All heads but Jack's turned to the forensic investigator. He had been a part of enough postmortems to know direct observations trump all theories. "Dr. Burcher. Would you like the honors, sir?"

All heads returned to the Medical Examiner. "This is not my mother's heart."

"I don't understand," Paul said. "We went to Rose's grave. I watched them dig up the burial capsule. It had Rose's name and dates. The heart was identified in 1970."

"I was ten at the time," Jack said. "My father was the medical examiner. He was drugged the night the bloody heart appeared at our house. My father never examined this heart.

"I did not know Dr. Albert Scruggs, the pathologist that stepped in to help when Ronan dropped out of the picture. Scruggs died a few years later. He was only there because he was available. Someone who could sign a death certificate in those tragic days."

"What are you saying, Jack?" Paul pushed.

"I'm saying nobody examined this heart in 1970. They assumed it belonged to my mother because she had been taken and it came to our house with a personal note to my father. You saw the heart we examined today. It had never been dissected. Not until today. This heart had never been x-rayed. They had no idea three silver stars were inside."

"Tell me how you know this is not your mother's heart. We are looking at a decomposed lump of meat that's been in the ground for more than three decades."

"Advanced aortic valve calcification, Paul. There are other names for it. Aortic sclerosis. Aortic stenosis. It's a condition that affects individuals over 65. My mother was 40. She did not have heart disease. There is no heart disease on her side of the family."

"You're telling me it is impossible for you mother to have aortic scler—"

"—osis. Yes. She did not have a congenital heart defect. She never had rheumatic fever. Those are the only other ways she could have it this advanced at her age."

"But there's still a chance," Paul argued.

Jack smiled. "There is no chance, Paul. They did not have DNA testing in 1970. We do now. The paper I just looked at confirmed the DNA is not a match." All eyes widened. "I believe the heart I dissected today came from a male, in his seventies.

"I knew this was not my mother's heart the moment I saw it. Males have larger hearts than females. Mother was a diminutive lady—only five feet. The aortic stenosis and the DNA confirm it belongs to someone else."

"Someone else was killed," Novak muttered. "The bloody beast used another's heart to deliver three stars and a note to the Burcher family."

"Not necessarily killed for this purpose," Jack said. "This heart could have been taken from a man who recently died from this advanced heart condition."

"A funeral home would present the best opportunity," Novak said.

"It's like our killer had a date to keep. Maybe this heart was his backup."

"My God," Paul sighed. "It just hit me. Your mother could be alive."

"I think that's a long way to go," Jack said. "I don't even know how to process that." He turned to the three stars nestled on the sterile towel. "Why go to all this trouble? Why pretend to kill my mother and put stars in the left aorta of a diseased heart?"

He walked to the lightbox and studied the x-ray. "I'm thinking a military or government motive. Then the Medal of Freedom would connect."

"Those are not just stars. We're looking at three Silver Stars," Paul said.

"Not a Silver Star medal," Bullitt said. "Those are gold and hang from a service ribbon. I know because my grandfather has one. It's a pretty high decoration for valor in combat. I think these are three Silver Stars. They may be all about rank, a senior commanding officer."

"I'll get our people on it," Paul said, taking a picture on his cell phone. "Research three silver star, military relevance. Jack, I need the DNA sent over. We will run it through CODEX."

"We may have another exhumation," Jack said.

"Who?"

"I don't know yet." Jack returned to the autopsy table. "My office needs to do some research. I want to know all males in their seventies that died in Hillsborough County around the time my mother was abducted. We may not have seen all of them here. We can review the death certificates issued in the county the weeks before the July 14 date in 1970. I say before because we won't know when the body was buried. A death certificate must be signed first."

"This heart was embalmed," Bullitt said. "The dead man could have been at one of the funeral homes around here. I'll check for reports of break-ins around that time."

"There's a good chance this heart was taken, and nobody knew it," Paul said.

"Is there any chance Ronan's brain is not—"

"—Ronan's?" Jack muttered. "No. Zero. We have a DNA match."

"The FBI is looking into Caroline Lawton's death in '75 and Harold Lawton's in '78. I should hear back this week."

"I will continue to wade through family archives," Jack said.

"We've posted police at the house 24/7," Bullitt said.

"I really don't think that's necessary." Jack touched his bandage and winced. "I guess I don't have to like it."

"You don't," Paul said. "Look at it this way. Your siblings will get off your back for staying in that big, old house alone."

"I won't be alone much longer. Patricia is coming back to pack up a few things. She's going to return to Boston and stay at our place in Cape Cod, indefinitely."

The four left the autopsy room. Staff would process the physical evidence and clean up the place. Bullitt and Novak broke away to synchronize efforts, in the parking lot. Jack and Paul stopped at the open doorway to Jack's office. The two checked their watches and continued to catch up on their text messages.

"We've got a lot of new information, Jack."

"Too much, Paul. We don't know what's real and what's our wild imaginations."

"I've always believed when working a complex case, you keep pushing. All of a sudden something comes along and blows it wide open."

"I hope soon. I'm losing ground, my friend. I've lived this family nightmare too long. I don't think I can go on much longer."

Jack turned and looked out his office picture window. He often got lost staring into the thick trees on the ten acres on the east side of their complex—set aside for future expansion. Jack could not get the shooting out of his head. *You shot a two-inch medallion out of Paul's hand and put a bullet in Francis Deron's spine. Why not just put a bullet in my head. Just put me out of my misery...*

Paul followed Jack's gaze. "He's not out there, Jack. If he is, you don't need to worry. The TPD is watching this place, now. This guy is too smart to risk daylight twice."

Jack nodded. *I'm not worried. I'm inviting it. I'm a divorced alcoholic with dead parents and a miserable nightmare.*

Jack's phone buzzed like a hornet in his pocket. He pulled it out and glanced at the screen—Kayda Webster. "I gotta take this, Paul."

"Fine. I gotta go, too. I'll be in touch."

Paul started down the hall. A flash of light from the woods caught Jack's eye. He squinted as he started to raise his phone. It exploded out of his hand as he watched a line climb his office window.

SEVENTEEN

Aloft Tampa Downtown Hotel – Friday, October 10, 2003 – 22:00

"I thought you did not want to see me again." Kayda Webster sat on the edge of the bed looking out the seventh-floor window at the shimmering blue lights on calm bay waters. She crossed her long legs and allowed her skirt to climb her firm thighs.

Jack left the small kitchen holding two glasses—one scotch on the rocks and one chilled glass of Chardonnay. He admired her perfect legs and alluring presence on his short trip. "I'm sorry. I certainly did not intend to send you that message."

She turned and caught him looking at her legs. She smiled —veiled approval—and reached for her glass. "Thank you." With locked eyes, their glasses touched. It was too soon for a kiss, if ever. Were they both waiting for the other to make the first move? The attraction was there, but they were uncertain. Loosening his tie, he backed to the sofa across from her.

"Does it hurt?" she asked.

He touched his bandage. "This? Not anymore. I've always been a fast healer."

"I was not expecting to see—"

"—a wounded warrior," he teased. "It's a long story. I got twenty-eight tiny stitches. Dr. Kelton swears the scar will be unnoticeable in six months. I don't know about that—it feels tight. But he is the best plastic surgeon in the Tampa Bay area."

Kayda sipped her Chardonnay and licked her lips. Jack sipped his scotch and felt his heartbeat in his ears. "I'm glad you called. I have thought of you often."

"I did not want to get you in trouble. There are things I need to tell you."

Jack unbuttoned his top button and pulled off his tie. "I don't think things are what you think they are, Kayda. My marriage is over. The resolution document is a piece of paper, a negotiated settlement to address legal matters of an excessive estate. Although we are technically married, it has nothing to do with matters of the heart for either of us. We are free to pursue relationships. If something were to enter the realm of matrimony, there would be some legal hoops to jump through, that's all."

"I think I understand. I guess I assumed your marital status meant—"

"—I could not have feelings for you?" he whispered.

She uncrossed her legs and adjusted her skirt watching him. "Yes."

Jack sipped his drink as he searched for the perfect words to express his situation. What he said next would comfort the girl he has been falling in love with or scare her further away.

"My family has a lot of money. Most is invested with other wealthy families—kind of like a rich club—people around the world we've known for many generations. When we learned my father had Parkinson's, we divested all interests in companies and sold family businesses. Today we are only invested in safe, long term, joint ventures with friends. Like us, they don't want their boats rocked. A divorce, and nasty litigation, puts their money at risk, too. If one of us pulled a lot of money out, it could create return-on-investment problems for others."

"I think I understand," she said with a flutter of her eyelashes and alluring smile.

"If we can avoid surprises and negative press, everyone is happy. It's as simple as that."

"I don't want to mislead you. I did not call you on a personal basis. I called because I feel I need to talk to you about something that could be important to you and your family."

"Okay," Jack said. *Maybe I misread you,* he thought. *I arranged for us to meet in the room where we spent our first night together. Thought you wanted what I wanted. How stupid of me. You just want to talk. This is not about us or sex. I'm such an idiot.*

"When you did not answer your phone, I started to have some second thoughts."

"You do know what happened? It was in the newspapers. I had to get a new phone."

"Yes. Someone shot into your building. Hit your phone." She jerked her head back to the windows as if she remembered she could be in danger, too. "Did they ever catch the person? It is a terrible thing. I know about your family nightmare, Jack."

"Yes, you do. You probably know more than most since you attended my FBI interview about the night—"

"—someone bad brought a terrible box to your house," she sighed.

"Yes. That night." He looked into his glass.

"The bad person, do you think he is the same one that shot at you?"

"I do. But I don't know anything for sure. And it probably won't be the last time. The police were patrolling the grounds to protect us. They didn't even hear the shot fired. They said the shooter used a silencer. I bet he was gone before they knew it happened. The bullet was from the same gun as before."

"I read about the first time in the Sentinel. It was on the day I was with you transcribing that terrible night. I was sorry to hear the Chief of Police was severely injured."

"That was too bad," Jack said. Kayda looked away. Her hand trembled.

"I'm sorry you have to even think about these things. I've been pulled in so many directions. I would have called you the night after I saw you at my office, but I felt things were heating up again. I didn't want to expose you to my problems."

She turned back and took him in as he spoke—his soft hazel eyes and strong jaw. She memorized all of him the first time they made love. But now she felt like a stranger. They desired each other but were forced to be apart, and Jack Burcher was still a married man.

Her heart fluttered and body tingled as she sat on the edge of the bed thinking about what it would be like to make love to him again. Her mind moved in and out of those private erotic places as she struggled to stay focused, to do what she had come to do.

I want you to take me into your arms now, she thought. Then she turned away again. Her long black hair fell off her soft neck as she stared at the night lights outside the seventh-floor window. *I must tell him what I know. It matters in so many ways.*

"Kayda, are you okay?"

I need you, Jack Burcher. Don't you know women? A man of your intellect and accomplishments. Didn't you see it in my eyes, when we met in your conference room? I struggled to focus on my transcription. I missed things, made mistakes. I felt you looking at me, taking off my clothes, and I liked it—

"You seem distracted," Jack said. "Is there something bothering you? Is it my situation with my ex-wife, the changes are not enough? Is it the family nightmare? I feel like you are afraid something bad will happen to you. No one knows where I am tonight. My ex-wife is not in Tampa. She lives in Boston. The next time she comes here, she will spend a few days gathering her things. She will leave. I don't expect her back ever again."

"I don't know how to—"

"I'm sorry I brought you here. This was a mistake. I felt—it doesn't matter what I felt. We can leave. We can go get dinner and talk. We can talk about anything you want, anything that will help you be comfortable. I just want to be with you. I've missed you terribly."

She stood up and looked down at him. "I'm not distracted, Jack Burcher." She moved to him; her knees touched his. "I am all here," She said. "I am exactly where I want to be." She sat on the sofa close to him, her mouth inches away. "But first there are things I must say. There are things that may be important. You must hear me." Jack saw his reflection in her big, glassy eyes. "It has nothing to do with how I feel about you."

"It doesn't," he whispered as he moved his hand to the small of her back.

"As medical examiner you hold inquests?"

He relaxed his hand. "Yes?"

"You look into deaths in Hillsborough County. Am I right?"

"Not all deaths. Only traumatic ones—accidents, suicides, homicides. And I look into natural deaths, when there is no attending physician or there are unusual circumstances. Why?"

"You handle many deaths each day?" She asked.

He removed his hand from her back and leaned back. "Yes. I do. It is my job."

"I read about a homicide in the newspaper. It happened behind the Calypso Sports Bar downtown on the night of September 10. There was a fight. A man was stabbed. He died that night. Do you know this homicide?"

"Michael Brule'," he breathed. "Yes. I do." His eyes found her trembling hands. He reached for them. "Why are you frightened?"

She pulled her hands away and reached for her wineglass. She sipped and looked away. "I don't know if I should—"

"Something's bothering you."

"It's not about me. It is about you."

"Okay?" Jack took her empty glass and walked to the kitchen. Watching, he refreshed his scotch and filled her wine glass to the top. "Is it about that man who died? There are things I can talk about, and things I cannot. It is an active investigation. They have not found the—"

"It's not about him," she said. "It's about the friend, Mr. Shandling."

"Thomas Shandling. Right. His name was in the newspaper."

"The friend and witness."

"Okay?"

She got up and walked to the window with her glass, and stood there in all her radiance, her back to Jack. "The newspaper said a man stabbed Mr. Brule' and marked Mr. Shandling's face with blood from Mr. Brule'."

"I guess it was in the Sentinel, too."

"I saw the picture of Mr. Shandling. He was unconscious on a bed with wheels. I saw the blood on his face." She turned to him. "I saw the mark of—"

"It's okay. You can talk to me about anything. When you say mark, you mean symbol?"

"Yes. It means something, Jack. It means something if it was made by a Japanese man."

"I think you mean Eastern Asian. Did the Sentinel say Japanese?"

Kayda returned to the sofa. "Eastern Asian means many things, many ethnic groups—Chinese, Korean, Taiwanese, Japanese, and more. In this country, you think all Asian's are the same. We are different."

"I'm sorry. I did not mean to be insensitive—"

"We have very different family history, customs, cultures, religions, anatomies, and politics. Maybe the East Asian man that marked Mr. Shandling is Japanese. If he is, it is very important for you to know what that mark means."

Jack lowered his glass. "What does it mean, Kayda?"

"A half-circle with parallel lines on a vertical axis means something terrible to Japanese people. It is symbol for *atomic bomb*."

"Oh God. Atomic bomb? I never... Why draw it on someone's face?"

"Survivors of Hiroshima and Nagasaki use the symbol to remember."

"To remember World War II?" Jack questioned.

"The reason their families are gone. Cherished histories and memories, gone."

"This is terrible. It was a very dark time in human history."

"Some Japanese people blame the American people. Some are still angry today. They unite behind this symbol. They protest the atomic bomb. For some it is their life mission."

"What is that life mission today?" Jack asked as he leaned closer to Kayda.

"Retribution," she said. "Inflict pain and anguish. Punish

those most responsible for this great wrong. In the eyes of the extreme radicals, the creation and deployment of the atomic bomb on Hiroshima and Nagasaki is seen as a criminal act that must be punished."

"I understand the pain—many innocent people died. Do they weigh in on Pearl Harbor?" Jack asked not expecting an answer. "The Japanese people attacked the American people. Many innocent people died that day, too. The Japanese attack forced America into the war, one we did not want. I think all sides lost innocent lives. All sides have great sadness and regret. War is hell for all involved, not just one side."

"The Japanese people are a humble and gentle people. It has been told by my father Shintoism—an ancient animist religion—was intertwined with Japanese nationalism and militarism. It became *Imperial Japan's* new national religion. Many did not accept it. He said it promoted a dangerous ideology—*Japanese superiority*. He believed it led to war."

"I did not know any of this," Jack whispered. "I'm sorry for not being—"

"An Imperial Japanese splinter group—the most extreme radicals—persists today. They do not see the Japanese role in war. They only see their loss and those who took from them."

"Are you sure this Imperial Japanese radical splinter group exists today?"

"Yes. Few and scattered. When I saw the mark, I knew they were here," Kayda said.

Jack lifted her chin. "None of this is your fault, Kayda, or the fault of the Japanese people. Like all nations there are extreme groups. They do not represent the people. We both know most people in this world are good. They have no intention to hurt anyone."

"I tell you this because maybe your family is a target."

"Why my family?"

"You have unexplained, violent deaths in your family over many years. Your mother and now father. Maybe more. You must look."

"I don't understand. Why kill Brule' and put a mark on Shandling?"

"Maybe to send message—a reveal."

"Reveal what?"

"Reveal an ending or a beginning."

"I don't know why my family would be a target. No Burcher served in World War II."

"No direct connection? Is there indirect connection? Must look at family tree, all branches. Look at marriages and relationships. Look at family investments. If something connects to Hiroshima and Nagasaki, this group could be in Tampa for your family."

"The Burcher family opposed the war, Kayda. We did not participate. Some friendships and business relationships were lost because of our stance. Some thought we were un-American. I don't see how we could be a target of this radical splinter group. I appreciate you talking to me about this. I love that you had the concern and courage to share this information with me, but I think my family has the attention of a very determined serial killer."

Jack's eyes softened as he got lost in Kayda's eyes, the lady he could not stop thinking about. The only good in his life. Then she leaned on him—her firm breasts pressed against his hard chest as the tip of her tongue touched her lip. She whispered, "You are a good man, Jack Burcher. I am sorry for your misery. You do not deserve bad things in life." Her pupils dilated as she looked at his lips. "I have been falling in love with you."

"I am falling in love with you, too," he whispered. Their lips touched.

They both smiled. They kissed. And then were consumed.

Hands pulled close and touched. He slid her dress up her legs and lifted her onto him. "I missed you," she breathed as her shoes fell to the floor. With her head back and eyes closed, her hair fell off her shoulders. Buttons popped. Her blouse opened.

Holding her close he lifted her. Kayda's legs locked around his waist and they kissed hard. He carried her to the bed where they had made love all night and would again. Their clothes flew in all directions as their hard bodies melded together. The bed moved. They made love, lost in the sparkling city lights that poured off Hillsborough Bay waters.

Across the city, on the 42nd floor of the Bank of America Plaza Building, a penlight moved along a line of black file cabinets. When it stopped, someone picked a lock. Files and an evidence bag were removed. Rubber gloves held the medallion under a light—the hole in the center was a miss. Deron was the target. He got lucky—dodged a bullet.

ONE YEAR LATER

EIGHTEEN

**Janice & Mesmer Neuropsychiatry Offices –
Monday, October 11, 2004 – 18:00**

A year had passed since the night of passion and sex at the
Aloft Tampa Hotel. Bizarre World War II revelations
and talk of an Imperial Japanese radical group and Jack's
matrimonial woes had faded as his relationship with Kayda
Webster flourished and his family nightmare waned. The
combination of events gave Jack a chance to look hard at his life
and make changes. As a child, he lost his mother. As a man, he
lost his marriage. As a Chief Medical Examiner, he held his
father's brain in his hands and could not solve his most
important puzzle of his life. Alcohol could not stop the pain—it
was killing him. Maybe Kayda could stop the pain. Maybe
Kayda could give him his life back.

A year had also passed since the FBI Regional Office break-
in. Classified case files and important physical evidence had
been taken. Because sophisticated security systems had been
successfully breached, the Bureau concluded the work of

professionals. They identified the most likely culprit, but they would never be able to prove it. One day after the break-in, attorneys for Scott Trent Preston filed a motion at Florida's Second District Court of Appeals. Preston's attorneys claimed wrongful prosecution on racketeering charges due to insufficient evidence and tampering. After the break-in, the insufficient evidence part was true.

Paul Shuck disagreed with the Bureau's conclusions and focus. He argued the break-in had been the work of the Burcher family perp. The Presidential Medal of Honor, with the bullet hole, had been taken and Burcher files ransacked. Because the cheap medallion is available in all government souvenir stores, and because all Burcher files were accounted for, the Bureau clung to their position and began to redirect resource accordingly.

At 18:00 Jack left the county morgue and drove to Bayshore Gardens, on the Interbay Peninsula. Shuck asked for a one-year-update meeting with all members of the Burcher family. He wanted to present information on the progress of Ronan Burcher's case. David and Melissa passed. Jack would have passed, but Shuck also had a proposition to make. The SE Regional Director of the FBI had a way to bring an end to the Burcher family nightmare once and for all. That bold statement would be enough. Jack would hear him out. Kayda would wait for Jack. She had planned another late dinner and more. Jack promised he would not be long.

The Janice & Mesmer Medical Offices were one block from the Tampa Neuropsychiatry Hospital on Barcelona Avenue. At first Jack thought the meeting site odd. However, after two meetings and two shootings at the county morgue, the FBI wanted a safer place. Nestled in a lush tropical forest surrounded by ten-foot walls and equipped with a plethora of high-tech surveillance, the modern (bulletproof) glass psychiatric office building on Bayshore Boulevard seemed ideal. Secured and convenient for Jack, the locale met the needs of Dr. Janice and Dr. Mesmer. Their reason for participation would unfold at the right time.

"Hello, my friend," Paul said. Jack entered with a smile and handshake. His eyes scanned the room. Novak and Bullitt stood at the edge of the small conference table. At the far end Francis Deron remained seated, his hands in his lap and a subdued smile. Next to Deron, Dr. William Janice got to his feet with a casual salute and smile. Jack greeted each as the doors closed behind. When he got to Deron, he saw the wheelchair—they had not been in contact since the shooting. Their last words were harsh.

"Hello, Francis."

"Jack." He reached up with a shaking hand. "Good to see you."

"I'm sorry about your situation, the chair and all."

"This? It's fine. Could have been worse. I' never got to thank you."

"I did what anyone would do." Jack turned to the hand gripping his shoulder from behind. "Hello, William."

"Dr. Jack Burcher." They embraced. William Janice looked more like an experienced casino dealer than a neuropsychiatrist. The short, plump, bald man with the handlebar mustache and round spectacles always wore a black pinstriped suit, red vest, and paisley tie. He and Jack had become good friends over the prior four years. Janice had taken an interest in the field of forensic psychology—the postmortem psychoanalysis of death scenes, victims, and killers.

"You look well for a man who spends a lot of time with dead people," Janice teased.

"You know I like patients that can't escape."

"I do know. And it's why I find your profession so alluring, sir."

"Allowing the FBI and TPD to use your august facilities is gracious of you, William." He included Francis. "And it will certainly help you with the pesky parking tickets." Deron smiled and looked away. "Tell me Dr. Janice. Are you here to announce acceptance of my offer to join the Institute of Forensic Science? I know you're in desperate need to dress up a bland resume'."

"I am and I would, but you know I don't think it would be fair to the criminal element if you and I were to collude full time." Dr. Janice pushed his glasses up his nose with one finger as he always did when making a point. The two smiled. Francis Deron sipped his glass of Cabernet and continued to look away.

The overhead lights flashed. Conversations stopped and eyes moved to Director Paul Shuck. "Since we are all here, and have our after-hour beverages, I would like to get started. I promised each of you an hour meeting. I will touch on some of the high points of the Ronan Burcher case to date. Then we will move to the *meat* of the meeting."

"Meat of the meeting," Jack whispered to Janice on their way down. "Interesting choice of words." Janice did not react. He stared at Paul Shuck in controlled anticipation of the curtain going up.

Novak handed Jack a scotch on the rocks and scrambled to his seat. The room settled. Papers rustled and ice cubes chimed in crystal glasses. Jack eyed the only new one in the room. Dr. William Janice. *Why didn't Paul tell me about you?* He wondered.

From the corner of his eye he watched Janice lean back in his chair and clasp his hands on top of his belly. The unique scowl on Janice's face caught Jack's eye. He had seen that look before—when a complex forensic case challenged him. Dr.

Janice had an uncanny ability to shut out all distractions and turn on genius—the scowl was out of his control. *What do you know about my family mystery?* Jack wondered. *What is your interest? You never once broached me on the subject over the years. Why are you here?*

"Loose ends," Paul said as he opened his leather binder and pulled a pen from its sleeve. "Let's begin with *ransom calls*."

"There have been ransom calls?" Jack bellowed.

"Yes."

"And you thought it not important to tell me?"

"Correct. Jack."

"What in the hell is going on, Paul. This is not how we have worked together. We had an agreement. Did you forget?"

Paul waited for the dust to settle. "May I speak?"

"Please do," Jack growled in a deathly silent room.

"Did you enjoy the last twelve months, Jack? Please think before you answer."

Jack looked at each person sitting at the table. He took a deep breath. "Yes. I did, Paul. But that does not matter. I did not know you and Deron were withholding vital information on my father's case. How could you possibly justify—?"

"Jack, you have been embroiled in your family nightmare since you were ten. It has been on your mind every day and every night. You have paid a great personal price. It is not fair to you. It is not safe, and it is not right. After much council and consideration, we decided to not bring every small setback and every development to you. It is our job to handle the Burcher family case. We must handle it like every other case. The FBI takes full responsibility, and we always minimize family involvement in the day-to-day details."

"I see. The Chief Medical Examiner is in your way."

"No, Jack. The Chief Medical Examiner is never in our way. However, Jack Burcher gets in the way sometimes.

"It's not fair we take you down every rabbit hole. The FBI should only give an update on the most important aspects of the case, on a regular basis not a daily or sometimes hourly basis. The FBI and Tampa Police are here tonight to update you and your family on the most relevant aspects and developments of your family's case over the last twelve-month period."

Jack turned to Janice. "Are you in this, William? Are you psychoanalyzing me, too?"

"You know better," Janice said. "You know how much the people in this room respect and admire you. You are an exceptional forensic pathologist and a good man. But you are not superman. None of us are. It is 2004. You have carried this burden 34 years. Your life has been shaped by a tragedy you witnessed as a boy. We all know you became a forensic pathologist because of your life mission to track down those responsible for your mother's death, and now your father's.

Dr. Janice pushed his glasses up his nose. "I was asked to help a dear friend of mine—you, Jack. It was my recommendation the FBI move forward with the investigation with minimal contact with you and family members for one year. I wanted you to have a chance to experience life away from the constant nightmare. I wanted you to have a chance to enjoy life for a change.

"Your reluctance to attend this one meeting tells me I was right. You like your life. You want to protect what you are building. You don't want to get lost in this relentless nightmare again. Jack, it is past time for you to accept help. You must let go."

He listened to every word with his eyes locked on the bottom of his empty glass. Without a word he looked up into William Janice's understanding eyes. Then he looked around the room. *You're right. What am I doing? You are attempting to solve my nightmare without me. That's a good thing. I did have a good year, for a change. The best year of my life. I don't want to do this anymore. Can I let go?*

"I understand. I will do my best. I'm not promising perfection day one."

The room released a collective sigh of relief. Paul nodded. Janice squeezed Jack's shoulder. Paul continued. "We received three ransom calls over the last twelve-month period. Two have been eliminated—confirmed bogus. There was no way they connected with Rose's abduction, or Ronan's disappearance. However, one ransom call remains open and under investigation. Although we are not able to eliminate it, we believe it is one more opportunistic attempt to get money from the Burcher family. We will know more soon."

Jack closed his eyes and held his tongue. *My 'loose-end' cup runneth over. A ransom call is viable until it is proven nonviable. This loose end could demolish the family vendetta theory. It would be about money. Stop thinking. They got this.*

"Next. The fires on Bird Island September 9, 2003. We have confirmed it. The act of arsonists. I say plural because evidence may support more than one. There were three fires."

"Wonderful," Jack scoffed. "Sorry. Continue, please."

"An aerial view of the island reveals three separate and repetitive burn patterns. Quantico has studied them. Each fire left a burn pattern, a half-circle with two parallel lines projecting from the open part. We are familiar with the symbol. It is outdated. It symbolizes the atomic bomb, a mushroom cloud with the column."

"I didn't know a symbol for the atomic bomb existed," Bullitt said.

"First seen after the bombs dropped on Hiroshima and Nagasaki, August 6 and 9, 1945. The horrific event gave rise to a fringe group inside the Imperial Japanese government. The symbol captured the pain and ire of survivors of the event that ended World War II.

"Today the symbol is rarely seen. A small group of trident defenders of Imperial Japan exists. Membership is small, most from the older generation that remembers those days."

Deron spoke for the first time. "We have seen this symbol twice in the Tampa area—the Bird Island fires and on the face of a murder witness. Both on September 9th, 2003."

"A murder witness," Janice gasped. "Can you tell us more?"

"There was a knife fight at downtown bar," Deron said. "A young man died—stabbed in the top of the head—I'm sure Jack remembers. The killer drew this symbol on the face of the dead man's friend. Witnesses saw the killer, an Asian man. He's still out there."

"Francis is correct. I did the autopsy of Michael Brule', the victim. His friend, Thomas Shandling, witnessed everything."

Paul flipped another page and sipped his bourbon. "We think this has some bearing on the abduction of Ronan Burcher. The homicide in downtown Tampa happened in the early morning hours of September 9. The fires were set on Bird Island later that day. Ronan was taken from his room that night, the early morning hours of September 10. All in a 24-hour period."

Jack leaned forward. "I'm not sure I see the connection to Ronan, Paul. What do you have I don't know about?"

"I didn't think about it until after the break-in a year ago, and the disappearance of the Presidential Medal of Freedom. It just didn't sit right with me. We kept important things in the offices on the 42nd floor—things not touched. Although the Bureau and I disagreed on who orchestrated the break-in, I asked myself why would someone go out of their way to take a cheap medallion with a hole in it? Was it a random keepsake? Or, did they come for it? Then it hit me. Remember when we found the impression on the edge of it? Looked like it had been pressed into the metal after it had been made?"

"I remember," Jack said. "We saw the 'C' and the equal sign. It meant nothing to us at the time—I thought a manufacturing flaw or damage from debris. Something that got in the way as they pounded out thousands."

"I think someone took that medallion for a reason. Maybe they did not want us—"

"—to see the symbol," Jack said. "They weren't trying to shoot the center of the coin. They missed their mark. They were trying to eliminate the symbol. They did not want us to see it, Paul."

"Exactly. Thank God I had my own photo. I carried it because I thought I dodged a bullet, and because it gnawed at me." He held up the photo and passed it around. "The question we must answer is why was a symbol of an atomic bomb on a medallion put in Ronan's brain?"

Kayda told me about the splinter group a year ago, Jack thought. *I didn't really listen—dismissed as a crazy notion because the family had nothing to do with World War II or the atomic bomb. We were patriotic like other Americans, but.*

Paul cleared his throat and flipped another page. "We did locate the owner of the heart we once thought belonged to Rose Burcher."

"That I do know. I found it," Jack whispered.

"Yes. And thank you. I'm sharing this information with the others."

"Right. Sorry."

"Would you like to take this one? You know more than me."

"Sure. We reviewed all our records at the county morgue. We looked at every death certificate issued in Hillsborough County on and around the date of my mother's disappearance. As I had suspected, the heart did belong to a 65-year-old male with advanced atherosclerosis. This explained the severe calcification of the left aorta found.

"The heart belongs to Ralph Martin, a retired city fireman doing home repair. Mr. Martin died of natural causes at his home with family present. Our monster took Mr. Martin's heart after embalmed at Griffin Funeral Home, Tampa's east side."

"I don't understand."

"Why would someone steal Ralph Martin's heart and make us think it belonged to my mother?" Jack said. "Before I answer, there's more. We exhumed Ralph Martin. We found he had all his organs. DNA confirmed my mother's heart replaced his heart. I suspect slipped under the hood before burial. Nobody would have thought to look."

"My God, that is bizarre," Janice muttered.

"We believe the Burcher killer does everything for a reason," Paul said. "He selected Ralph Martin's heart. When we find out why, we will have another piece to this puzzle."

"There's a ritual of disclosure," Jack muttered. "I think it's as important as the kill."

"We identified the redheaded nurse at the Sun Bay facility," Paul said.

Jack blinked at the change in subject. "You identified our mystery nurse?"

"Mai Kohana," Paul said. "A 44-year-old Japanese florist from Little Rock—"

"—Arkansas," Jack muttered as he scratched his head. He never scratches his head.

"Yes."

"What was she doing in Tampa?"

"We don't know," Deron said.

"We do know her mother, MaSato Kohana, was the only Kohana family member to survive the bomb in Hiroshima. Age ten. Away from home when it happened. Before the bomb dropped on Nagasaki, MaSato had returned to bury her family. Fourteen years later she gave birth to a girl, Mai. The next year MaSato died. Cancer. Mai was placed in an orphanage. We don't know how or when she got to this country. Documents of American citizenship, forged. Her history here begins in the spring of '94. Lived alone. Worked at Sully's Flower Shop in a suburb of Little Rock."

"Anything that would suggest she joined the radical group?" Jack asked.

"Her tragic family history. She could have been an angry. We have no way to know how she processed her losses, or her view of this country. Most people moved on, both sides."

"I still don't understand how any of this connects to my family," Jack said. "We had nothing to do with World War II. I researched all the family businesses and investments. We had zero interest in anything related to the war effort. My family had nothing to do with the creation and/or deployment of the atomic bomb.

"Not one member of my family served in the military, any war ever. Personally, I find that reality disturbing. However, it should eliminate the Burcher family."

"The only take-away we have is Mai Kohana—a Hiroshima survivor—came to Tampa, found a way inside Sun Bay, and delivered your father to a killer. After she did, she landed in a dumpster with a broken neck. Miss Kohana could have been forced to comply, manipulated."

The room sat in silence as the unanswered questions swirled.

"I suggest we break," Chief Deron said.

"Good idea." Paul closed his binder. "When we return, I will present a formal proposition, one I believe will put us on the elusive path to resolution. We will get started in ten minutes."

Deron backed away from the table and wheeled up to a window, where he sat alone.

"Let's all get back in ten, please," Paul said.

Jack smiled inside. With veiled skepticism, he watched the room empty. Each attendee filed out leaving him alone as if they had practiced. Not a time for chitchat. They were working up to something.

Where is this going, Jack wondered.

NINETEEN

**Janice & Mesmer Neuropsychiatry Offices –
Monday, October 11, 2004 – 18:30**

I n the dark of night, the torrential rains slid across Bayshore
Gardens. Left alone to wander before the FBI's *proposition*,
Jack took the opportunity to phone Kayda. He walked. They
planned dinner and the rest of their evening. When he
disconnected, he found himself lost on the second floor
mesmerized by the sheets of cascading water and bending
palms framing the lush grounds. *How far can you bend before
you break?* He wondered as the they dipped. *I guess that's the
question—survival in life's storms.*

He leaned to the glass and read the words cut into a marble
slab on the edge of the gardens. "Psychoanalysis is a tool to
explore the unconscious mind to relive painful emotions and
increase self-awareness." *Maybe if my mother had never been
taken, I would have pursued a different medical specialty. Or
maybe medicine would have never been a consideration.*

Jack arrived more than ten minutes late. He opened the

meeting-room door and froze. The lighting and furniture had changed. The conference table he left twenty minutes ago had disappeared. Three high-back, cushioned chairs sat on a small stage in front of a dozen chairs arranged in two rows: a semi-circle configuration with an aisle down the center. When his eyes adjusted, he saw the faces in the chairs. Paul sat on stage with an odd smile. Two strangers stood in the shadows off stage.

What the hell, he wondered as he clung to the doorknob and started to back away?

"Jack. Wait," Paul called. "You're late. Please. Join me up here."

Jack made out Deron in his wheelchair on the edge of the front row and the faces in the chairs near him. He expected Janice, Novak, and Bullitt. They were here before. He did not expect Milton Crabtree (FBI), Raymond Gompers (CSI), Sheriff Babcock, Judge Benatar, Deborah Quin, or Mack Sutton (SWAT). They were new. And he did not expect Melissa and David. They sat on the front row. *You never said a word about coming to this thing. As a matter of fact, you said there was no way in hell you'd take part in another FBI dog-and-pony... Guess you changed your minds.* Then he saw four more strangers. That made six in the so-called private meeting with the Burcher family.

"What's this all about?" Jack barked. "I don't like surprises. Looks like I'm the only one in the dark, and I'm not just talkin' about room optics."

"No surprises here, Jack. We're doing something new, something I believe can solve your family mystery. I told you I had a proposition."

"Your proposition calls for these theatrics?" Jack scoffed.

"This is not intended to be theatrical. The setup has a purpose. If you had been here on time, you would have participated in the rearrangement. It's intended to accommodate the needs of this part of our meeting. Everybody helped move the tables and chairs around.

"As always, you have the final word on whether we go forward or not. Now please, come up here with me. Give this a chance. I think it's important."

Jack perused the staring manikins and weighed his options. *I could turn around and leave, but then all I could do is wait to die like the rest of the family, never knowing why. No! I gotta go through with this. If it has any chance to bring an end to the family nightmare, it's worth the discomfort. Close the door. Go up there. Keep an open mind.* "Okay."

Jack let go of the knob. The door muffled closed as he walked through the whispers floating from the shadows into the soft light that fell off the peculiar, little platform.

"Thank you. Please. Sit with me."

Paul pulled out index cards and spoke to Jack as if they were alone. "I've had a lot of time to think about your family. Fourteen years, three months, one week and four days counting today. I think the last year was the real eyeopener for me.

"I spent a fair amount of time alone with the case files. I laid them out on my office floor and went through every piece of paper in every file, every article of evidence, every photograph, and each video and audio files. I spent months looking for the kill-trail that has eluded us.

"I used all my resources and the top professionals in the FBI to examine all the evidence. I did not want to miss one thing. We conducted investigations from the 1948 death of Leonard Burcher to the 1970 death of Rose and the 2003 abduction of Ronan, including the delivery of his brain to your home. We looked at all the bizarre incidents following his abduction. We have another year of evidence, another year of loose ends, and another year of questions."

The audience shifted in their chairs as Paul recounted the uncomfortable extent of the Burcher family nightmare and failed investigations. Where would Paul Shuck go next? What was the great revelation that had led to this meeting and a veiled proposition?

"Sitting on my office floor one night, looking at the carpet of endless files, it hit me." The stage lights touched Paul's face in an eerie or celestial way depending on one's mood. "We do the same thing with every new piece of information, and we always get to the same place—a multigenerational killing spree of unknown origin and purpose.

"After all these years, and all these investigations, we just have theories. Nothing holds together. Nothing adds up. Nothing makes sense. Why the Burcher family? Why? Why?"

Whispers fluttered across the dark room. "I agree with every word," Jack said. *Who are the shadows off stage,* he wondered? *Where are you going with this, Paul?*

"We have learned, after all these years, we will not get where we want to be if we continue to do the same things the same way."

"Okay. That makes perfect sense," Jack muttered.

"Albert Einstein once said, 'You can never solve a problem on the level on which it was created.' Those words spoke to me. We've allowed ourselves to be misled. Our thinking is flawed. It has dropped to the level of the monster we hunt. We are fed a mixture of truths and lies, and we consume them like children eating candy. We are being played. Everything around each tragedy is intended to send us multiple directions—controlled chaos. We are manipulated masterfully. It is time for a new approach.

"My proposal is composed of two recommendations. If we do as I have outlined, I am certain we will solve this mystery and catch the monster. My first recommendation is we must gain access to the earliest and most vital information that is available to us and has yet to be pursued. It holds the purest and most important clues, the keys to solving this case.

"My second recommendation—"

Jack scanned the room. Faces were intense, fixed on Paul. *Do you people know what information he's talking about— earliest, most vital, and purest not pursued?*

"—we must give this new information, and all the Burcher case files, to someone untainted by decades of personalities, positions, politics, and worn-out theories. This person must be an internationally acclaimed expert in the field of homicide investigation. They must be able to commit to this project full time for a minimum of six months."

"Someone without preconceived notions," floated anonymously through the room.

"Is that it?" Jack said as Paul shuffled his index cards. "I too am reminded of something Albert Einstein said. 'Information is not knowledge.' For some time, I've felt we've lifted every rock in our mystery river. We have no idea what river we are in or where it goes."

"That is a perfect analogy. If you agree, we can now move forward on that river."

"For now, I can agree with your general concept," Jack said. "But I—"

Paul jumped to his feet. "Dr. William Janice. Please join us."

With a fatherly and professorial aura, Janice climbed onto the small stage. He would soon take control of the audience. In the subdued setting, he sat down, removed his glasses, and slid them into his tight breast pocket.

Janice flashed a smile, ran a slow finger across each bushy eyebrow, and his eyes found each person in the room. The acclaimed psychoanalyst knew how to connect and control.

"Your family tragedy has been with you for a very long time," he said without looking at Jack.

"It has been with *all members of our family* a very long time," Jack corrected.

"Of course. The family members—David and Melissa and your father, up until the onset of his unfortunate medical conditions," Janice reasoned in a veiled effort to maintain his point.

Jack would not let it go. For him, accuracy matters. "No, doctor. Even after the onset of Parkinson's and dementia Ronan carried the memories and the pain. The night of his abduction, he spoke of my mother and his feared expectations—that he was next."

"I understand, Jack. I contend the Burcher family tragedy has weighed you down the most. Will you accept that clinical observation?"

"No, I will not. We each handle tragedy and pain different ways. I cannot say I have carried more than my brother or sister or father. I don't know where you're going with this, but I am not the one most weighed down. It has been a lifelong burden for my entire family. If you are asking me, I cannot quantify, differentiate, or distribute such complex emotions."

Dr. Janice smiled differently this time. He had cleared the first hurdle—Jack Burcher's stubborn resistance to acknowledge his obvious burden well beyond that of his siblings.

"Let me give you more information, it will help us move forward together," Janice said. "When your mother was taken from your home, that hot summer night in 1970, you were ten years old. Is that correct?"

"Yes. I was ten."

"Melissa was almost five and David two," Janice said.

"Yes. That's right."

"You were old enough to remember your mother well. Is that a fair statement?"

"*Well* is a subjective word," Jack said as he scrutinized the psychoanalyst. "I do remember my mother, of course."

"I contend you carry far more of a burden from your family tragedies than your sister or brother combined, a contention you—Dr. Burcher—feel compelled to reject."

"Not reject. Put into proper perspective," Jack rationalized.

"I say *reject* and *deny*," Janice boomed. "Would you like to know why?"

Jack smiled. "I'm not sure it's a necessary or a relevant—"

"—matter to dissect," Janice pushed. "There's a word I know you are familiar with. I do think it is necessary and relevant and important to *dissect* so we can move forward together with the FBI's first recommendation."

Jack sat up. "I don't see how this—"

"Allow me to be very clear on what we are talking about here. I contend you not only carry more of the burden than your siblings, I contend you carry many multiples more and it has touched every aspect of your being—your every thought, behavior, and all your life choices."

Jack leaned back in his chair. With cold eyes, he stared at Janice—*ambushed*.

"This is *my* area of expertise, Dr. Burcher. I will explain the basis of my conclusions because it is an underpinning we must rectify if we are to move forward with step one.

"*Cognition* by definition is the mental process for acquiring knowledge and understanding through thought, experience, and the senses. What do we know about *cognitive development*? We know there are four cognitive stages of childhood development. From birth to two years of age children learn about the world through their senses and manipulation of objects—including people. They are egocentric—they only know of themselves. Age three to seven children begin to develop imagination and memory. They understand things symbolically. Age seven to eleven children become aware of feelings other than their own. They recognize external events. They begin to understand others do not always share their thoughts, beliefs, or feelings. It is when a child becomes aware of others, especially mothers, fathers, and siblings.

"Jack, these are three of the four stages of *childhood cognitive development* relevant to our conversation. David was two when Rose Burcher was abducted. David did not know his mother other than an object meeting his sensual needs. Melissa was almost five. She knew of her mother but was just beginning to develop a memory. Thirty years later I'm quite certain that sliver of a memory vanished. You were ten, Jack. You knew you mother better than any other person on earth. She was the person you spent the most time with. You knew everything about her. You knew her smile. Today you remember how she smelled, her gentle touch, her love and anger and her protection. Through your mother you learned your feelings were often different from others. At ten you were beginning to grasp external events. That's why you had to be in that field at night to look at the stars and to dream big dreams in a vast universe.

"You remember well the night the *external world* tore apart your world, Jack Burcher. You remember the moment you were taken from your stars and innocent dreams. You remember the monster that took your mother away. You saw the blood in the house—you walked through it looking for help. Then you saw police everywhere and felt nothing happening. They just didn't care like you cared.

"The next night you saw even more horror. They said something to your father. You watched him collapse. They took him away from you for three weeks. No one talked to you.

They did not even attempt to comfort you when your whole world imploded in 1970.

"A ten-year-old boy watched a monster deliver a box with his mother's heart inside. They tried to keep it from you. I think you found out that night. I think you looked inside that box because you knew they would never tell you the truth. You were beginning to understand the outside world. It was a dark and dangerous place filled with monsters and liars. Everyone lied to you. It was then you knew you could trust no one ever again."

Dr. Janice paused. Through glassy eyes Jack stared at the psychoanalyst. "You were swallowed that night, Jack. Your pain had reached a level Melissa and David could not comprehend at their tender ages or ever after. You were hurt, confused, and alone. The lines between imaginary and real those nights were forever blurred. And you blamed yourself for not saving your mother—something you have never spoken about. Your secret would define the rest of your life. The world is a dangerous place! How could it take the most perfect person from you? All people lie! The police, the news, your friends and neighbors, counselors, and your father. The only one you could count on would be Jack Burcher. That was when you decided you would find the monster on your own. That was your only reason to live."

A single tear left Jack's eye. "It's true," he whispered. "All of it."

The room stirred. Jack sat up and wiped his eyes looking first at David and then Melissa. "I have known a long time, William. It has always been with me." He forced a smile. "For heaven's sake, it was why I went to medical school. I needed to understand all these feelings. Maybe I could fix them. And yes, the other reason I went was to learn everything I could so I could find the person who—"

Janice rested a hand on Jack's shoulder. "I'm sorry. This was necessary. Now. Not only to begin the healing process, but so we can move forward together with the FBI's proposition. You must allow us inside, Jack. You are a brilliant forensic pathologist and Chief Medical Examiner. You are a good man. But you are not superman. A confused, ten-year-old boy lives inside you. He has too much control. He has mastered sidestepping your brilliance and your adult intellect because someone must carry your burden. You will not let him go, on your own. You need help. We will talk to the boy. It is our first step in this most promising FBI initiative. Only then will you let him go."

"I'm not sure I understand what you mean," Jack said.

Paul returned to the edge of the stage. "Jack, we must access early and vital information that we have never pursued properly."

Chief Deron wheeled out of the shadows. "I am a big part of your problem, Jack. You've never forgiven me for my handling of the 1970 investigation. I now know my failure to properly vet you pushed you deeper into a dark abyss."

Janice interrupted. "No one could expect a homicide detective in 1970 to behave like one in 2004," he said. "In 1970 we did not know how to conduct a careful and critical examination of tragic facts with a child. That psychological knowledge had not yet been developed. In those days, kids were to be seen not heard. We've come a very long way."

Paul approached Jack and stayed at the edge of the light. Jack could not see his face. He could not read him. "You possess vital information from the two most important nights in 1970—July 14 and July 15. You are the only eyewitness. You have never been vetted. We know the ten-year-old boy inside you has information that will unlock secrets and shed new light on your mother's and possibly your father's cases. When we extract that information, it will be infused with all we know thirty years later. I'm confident we will learn why your family has been terrorized—"

"—and we will find those responsible," Deron said as if his every word had been scripted. Janice smiled at him but took note. There could be no lingering obstacles. Jack may only have one shot at it.

Jack rubbed the growing ache in his neck. The room waited for his next words. Would he accept the proposed process or reject it? Then he looked at each person in the room. He had just been stripped naked in front of his sister and brother, friends, associates, and strangers. Would he shut it down, leave, and go it alone like always? Or did Janice give him a new strength?

You are right about many things, Jack thought. *But not all things.*

"That ten-year-old boy you want to talk to is a long way from home now," Jack said. "Thirty-four years away. I'm sorry, but I can't give you what you want. God knows I've racked my brain to remember more about those two nights." He shook his head and ran a hand through his hair. "I'm sorry. That's all I can say. I've got nothin' more to give. I cannot pull things out of thin air...

"I have listened," Jack said. "I'm sorry. I think we are done here." He started to stand.

"Yes, you can," Janice said. Jack froze. "We can pull things out of thin air, Jack, because they are there. You saw them with your own eyes. Your brain is just not sharing them with you."

"There are ways to let you see," Paul said.

"No. There are not. Dr. Janice just told you why—I was ten. I was just beginning to be aware of external events. Francis is right, too. Although I blamed him for not listening to me, I still cannot separate imagination from reality. For God's sake, I thought I saw a UFO land on our property both nights. I saw a long, gray thing with black windows and fins. I heard it growl at me. The UFO hovered in the night fog above the ground. Then it left in a flash of light. That's all I got, Paul—a frightening world through the eyes of a ten-year-old boy lost and confused and scared to death."

On Jack's last word, a shadow off stage stepped into the light. "There are ways to help that ten-year-old boy see. I can show you."

TWENTY

The tall, gray-haired man stepped from the shadows. "There are ways to return to 1970, Dr. Burcher," he said. "We can talk to the ten-year-old boy like it happened yesterday."

Dr. Janice pointed to his friend. "Allow me to introduce my associate, Dr. Eric Mesmer."

Mesmer leaned his gentle smile further into the light. The wiry, old gentleman in the black suit looked like he had walked off a silent-movie set. His pallid face, framed by a pair of bushy sideburns and nest of curly gray hair atop his long forehead, put the room at ease like a beloved Dickens character.

"I asked Dr. Mesmer to be a part of this," Janice said. "He is a brilliant doctor of psychiatric medicine. However, it is his unique specialty that has application here."

"Dr. Mesmer brings an expertise we need," Paul said as he tucked his index cards into his pocket and watched Jack study the surprise guest. Mesmer approached Jack with an extended hand. After staring a few long seconds at his boney fingers dangling from the starched French cuff, Jack shook it with a forced smile.

Who is this man? Jack wondered. *I know you're William's partner—another shrink—but I don't know your specialty. What is your claim to fame? Why does the name ring a—*

"We've identified Jack Burcher as our *only* eyewitness to the events of July 14 and 15, 1970," Paul continued. He waved for Mesmer to take a seat on the stage. "We believe there are valuable clues in this eyewitness's testimony. We hope to recover all of them. These clues may solve the Burcher mystery once and for all.

"Jack did share his feelings about all of this earlier. He does not believe he can go back there—he cannot remember much more than he's already shared about those perilous nights. He is convinced he is unable to interpret the observations of that ten-year-old boy sitting alone in a field outside his bedroom window." Paul turned to Jack. "Have I accurately stated your feelings on this matter, Jack?"

Jack's eyes moved from Mesmer. "Yes, Paul. I have tried. I must agree with Dr. Janice. The tragic events of 1970 were witnessed by a boy with limited cognitive development. Separating facts from a boy's wild imagination decades later is impossible."

"Dr. Mesmer, please tell us if you can help," Paul said.

The old man crossed his spindly legs like a tall, skinny girl. He clasped bony fingers with arthritic knuckles on his lap and flashed an awkward smile. "Can I help...? Well, that sir would be up to Dr. Burcher." He turned to Jack with soft but now penetrating eyes. "If this young man can find a reason to trust me, we can get the information everyone seeks, including Dr. Burcher."

Whispers fluttered through the dark room like a hundred disturbed moths. With elbows on the chair arms and pyramid fingers propping his chin, Jack studied the old man like one of his cadavers. *Mesmer... Mesmerize... I know where this is going—*

"Please educate them, Eric," Dr. Janice said with great authority.

Mesmer turned back to the audience. His face changed. "My distant, multiples-of-great grandfather was born in a small village—Iznang, 1734. A place *nowhere,* on Lake Constance in Swabia, Germany. A place many have never heard of. He was the son of a master forester. I don't know how he found his way to become a world-renowned expert on the influence of planets on the human body, but he did just that.

"A student of Isaac Newton's theory of tides, my multiple-of-greats grandfather believed tides are in the body. Like ocean tides, they too are influenced by the movement of the sun and the moon. His theory was formally termed—*animal magnetism.* He believed absence or disruption of these natural tides in the body created a long list of abysmal conditions—hysteria, insanity, and disease. He theorized our health requires the free flow of these *tides of life* through thousands of internal channels. When nature fails to produce or manage them, disease and other dreadful conditions manifest. An unhealthy state prevails. The only cure is intervention. One must get the internal tides flowing properly again.

"To do this, he developed a treatment regimen. First, he needed to alter the patient's state of mind: focus their attention, reduce their peripheral awareness, and enhance their capacity to respond to suggestion. *Franz Friedrich Anton Mesmer,* my multiples-of-great grandfather and a German doctor with interests in astronomy, died in March of 1815. He died not knowing his theory of *animal magnetism* was a farce. Nor did he know he had discovered *hypnosis.*"

"Your specialty is hypnosis," Jack said. The crowd whispered.

"Yes," Mesmer said. "I suppose my interest resides in my genes."

"I see. Well, I appreciate your genes and your desire to help. Please don't take this the wrong way, Doctor. Hypnosis does have a place, but not with me. I am not a candidate. I am a skeptic, untrusting, and strong willed. I would not respond to any form of suggestion therapy."

"On the contrary, Dr. Burcher," Mesmer said softly. "I have taken the time to know you. I've observed all your interviews with the FBI and Tampa police. I've watched your televised appearances as Chief Medical Examiner amidst difficult situations. And I've observed you today. Your ability to listen, share, challenge, and take risk tells me you would be the perfect candidate for hypnosis therapy. I know for a fact we can go back to 1970 and talk to that ten-year-old boy. If I had any doubts, I assure you I would not be here today."

"I'm sorry. But I just cannot do—"

"—you can do this," Janice bellowed. "You must do this. You cannot leave a single rock unturned. This nightmare can be solved. Tell us what you're really afraid of, Jack."

"Hypnosis is a human condition," Mesmer said. "It involves focus and the elimination of peripheral awareness. When we accomplish that, you experience an amplified capacity to respond to suggestion. If I earn your trust you will go beyond most who enter a hypnotic state."

"How do you know that to be true?" Jack challenged.

"Because you are a forensic pathologist desperate for answers. Your life is all about solving complex puzzles and utilizing all tools available. You seek truth. Your deductive reasoning skills and forensic intellect will allow you to learn while in the hypnotic state. At some point you will not need me. You will take control of your own process."

"What does that mean?"

"Hypnosis is like going under water—a new environment governed by new rules. Some patients refuse to do anything more than put their face in the water—they are afraid. Others will go under but stay near the surface—not risk takers. All hold my hand."

"And what will I do?"

"You will dive deep, Dr. Burcher. You will leave the light and move into the dark without fear. You will be driven by your innate sense of curiosity and new-found freedom to explore places never before available to you." A broad smile grew on Mesmer's face. "You will let go of my hand, Jack Burcher. My challenge with you will not be about getting you under the water. It will be about keeping you from going too deep too long."

"And if I go too deep, then what?"

"I don't know. I've never been there before. We must trust each other."

"I see. An unknown risk with questionable rewards. I don't know if—"

"—I can promise you this. Whatever you saw the nights of July 14 and 15 in 1970, you will see it again. But this time you will be able to examine it with your forensic brain, not the underdeveloped brain of a child. I will ask questions. You will tell me everything you see. I will record the session. In your own words you will describe what you see. You will see and know far more than you think right now. If you felt something then, something you did not understand, we can dissect it together. We will separate fact from fiction, reality from imagination."

"I say do it, Jack." The words exploded in the dark room.

People jerked. David jumped to his feet and ran up to the edge of the stage. "Please, Jack. Let him hypnotize you."

"He's right." Melissa joined David. "Everything these doctors have said is true, and you know it. Mother's death destroyed *your* life, Jack. You gotta let go of it. David and I don't remember any of it like you. We loved our mother, but we don't have the memories you have. We don't know her or the nightmare you live every day. We never will."

"Let Dr. Mesmer hypnotize you," David pushed. "I don't care about finding a monster anymore. We want you better, Jack. We want you to stop drinking away your life. You are living a slow death sentence. It's time—"

"—David. Melissa. Thank you, but I need you to sit down now. I appreciate your words, but we have more to do tonight.

"Dr. Mesmer. Dr. Janice. Thank you, gentlemen. Please take a seat in the front row." Paul flipped through his small stack of dog-eared index cards.

"Are you done with me?" Jack asked as he started to get up from his chair.

"No, Jack. Please. Sit. Stay here—"

TWENTY-ONE

Paul scanned the shadows and stopped on the tall silhouette in back. He returned his attentions to the small group of professionals and family members with their own vested interests in the outcome of the meeting. "I appreciate Dr. Mesmer's and Dr. Janice's personal and professional investments in the Burcher family mystery. At this time Jack and his family do not need to make any decisions—"

"—there is more to consider," Deron said as he bumped the stage and locked his wheels.

"Frank. Please. I got this." Paul studied his top card. "As I said at the onset, the FBI proposition is composed of two recommendations. We see them as connected. Implementation of one and not the other will not give us the opportunity we must have to achieve our objectives—capture a killer and close the Burcher case. At the end of this meeting the proposition must be adopted in its entirety without modification. That is when we will need a family decision."

Jack leaned forward. "And if it is not adopted or—"

"—fully embraced as outlined," Paul said. "The FBI will shelve the Burcher case. We will be done, Jack."

"Done?"

"The FBI will move on. We will shift attentions and resources to other cases in the central Florida region. We have more than enough waiting."

"You can't be serious," Jack said. "You can't shelve our case."

"I'm sorry, Jack. We can and we will if our requirements are not met."

"The FBI can't dictate—"

"—matters affecting the deployment of our limited resources. Yes, we can. I went to the wall to get this proposition approved because I know it will work. After all we've been through, I hope you will give me some credit. This will be the FBI's last major effort to solve the Burcher family case. We walk away. It is not our first cold case."

"Your position has holes. I will go over your head."

"The fact remains the FBI has limits. As a county medical examiner, you should understand limits better than anyone. There are times we all must let go of an unsolved case because other cases wait.

"You can go over my head. It won't change a thing. The Bureau doesn't even want to support my proposition—too costly. A call from you may only expedite the termination order. Maybe instead of fighting me you should ask yourself why I'm so committed to this."

Jack turned away in a huff. *He's right. I'd get nowhere.*

"Let's move on," Deron said. "If Jack cannot get on board after he's heard the whole proposition—"

"—or if he can get on board all this is moot," Dr. Mesmer said. Paul nodded.

"The *second recommendation;* information obtained from the *first phase,* and all Burcher case files, will be given to someone untainted by decades of personalities, positions, politics, and theories. They will be experienced in international homicide investigation and available on a full-time basis for a minimum of six months."

"Great. More *new eyes* to slow us down," Jack muttered. *A classic time waster—*

"Dr. Tate Worthington," Paul announced. "Please join us up here, sir."

The silhouette in back walked down the aisle and into the light. The handlebar mustache and sunglasses climbed onto the stage and took the chair next to Jack. The ironed jeans, brown corduroy coat, and white cotton shirt with an open collar sat down. He casually brushed his sleeves, tugged at his cuffs, and removed a tiny piece of lint. He dropped it to the floor with a hint of irritation.

"Thank you for coming, Dr. Worthington," Paul said.

"Certainly."

"For those unfamiliar with the *Worthington Private Investigation Agency,* allow me to introduce the founder/owner/namesake. Tate Worthington is an internationally renowned PI. He has successfully handled over a hundred complex cases around the world working with top law enforcement organizations including the IPA, INTERPOL, the International Law Enforcement Academies, Scotland Yard, Royal Canadian Mounted Police, FBI, and CIA.

"Tate Worthington has stopped some of the most prolific serial killers in the world, disrupted the most despicable cohorts engaged in lethal counter espionage, brought in South American drug lords and human trafficking kingpins, and has solved numerous, high-profile abductions for ransom—most of which never made it into the newspapers.

"I had the opportunity to meet Tate while working on the *Range Strangler* case—an elusive serial killer active in the central U.S. The FBI began their investigation in June of 1989. We soon realized we were dealing with a horrific killing machine. Our investigations took us into eight states where we worked with seventeen state and local law enforcement offices. Five years later we had collected enough physical evidence to sink a boat and place the Range Strangler at thirty-four crime scenes. That's all we had, evidence. Zero workable patterns to predict targets or next moves. We had a profile but no knowledge of where the monster came from or where he was going. The Range Strangler kept us on our heels. He was either smart or stupid lucky. Weren't sure which. All we had were smoldering crime scenes and cold trails.

"Someone recommended Tate Worthington," Paul said. "I remember I thought adding a PI was a bad idea—just something else to slow us down. What could this guy bring? We already had five regional FBI offices and 17 law enforcement agencies crawling all over the case."

Paul shook off memory lane. "Worthington brought new eyes to a dead case. I remember when he walked in my office the first time. All I saw was a tall Texan with a big mustache, jeans, and cowboy boots." Paul chuckled. "I thought, here we go. I was not in favor of bringing in an overrated PI. We're the damn FBI. We got this. Fact was, it had us.

"The Texan didn't talk much. Just hung his hat on a peg and took the lid off the first box—the Range Strangler's first kill. Tulsa, Oklahoma. Over the next few weeks, he opened every box and studied every case file. Every piece of paper. Every piece of evidence. Then he talked to the witnesses and went to each crime scene. At the end of the first month he focused on one item of physical evidence. Something we recovered at the first crime scene. At the end of the next month he brought in the Range Strangler. The monster was in the act. Tate got him before he killed number thirty-five."

"We need more, Paul," David said. "We have a lot of experts. I identify more with your and Jack's initial feelings about someone new. I thought we were getting close. With Dr. Mesmer and Jack's eyewitness testimony, we could get the information we need to find the sick bastard haunting my family. I don't see how a PI is gonna help. No offense, Dr. Worthington. I see *new* slowin' us down. Maybe tell us how he solved the Range Strangler case. What made him smarter than the FBI?"

Paul walked to the edge of the stage. "We found a rag, a scrap torn off an old t-shirt. It was at the first crime scene. Killer used it to gag the poor victim. He raped and strangled her. We processed that rag in the lab. Got DNA. Ran it through CODIS—no match. We had a lot of other items from the crime scene to process. While that went on, we moved to other cases. Well, about a month later Tate came on board. He took a long look at everything and decided to stay with the old t-shirt. Tate said that one piece of evidence spoke to him the most. It presented the greatest opportunity.

"After his extensive analysis, he found a faint and partial ink label on the fabric. Tate reconstructed four letters— MACC. After a lot more research, he had a hunch the letters were an acronym for the Mack Alford Correctional Center, a minimum-security prison just outside Stringtown, Oklahoma. That small prison put MACC on their property items—an ink stamp. Tate believed the southwest quadrant of Oklahoma made for an ideal *home base* for the serial killer—it fit his theories for the eight-state killing pattern.

"Well, the Range Strangler DNA taken from that old rag did not match any of the inmates or employees at the Mack Alford Correctional Center. We had reached another dead end. Tate felt differently. He continued looking. Convinced that old rag found at the first crime scene was the Range Strangler's one big mistake.

"Tate learned the Mack Alford Correctional Center employed many people from in and around Stringtown. MACC was also very active in community outreach programs. They supported Stringtown charities, including Goodwill. Each year MACC donated their old furniture and piles of worn soft goods—old towels, sheets, shoes, and t-shirts. Tate put a detail on the Stringtown Goodwill location. They looked for men that fit our profile. One week later he had five suspects. Seemed like too many. Another dead end, but Tate stayed with it. He went around and collected DNA samples from each suspect. Went through their garbage. Picked up discarded soda cans, half-eaten sandwiches, and other sorts of trash.

"To our surprise, Tate got a match—Frederick Donley. A truck driver. Creighton Freight. Tate analyzed the man's routes. He had been with CF five years. Matched our kill timeline. Tate got the man's drive schedule. It confirmed everything. Donley was at all thirty-four crime scenes on the kill dates. He ran. Almost got away. Tate tracked him to Kansas City. Pulled him off victim number thirty-five. Donley confessed to all the killings and more. Got the death penalty.

"I'm not saying the FBI would have never stopped the Range Strangler. I've been in this business long enough to know sometimes the solutions come from unexpected places."

"The Burcher case has generated a similar mountain of evidence," Chief Deron said. "Paul thinks new eyes will increase chances of finding the smoking gun. And now we have an eyewitness we can talk to—Jack saw everything in 1970. Dr.

Mesmer says that information can be accessed. I don't know about that. Like Jack, I have my doubts. Yes, the FBI could be barking up another wrong tree. I guess you gotta do both or none of it, Jack."

"We do need a new set of eyes," Paul said. "Tate Worthington can help us."

Jack observed the renowned international PI as Shuck and Deron spoke. "You've been awful quiet, Dr. Worthington. Do you have anything to add?"

Worthington turned to Jack for the first time. "What do you need from me?"

"What do I need from you?" Jack sighed. "I need to know if you're right for this."

Worthington's mustache moved but hid his smile. "Maybe I'm not right for you."

"Maybe you're not right for us?" Jack breathed. He turned to Paul Shuck. "I think you should have coordinated your proposition with Dr. Worthington first. He has doubts."

Paul smiled and sat down. "That's not what he said, Jack."

"Excuse me? We all heard—"

"—my words, Dr. Burcher. You side-stepped my meaning. Something you do depending upon *which one of you* is setting the agenda at any given time."

"I don't understand. What are you saying?" Jack shot back.

"You're a physician first, Dr. Burcher. A forensic pathologist second. A *chief* medical examiner third. The son of a mother abducted and killed, fourth. The son of a dead father, fifth. You held his brain in your hands."

"I don't know what—"

"Sixth, you're the ten-year-old eyewitness to a kidnapping and delivery of a heart, and now brain to your house. You saw your monster! Seventh, you're the eldest sibling, therefore the most responsible for the family tragedies. And eighth, you are the self-appointed leader of this unending investigation to find some *invisible monster* to end a nightmare you are ill-equipped to live without. Have I left 'any of you' out, Dr. Jackson Ronan Burcher, Junior?"

"Nice. You're playing a game," Jack scoffed.

"I don't play games. I did not come here to do battle with your eight personalities, or to be ordained 'by you' to do what I do quite well." He spun a silver-dollar cufflink and leaned into Jack. "I solve hideous cases and catch monsters, Dr. Burcher. Based on what I know about this mess in Tampa, and what I've witnessed in this room, you don't want or need me here."

"You don't know what I want or need, Dr. Worthington," Jack bellowed.

"You demean those most committed to solving your case when you should be embracing them. You criticize and reject what you do not understand. You are defensive, closed-minded, and arrogant. Those traits get in my way more than the demons I hunt—

"No sir," Tate said. "You've adapted to your life of misery. You derive a twisted security from staying lost and at risk. If you were honest, you would admit you do not want to solve the family mystery because you do not know how you would live without it."

The room reeled. Whispers fluttered. "Why do you think that is?" Burcher breathed.

"You know why," Worthington said as he brushed his sleeves.

"I want you to tell me."

The PI looked around the room. Paul nodded. Janice nodded. Mesmer nodded. Tate leaned even closer to Jack, faces inches apart. "A ten-year-old boy runs your life."

Jack's pupils dilated as he paled.

"The FBI proposition has two parts for a reason," Tate said. "You must deal with the ten-year-old boy so I can do what I do. If you cannot, Dr. Burcher, I must accept I'm not right for you, and I will catch the next flight back to Dallas.

148 DAYS LATER
March 7, 2005

TWENTY-TWO

Ballast Point Tavern – March 7, 2005 – 21:00

The rain swept across Hillsborough County for a third day. It had already set a fifty-year record for the month of March.

Jack watched through the fogged windows at the Ballast Point Tavern as sheets of water slid by and stirred the lush foliage along Interbay Boulevard. Across from Big Ray's the storm had already bent the stop sign forty-five degrees and dropped a giant palm.

As he butted-out a cigarette, his eyes climbed the foggy glass to the old-tavern wooden sign outside—it swung wildly. Like scraping fingers on a chalkboard, the rusted chains whined. He pulled out another cigarette and stuck it in his mouth. *That things gonna—*

"—don't worry, Doc." Barry appeared with a lit match. Jack nodded as he puffed. Barry slid a new beer on the table and picked up the two empty mugs. "I been told that old sign's handled fiddy years of Tampa weather. And that-there includes the hurry-canes."

"Right. But it wasn't up there for the Tampa Bay hurricane of 1921," Jack said as he checked his watch with smoke spilling from his nose. "Then again that was an October—a lot more fronts with big temp swings." He gripped the new mug and looked up at Barry Bright, who blocked the room. "I do not think we've seen anything like it since."

"Nice factoid, Doctor Jack. Guess that's why yous a doc. Gotta know lotsa stuff nobody cares 'bout." Jack smiled in his beer.

Barry Bright (Bear) emptied the pile of butts into an empty mug and tidied the table. The obese New Yorker looked more like a heavyweight wrestler than a jolly, fat person. Jack had always assumed Bear had a football background, offensive guard or tackle. He was the protector type. Bear purchased the Ballast Point Tavern in '95. Sold his bar in Manhattan when the taxes went up three times in two years. He figured New York politicians would bankrupt him in five more, so he got top dollar for the place from a builder interested in location. Enough money to buy the struggling Ballast Point Tavern and a five-bedroom house on the north end of the peninsula. Ten years ago, Bear moved his family of eight and never looked back.

"Hey Doc, ya gonna eat tonight?" He dropped a newspaper and menu on the table.

"I don't know, Bear. It's almost nine." Jack's eyes moved from his watch back to the window and swinging sign. My brother and a friend were supposed to be here at eight."

"Comin' from the city?"

"I believe so."

"Heard on the radio in back, Selmon Expressway's flooded. Bayshore Gardens—"

Bayshore Gardens, Jack thought, *it's been a while since I thought about Bayshore Gardens. I do not know if I did the right thing, but I do not like a plan where I'm the problem.*

"—they're routin' traffic onto Granada then Concordia somehow past Pinky's and then down Ferdinand back onto Selmon. Gonna slow up a lotta people."

"Flooding?" Jack said. *I guess passing on it didn't matter anyway. Everything's been quiet. No one's gotten hurt for six months. Nothing mysterious going on. Without the FBI and Tampa PD stirring up things for a while, my life's been rather calm for a change. And Kayda—*

"I'm not sayin' you gotta eat right now, Doc. We'll be cookin' burgers and fries all night. But if ya want a ribeye or somthin' nice, we gotta get an order in before Jimmy closes things down. I'm thinking we're good for thirty minutes. After that, menu's out the window."

"Got it, Bear."

Am I the problem? Jack wondered. *All those things Worthington said, are they true? Am I eight people controlled by a ten-year-old boy? Maybe he influences me, but I don't think he controls me. Everyone has bad childhood experiences that affect them; like fear of spiders or feeling inadequate around girls or never measurin' up. Don't know. Maybe should have done it.*

"Okay, Doc. Enjoy the beers. And I brought ya part of today's paper to keep ya company. Some little guy left it behind. Only one section. Who does that? Anyway, it's right down your alley. Obits. Somebody important to somebody keeled over."

"Thanks." Jack chuckled as he reached for the crumpled Sentinel. He flipped it over. Bear disappeared and the noisy bar retook the room. *It doesn't matter if they come or not. I'm not leaving this bar until after eleven.*

His eyes found the heading—Obituary. *Thanks Bear. It is*

odd someone would leave just this section behind. His eyes jumped to the largest picture. *What the hell! Looks like Otto. What's my grandfather doing in today's newspaper? He died in '55, cancer.* Jack read the bold print under the picture. *Hans Albrecht Bethe, the Father of the Atomic Bomb, Dead at 98.*

Headlights washed over the wet window. David and Paul pulled up. Jack returned to his paper. *Where did I see this picture before? The night I was attacked—that's right. I got my wonderful facial scar. One of the Manhattan Project guys died— Edward Teller. They had pictures of the Manhattan Project team. I saw this picture and thought it was Otto—*

"That was a bitch," David groused as he hung his dripping coat on a peg.

"Hello, Jack." Paul shook his wet coat. "Been 148 days since—"

"—our last disagreement. Hello Paul. Good to see you." Jack had positioned himself in the center of his bench. The two would have to sit across. "I heard they rerouted Selmon."

David slid to the window and blew into his cupped hands. "Lost an hour. Damn Tampa PD screws up everything they touch." He waved to Bear. "Shit. He's not lookin'."

Paul eyed the newspaper as he sat down next to David. "Long time no see."

"How's FBI Director Shuck?" Jack caught Bear's eye. The big man smiled and rounded the bar with a couple of mugs in one hand and fistful of menus and silverware the other.

"You boys eatin' tonight?"

"Not me. Just a beer or two," David said.

"I'm good, too. A couple of beers and I've gotta run. What's with the newspaper? You checking on your clients," Paul teased as Bear dropped his load onto the table.

"I think we're all just drinking tonight. Maybe a bowl of pretzels."

"Got it, Doc. I'll watch the mugs."

"Obituaries. Someone left behind this section of the Sentinel. Barry felt sorry for me. He thought I needed entertainment other than weather. He didn't know I never look at the obits. I like to keep my distance—stay clinical."

"I'll bet Novak looks at 'em every single day," David said in his mug. "He's always investigating. The man creeps me out—has a little British *Alfred Hitchcock* thing goin' on."

"You watch too much TV." Jack lit another cigarette.

"Before we get too deep into things—God knows what Paul wants—have you talked to Patricia?" David asked.

"Nope. And I don't intend to. Why do you think I'm sitting in a Tavern on a miserable, wet Monday night instead of my den with a good bottle of scotch?"

"You avoiding her?" David asked.

"Not avoiding. Staying out of her way. She's got the house all to herself. Patricia's on her last lap picking and packing the rest of her things, whatever she wants."

"Don't tell me she's gonna get the signed first editions," David groused. "Not the Dickens books. You should have warned me. I would have gotten them out of there."

"She's a good person. We grew apart, that's all. It happens. The family nightmare did not help. She's had enough torment in her life. Patricia can have anything she wants, David."

"Your wife is in town?" Paul asked after pocketing his phone.

"Ex-wife, Paul. Yes."

"She's at your house now?"

"Yes. Patricia is at the house. She got here this morning and is staying one night. My plan is to stay out of her way. I stay here until eleven, go home when she's in bed, and then leave in the morning before she gets up to catch her ten o'clock flight."

"You think it's a good idea for her to be in that house alone?"

"Stop, Paul. She's fine. It's been a long time since—"

"—someone's been killed there," David said.

"Yes. It's been 544 days, but who's counting." Paul lit his first cigarette.

"Patricia will be fine," Jack declared. *What are you working up to?*

"There's that picture," David grabbed the Sentinel. "The guy that looks like Grandpa Otto. What's he doin' in the paper again?"

"Hans Bethe. A member of the Manhattan Project team. He died, David. The first time you saw that picture was when Edward Teller died, another member of the Manhattan Project team. Mr. Bethe died yesterday, March 6th. He was 98."

"I remember that night. You had a visitor. He gave you that scar." Paul loosened his tie and unbuttoned his collar. "I guess we haven't talked since Bayshore."

"Right."

"As a result of your decision to reject my proposition."

"I did not reject your proposition. I wanted a modified version."

"Jack. You demanded we do exactly what we said we would no longer do. You got in the way of the investigation again. I'm surprised you still don't see the problem."

"You mean me. I'm the problem, Paul. You're right. I don't."

"No one said you were the problem. Very smart people explained why we need to take you back to those two nights in 1970. We explained why a person like Tate Worthington needed to be involved. The investigation was going in circles. It is time for a change."

"I disagree. We were making progress."

"I did not ask to meet here tonight to go back over

Bayshore," Paul said. "There are things you, David, and Melissa need to know. Where is Melissa? She was supposed to be here."

Jack butted out another cigarette. "She's with her birds. The weather's a problem."

"Go ahead, Paul," David said. "We'll bring her up on whatever."

Paul took a deep breath as he put his palms on the table and spread his fingers. He stared at the backs of his hands, and then looked up at Jack. "We had twelve separate investigation tracks in progress the night of the Bayshore Gardens meeting. Eleven were internal. One was external—meaning contracted outside the FBI. Your decision to reject the Bayshore proposition triggered the termination of all twelve investigations that night."

"What do you want me to say?" Jack snapped. "I got in the way again?"

"Against orders, I allowed one track to continue. I was debriefed Friday."

"Is this where I'm supposed to say thank you?" Jack scoffed.

Paul took a swallow of beer and wiped his lips with serious eyes on Jack. "The outside investigation was to be a deep dive into your family tree, Jack. Deeper than ever before."

Bear slid beers onto the table and grabbed the empty mugs. Paul waited for him to leave. "We engaged the top genealogy experts in the country to go back as far as they could on both sides of your family—Rose's and Ronan's."

"Why do that?" David asked. "There's nothing to—"

"I had asked them to, David." Jack turned back to Paul. "What did you find that has you carefully measuring your words tonight?"

"Actually, your question should be what did Tate Worthington find?"

"Oh. He's also a genealogy expert?" Jack sighed.

"No. He holds exclusive contracts with two of the top genealogy experts in the country."

David laughed. "Why the hell would—"

"Shut up, David," Jack barked. "Worthington's a smart guy. Lines of descent sometimes answer elusive questions. Life is full of untold stories. Go ahead Paul, what did he find? What's got you hyperventilating?"

Paul pulled the newspaper over and looked at the picture of Hans Bethe. "What do you know about your grandfather— Otto Burcher—his life before Ballast Point?"

"How far back?"

"His birth."

"I know Otto was born in Germany sometime in 1906," Jack said. "I don't know the birth date because Wilhelm and Edwina Burcher did not keep records, other than notes in the family bible. Like a lot of people those days, they moved around. Wilhelm took on odd jobs. They lived all over Germany. While on the road, Edwina gave birth to Otto."

"Where? What hospital?" David asked.

"No hospital records. Born wherever they were living," Jack said.

David leaned in, "I didn't know that."

"You don't know a lot of things because you never pay attention." Jack turned back to Paul. "I can't verify any of it. I've tried, but the family archives are weak. Especially that far back. Notations in the Burcher family Bible start with their marriage—Wilhelm and Edwina, the spring of 1902, Saint Peter's Church, Strasbourg, Germany."

"What exactly do they say about Otto?" Paul asked.

"I found a few lines that recount Edwina giving birth to Otto on the road in the fall of 1906. And I found references to an adoption, too. It said an unwed migrant worker died giving birth to a baby boy. The note said Wilhelm and Edwina adopted the orphaned child and named him Otto, but I could not find adoption papers. I had two stories. Which one is true is anyone's guess. Not sure it matters a hundred years later."

Paul pointed at the picture. "Hans Bethe was born in Strasbourg, Germany in 1906. By your own account, that's where Wilhelm and Edwina married and lived from 1902."

Jack and David stared at the man that looked like Otto. Hans had a full head of hair and no mustache. Otto was bald with a mustache. "Are you saying the Burchers knew the Bethes?"

"No, David. We don't think they ever met," Paul said. "That's still being researched in Bethesda."

"Just get to it, Paul," Jack pushed. "Drop your bomb."

"On July 2nd, 1906, Albrecht Bethe took his wife Anna to *Hospital civil de Strasbourg*. Later that day Anna gave birth to twin boys—Hans and Karl. Sometime in the early morning hours, the hospital staff discovered a newborn missing from the nursery. Karl Bethe had been taken—kidnapped. The whole town of Strasbourg got turned upside down. Albrecht Bethe, a respected professor of physiology at the University, had enormous community support.

"In those days, it was not unusual for children to go missing. Many were found working in factories or on farms or dead. Others were never heard from again. Times were hard. Families were desperate, known to leave their female babies in the woods to die. Others kidnapped males to work their farms. A year after Karl disappeared, the search was abandoned. The Bethes left Strasbourg with one son, Hans. They settled in Kiel, Germany."

"Are you saying—?"

"In July 1906, Wilhelm and Edwina Burcher left Strasbourg in the middle of the night around the time of the kidnapping. At that time, your great grandparents had no children. When they resettled in Hamburg a year later, they had a child. A boy. One year old, Jack. The official records in the city of Hamburg's archives show Otto Theodore Burcher as home birthed—mother, Edwina Burcher."

"Okay," David said. "So, the adoption story in the Burcher Bible is wrong. I think we gotta go with the birth story and the official records in Hamburg. In those days, I'm pretty sure people birthed babies at home more than hospitals."

"They kidnapped Karl Bethe," Jack said under his breath.

"Did you hear anything I just said." David slammed his mug on the table.

"Edwina Burcher was barren, David," Jack said.

"That's true," Paul said.

"How do you know? And what the hell is barren?"

"I found a box of medical records in the cellar, the mountain of family archives you and Mel refuse to acknowledge or explore. Edwina Burcher had a medical condition—endometriosis. Today, hysterectomy is not the treatment of choice. However, her condition was described as advanced and life-threatening in the early 1900s."

"What the hell is endo—?"

"—endometriosis is a condition where the lining of the uterus is on the outside instead of the inside. That condition is dangerous. It causes pain and uncontrolled bleeding. In Edwina's case, she was in danger of bleeding to death."

Paul nodded. "We located the operating records; Edwina's hysterectomy was performed at the *Hospital civil de Strasbourg* in 1903."

"When they settled in Hamburg a year later with a child, they had to come up with a story," Paul said. "Adoption of dead migrant's child. They needed paperwork. They couldn't produce the certified documents—who, when, where—for

Hamburg officials. So, home birth would be the best story to go with. Edwina's personal medical records were not public nor were they required. I suspect the adoption entry in the bible was forgotten."

The three stared at the picture of Hans Bethe in cold silence. Two processed the myriad of implications. One sat in denial. Could this be the breakthrough information they had been waiting for, or was it another detour on the unending highway to hell?

"Okay. Otto Burcher is that dead man's twin brother—so what?" David muttered.

"This connects the Burcher family to the Manhattan Project," Paul said. "If the world knows, as we talked about it is possible someone is punishing your family for the atom bomb."

"Edward Teller died the day before Ronan was taken," Jack said as he ran a finger down the small print beneath Hans Bethe's picture. "Here it is. He died September 9, 2003."

"That's peculiar," Paul muttered.

He looked up. "My God!" Jack slid out the booth. "Get the police to my place now."

"What is it, Jack?" Paul asked as he pulled out his cell.

Jack spun around and leaned onto the table punching in Patricia's number. "I could not explain the time lapse between the deaths of my mother and father. Now I can! It says here that Lieutenant Colonel Leslie Groves, another member of the Manhattan Project team, died on July 13, 1970. That is one day before my mother was taken!"

"Jesus! Hans Bethe died yesterday! Go Jack. I'll catch up." Paul punched numbers into his phone. Seconds later Jack fishtailed out of the Tavern parking lot.

"Are you gonna tell me what the hell's goin' on?" David demanded. Barry approached from behind. This time with no beers."

Paul turned his back to both, his phone pressed to his ear. "Yes. This is Shuck, FBI. I want an APB, armed police at the Burcher estate now—lights and sirens. You have the address. There's a serial killer on the premises stalking Patricia Burcher. Proceed with extreme caution. Also contact Homicide Detective Moe Bullitt and Chief Frank Deron—they will want to know. Tell them we need a roadblock set up around Ballast Point—ground and water. They'll know what to do—"

Paul pocketed his cell and turned to the wide eyes of David and Barry. "David, someone has been killing a member of your family each time a member of the Manhattan Project dies of natural causes. I think we now have a pattern—your mother and your father. I'm certain there will be more deaths in your family that fit this. Otto Burcher is your family's blood connection to Hans Bethe, one of the chief creators of the atomic bomb. Your family may have been targeted a long time ago."

"But why did Jack run out of here?" David asked. "Where—"

"—is he going? I'll tell you. Listen to me very closely, David. Hans Bethe died yesterday. He was on the Manhattan Project team. Patricia, your brother's ex-wife, is alone at the family estate. She is the most exposed and an obvious target. We think a Burcher family member is killed one day after an elite member of the Manhattan Project team dies of natural causes. Do you follow what I am telling you? Do you get it?"

Paul passed a Ulysses S. Grant to Barry and did not wait for a response. Paul grabbed David's lapels and pulled him close. "Listen to me. Find your sister. Now! She is in great danger. Someone could be coming to kill her. Tell the police where Melissa is right now. We need her and you protected. All of you are targets. Your family killer will get one of you tonight."

"But I don't know where—"

"Just find her," he yelled. Paul released David and pulled car keys from his pocket. "I'm taking your vehicle. Stop hyperventilating and start helping or people die—"

On his last word, Paul ran out of the tavern. Locked in terror David trembled at the edge of the booth watching the rain hit the window. Bear heard enough. He appeared and wrapped his big arm around David's neck. He pulled him close, like a small child, and calmly spoke inches from his face. "We got this, David. No problem. Now. Tell me where you think your sister is tonight. Let's give her a call on her cell phone. Pull out your phone, David."

TWENTY-THREE

Burcher Estate – March 7, 2005 – 22:00

Patricia did not answer her cell.

Wipers could not beat back the pounding rain or swirling leaves. Jack skidded to a stop on the gravel driveway and sprayed wet stones onto the front porch. His headlights burned through the windows of the dark house—death waited inside.

He left his car door open and engine running—he could not lose a second. Drenched and unarmed he hesitated at the front door. It moved. Maybe the wind. With a finger he eased it open. A familiar smell dripped from inside. He knew what he would find. He smelled the smell many times—the smell inside his autopsy room. The sweet smell of carved human flesh and blood could not be mistaken. *Please don't let me be too late.*

He swallowed hard and stepped from the steaming car lights into the cold dark house and surrealistic world of unbridled terror. Surrounded by dark halls he thought—*please*

God, please help me find her. Let her be alive. She's not a part of this hell.

He felt the wall until he found the light switch. He toggled it—nothing. *You cut the lines. Organized this time.* Jack moved through the dining room into the next hall. There he stopped a second time, his back pressed against the wall. The monster loomed in his head. *Are you here now? Are you waiting for me? Or is it about one-for-one, Patricia for Hans Bethe?*

The smell of blood seeped through the cracked kitchen door. He moved down the hall and avoided each warped floorboard. Jack had memorized the whiners and the moaners a long time ago. He felt his way through the dark like the ten-year-old boy sneaking out of the house thirty-four years ago. This time the repulsive odor of death hung in the house. This time would not be another carefree adventure. This time the nearby realities consumed him. This time the horrid stench destroyed all his childish memories.

With his hand on the swinging kitchen door and head on his hand, Jack reached deeper for the courage. He prayed for anything but what he knew he would find. *Please let Patricia be alive. Help me this night. I'd understand if you did not help me, but I pray you help Patricia. Please forgive me for my stubbornness. Give me one more chance to make things right. Let Patricia have a life away from this hell.*

He pushed open the door and peered around the side of the refrigerator. He studied the shadows inside the shadows—nothing moved. Would he find Patricia dead or alive? Did the monster leave, or did the monster wait for him? Would tonight be Jack Burcher's turn to die? *I've been as bad as you,* he mused. *I allowed you to exist longer than you should. I allowed all of this to happen.*

There was a time I wanted to solve this nightmare—you took my mother from me. She left me alone in a cold, empty world. I failed her that night. I did nothing to stop it. He pushed the door open further. *Then I decided I would fix everything. I prepared. I studied. I chose the life of a forensic doctor. But when I got out of medical school, I knew I could not stop any of it. I understood then my family nightmare would be a part of me. I needed it more than I wanted it gone. They were right. Janice, Mesmer, Paul, and Worthington. They were all right.*

Sirens screamed in the distance. Squad cards invaded Ballast Point. In minutes, they would surround the Burcher estate and storm the house. They would hunt a monster and find a body. Jack blinked away the tears. He struggled to see. *The unknown... the pain... the terror... it's all I knew. It's how I lived. It's how I navigated my dark world. I needed the hunt like I need blood in my veins. But now the twisted world I perpetuated has taken the life of a girl I once loved—NO—a girl I do love. She does not deserve any of this.*

The rain stopped. A single beam of moonlight from a sliver moon broke through an opening in the clouds. It passed through the kitchen window and stopped on her eyes. She blinked. *Patricia? You're—*

Jack rushed into the kitchen; his eyes locked on hers. Then the rest of the carnage came into view. She laid on her back on the island—a cold slab of granite. Naked. Ankles and wrists tied. Jack saw the incision. It ran from the bottom of her throat to the top of her groin. Jack gently rested his hand on her forehead—she could not survive. "Patricia," he whispered. "Patricia, I'm so sorry for everything. Our life together. Patricia, I love you."

Her eyes took him inside her. "I know. It is okay, Jack. I waited for you—"

"I'm so, so sorry."

"Leave him with me, honey. Leave the little boy that lives

inside you. Leave him with me. Let me take him away. You need your life back, Jack. It's time."

She had lost too much blood, and something else. An organ. But which one and why? "I don't understand."

Then Jack heard the breathing. He felt the hot breath on the back of his neck. Before he could move, the arm wrapped tight around his chest and the bloody knife pressed against his throat. Jack did not struggle. He wanted to die. He could not live with it anymore. But before he died, he had to see the face of the killer—the beast that ravaged his family. The demon who just butchered his wife. Jack broke free. He battled anew. Then everything went dark and empty.

TWENTY-FOUR

TGH Urgent Care – March 9, 2005 – 07:30

"How long is Dr. Burcher going to be out?" Paul asked, only his head in the door.

"Are you FBI?" asked the surgeon.

"Yes." He flashed a badge. "Southern Regional Director, Paul Shuck."

"He could come out of the sedation anytime, now. We lost him twice last night—once in the ambulance and again the ER. When he gets out of here, he's got a couple of steaks to buy some incredible paramedics. Those guys don't even slow down to tuck in their capes."

Paul smiled and stepped into the room. "What do you mean, lost him?"

"Cardiac arrest. Heart stopped. Dead." The surgeon lifted the neck bandage and adjusted a drain tube. He checked the blood bag. "Dr. Burcher took ten pints. Lost most of his. Five before they got him on the ambulance. The neck wound was bad. Nicked both carotids. The guy knew how to create medical havoc. I thank God we had some O-neg on board."

He eased closer but stayed out of Jack's direct view. "I found him in a pool of blood. I didn't know whose. His wife was in bad shape. Dead. I thought Jack was dead, too."

"I heard Chief Deron sent an ambulance, when he sent the squad cars," the doctor muttered. "That's not standard operating procedure for those guys. Deron told them to throw in a dozen bags of O-neg. Francis Deron gave Jack Burcher his life back."

"Now they're even," Paul breathed. *Never would have occurred—*

"You say even?" the surgeon asked.

Paul's phone vibrated. "Sorry. I need to take this." He eased out the room.

Another thirty minutes passed before Jack opened one eye halfway. The surgeon rounded the bed and rechecked vitals. He leaned into his patient's face and lifted the other lid. "I've been poking you all morning. You got my premium-service package, Dr. Burcher. Welcome back."

"Back? Where have I been?" Jack mumbled, unable to control his eyes.

"Outer space. I'm Dr. Roland Pouncer. I saved your life."

Jack smiled on one side of his mouth. His eyes crossed. "Nice name. Roll and pounce on her." Jack's weak chuckle evolved into a dismal cough.

"Nice one. God knows I've never heard that before," Pouncer rolled his eyes and patted Jack's arm without tubes. He rechecked the neck bandage and drains. "Try not to make too many bad jokes. It's not good for that nasty little cut on your neck."

Jack tried to move his arms. He was strapped in tight. "You sound familiar. Do I—"

"—you do. Yes. We met at one of your autopsies last year. I'm sure you don't remember. I lost a patient. You helped me sort out a complicated disease process. She was terminal. Gave her body to science to help others beat her rare condition."

"Evelyn Tessler—a lovely lady. I am sorry I did not recognize your voice. I can't see too good at the moment. Everything's a blur—modern art real time."

Pouncer put drops in each eye. "I must say I am surprised you remembered Miss Tessler. You have enough morphine in you to relive Woodstock. Morphine affects people in different ways."

"I know. I'm a doctor," Jack poked.

"The important thing is to remember I saved your life," Pouncer countered.

"Thank God someone did. I hate to sound like I'm not paying attention, but I have no idea why I'm in this bed, or why my head and neck are sore."

"I'm not sure if that is from the head wound, the morphine, or both," Pouncer said. "You were attacked, Dr. Burcher. You sustained some nasty injuries. It's clear someone hit you on the head, and then tried to cut you in a way to regulate your bleed rate. You took a lot of—"

"How much?"

"148 stitches. 10 pints."

"That would explain my visit to the pearly gates."

"Two visits. We lost you twice, my friend. You had us hoppin' last night. Nobody wants to tick off a Chief Medical Examiner." Pouncer tore off two feet of EKG tape and studied it.

Paul stuck his head in the door. "Can I see you a sec, Dr. Pouncer."

They met in the hall. "I see he's awake. I need to talk to him."

"He's stable. Struggling with the drugs. We loaded him up with morphine. He's in and out of la-la land if you know what I mean. We can't bring him down for at least twenty-four hours. The pain would be too much. He just asked me what happened to him."

"Can he handle bad news?" Paul asked.

"He's physically capable. I don't know about his mental condition. He is a doctor, so I doubt he will overreact—pull out his tubes and go storming off. I suspect, if he did pull them out, he'd do it aseptically." Pouncer said.

"I won't take too much time. I need him alone."

"Sure. That's fine. Press the nurse button if you need us."

Paul took a deep breath. "There are things he saw. I gotta know—"

Pouncer put his hand on Paul's shoulder. "You FBI guys think you should be able to handle everything. You can't. You see the worst of mankind. I know Jack Burcher is a close friend of yours. All of us are concerned for him and his family, the terrible history and ongoing threat. Jack needs to see Paul, his friend, more than Paul the FBI man. Keep that in mind."

"There's a serial killer out there. Last night he killed Patricia Burcher, Jack's ex-wife. I found Jack next to her, unconscious and bleeding profusely." Pouncer squeezed Paul's shoulder. "Patricia was tortured to death. I don't know if Jack remembers any of it."

"I talked to Dr. Quin last night," Pouncer said. "She wanted to check on Jack. She told me it was the most heinous mutilation she had ever seen as a medical examiner. We are all here to help. Do what you must to catch this monster."

"Thank you. We will."

"Jack will be moved from ICU into a private room later today. I assume you have made some arrangements for his protection."

"We have."

"Good." Pouncer turned to leave.

"Dr. Pouncer."

"Yes."

"Thank you." Paul grabbed the handle and took a deep breath.

* * *

The morning sun cut through the venetian blinds and turned the room into a prison with fat shadow bars on the walls and bed. Paul sat in a chair next to Jack's head and waited. Jack had drifted off while Paul and Pouncer met in the hall.

"Is Patricia—"

"She didn't make it, Jack. I'm sorry."

He pinched his eyes closed. A tear rolled to his sideburn. "I know, but hoped maybe I had one of my nightmares," he breathed. "I got there too late. I should have—"

"No, Jack. When we figured some of it out, you took off and risked your life for Patricia. Maybe I should go. I'll come back later. You need time. I'm sorry." Paul got to his feet.

"Stay, Paul. I'm as good as I'll ever be about it. Do me a favor. I want you to untie the arm without tubes."

"I don't think I—"

"I'm a doctor, Paul. I'm not gonna do anything stupid."

When his binding dropped to the side of the bed, Jack rubbed his eyes. "I saw him."

"You saw him?"

"It was dark. We fought maybe twenty seconds. Well, I struggled, he fought. I figured I was gonna die, anyway. Before I did, I wanted to see the face of the man that killed my family." Jack closed his eyes. "I'll never forget him, Paul. His eyes, they were empty."

"Eyes empty," Paul muttered.

"He is Asian."

"We can put a check mark in that box. What else?"

"He fits one of our profiles."

"Good. We can toss the others."

"We can't throw out anything. No way this guy killed Leonard in Pasadena. He was maybe fifteen years older than me. I'm guessing a strong fifty-five-year-old man. He would have been around three in 1948. He could have killed Rose, Carolyn, Harold, and Ronan. We need to figure out how he's connected to Leonard's killer. Is it family? Is he a member of this radical group, the IJRG? Or is he something else?"

"Right," Paul looked down at a message on his phone. He smiled but did not share. "What else can you tell me about the man?"

"Five-feet-six. I know for a fact. We squared-off once. I could see the second knob on the kitchen cabinets above his head. We used those knobs to measure us kids growing up." Jack forced a swallow. "Jesus... Okay, I'd say he's around 150 pounds. He's a strong man. A sinewy mesomorph."

"You mean muscular."

"Right, but not visibly. He looked lean but was very strong. I was no match." Jack touched his neck bandage. "This thing is starting to burn."

"He tried to cut your head off, Jack."

"No. He did not, Paul."

"You haven't seen the wound. He sliced two-thirds of your neck."

"He was doing surgery, Paul. After he knocked me out, he was looking for my external carotids—slower bleeders than the jugular. If he wanted, he could have cut my head off in less than a minute. He knew exactly what he was doing and was good with a knife."

"I don't understand how you can say—"

"He performed an *autopsy* on Patricia, Paul. He opened her like we open a corpse. Sagittal to the midline and an upper-chest vee. He even clipped the ribs. He's done this before."

"Professionally?"

"Maybe. Probably."

"A doctor?"

"I doubt it, but maybe a *deaner*. I have three. They assist during autopsies. They do most of the cutting for me. Pass organs. If I did all the cutting, I could only handle a few cases a day. We handle a half-dozen by noon on a slow day.

"An experienced deaner can develop surgical skills well beyond most surgeons. It's volume and repetition. Some deaners have thousands of autopsies under their belts. Each case is a careful dissection of human anatomy."

"So, we're looking for someone with surgical skills," Paul said.

"Yes. Knowledge of human anatomy. Someone good with their hands. Could be medical. Could be a mortician. Also, we should consider woodworkers, sculptors, artists, typists, pianists, and the like. Since he did not cut my jugular, I know he wants me to live for another day. That is confusing because I got a good look at him, and he knows it."

The door opened. Bullitt appeared. Then Deron wheeled in and bumped the bed. "Mornin', Jack." An odd hint of delight dripped from Deron's words. Something detectable only by someone that had scrutinized the man over a lifetime.

What do people see in you? Jack wondered each time he saw Deron. *You're a below-average homicide detective. You failed to interview your only eyewitness to an abduction, and you get promoted to Chief of Police! Good lord. Not only did you screw me up, you eliminated all possibilities of catching a killer 35 years ago. Sometimes I feel like you're orchestrating my mental breakdown. You live a charmed life. Even now, you look better than you ever have. After eighteen months in a wheelchair you look more like a marathon runner than an emaciated victim battling paralysis—*

"Moe. Francis." Jack muttered.

"I'm sorry about Patricia," Bullitt said.

"A lovely lady," Deron said. "Please accept our condolences."

"Thanks, but I take responsibility for her death," Jack said.

"That's the morphine talking," Paul said. "Dr. Pouncer said Jack would have moments."

"The way I heard it, you risked your life to save her," Deron said.

Jack held up his free hand. "Janice got it right. I allowed a ten-year-old boy to run my life. Those nights in 1970 changed me. I hated my mother for leaving me alone."

"That's ridiculous," Deron said.

"I hated her, and I blamed me for not helping her," Jack said. "My punishment is a life dedicated to hunting the monster I failed to confront in 1970."

"That's not a punishment," Paul said. "Dr. Janice said guilt is a normal emotion for a kid that loses a parent. It is normal for you to want to find the missing parent and those responsible for hurting them."

"You don't understand," Jack sighed.

"I do," Deron said. "It's about the *hunt*. It's all you have left."

"The hunt fills the hole in my life. Worthington and Janice understood that. Both knew I would fight them. They tried to break me but couldn't. I walked out. That's why I'm the one responsible for Patricia's death. The boy inside me has an agenda. The boy inside me will not allow the FBI or anyone else to take over the hunt because it could end. I would have nothing left to live for."

"When did all this surface?" Paul asked.

Jack turned to the blinds and squinted at the gaps filled with sunlight. "I always felt it, like a locked box floating. Always out of my reach. I got close two times. The first, when I held my father's brain. The second, when I held my mother's heart. And then—"

"It's okay, Jack," Paul whispered. Deron squirmed in his wheelchair.

"I looked into Patricia's eyes. I held that box. She floated between two worlds and spoke to me. She told me to leave *the boy* with her. She said it was time for this to be over. She told me to trust her. I would have a life after the hunt ended."

"The epiphany you needed, Jack," Paul said. "We all live with confusions. We all get lost. I believe it's part of life. When we finally do understand something, I don't believe it's right to blame ourselves. You need to clear the last hurdle, Jack. Then you can move forward."

"He's right, Dr. Burcher," Bullitt said. "You're the smartest man I know, but you're still a man. We've all got to deal with things we don't understand. You are not responsible for what you don't know."

"Thanks, Moe and Paul. I don't know if I can clear the last hurdle."

"You can and will sooner or later," Paul said.

"If it's not too late, I want to accept the Bayshore Gardens proposition without modification. And I want Tate Worthington on the case. I will let Dr. Mesmer hypnotize me as soon as I'm physically able."

"Are you sure that's a good idea?" Deron broke his silence.

"You having second thoughts, Frank?" Paul asked. "You were all for this before."

"Not at all. Just thinking about Jack, his revelations and taking responsibility for Patricia's death. It had to be hard seeing her butchered like—"

Paul opened the blinds. Sunlight poured into the room. "I think Jack will be fine, Frank. And I have some good news. Tate Worthington has been working on the case for six months."

"You went forward without my—?"

"—blessing. Yup. I told him you were close to seeing the light."

"You know me better than I know me. And he was good with that?"

"Actually, he said the Bayshore Gardens meeting cemented the deal for him. He had spoken with Dr. Janice earlier. Turns out Tate has a history similar to yours, Jack. He lost his father as a child. A grisly homicide. It changed his life, too. It was the reason he became an international PI and climbed to world-acclaimed status. He told me he got his demons under control. After the Bayshore Gardens meeting he knew you were very close to facing yours."

"I should have done my research on him," Jack muttered.

"I have some news," Moe said as he slid his phone into his pocket.

"Just a moment, Moe," Paul said. "Your shared life-experience is not the only reason Tate is on board. He said the Burcher family case may be his greatest challenge. He has just connected the dots to Hiroshima. He's over there now."

"No question our dots connect to the Manhattan Project," Jack said.

"Tate has not briefed me yet—the orient trip and all. He wants a meeting with us after your hypnotic tour of the infamous nights in 1970. He and Dr. Janice are quite certain after Dr. Mesmer's done with you; your demons will be on the run."

Out of the corner of his eye, Jack watched Deron fiddle with the leather on the arms of his wheelchair. He picked at it as he looked out the window. *What's going on with you?*

"Tate has uncovered more information from the past. Like the Range Strangler case, he's looking for the beginning of the trail. Remember, when you have a lot of cold trails you must get on the first one."

"Right. We need to know where it starts," Jack said with a wince.

"You need the doctor," Paul said.

"I need morphine, but before Pouncer I want to hear Detective Bullitt's news."

Moe rounded Deron's wheelchair. "We got to your place fast last night, Doc. And we set up roadblocks fast. Containment works sometimes. I just learned we took an Asian man into custody. Found him hiding in your boathouse this morning."

"Are you sure about that?" Deron asked. He turned his chair to Moe. "Is he talking?"

"Yes. Of course, I'm sure, Frank. And yes, he's talking. I will find out more when I get to the station. He's in lock up. Paul you need to come with me."

"Someone. Get the door," Deron barked. Moe opened it and they watched Deron bump his wheelchair into everything on the way out.

"What was that all about?" Jack asked.

"He's not happy," Moe said. "Forced retirement. Not in control of things anymore."

"Acts like he's concerned about the Asian man talking," Jack said. Paul nodded.

"Nah. He's just being crotchety," Moe said. "Wheelchair, too. He'll get over it."

"I'll check in on you later," Paul said. The two left Jack's hospital room and the door muffled closed.

What's going on with you, Francis? Jack wondered. He pressed the button for Pouncer. His neck burned. He would never forget the eyes of the killer. They danced.

TWENTY-FIVE

Rose Hill Cemetery – March 9, 2005 – 10:00

Although the rain had stopped two days earlier, the ground stayed soft. The limited access would be an unexpected gift.

At 10:00 a.m. friends and family parked in a line on the only road inside the Rose Hill Cemetery. Inside the half-tent were chairs with black suits and veils and hung heads. The white-haired priest in black robes held an open bible over a closed Lincoln Blue casket. Across from him, surrounded by flowers, Melissa Burcher sang *Tears in Heaven* a cappella.

The uninvited parked on East Chelsea and in the fields like a county fair. Inside the cemetery gates, twenty yards from Burcher's tent, crowds churned behind fat ropes and a line of off-duty police. The masses had come from all over the state. Most were murder-mystery buffs. Some wanted to pay their last respects. All were there to be a part of Florida history. The funeral of the billionaire, Medical Examiner's ex-spouse would be one more juicy chapter in the true-crime novel, the ongoing, unsolved Burcher family murder mystery.

The *Tampa Sentinel* dedicated a whole section to the Burcher family funeral but devoted only one paragraph to the deceased—Patricia. Like a cheap tabloid they covered the infamous Ballast Point family murder mystery and 1970 abduction of Rose Burcher. The abundance of unsubstantiated speculation and absence of detail left readers wanting. Glaring holes in the half-baked narrative would have to linger until the murders were solved. Neither the Tampa PD nor the FBI would discuss active investigations.

The tent held fifteen. Jack sat on the front row next to Melissa's empty chair and Emily Monroe Burcher (Grandma-Em). Patricia's family flew in from Boston the night before and stayed at a hotel. Her mother, father, sister, and brother were also on the front row. Attendees were lost in the music and moment. Jack stared at the oleanders touching Melissa's dress.

"Who took care of the flowers?" he leaned and whispered to David one seat over.

"How do I know? What's with you and flowers," he breathed through his cupped hand. "Funeral homes handle that stuff, Jack."

"It would be nice to know who," he muttered. *Who brings oleanders to—?* He leaned for another angle. *Ah... there it is. The card on its plastic stick.* "Never mind," He whispered. David shrugged. Melissa hit a high note.

Jack had suggested Grandma-Em not risk the journey outside Sun Bay. The feisty 93-year-old matriarch would hear nothing of it. She still had her mind (most times) and stubborn streak (all times). Patricia held a special place in the old lady's heart. G-Em was the reason Jack and Patricia worked an extra year on their dead marriage.

The Lincoln Blue casket had been sealed at the funeral

home. The mortician could not remove the terror from her face, and her body had been irreparably ravaged before the added damage from the autopsy by Dr. Quin. Jack had left orders with the funeral director—gently bathe her, dress her in her favorite nightgown, place her between the white-satin sheets inside the Lincoln Blue casket, and seal it. Patricia had been through enough.

The poignant, graveside service ended at 10:35. The tent emptied in ten minutes and the cemetery in another fifteen. By 11:00 East Chelsea was barren. Jack and G-Em stayed. They would witness the entire interment.

Paul Shuck, Moe Bullitt, and Hugo Novak gathered outside the tent to stand vigil. Unmarked cars patrolled the area —Jack still not safe. The Asian man found in the boathouse had been released. The FBI determined the drifter had no connection to Patricia's death. The man was unable to feed himself much less manage a diabolical killing spree over thirty-plus years. He had wandered onto Ballast Point. To get out of the rain he took the nearest shelter, an empty boathouse. The killer got away, but this time the FBI had a detailed description. Jack had helped reproduce a composite drawing. It would be in the hands of all law enforcement.

"Im glad you came, Em," Jack whispered as he tugged at his neck bandage. "Patricia thought the world of you. I guess it was unthoughtful of me to suggest—"

"—I stay put at Sun Bay?" she said with eyes on the casket as it sank into the hole.

"I tend to be overly protective."

She changed the subject. "I don't want you to feel bad about your divorce, Jack."

"How do you know how I feel?"

"I know it's rolling around that head of yours?" She pinched his chin. "You can feel bad about losing her. And you can be mad at the person who took her from us. But you cannot add Patricia's death to your list of things to—"

"—blame myself for?" He dropped his head like a runner at the end of a long race coming in last place. "I hear you, Em."

"Do you? Do you really hear me, Jack?"

"There are things you don't know," he said. "I'm not as innocent as you think."

"I know the important thing. Patricia's death opened your eyes."

"And how do you know that?" he whispered and looked around.

"Because I know you." They watched three shovels move dirt into the hole. "I have seen the change in you since her death."

"You have?"

"You don't remember, I was there the night after we lost your mother."

"You're right. I don't remember."

"I was there. I knew you had to go back outside—your safe place."

"I had to?" he sighed.

"Yes. You did. That field outside your bedroom window," she said as she closed her eyes. "You found that God-awful box in the driveway." She grabbed Jack's hand and squeezed. "The darn police were everywhere except where they shoulda been, Jack," she groused. "You shoulda never have been the one to find that box."

"I guess you're right," he muttered.

"Of course, I'm right. I was an adult and I was there. I was very aware of what was goin' on," she cackled. "And I saw your face change that night. You were scared. You lost your mother forever. You watched your father breakdown. They took him to the hospital that night. You did not see Ronan for three of the most important weeks of your life. A terrible thing."

I was alone, he thought.

"They drugged him up, Jack," Emily said. "The contents of the box almost killed him. I think he died inside that night. The box hurt you too, Jack."

Jack looked past the men with the shovels to the trees on the edge of the cemetery. He got lost in the clouds and his broken memories. *I wish they had drugged me, too. Maybe I would have had a chance.*

"That day you took on the whole load. There was nothing anyone could do." She leaned close. "You saw things you should not have seen. You saw things few outside the police saw. Nobody would listen to you. Back in those days' adults didn't talk to kids about bad things. And they sure as hell stayed away from smart kids with imaginations like you.

"That night you were angry, scared, and lost. I was afraid then you would find a way to blame yourself for your mother's abduction, and later, her death. Quilt is a terrible thing."

"I didn't understand much," Jack said as the three shovels took rhythmic turns tossing dirt into the half-full hole.

"Your father tried to get you help, but you weren't havin' it. We were advised by the smart doctors to handle you in a way that would not add to your trauma. Ronan had psychologists come to the house disguised as au pairs and tutors and maids.

"After a year, the doctors said they could not fix your biggest problem—you felt alone in a cruel world and trusted no one. They said you had to figure it out on your own.

"I thought you needed someone special, in your life," Em continued. "I thought that person would fix you. I thought Patricia would be that person. I was wrong. Turns out she would not be special until she died in your arms, Jack. I don't know why or how, but somehow she opened your eyes."

"Opened my eyes to what?"

"I think she told you to leave the little boy with her, the one from those terrible nights. I know she stayed alive for you. Patricia knew you would come. She knew she was dying. You did come. You were with her in her final moments. Her love, and your trust and pain, allowed you let go."

Jack wrapped an arm around the fragile old lady. In silence, they watched the shovels, swirling leaves, and swaying branches. It was the first time Grandma Em had talked to him about the events of 1970. *By letting go of the ten-year-old boy,* he thought, *I realized an end to the nightmare did not mean an end to meaning in my life.*

"There's something I need to ask. I'll understand if you don't want to talk about it." He watched her watch the shovels shape the mound. "Was Otto adopted or—?"

A soft smile grew on her wrinkled face. "I carried his secret for 77 years. Otto told me the night he asked me to marry him. One year before we got married, the spring of 1929."

Jack waved off Paul Shuck and watched him back away from the front edge of the tent.

"Otto wanted to spend his life with me. He did not want any secrets between us."

Jack cupped her small hands in his. "That's nice, Em."

"I never had a secret until that night," she sighed. "After he told me, I didn't know what to do. I was scared one day someone would ask and I would have to lie. I never lie, Jack. Nobody asked. I pretty much stopped thinking about it."

"I wouldn't ask if it wasn't important. I know some things. I want to hear it from you. I can't be sure unless I hear it from you, Em. It matters."

With sad eyes she turned to him. "Otto was not adopted," she said. "And Edwina did not homebirth him either," she whispered.

"Okay, but—"

"Wilhelm and Edwina Burcher were desperate for a child. You see, she had a medical condition. Back then an operation was the only way. But there was a terrible downside. Edwina could never birth a child. The lifesaving operation would remove her feminine parts. They both decided to go forward with the operation. They thought they could live with the consequences.

"Well, the operation was a success. Still, Edwina went into a terrible depression. She found she could not live without a child in her life. I was told that her depression got very bad— suicidal. Otto said his father was lost, desperate. Wilhelm just could not lose her. He had to do something. Then, late one night in July 1906, he left without telling her. Wilhelm took a newborn baby out of the hospital nursery in Strasbourg, Jack. He kidnapped a baby boy, Otto.

"My God." *It is true...*

"They left Strasbourg the very same night. Roamed the countryside like gypsies for a year. Lived in their car and a tent. Wilhelm took odd jobs. They avoided family. A year later they settled in Hamburg. When they did, they had a child with them, one they had to account for. Otto was about a year old. They needed paperwork for schools and census. That's when they decided to say Edwina home-birthed Otto. I suppose that story was the easiest. People had babies at home all the time. Wilhelm and Edwina could never begin to prove adoption."

Jack gave Emily his handkerchief for her wet eyes. "On his twenty-first birthday, Otto was told everything. Wilhelm said it was the age of responsibility. He told Otto but did not tell Edwina he told Otto. I think Wilhelm could not carry the lie to his grave. Now, it was a lie he had passed onto Otto. He never should have done that to Otto."

"What did Otto do?" Jack asked.

"He was devastated. In 1927 he went to see his real parents —Albrecht and Anna Bethe. They lived in Kiel, Germany. Otto watched them for several days. He tried to get up the nerve to approach them, but then he saw his twin brother —Hans."

Emily closed her eyes. "Otto just could not do it. He could not turn their lives upside down. They were happy. They had moved on. I encouraged him to meet his real parents and his brother. He resisted. I think he wanted to, but he worried Wilhelm and Edwina could get in trouble, be prosecuted for kidnapping. He didn't want them hurt."

"You and Otto married in 1929. You moved to Florida in 1930. Why?"

"We did. Otto had to get away from the lie. Uncle Horace invited him to the United States many times. Horace always liked Otto. Horace manufactured Cuban cigars in Tampa and was doing pretty good. He wanted Otto to take over the investment side of the tobacco business. Otto was the son Horace never had. I guess you know the rest of the story."

"Did Otto ever connect with Hans Bethe?" Jack asked.

"He tried after Wilhelm and Edwina passed. I pushed him —he did nothing wrong. He should meet his brother. Otto finally agreed. It was 1941. He was 35. Still had his hair and was doing pretty good financially with the cigar business. The Cuban farmers loved him."

"I would have to agree. He was on the road to billionaire status," Jack teased.

"Otto wanted to get Christmas out of the way. He planned to go meet Hans January 1942. But then on December 7 the Japanese bombed Pearl Harbor—"

"—Jesus. That's right. December 7, 1941. We were pulled into World War II."

"Otto didn't get involved in the war," Emily said. "Wasn't

that he didn't love America. He just hated wars. He grew up in constant turmoil in Poland."

"Hans Bethe was a famous scientist then," Jack said. "Hans got pulled into the war."

Emily smiled. "Hans Bethe was something new to us back then. He was a nuclear physicist. Still don't quite know what that is. Otto used it as another excuse not to meet him. Said his brother was a big shot. Wouldn't have time for him. Hans Bethe was deep into secret projects for the government.

"If you really want to know, I think Otto didn't want the CIA or FBI sniffing around his tobacco business. Otto started to think smoking tobacco had made him sick. Maybe tobacco was not a good thing. Maybe it caused his cancer."

"What about meeting with Hans after the war?" Jack asked.

"Otto was starting to get sick by then," Emily said. "He figured we were the only two people alive that knew the truth about them, and it wasn't hurtin' anyone but him."

"And he thought that was okay. I get it. But are you sure he never met Hans Bethe?

"Why must I answer that question?" she asked as she fidgeted with her lace shawl.

"It's very important for reasons I just can't talk about right now. You've got to trust me."

"Do you trust me?" she asked.

Jack smiled. "Of course, I do. I always have and always will. You are the only one in the world I can say that to." He watched a single tear roll down her cheek. Her hands trembled. The back-tent flap opened halfway. Paul held up five fingers. Jack nodded. "You can tell me, Em. It can't hurt anybody now. Maybe it can help."

She blew her nose. Jack waited.

"Otto met Hans Bethe in the winter of 1946 after the war.

Otto got a phone call from him. Darn near had a heart attack. Why would the world-famous nuclear scientist—one of the men who ended World War II—call Otto on the phone? Well, it was a fundraising inquiry. Otto's net worth had gotten up there—almost the billion-dollar mark. After the war, the government had a new program. They got their top people to reach out to the most patriotic and richest people."

"I read about the Freedom Train. The government sought wealthy patriots to fund new research to advance science and technology for freedom. Nobody wanted another war."

"Otto donated a large sum of money along with a lot of other people. He attended a dinner in Washington DC, winter of 1946. He finally got to meet his brother, face to face."

"Did their *mutual beginnings* come up?"

"Oh no," Emily puffed.

"Are you saying Hans did not recognize their similarities? They are twins."

"That's exactly what I am saying. And no one else did either. Otto had grown a mustache and shaved his head. You must remember in '46 the chemo had started to change Otto. He was losing muscle. His face looked very different that year. He battled another nine years."

"I'm sorry. Of course, you're right," Jack whispered.

"Otto has one picture of him and Hans together at that dinner. I don't know why it was picked up by all the newspapers. That picture made the front page of the Washington Post and the New York Times and papers across the country. I suppose they followed Hans Bethe around. He was one of six we gave credit for ending World War II. If we had lost, I think it would have been the end of freedom and democracy. I bet half the country would be speaking German and the other half Japanese."

Emily opened her white-pearl purse and dug deep into a

side pocket. She pulled out a folded newspaper clipping and passed it to Jack. "I haven't looked at that for years. I carry it around with me because it's the only picture I have of Otto with his brother. Otto was so happy and proud that night. He admired his brother. I think, in a way, Hans was drawn to Otto. They say the man rarely smiles. Well, he's certainly smiling with my Otto."

Jack unfolded the brittle clipping. The faded picture of Otto and Hans leaning together was special. They each smiled with their wine glasses held high. The headline said it all. "The father of the atomic bomb and a true patriot that made it all possible." Jack then read the first line under the picture. "Nuclear scientist Hans Bethe celebrates the end of WWII with billionaire patriot Otto Burcher, a successful American businessman committed to supporting continues nuclear research and development."

Oh my God, Jack mused. *The Burcher family was outed in December 1946!*

"A few years after that picture we lost Leonard. He died in California. A terrible car accident. I think losing Leonard in '48 killed Otto more than his cancer."

"I'm sorry, Em." *The radical bastards didn't waste any time,* he thought.

Paul Shuck and another man approached Jack and Emily. "Excuse me. I'm sorry to interrupt. Mr. Filbert is with the Sun Bay Center. He is here for Mrs. Burcher. I understand this man is on a very tight schedule and you need your meds, Mrs. Burcher."

"A few more stops," Filbert said. "Yes. Mrs. Burcher's noon meds cannot be missed."

"Of course," Jack said as he helped Emily to her feet. The four left the tent. Jack looked back at the mound. *At the end of the week the Makrana marble headstone from Rajasthan, India would be placed on Patricia's grave,* he recalled. *I'll bring Emily back. She'll like that...*

They watched the Sun Bay van pull away. "We're also on a schedule," Paul said. "Your session with Dr. Mesmer is tonight. He wants you to eat a hardy lunch and take a nap, no dinner. You need to get to the Bayshore Gardens office at 18:30. And remember, absolutely no—"

"—alcohol. I got it, Paul. You do remember I must go to the office. I have a few cases pending. Meeting Mr. Novak. We must get them out. I will keep my appointment with Dr. Mesmer. Don't you worry. I will be there this time."

When the van crawled out the cemetery gates onto Chelsea, Jack turned and ran back into the tent. Paul caught up.

Jack pulled a pair of surgical gloves from his pocket and snapped them on. He slid the pot of oleanders from the wall of flowers, pushed through the foliage, and removed an envelope by the edges. He carefully opened it on a chair seat.

"What are you doing?"

"Oleanders, Paul."

"Wonderful. Flowers at a funeral. How bizarre," he scoffed.

"Oleanders were in my father's room the night he was taken."

"Okay. It is a common flower around here, isn't it?"

"I wondered who gave oleanders to Ronan that day. I asked everyone. David and Melissa had no idea where they came from. Sun Bay didn't put them there—they have a policy. Their personnel are prohibited from delivering or removing patient flowers. Some sort of liability issues. I could never find out who put the flowers in Ronan's room."

"Why would gifted flowers bug you, Jack? There are so many other things to—"

"—worry about? Did you know oleanders were planted outside our gates the night after my mother was taken?"

"No. I did not. How do you—?"

"They are giant bushes now, thirty-five years later."

"Okay. I see the connection. Still, it could be just a coincidence."

"I checked with Buford Penland, our gardener. Been taking care of the estate for as long as I can remember. Buford's an old man now. Still putters outside most days. Ronan told him fifty years ago he could take care of the place as long as he wanted. He's like family..."

"I asked Buford about the oleanders along the rock wall outside the gates. He told me they were planted the day after Rose was taken. I didn't think much of it, until he acted nervous. He stuttered around. Said he thought someone in the family planted them in memory of Rose."

"That's a little peculiar but likely a harmless event."

"He's been feeding and trimming 'em ever since. Today the oleander bushes run fifty feet from the gates along the wall up Crescent Drive."

"So, you think oleanders are connected to the killings?" Paul asked.

"I do. They gotta mean something. Maybe a twisted clue. Maybe part of a ritual or process. Why did these oleanders appear at Patricia's funeral? Everyone killed gets these flowers: Rose, Ronan, and now Patricia."

"What does the card say?"

Jack held the edges. "It says when children die, they do not grow." He flipped it over and checked the envelope. "No signature. No return address. Nothing. What does the note mean?"

"I don't know. Chilling thought. Someone will know in

Quantico. They're good with puzzles." Paul held out an opened evidence bag. Jack dropped it inside.

"Something else we need to talk about. My visit with Emily just now. "She confirmed the story about Otto being kidnapped. But I got more. You and Tate will be very interested in this."

Paul wrote on the evidence bag. "Okay. Give me the highlights?"

"Otto's biological brother is definitely—"

"—Hans Bethe. We know that. For a week now. What do you have new?"

They stopped outside the tent. Jack looked at the sun. "I know where the trail begins..."

TWENTY-SIX

Janice & Mesmer Psychiatric Offices – Bayshore Gardens – 19:00

Tate Worthington stood next to Paul Shuck behind the two-way mirror.

"He wanted to wait," Paul said. "Talk to us together, since you would be here tonight."

"Don't take this the wrong way," Tate said. "Are you sure he said—"

"—I know *where* the trail begins. Yes. I am."

"If that's true, dovetailed with what I've learned over the last few months, we may have something here. I wonder if it starts where I think it starts."

"You will find out soon. Great minds, right. Did you ever interview Emily Burcher?"

"I did. A week before our failed October meeting. She put on a very professional act—the fragile little old lady with dementia," Tate scoffed. "Grandma Em's been hiding somethin' for a long time. She's gotten good at dodging. She has a secret and no plans to share it with me."

"Well. She shared it with Jack. They had a cozy little chat at the cemetery."

"Today? After the services?" Tate asked.

"Couple Jack's new information with yours, and what comes out of this session, we could make real progress over the next few days."

"You've known Jack Burcher a long time. I told you I saw the conflict inside him. I know it because I had it, too. He wants to help, but his inner demons keep getting in his way. I think he's winning the battle. But, if not soon, I'll give you what I've learned. I gotta be leaving. I've given the Burcher case more than my allotted time already. I've got things piling up in Texas."

"I've known Jack a long time—fifteen years." Paul turned from the glass. "No doubt, there has been something controlling him. You said as much. I'm now convinced that all ended the night I pulled him off his wife."

"How do you mean, all ended?"

"I talked to him at the hospital the next day. Jack had an epiphany."

"I hope you're right. It's past time to get this thing solved."

Paul smiled as he turned back to the two-way mirror and Jack Burcher lying on a couch twenty feet away. "Jack met the ten-year-old boy that witnessed his 1970 nightmare."

"You mean he met himself as a ten-year-old boy?"

"Yes. The boy inside that controlled him. The boy that has hijacked our investigation. When Patricia died, she told him to let the boy go with her. She told him to get his life back."

"That is a touching story," Tate said. "I just don't know if it's gonna be enough. He might be the kind of man changed only by justice. Some are that way."

"The mission is all the boy ever had. He took control of Jack. He defined Jack from those days forward. He is why Jack became the Chief Medical Examiner—"

"You just validated my position," Tate said. "The boy inside Jack Burcher is all about the hunt for his mother's killer. Why would he get in the way of the investigation?"

"Janice calls it a *psychopathic conflict*. A struggle from within. He explained that inner struggle can only be resolved by Jack. Patricia's death triggered awareness. Before that he did not know the boy. When he ran into him that night, he let him go and took back his life."

"So, you are saying he turned the boy over to Patricia Burcher," Tate muttered.

"Yes. He knows what he must do tonight. He must take control of the ten-year-old boy and look into the eyes of the monster that visited his house in 1970."

"And visited others," Tate breathed. His words fogged the glass.

Paul's eyes moved to the old man in the black suit sitting next to Jack. "I pray Mesmer can help him get there tonight."

They perused the dimly lit room decorated in turn-of-the-century furniture, heavy drapes, oriental rugs, and dark oil paintings with medal-adorned generals in red coats on white horses. Paul turned the volume knob on the small control panel by the glass. "Dr. Mesmer told me Jack would see everything tonight."

Jack laid in a supine position on a brown-leather couch. No shoes. Collar unbuttoned. His hands at his sides, palms down. Janice and Deron were seated against the far wall behind Jack. Mesmer sat in a matching brown-leather chair at Jack's side. His long legs were crossed with an opened notebook on his lap.

The tip of a fat Mont Blanc pen moved on Mesmer's lips as he considered the recessed panel on the arm of his chair, the array of knobs and switches and lights. He controlled the room environment—temperature, airflow, and lighting. He also controlled the hidden audio/video recording devices and feeds into the observation room. Like the Wizard of Oz, the unpretentious old man had complete control of his peculiar world.

"Are you comfortable?" he asked.

"I am," Jack sighed. "I guess I should be. I've been lying on this couch for more than thirty minutes waiting for—"

"How was your day, Jack?"

"My day, today?" He scratched the leather. "Okay, I suppose."

Mesmer made a note. "You buried your wife, today."

"Yes. Well, ex-wife. We are divorced. Well, were divorced at the time of—"

"So then, I stand corrected. You buried your ex-wife today," he whispered with his head down and eyes peering over his round wire glasses.

"Patricia. I think her name is what I want to say. I buried Patricia, today."

"How long did you know *Patricia*, Jack?"

He rubbed his forehead and squinted. "We were married eight years. Separated two. And before that we dated three. I finished my pathology residency and went to Boston for my forensic specialty work. We married that June. That would make it thirteen years."

"Is thirteen your answer?"

"Yes. I buried Patricia thirteen years after we met," Jack muttered.

"Thirteen," Mesmer repeated as his pen moved in his small notebook.

"Yeah. I'm not sure why you ask. I don't know what you're looking for."

"I'm not looking for anything, Jack. I want you to answer my questions, say what you feel. Try to visualize your answers. Less critical thinking. Can you do that?"

"Visualize. Less critical thinking. I can try." Jack tugged at his collar and undid another button. "Tell you what. Why not just skip the customary pre-hypnosis chitchat?"

"Pre-hypnosis chitchat?"

"We're both doctors here. As I told you and William before, although I agreed to do this, I doubt we will have success. I told you I'm not a good candidate for hypnosis. I have one of those controlling personalities, and I am a doctor—I know what's behind the curtain."

"Behind what curtain?"

"The hypnosis curtain. The process. The steps: relax, follow the swinging pendent, your eyes are getting heavy, etcetera, etcetera. The process is no secret. I'm just not—"

"—I'm sorry to interrupt, Jack. You are right about time. It is important. Time is of the essence, they say. May I do something to help you with what you refer to as *the process*?"

"Please do," he sighed as he rolled his head toward Mesmer. Jack took in the skinny, pale, white-haired, old man in the shiny black suit, and he perused the long, spindly legs and boney fingers wrapped around a fat pen and tiny leather notebook. *What am I doing here? I feel like I'm negotiating with a troll from a Harry Potter movie,* he mused.

His inside smile faded when Mesmer started to speak. The irritating buzz of uninteresting words flowed in the background as Jack's mind wandered. *I've never believed in the 'powers of suggestion' stuff, not even when they tried to sell it to me in medical school. This will never work. Why did I agree to do it? I wanted to do something after losing Patricia. But maybe I could have found a better way to participate, to demonstrate my new awareness, to show my solid commitment to the team...*

Those last moments with Patricia, I met the ten-year-old boy —I met me! I can't believe he lived inside my head. He kept me in limbo. One day I wanted to find the killer. The next day I wanted to stop everything. William Janice said my fears as a boy controlled me as a man. I had a split personality—a kid and me. When I saw Patricia take her last breath, it was time to retake control of my life. Her brutal death opened my eyes. The monster had to be stopped. She helped me. She sucked that boy out of me, gave me the strength to break away...

Stop thinking. Listen to Mesmer. Try to cooperate. This might work. Stop being an obstacle. You want to end the hunt. You want to catch the monster. So do they. You want this nightmare over. Kayda is my new life. Finish the hunt. Get justice. Find peace—

"Did you hear me, Jack?" Mesmer asked.

"Sorry. Yes, I did." *Focus...*

"I want you to know something about me, something I have shared with very few in my life. I can count on one hand. This personal information will help you—"

"—help me? No. I don't think so, Eric." *What are the words to gently pull the plug on this circus event,* Jack stressed? *There's gotta be a better way for me to—*

"I'm sorry, Dr. Mesmer. I just do not do well with personal information. It conflicts me. I withhold truth so I don't hurt people. That burdens me. It's just another distraction. I end up feeling obligated and it makes me very uncomfortable, edgy. So, please don't—"

"I remember everything perfectly, Jack. Total recall." Mesmer smiled. Jack froze. "I remember every detail of every experience I have had from my early childhood to this day."

Jack blinked, swallowed hard, and stared with an opened mouth.

"I know. It is difficult to grasp such a preposterous

capability. It sounds utterly absurd. Ridiculous. Contrary to reason and common sense. It is impossible.

"Most think it a gift—one in the *superpower* category." His cackle turned into a cough. He cleared his throat and blew his nose as Jack stared. "Excuse me. I'm sorry. Aging is not easy. "Where was I? Oh yes. Perfect memory, total recall. I suppose it can be an asset at times. Helpful in some situations, like now. Most of the time it is another affliction I must manage."

"A perfect photographic memory and total recall," Jack murmured.

"Yes. For example, I remember every word you said the evening of October 11, 2004, in this building, in our main conference room between 6:14 and 7:38 pm. It was such a miserable, cold, and rainy night." Mesmer looked up and rubbed his turkey neck. "I should have been at home by the fire with a bowl of hot chicken soup," he muttered. "But someone I respect asked for my help. He wanted me to help his friend, Jack Burcher."

Mesmer smiled. His eyes dropped to the small notebook and his words took on a chilling tone, when his eyes returned to Jack's. "I not only remember everything *you* said that night. I remember everything Dr. William Janice, Paul Shuck, Francis Deron, Melissa and David Burcher, and Tate Worthington said that night. I tell you my secret for a reason. I want to remove one of your suffocating, self-imposed burdens."

"Burdens," Jack breathed.

"You are not responsible for me, Jack. You do not need to remind me of anything, ever. You can focus completely on you and your experiences. I believe that's quite enough for anyone to have to deal with."

Jack swallowed hard a second time. He stared at the old man, who minutes ago he had berated—an old and incompetent troll. *I hope you don't read minds, too.*

Mesmer smiled. "You're a disciplined forensic pathologist, a Chief Medical Examiner. You are trained to reach conclusions based on objective facts. You set aside the subjective, the unprovable information. I know you are struggling to believe my claim, Jack. A photographic memory is possible, to a degree. You accept that I possibly could remember some things better than most, but total recall is a stretch. Let us take a little journey together. Let us return to the evening of October 11, 2004, in this building—"

"—I don't know, Dr. Mesmer. This is a lot for anyone to get their head around," Jack said. "A photographic memory is not that uncommon. Total recall, well, there have been very few verifiable cases ever reported. I really don't think a demonstration would help me—

"'—he cannot interpret the observations of the ten-year-old boy alone in the field outside his bedroom window,' Paul Shuck said as he turned to Jack. 'Have I accurately stated your feelings on this, Jack?' Jack's eyes jump from Mesmer to Shuck. 'Yes, Paul. As I have said, I have tried many times before. I am unable to get beyond the information I've shared. I agree with Dr. Janice. The tragic events of 1970 were witnessed by a boy with limited cognitive development. My interpretations of the most frightening nights of my life are vague and jumbled. Separating facts from the imagination of a boy three-plus decades later is simply impossible—'"

"—that's enough," Jack said. He rolled his head back on the leather couch and stared at the ceiling. "I stand corrected. I think we can move on."

"Good. Going forward I want you to visualize your answers to my questions."

"I will try, but I don't know if—"

"—you can visualize answers? That is a fair concern. I can help you. Let's try a simple exercise. I will say a word.

You will visualize your answer and tell me the first thing you see."

"Okay. It's just not how I think—"

"Hospital," Mesmer said.

"Operating room," Jack said. "I see a surgical team and a patient on the—"

"Only the first thing you see, Jack... House."

"My home on Ballast Point."

"Good, but one word, Jack... Thanksgiving."

"Family around the table. A busy kitchen—"

"I want you to relax, Jack. Visualize. Remember, one word."

"Right. I'm not good at games."

"Saltwater."

"Bay."

"Good... Steak," Mesmer said.

"Juicy," Jack shot back.

"Kitten."

"Fur." *Soft and fluffy,* he thought.

"Very good. Snow."

"Shivering," Jack said. *Patricia and I were freezing that time in Boston—*

"Smoke," Mesmer said.

"Bonfire." *We stayed for the blazing fire and hot drinks. It was the best day of my—*

"Burning leaves."

"Piles." *Raking leaves with, father—*

"Cicada," Mesmer said with a softer voice. *That's right. See it. Feel it. Own it. Then say it,* Mesmer thought with a finger moving a cuff off his Rolex. He turned a dial on the arm of his chair. Warm air fell from the vent above the couch. Jack's hair moved. A hum grew in the room.

"Night," Jack responded with a smile. *I remember those hot summer nights. I was swallowed by a magnificent world.*

Everything was perfect. Just me and the lightning bugs flickering and cicadas screaming up and down the sparkling coast of Hillsborough Bay. I can see the—

"Stars," Mesmer whispered.

"Wonder," Jack whispered back. *I'm in the field engulfed by an endless universe—*

"Wildflowers."

"Safe." *No one can see me in my nest—*

"Bedtime."

"Mother." *Tucking me in last. You always came to me last—I am your favorite. I can hear your soft voice. I feel your kiss on my forehead. You always moved my hair from my eyes and just looked at me with that smile. I smell your perfume—*

"School," Mesmer snapped.

"Study," Jack snapped back. *I cannot fail. I must be ready to hunt the—*

"Flowers," Mesmer whispered.

"Oleanders," Jack snapped.

"Driveway."

"Box." Jack closed his eyes. *No. I see—*

"Iron gates," Mesmer said. *You are on the fringe of your dark place,* he thought as he made another notation in his notebook and increased the warm air flow. Mesmer adjusted the hum from steady flow to a pulsating flow.

"Box," Jack whispered. *God! I know. Mother is dead. The blood. He cut out her—*

"Rock wall."

"Box." His whisper trailed off. His body relaxed. He exhaled. *I can see everything from here. I'm floating above the couch, the house. I'm floating above Ballast Point, the bay. It's beautiful, so big. I feel the warm wind in my face. I see the lights on the channel and smell the smoke from our chimney. Why smoke from our—*

"Jack. You are safe. I'm going to count to three. When I say *three*, you will sleep. You will be able to see everything you want to see. Nothing can stop you. I will be with you. You will only hear my voice. I am your guide, your only trusted friend on this journey. When we complete our journey together, I will snap my fingers and you will wake up. You will be refreshed and have no memory of our travels. Nod if you understand me."

Jack nodded with eyes closed.

"One... Two... Three..."

On three Jack sunk deeper into the couch. Mesmer smiled and held his hand up for all to see. Then he touched a finger to his lips. Jack Burcher was in a deep hypnotic trance.

"Jack. Are you comfortable?"

"Yes."

"Where are you now, Jack?"

"I'm in Bayshore Gardens at a meeting with Dr. Mesmer."

"Jack, the meeting is over. You are now floating in a bathtub full of warm water—the perfect temperature. It is late on a Sunday afternoon. No one needs you. It is your time, Jack. You're in a bathtub completely submerged. Only your mouth, nose, and eyes break the surface."

Paul Shuck leaned closer. He touched the tip of his nose to the glass. "I can't believe it. He hypnotized Jack Burcher in less than three minutes. One minute they're talking and the next playing a word game—boom. Now, Jack's floatin' in an imaginary tub of water with a ridiculous smile on his face."

Tate chuckled. "Mesmer is a consummate professional. His benign persona combined with genius intellect has put him at the top of his game in the least-understood profession. He has a reputation, on the world stage. I doubt Tampa knows they have this treasure, in their fair city."

"I knew he was a hypnotist, but nothing like this. And that photographic memory—"

"Only two people know everything that happened in 1970, the killer and Jack Burcher. Get a bag of popcorn and sit back for the show. Mesmer is the best in the world at this. We're going to travel back in time and revisit the 1970 abduction and maybe, homicide."

"I hope you're right. But why are you so sure?"

"I've seen it with my own eyes. I contracted with Mesmer, two cases a few years ago. I watched him in action." Tate turned back to the glass and the doctor writing in his notebook. "He's ready, Paul. He knows how to get Jack Burcher productive."

"Productive?"

"If Jack saw it, touched it, smelled it, or felt it, Mesmer will unlock the experience so Jack can revisit it—dissect it if you will. The only variable in Mesmer's process will be Jack. Hypnosis or not, Jack decides whether he will or won't share it with Mesmer."

"I hope he shares everything," Paul muttered.

"We're looking at *Franz Friedrich Anton Mesmer* reincarnate. The man who led the way to the modern medical practice of mesmerization, or the term we now know as hypnotism. If Mesmer can't get Jack to share, nobody can."

"Are you floating, Jack?" Mesmer asked.

"Yes. Floating."

"Good. I want us to go somewhere together, Jack. You can travel with me while you float in your perfect, warm bath. Let's call it *mind travel*. Is that okay, Jack? Are you ready, Jack?"

"Yes, it is perfect, and I am ready to travel." Jack's smile never left his face.

"Okay, Jack. Let's go to the Sun Bay Rehabilitation Center and visit your father. The date is September 9, 2003. It is

Tuesday. The time is 7:10 p.m. You are in Ronan's room with David. You just got there. Tell me what you see, Jack. Tell me what Ronan is doing."

Jack's smile melted for the first time. His face tightened. "Pop. What's bothering you today? David and I are here to help you. Tell me what's got you all upset."

Jack sat up on the coach, with eyes closed. His arms trembled. "Is it the fire on Bird Island? Is that upsetting you, Pop?" Jack shook his head, no. Then he spoke in a low voice, his father's voice. "He—is—coming—for—me. It—is—my—turn. I am—the next—to be—sac—sac—sac—"

"Finish Ronan's word for him, Jack," Mesmer ordered. "You know what he is saying. Tell me what Ronan is telling you, what you do not want to hear. I demand you tell me, Jack."

Jack's shoulders dropped. His posture sagged. His chin touched his chest.

"You can do this," Mesmer said. "You are safe, Jack. You can say it out loud."

Jack's head and shoulders lifted. "Sac—sac—sacrifice," he said. He took a deep breath and stuck out his chest. "Uncle Leonard and mother, they were sacrificed. Ronan—now it is his turn. I don't understand why." Jack opened his eyes and looked at his palms. "I see the others sacrificed. I know, but I do not know why."

"Who do you see, Jack? Who else in your family was sacrificed? Tell me now."

"Uncle Leonard in 1948. Aunt Caroline in 1975. Uncle Harold in 1978."

"You getting' this?" Paul said behind the glass. "I suspected all three were but—"

"It ties to my investigation," Tate said with his nose in an open file on the window ledge. "It confirms what I know, but I don't know how they were killed."

"Mesmer needs to ask Jack how he knows. Granted Caroline and Harold Lawton's deaths are suspicious, but everything is circumstantial. I agree. We need more on them. I've got enough to link Leonard's homicide in '48. Come on Mesmer, ask—"

"How do you know your Aunt Caroline and Uncle Harold were sacrificed, Jack?" Mesmer asked. Tate and Paul smiled.

"He can't hear me, right?" Paul whispered behind the glass.

"Nope. He's just that good."

"Nerium oleander," Jack said. "Apocynaceae Gentianales."

"I don't understand," Mesmer said. "What are you telling me, Jack?"

He moved his hands, as if turning pages of an imaginary book. He stopped and leaned forward like he was reading. "Oleanders. An ornamental plant used throughout the world for good things. Also, one of the most poisonous plants on earth. Some oleander-related deaths in the world are accidental. Some are suicides. And some are homicides."

"I need more, Jack. Your aunt and uncle. How do you know—?"

"Causes nausea, vomiting, diarrhea, weakness, dizziness, headaches, stomach pain, and heart problems," Jack said. "And oleander seeds make deadly poisons when absorbed into the body." Jack blinked and lowered his hands to the side of the couch.

Mesmer pushed. "Aunt Carolyn and Uncle Harold died from—"

"—a toxic cardiac glycoside found in the oleander plant. It increases output force of the heart. It increases rate of contractions by acting on cellular sodium-potassium ATPase pump—"

"Okay. Good. I have enough. Thank you, Jack." Mesmer made a note, looked at the two-way mirror and nodded, and then adjusted knobs on his console. "Is there anything else you want to tell me about your visit with Ronan, Jack...?"

"Poisoning," Paul said to Tate. "I get it with Carolyn's file. It could fit. But Harold Lawton fell off a scaffold. Died from the fall. We were looking into the possibility someone pushed him, not a poisoning."

"Remember, the oleander poison causes dizziness and weakness," Tate said. "Maybe the guy was poisoned. like in a sandwich, on a break. Maybe the intention was for him to get dizzy, disoriented, and fall to his death. Boom. Another Sacrificed. Would be nice if we could get a hold of their remains to run a toxicology screen—"

"—if we can even find remains. I believe they were cremated. I will double check that. I did not bring their files."

"Toxicology on Ronan Burcher's brain did not reveal oleander poisoning," Tate said. "But that could be an oversight. Interference from our ten-year-old boy."

"Yes. There's that," Paul said. "Today, Jack talked about oleanders. He brought it up at the cemetery."

"To what extent?"

"A lot. If he had said anything before, it was in passing. Nothing made it into the file. Today, he said there was an oleander plant inserted into the funeral arrangement by the casket. A card was with it, but unsigned—anonymous. He also talked about an oleander plant in Ronan's room the night he was taken. Again anonymous. What is most bizarre, he told me someone had planted oleanders outside their gates in 1970, the night after Rose Burcher was taken."

"Now that is bizarre. Maybe some kind of ritual," Tate said. "I wonder the significance?"

"It's a pattern. Must have some meaning."

They turned back to the window and watched Jack

Burcher. He was sitting up staring into space. Then Dr. Mesmer put down his notebook and watched him.

"What is it, Jack," Mesmer asked. "You're not through? There's something you want to share. It's bothering you. I am here, Jack. It will feel good to say whatever it is."

Paul and Tate leaned closer to the glass. Janice and Deron leaned back.

With eyes closed, Jack swung his legs off the couch. His feet dangled. He stuck out his chest like challenging someone or something. "Say it, Jack," Mesmer prodded.

"The oleander flower is the official flower of Hiroshima. The first flower to blossom after the devastation by the atomic bomb in 1945."

On his last word, he collapsed backwards, onto the couch. Mesmer ran to his side. Jack's arms trembled as he dug fingernails into the leather.

TWENTY-SEVEN

**Janice & Mesmer Psychiatric Offices – Bayshore
Gardens – 20:00**

"We have returned from Sun Bay," Mesmer said. "You are floating in your tub of warm water. Your first journey went very, very well. You saw things, you shared, and you are safe. Do you feel the warm water, Jack?"

"I do," he said with an edgy tone.

"Let's make your water temperature perfect. There. Is that better, Jack?"

"Yes." He settled into the couch. "It is perfect," he whispered.

"Good. Now, I'm going to ask you to hold your breath and go under water. I will tell you when to come up for air." Mesmer looked at his watch. "Ready? Go under now."

As instructed Jack sucked in air and slid down the couch submerging himself in his imaginary tub of water. Mesmer adjusted a few dials on his console. He turned off the low-pitched hum, turned down the room temp, and stopped the warm stream of air on Jack's face.

Thirty seconds passed. Jack started to struggle. "You—can —come—up—now."

Jack pushed his head up the couch, broke the surface of water, and gasped for air. Mesmer turned up the airflow. A stream of cold air and fine mist shot from the stealth ceiling jet. It lifted his hair and small droplets of water ran down his face. When Mesmer restored the familiar, but undetectable, background hum, Jack's arms and legs went limp. His face airdried. The distressful ordeal worked. Mesmer had prepared Jack for the next journey—the reason for his hypnosis. Jack would now return to the night his mother was taken from their home. And the night a bloody heart was delivered to the gates of the Burcher estate. This journey would be the most demanding. It would present the greatest risks. Jack would either gain strength or fall deeper into the abyss. It depended on his reaction to the information he had avoided all his life.

"You look good, Jack," Mesmer said. "Everything is perfect. Your water temperature is perfect. You feel more refreshed than ever before. I know you want to travel again. Am I right Jack?"

"Yes. I feel refreshed." His smile grew and his hands played with the imaginary water. Mesmer adjusted the airflow temperature from cold to warm.

"Good. Since you did so well on our first journey, I think we can travel anywhere we want. Before we go, let's talk about the ten-year-old boy you met earlier this week. You met him the night Patricia died. I want to talk about him because we will see him where we are going. You may want to talk to him, Jack. He may want to explain or show things to you."

Jack's smile melted as both hands closed into white-knuckled fists.

"Jack, I don't want you to think about what happened to Patricia. We will come back to that. I promise. Now, I want you to focus on the ten-year-old boy?"

Jack's hands relaxed. He rocked his head side to side.

"From now on we will refer to the ten-year-old boy as *the boy*. Is that okay, Jack?"

"The boy," he said.

"When did you meet *the boy*, Jack?"

"I met him on March 7, 2005, around 10:00 p.m. I had to let him go that night. Patricia told me with her eyes to let him go. She helped me. It was time. She took him with—"

"Did you know *the boy* before that night, Jack?"

"No. I knew *of him* from a long time ago. It was different."

"Different. How do you mean?"

Jack smiled. "I was *the boy* up until the night my mother—" Jack froze. Mesmer watched the blood leave his head. Jack started to pant. "The night my mother—"

"Slow down," Mesmer whispered. "You are floating, Jack. You are safe. What night?"

Jack swallowed hard. "Up until the night of July 14, 1970, I was *the boy*. He died that night with my mother."

"Why do you think he died with your mother, Jack?"

"Because everything changed for me. I was different. Empty. Alone. Scared. I was someone else. The world was no longer filled with wonder. It had a darkness. The world was not safe. It was a dangerous place. I thought *the boy* died that night, but I was wrong."

"How were you wrong, Jack?"

"*The boy* did not die. He found a place to hide inside me. He hid from me. He abandoned me, like my mother. *The boy* did things to me without me knowing. He controlled parts of my head, my life. I felt something, but I didn't know until Patricia—"

"She told you about the boy with her eyes before she died," Mesmer said. "I can see you are confused, conflicted. I am confused, too. I think we can resolve our confusion, Jack. Would you like to resolve our confusion?"

"I would."

"Good. I've decided we will go to your house, the night of July 14, 1970. You will be invisible to everyone but me, Jack. You will be safe. No one can hurt you. You will not be in danger. You will see everything you want to see and understand everything you want to understand. Are you ready to travel with me, Jack?"

"I am invisible. I am safe. I can see everything," Jack said. His smile grew. "Yes."

"Here we go. You're flying above a layer of thin, wispy clouds floating over the Florida peninsula, Jack. You're going toward your home—the Burcher estate. You're soaring like an eagle. Look down, Jack. You can see the sparkling lights beneath the thin clouds."

Mesmer turned dials on his console. From the stealth ceiling nozzle, the small stream of air on Jack's face increased. Mesmer darkened the room. A thousand pinpoint lights, embedded in the ceiling and walls, twinkled. The sound of rushing winds filled the room. "Can you see the city lights below?" Mesmer yelled. "Can you feel the warm Florida air on your face?"

"I can. My God, it's beautiful. I can see downtown Tampa. I see the lights on the Interbay Peninsula and the line of cargo ships on the channel in Hillsborough Bay. I can see—"

"—there's Ballast Point, Jack. There's your home nestled in the field of wildflowers and giant live oak trees. There's the old house where you grew up. You can see the dock where you fished and the boathouse. Do you see the boats bobbing in the water, tugging their ropes? And the fireflies. They're just a few flickering on the water's edge and in your most favorite field." Mesmer turned up the soundtrack of the cicadas. He had thought of everything. "What's that? Is that the cicadas?" Mesmer had reproduced Jack's night of thirty-five years ago.

"I hear them," Jack gushed. It's beautiful. It's when my life was perfect—"

"It's midnight, July 14, 1970," Mesmer said as he softened his sound effects with the turn of a few dials. He had Jack where he wanted. "You are sitting on the roof outside your bedroom window. You are looking down at your field of wildflowers. Tell me, Jack. Tell me what else you see?"

"I see *the boy*," Jack whispered. "He's sitting in my spot. He is me before—"

"Before you changed? Does that clear up your confusion?"

"Yes. I am *the boy*," he sighed.

"Go down there, Jack. It's okay. Now. What are you doing?"

"I'm lying on my back. The wildflowers around me. It's my nest. They protect me from danger. That's why I'm not afraid to go outside alone at night."

"What do you do every summer night, in your field of wildflowers, Jack?"

"I'm looking up at the stars. I always get lost in the stars, and the fireflies, and the cicadas, and my dreams."

"Enjoy your fields and stars and fireflies and cicadas, Jack," Mesmer whispered as he wrote in his small notebook and increased the gentle airflow on his face.

"They're moving again. I always waited. The rolling waves."

"Can you see the bay, Jack?"

"No. Not from my spot. The summer winds leave the bay and slide across Ballast Point. The wind crosses my field. My wildflowers roll like waves in the ocean."

"Now I understand. Thank you for explaining that to me, Jack."

"The cicadas scream all night. Mother told me the males make that sound when they are looking for a female so they can have sex." Jack's light laughter waned. "But—"

"But what? Jack."

"The cicadas, they stopped. The wind stopped. Everything is quiet and still."

"Is something wrong?" Mesmer asked. Jack put his hands over his face.

Paul turned to Tate behind the glass. "Something's gonna happen. Jack's there, in the field the night Rose Burcher was taken from the house."

Tate wrote in his file and looked over his glasses. "Mesmer will get it all."

"Jack. You are safe. Remember? When you remove your hands from your face, you will see through the eyes of *the boy*. He did not get hurt that night, Jack. Do it now."

Jack lowered his hands and blinked. "I see through *the boy's* eyes—"

"Good. What's happening? Everything got quiet. What do you see, Jack?"

He sat up on the couch and crossed his legs Indian style. He stretched his neck and looked left, right, and straight ahead at the two-way mirror on Mesmer's office wall. Then he looked up. "I see a shooting star."

"That's good. Time is not a factor. What next do you see or hear or feel?"

"I hear a UFO—it's growling. The cicadas are still quiet—they're cautious. I smell a UFO. It's close, but where? I read about encounters of the fourth kind—abductions. I don't want 'em stickin' needles and things in me." Jack jerked his head left. He looked at Mesmer but did not see him. "There it is. I found it. The UFO's floating above the road outside our gates."

Mesmer increased the warm airflow on Jack's face and softened the twinkling lights and background hum. Jack had taken over. He had his own effects cascading into his experience.

"There's a flash of light—a square on the side of the gray thing. It's gone. I see a shadow. An alien. He's running to the house, staying low to the ground. He stopped on the driveway—"

"*Who* do you see, Jack?"

"I'm not supposed to be out here. I'm gonna get in trouble this time. My mom said not tonight. She didn't need any incidents with dad out of town. I better climb back up the trellis. But I think it's still broken. I better get back into bed, but—"

"But what, Jack?" Mesmer asked.

"*We* want to look at the flying saucer. *The boy* is more curious than he is scared. We're gonna sneak up close."

"*The boy* wants to do this, or is it you?"

"I'm *the boy* now."

"Okay." *You've made the complete transition,* Mesmer thought with a triumphant smile. "Please tell me everything along the way. I want to go with you."

"I'm climbing the rock wall. I know each rock to step on. I'm under thick trees. They're overgrown," he said breathing hard. "Need to be trimmed. Nobody can see us up here.

"It smells like gas, the kind they put in mowers. I smell oil, too. I see smoke shooting out of the gray thing. It has black windows. That thing is floating in the fog. No lights.

"Wait! I hear screams coming from the house."

"Is the alien shadow gone, Jack?"

Jack turns and squints. "No. He's still in the driveway."

Paul leaned closer to the glass. "Could there be two people? We never thought—"

"Now this is getting interesting," Tate muttered.

"Jack, are you sure about the screams coming from the house?" Mesmer asked.

"Yes."

"Are you sure the alien shadow is standing in the driveway?"

"He's not standing in the driveway. He's squatting. He's watching the house." Jack turned from the house to the gray thing. "I think it's a boat. No. Not a boat," he whispered. "It's not a UFO. It's a big car or a small truck. Has big fins. I need to get closer. Quiet!"

"What is it? Why did you stop talking?" Mesmer whispered.

"Someone's coming. I see two shadows carrying something. I think it's a rolled rug. Why would they take a rug from the house?"

"The missing rug from the foyer," Paul sighed.

"They don't see me here," Jack whispered. "They're putting the rug in the—"

"Putting it where, Jack?" Mesmer snapped. "Does *the boy* see?"

Jack looked around the room, and then back at the two-way mirror. "They're putting my mother into a gray 1960 Cadillac Coupe Deville. I don't know how I now know the name and make of that car. *The boy* does not have that information. I'm getting confused."

"You're okay, Jack. You are both seeing," Mesmer said. "You are *the boy*. You bring your adult-knowledge to the boy's experience. It is okay to do it. Now, tell me exactly what the two men are doing at this moment, Jack."

"My mother is rolled in the rug. I see her hair. *The boy* does not see. He is confused. He does not know mother is in danger. I see a rag tied over her mouth. She is limp. Two shadows put her in the back seat of the Cadillac. One shadow is now opening the trunk. He has a shovel in his hand. The other man is carrying a potted plant—"

The oleander, Mesmer thought. "Are they approaching you, Jack?"

"Yes. We gotta hide." Jack and *the boy* dropped to the ground behind the rock wall. "I hear them digging," he whispered. "I'm moving. I gotta get the license plate number."

"Good idea, Jack." Mesmer held his pen over his notebook and waited for it to play out.

"The car's pulling away," Jack huffed. "It crawled by me. I should be able to see. No plate. The car is sliding into the fog. A flash. Headlights! The old gray Cadillac is gone."

Mesmer watched Jack fall back onto the couch, like a man after running a marathon. He showed all the signs of physical exhaustion. Mesmer only worried about Jack's mental strength. "Did either of you see the faces of the two shadows?"

"No. Only shadows," Jack said. Then he sat up on the couch. He looked around the room. "I'm not done."

"Are you ready to revisit the second night, Jack? The night the box—"

"—is delivered," Jack finished the thought. "I'm there, now. The first day went fast after the police came. No one would talk to me. They did not ask me one question. Detective Deron told me to go to my room. Go to sleep. He would handle everything. I'm trying to talk. He grabbed my throat. He's pushed me into my room. He is angry. He locked my door."

All eyes but Jack's found Francis Deron sitting by the wall. Deron ignored them. Tate wrote in his file—*locked boy in room*. "Are you *the boy* and Jack, now?" Mesmer asked.

"Yes. Seeing through *the boy's* eyes has confused the flow of events. Something is wrong. Something is not right about last night," Jack said. "I'm trying to sort things out."

"Maybe he didn't see two shadows," Tate whispered to Paul.

"Major information like this is not confusing," Paul said. "It's gotta be timing, sequence of events. Something's out of order. It's gotta move between *the boy's* eyes and Jack's brain."

"What are you doing right now, Jack?" Mesmer asked. "Give me the time."

"After bedtime. We're sitting in the field. It is July 15, 1970...

"Wait," Jack snapped. "*The boy* is going somewhere. I need to keep up. It's almost 11:00 p.m." Jack turned to Mesmer but did not see him. "I know the killer is coming back. I am starting to think *the boy* knows it too."

"How would *the boy* know?" Paul breathed onto the glass.

"There's no way he could," Tate said, "not unless we missed something significant."

"Where is *the boy* taking you, Jack?" Mesmer asked.

"The house. Not the gates. I'm confused." Jack slid off Mesmer's couch and squatted next to it. From there he panned the room. "We're hiding in shrubs on the other side of the driveway. The junipers along the north side of the house. *The boy* is watching the house.

"Police are inside the kitchen. I see them through the window. There are five or six. I see an enormous tape recorder sitting on the counter. Police are gathered. They are talking. One is pointing at our phone. They're nervous, on edge. Something's happening."

"I was there," Deron whispered to Janice. "I was in the kitchen at 11:00 p.m. on the second night. We got a phone call at 11:00. Everyone came into the kitchen. We let it ring five times. Turned on the recorder. I remember staring at the phone

—I prayed it was a ransom call. That would mean we had a chance. Rose could still be alive."

"What's going on now, Jack?" Mesmer nudged.

"The bushes next to the house, some are shaking by the cellar doors," he whispered. "One cellar door is opening. One shadow is coming out. He is closing the door. Bent over, he's going down the driveway. He is staying on the edge of the grass under the trees. He's carrying a box. We're following him. We're staying behind bushes. He doesn't see us..."

"Jack. What's he doing?" Mesmer asked after a long stretch of silence.

"He's at the end of the driveway. Looking around and counting steps. He set the box down. He's counting more steps and moving the box."

"Oh my God," Tate gasped.

"The heart in the box came from the Burcher's cellar," Shuck sighed.

"That's why Jack got confused," Tate said. "He wasn't watching them take Rose from the house to the car." Tate closed his fat file. "He was watching them take her from the car to the cellar. Why would they take her back to the cellar the second night? The place was crawling with Tampa police and FBI? I wonder. Was Rose Burcher alive?"

"What are they doing in the cellar?" Shuck bellowed as he pulled out his cell phone and hit speed dial. "This is FBI Director Paul Shuck, ID 121149. I have a 10-31 at 14920 Crescent Drive—the Dr. Jackson Burcher estate. I need SWAT to surround the property immediately. This is a stealth operation. I don't want anyone to know we are coming or that we are on the grounds. I want Sergeant Mack Sutton to lead this operation. He knows what I want. Tell him to deploy and wait for me at the northwest gates. My 10-77 is ten minutes. Mark. Tell Sutton I will give him more details en route.

"I repeat—this is a code 2. The Burcher family killer or killers could be in the cellar of the house now." Shuck pocketed his cell and checked his gun, on the way to the door.

"Hey, I'm coming," Tate said closing his briefcase.

When Shuck opened the door, Jack Burcher's words on the private speaker stopped them in their tracks. They looked back through the observation window. Jack sat on the couch with eyes locked on the ceiling.

"I don't understand, Jack," Mesmer said. "Help me. Please tell me what you see."

"I see smoke. It is coming out of our chimney. I see sparks spraying and dying in the smoke. All of it is floating above the trees into Hillsborough Bay."

"Is there a fire in your fireplace, Jack? Can you see your fireplace?"

"No fire in our fireplace. We never have fire in the summer. Never in hot July."

My God, Paul thought. He hit speed dial again. *They dismembered and burned the body parts under our noses.*

"Shuck again. Get Hugo Novak to the Burcher residence, too. Tell him to bring a forensic team. Not sure who goes in yet. Tell Novak the crime scene will be complex—multiple cold cases at one site. I need him on standby at the gates."

"Wicked evil," Tate muttered as the door to the observation room closed behind them.

TWENTY-EIGHT

Burcher Estate – March 13, 2005 – 21:00

"I love a crisp, low-humidity night in Tampa," Moe Bullitt said, as he leaned against the rock wall by the iron gates and loaded his gun.

A sliver moon hung in an empty night sky over Ballast Point. The Tampa SWAT team had arrived at the Burcher estate seven minutes after the FBI's call. Sergeant Sutton positioned his retired Navy Seals off the banks of the Hillsborough Bay on the eastern edge of the property. They would neutralize any-and-all escape efforts by water. Land-based tactical forces, deployed in the wildflower fields and live oak trees, kept vigil along the southern and western borders. The rest of the SWAT force took the northern sector with Big Boot.

"How can you talk about the bloody weather when you could die minutes from now, old boy?" Novak pocketed his clip-on bow tie and forgot to unbutton his collar as he eyed the gates.

In tactical gear holding an M4 carbine, Sutton stared at Bullitt and Novak talking on the other side of the opened gates. When the two glanced his way, Sutton's finger zipped his lips with a swift jerk—then he showed his teeth. Bullitt nodded and smiled—*the man's always intense.*

Headlights approached. They popped off. The black Suburban crawled under the trees by the rock wall. Bullitt watched and cocked his gun. He pointed it to the ground. "To answer your question, Mr. Novak, this is what I do for a living. I often work under dangerous conditions. If I were to fret each time—I could die—I would be one miserable sot most of the time. I prefer not to be miserable, old boy." He chuckled. "I would think of all people you would understand. You are a forensic investigator, for God's sake. You are deluged in horrific, mutilated deaths every day of your life. Talk about a miserable existence."

"Yes, I am deluged in gut and gore. That, I will agree. But I am an *after-death* bloke, Mr. Bullitt. My life is not in jeopardy unless I do something quite stupid, like trip over a bloody corpse or mishandle some deadly device or potion. I can tell you this, my good man, I much prefer my arrival time to be after *danger* has departed."

"That's my point. You can slice and dice people all day long. I cannot. That would give me nightmares. I could not live with all that, as you say, gut and gore. And Mr. Novak, you cannot live with danger. We've both chosen our poison in a cruel world."

On Moe's last word, Shuck and Worthington passed by on foot with a nod on their way to Sutton. Bullitt and Novak put their debate on hold and tagged along.

"Thanks for coming to the party, Mack," Shuck said. "As I shared on the way out here, we believe one or more of the Burcher family killers are in the cellar of that house."

Sutton nodded with eyes of steel and thumb rubbing his M4 carbine like a puppy.

"What did you bring me?" Shuck asked as he panned the grounds.

"Twenty. In position. Perimeter's set—nothin' gets in or out. I'll tighten the noose when we are ready to go in." They eyed the house, the largest shadow in the darkest cluster fifty yards out. "How do you want to do this?" Sutton huffed.

Shuck unfolded a layout of the grounds with a house floorplan. "Here's where we're going in—the outside cellar doors. If we're lucky, we'll find our targets in there. Expect them to be armed and not happy to see us. I'd like to surprise them if possible, but they could already know we're here. We don't know their surveillance capabilities."

Sutton nodded. "Go on."

Paul ran a finger across the floorplan. "There are two ways into the cellar. The stairs through the kitchen pantry—here. We'll use the outside cellar doors—here. You can see they are located center-point of house. They're under thick junipers along the exterior wall. I suspect the family forgot about this cellar entry years ago. It's never been brought up. We first found them when Jack was attacked in the basement but failed to examine them closely. Padlocked outside. Tonight, we'll take a closer look."

"Ten-year-old Jack knew about 'em," Tate muttered. "In 1970 he watched someone come out those doors with a box— the one found at the end of the driveway with the heart inside."

"We now know one or more people have used this access. We don't know why or how often. It could have been only one incident, or it could be more. My gut tells me, more. I believe someone has been using the Burcher cellar for nefarious purposes for some time, doing it under the noses of the family and law enforcement for reasons yet to be defined—"

"—a sickness," Tate muttered.

"They could have butchered a lot of people down there," Paul said. "Toss body parts into an old coal-burning furnace." Sutton's eyes narrowed as he squeezed his M4 and turned to the dark shadow of the house.

"I researched the Burcher estate," Tate said. "They installed a gas furnace in the attic in 1950 and abandoned the coal furnace in the cellar. It was installed when they built the place in 1930. The iron behemoth was too big to move when abandoned. They just left it there to gather dust. No use or market for it anymore."

"Novak. For now, I want you to stay put," Shuck said. "Be ready with your team. I don't know when or if we want a forensic sweep tonight. Where are your people?"

"I assumed you might want quantity and quality, sir. We will have all forensic specialties represented and on site shortly —should you need them."

"I don't like they're not here, now. Do I need to make a call?"

Novak smiled. "No sir. I have complete authority. At the moment I'm quite certain my team is gathering their thoughts, clothing, and complex forensic toys. Several are not accustomed to venturing into the thicket, in the wee hours. Those are my scientific nerds, sir. The proverbial lab rats. When I got the message—the Burcher's cellar—I felt this time everyone needed to be on site. The family has been through much, sir. If the monster has been under the house all this time, we cannot miss a thing."

"Thanks." Paul turned to Sutton's cold eyes and cradled M4 carbine. "You good to go?"

He patted his carbine. "Say the word."

"Remember, stealth not storm. We may want to vanish without a trace later."

Sutton's thumb popped up. "I prefer surgical strikes."

They stayed under the trees along the north wall parallel to the driveway. When they reached the house, Sutton touched his throat-mic. His lips moved, "Approaching target. Tighten noose." Although the words were undetectable by those around him, his SWAT force positioned across the Burcher grounds began to close their perimeter.

Sutton crossed the driveway and squatted. A dozen, giant junipers swayed in the night breeze between him and the north side of the house. He eased into the thick evergreens followed by Shuck, Worthington, Bullitt, and his second in command, Pierce. Sutton navigated a convoluted and meandering route to the two cellar doors. His route preserved potential evidence that might be found on the more direct routes.

Beneath the massive juniper limbs were the cellar doors. Resting on a century-old stone footing, the rotted wood laid at a forty-five-degree angle against the house. Shuck and Sutton used high-tech, spot penlights to inspect the immediate area for signs of activity. They found fresh breaks on tips of overhanging juniper limbs. The linear damage aligned with the centerline of the two doors—the limbs were pinched. The mechanical damage confirmed recent activity.

Along the edge of the stone footing at the base of the entry, they found fresh scuffmarks across a thin layer of moss. Adjacent to the first stone step were fresh boot prints in the soft soil. Shuck stuck in a small wire flag to mark and preserve the physical evidence. On the cellar doors were four steel leaf hinges with crumbled layers of paint and rust buildup. It confirmed decades of age and neglect. Upon closer inspection, raw gouges on the steel pins at each barrel-knuckle joint confirmed the doors had been used often and of recent.

Sutton removed his headset, inserted stethoscope ear tips,

and held the drum to the exterior wall. After moving to several locations, he shook his head—quiet inside.

Shuck checked his watch. *It's late. If anyone's in there, they could be asleep—been a long day, Patricia's funeral and all. Or maybe they know we're here.* Shuck's eyes met Sutton's. *Could be a trap.* Sutton nodded. No one moved.

He touched his throat-mic. Only his lips moved. "Position status? Check off."

"East, check."

"South, check."

"West, check."

"North, check."

Mission parameters had been set in route to the estate. Objectives were explicit. This would be a stealth invasion. Disrupt nothing. Leave zero evidence of presence. Locate targets, neutralize and detain. No kills. FBI wanted answers, not bodies. And preserve site.

The hinges were removed from one door. It could be lifted off to provide stealth access. Shuck nodded. Sutton touched his throat-mic again. He gave the order. "GO!" A four-man assault team broke from the perimeter SWAT force and moved to the house.

Shuck and Bullitt removed the cellar door. Sutton and Pierce entered. With night-vision goggles, they descended into the pitch-black stairwell and eased into the basement. Colt M4 carbines were strapped under their arms. The noses of their Glock G17s led the way around the stacks of boxes and decades of clutter and broken furniture. Unequipped for the impromptu night mission, Shuck and Bullitt and Worthington followed their leaders into the dark, musty cellar.

Within ten seconds the four-man assault force had scaled the house and accessed the second floor. In ten more seconds, they had searched and secured that level and moved to the ground floor. In another ten, they had secured the first level and moved into position to support the cellar offensive. They would wait for orders, with fingers on earbuds and hands on AK-47s. They would move only if something went wrong or a new danger presented.

Sutton and Pierce parted to surveil opposite ends of the basement. Worthington stayed by the exterior stairwell. Shuck and Bullitt felt their way along behind Sutton, who moved from pillar to pillar and then skirted the wall on his way to the east end of the cellar—there the enormous coal furnace melded into a wall of stone, like it had more than seventy years ago.

After several minutes of navigation in dark silence, Sutton barked orders to all inside the cellar. "Everyone stop. Hold positions. I do not like this." The most experienced on the SWAT force panned the basement. He scrutinized the foggy neon-green images in his night-vision goggles, and then pressed his throat mic. "Swat-4. Descend with caution, now."

On his last word, the four specialized assault team stood at the base of the staircase with AK-47s pointed in four directions. Without night-vision goggles, and against orders, Tate left the exterior cellar doors and moved to the center aisle between the boxes. He moved toward the east stone wall. Sutton, Shuck, and Bullitt had hunkered down and were looking around the cellar with flashlights sliding across the walls. Tate stopped twenty feet from the coal furnace.

Pierce walked up behind a pillar. "West end is clear, sergeant," he said into his mic.

The SWAT-4 crouched behind boxes, uneasy. They too sensed something amiss. A dozen pillars supported old crossbeams draped in empty cobwebs. Some hung broken.

Shuck stayed down by a large, smelly pile of oily rags and paint tarps next to the furnace. In the dark, he felt for the iron door. He opened it and aimed his penlight inside. No one moved. The cellar clutter showed no signs of unusual activity—especially the wholesale butchering of people as suggested by Jack Burcher's 1970 relived experience. Maybe a man did not leave the cellar with a box containing a heart.

Sutton repeated. "Everyone, hold positions."

"What the hell," Tate bellowed, in the dark. "There's nothin' down here but all these boxes and a few dead rats in long-forgotten traps. He shined his light on one. Hell, that one's been here so long it doesn't smell anymore. I don't know why we're tippy toeing around here. Nothing in my investigation points to—"

"Nobody moves," Sutton ordered. His flashlight moved slow on the stone wall.

Fresh ashes in an abandoned furnace, Shuck thought as his penlight beam moved inside the iron belly of the old furnace. "This has been used recently," he breathed. "I think there's a second furnace door on the back." *That's odd. Is there another room—*

Tate took a step forward. "That means there's a room behind that stonewall—"

A loud pop came from the northeast corner of the cellar. Then a second. And then a third. Everyone dropped to the floor.

"Hold fire," Sutton ordered. "No one move."

They waited in silent darkness. Then came the groans. "Give me lights, now." Six bulbs, hanging from the ceiling across the length of the cellar, came alive "Is anybody hit?" Shuck queried with his face pressed to the floor by the furnace.

"Right arm," Bullitt said as he unbuttoned his shirt sleeve. "Grazed."

"Sound off people," Sutton ordered.

"Miller."

"Fenton."

"Casper."

"Jacobs."

Each stepped out from behind a pillar or a stack of boxes. Their guns were locked on the corner of the cellar.

"Pierce," Sutton bellowed. "Sound off."

"I'm here, sir." Pierce got to his feet with a hand on his chest. He winced. "Flak jacket stopped one. I'm okay, but—"

The SWAT-4 filed along the walls and closed on the east stone wall. "Rifle nozzle, sir. In the wall. Upper-right quadrant. Appears mounted in—"

"Where's Worthington," Shuck yelled. "Tate. Where are you?"

"He's here. With me," Pierce said. He got hit. It's not good."

"Everyone stays under cover and holds positions," Sutton barked. "We've got motion detectors. We don't need to trigger another."

With his face still pressed to the floor Shuck yelled, "We need paramedics."

"No. We don't, Mr. Shuck. He's gone," Pierce said. "Mr. Worthington was hit in the head. He's dead, sir."

"No," Shuck yelled.

"Sergeant," Casper called out.

"I repeat. Hold your positions," Sutton ordered. "What is it Casper?"

"I found a way through the wall, sir. It's a hidden door."

"Can you open it?" Sutton asked.

"It's ajar, sir. Maybe left like that for a reason."

"Check for a trap, Casper. Open with caution," Sutton said.

Casper pulled on the section of wall. He inspected the interface—nothing. He opened the door a few more inches— nothing. He aimed his light inside the dark space behind the wall. "There's a room back there. A big one. More stone walls." He moved his beam.

"Do you see the shooter. The weapon. Anything," Sutton barked.

"I'm moving the light along the walls and now ceiling," Casper said. "Found it, sir. Ceiling mounted. A rifle. The barrel poking through the east wall of the cellar, sir. I can see some kind of electronic triggering device. I see wires."

Motion detection, Sutton thought. "Okay." He pressed his mic. "SWAT-4 enter the room behind the east wall of the cellar with extreme caution. We have motion-triggered weaponry on site. Search and secure. Standard procedure. Report back when you confirm danger neutralized."

"Disturb nothing," Shuck whispered to Sutton. "We do not want anyone to know we've been here."

Sutton nodded. "Disturb nothing, SWAT-4... If you find the shooter, kill the bastard. That's an order. Now go!"

TWENTY-NINE

Burcher Estate – 21:30

"No," Shuck shouted. "Do not kill anyone. I want them alive, Mack. We need answers."

Sergeant Mack Sutton growled as he turned back to his men. "Let the bastard live. Now go!" The four scrambled through the portal. The others held their positions. Sutton stood ready to shoot the first thing that pissed him off.

With head low, Shuck crawled to Tate. Pierce backed away and covered the FBI director with furtive eyes and an M4. As Shuck neared the body, he could see the growing pool of blood under Tate's head. He saw the gunshot wound in his forehead. Tate died instantly.

With a pass of his hand, Shuck closed Tate's glassy eyes. *I didn't know you long, my friend. I guess this was gonna be the only way you'd leave this world—hunting a monster. Me too. I promise you—we will get this one.*

Bullitt threw an old army blanket over the body. The two straightened it and sat in silence as Sutton's men did their jobs.

The hidden door moved. Guns raised. "It's me." Casper's muffled words came from behind the door in the stone wall. It opened without a sound. Casper leaned his head out, his mic and earbuds hanging from his neck and goggles on his forehead.

"Status report, lieutenant," Sutton ordered.

"Empty, sir. Four rooms. First one is biggest. Then a narrow tunnel or hallway connects three smaller rooms. No one back there, sir. Place is empty of life. Team's lookin' for other ways out, sir. Place is secured."

Sutton held up a hand. "More on layout, Casper. We'll get to contents later."

"The big room has stone walls like the cellar. The tunnel-hall and other three rooms are mostly cement with rocks here and there. Ceilings are boarded. There are stabilizing pillars."

"I doubt there's another access point," Shuck said. "But keep looking."

"The mounted rifle shot three times," Casper continued. "A wired trigger mechanism—motion detection. We left it alone. It only had three rounds. They were spent. No other traps."

We missed the damn rifle, Sutton mused. *No excuse.*

"There is a lightbulb hanging from the ceiling in each room. The big room has two. One over a large table. The other near the old furnace. The place stinks, Sergeant."

"We're coming in," Sutton barked.

Each stepped around the pile of oil rags and passed through the eye-burning stench of turpentine to enter the hidden lair. The six-foot by three-foot hinged door had chiseled rocks cemented to a wire mesh. When closed, it blended perfectly with the east rock wall.

When they entered the room, the stench of turpentine faded and the stench of decay, fresh blood, dirt, and mildew grew. Shuck first examined the rock wall on the other side. "This has been treated with epoxies and silicone sealants."

"Hermetically sealed," Bullitt muttered.

"Explains why the dogs didn't find this place. The turpentine-rag pile and the silicone barrier treatment isolated it. I suspect the all walls and ceilings have been treated."

"A bit more advanced than I would have envisioned," Bullitt groaned.

"Everyone," Sutton barked. "A reminder. Eyes open. Still could be more traps. We don't need to lose anyone else tonight."

"We will hold off on forensics until we are sure it's safe," Shuck said. "And people. Do not disturb anything. Eye's only."

"There's gotta be a lot of good evidence in here," Bullitt said.

"I agree. And it will be here later. Right now, no one knows we found this place."

"We've been all over this property," Moe muttered. "I can't believe we missed this."

"I'm sure our killer thinks his secret is still safe," Shuck said. "We may use that."

Sutton walked a beeline to the front corner of the room and ran a slow light over the dusty rifle mounted in the ceiling. "Casper's right. Muzzle's pokin' through the wall into the cellar. Set off by motion detection in one targeted location. A scrutiny point."

"Tate stepped into the wrong place," Shuck sighed.

At the opposite corner of the large room, Bullitt lifted the edge of a collapsed cardboard box atop a stack of 20. "The infamous box." He took a picture of the logo with his cell.

"This place is too elaborate for a root cellar," Shuck said.

The Bullitt family-tree got planted in Florida in the 1800s," Moe said. "My ancestors did a lot of things: chimney sweeps, woodcutters, coal delivery service, horse breeders, and farmers. I was the first cop. Anyway, we never had a root cellar. They were not common. Hell, cellars were rare. The ground around here is 90% sand. Looks like the Burcher family spent a lot of money digging this thing and building the stonewalls. I read root cellars can keep food around 40° Fahrenheit year-round. It was the pre-refrigeration era when they built this house. I suppose rich people could do just about anything they wanted."

"They built this house in 1930," Shuck said. "I suspect the root cellar had a food storage purpose in the beginning, Moe." He peered into the tunnel. Soft light poured from the other three rooms onto the dirt floor. "Something changed... Maybe 1948. The death of Leonard Burcher in Pasadena. Maybe Otto Burcher knew more about that than we know today."

"I gotta agree," Bullitt said.

"This place sheds new light, on the Burcher family mystery. Otto had some unusual concerns. He had to know about the conversion of the root cellar into a secret place." Shuck leaned over the single large piece of furniture in the room as his words sunk into moment. "Maybe meant to be a saferoom."

The long heavy table, with fat legs implanted into the cement floor, had a gnarled surface riddled with cracks and pits and deep gouges. At one end two blood-encrusted iron spikes were hammered an inch into the wood. At the other end, a single large spike stuck out of the wood.

Shuck moved a slow penlight over the surface. He examined stains. "This table had to be repurposed by a monster. It is where victims were dissected. Forensics will tell us who."

"This is a horror show," Bullitt muttered.

Sutton's impatient eyes darted around the room as he waited for the next report from his men. "The small spikes probably pinned ankles to the table," Shuck continued. "The big one pinned the upper torso. It would be pounded through the throat."

Bullitt opened an old chest under his end of the table. "Found his toolbox. We have knives, mallets, a hatchet, saws, icepicks, pliers, scissors, and a scalpel with replaceable blades."

"Sick," Sutton growled.

"And a bloody sledgehammer behind you, Moe." Shuck's eyes found blood-soaked ropes draped over a hook in the ceiling. "Bet those tethered victims. Seen it before. On a torture-table like this one. They tie a wrist, run the rope under the table, and tie the other wrist. Pull it tight. Leaves the person helpless—cannot escape what comes next."

Bullitt leaned over an imbedded spike. "Fresh blood on this one," he said.

With the toe of his boot, Sutton eased a large stainless-steel pail from under the table and shined a light inside. He snapped it off and looked away. "Clotted blood and scraps of flesh."

"Probably put body parts in the bucket," Moe said.

"Carried it to the furnace." Shuck opened the iron grate. The hinges whined. "Burned whole bodies one piece at a time." His light moved in the belly of the furnace. The beam found the charred head of a femur poking out of the ashes. *Bet we're gonna find Rose and Ronan here.*

"This explains the smoke Jack saw the second night," Shuck said.

"Hypnosis?" Bullitt asked. "Jack agreed? I did not know. When?"

"Tonight. Few attended. Me and Tate watched from an observation room. Frank Deron and Dr. Janice were in the back of the room where Dr. Mesmer hypnotized Jack."

"Deron was there?"

"Yes."

"You do know Francis Deron is no longer with the Tampa Police Department, right?"

"Yes. I do."

"You know they retired him against his will and made me interim Chief, right."

"I know that too, Moe."

"He should not have been there, Paul."

"I assumed you sent him. When Tate and I arrived, Deron and Janice were in the room with Jack and Mesmer, and the session had already begun."

"I need to handle this with Frank. Right now, Jack's new information is our focus." Moe took in the dismal surroundings. "We are standing in a devil's workshop."

"I'm sorry for not thinking, Moe."

"Not your fault. Francis Deron knew exactly what he was doing. Let's move on."

You knew what you were doing, Bullitt fumed. *You are barred from the Burcher case, the only specific directive on the day of your release. Why risk losing your severance package? A cop all your life. Don't you need the money? Why did you need to hear Jack under hypnosis? We're all trying to cut you some slack, but this is more than crossing the line.*

"Dr. Mesmer took Jack back to 1970," Paul said. "Jack described smoke pouring from their chimney the second night. Jack, the ten-year-old boy, said his family never had a fire in July. That makes perfect sense. Under hypnosis Jack knew someone was burning something in the old furnace in the cellar, and the police were just standing around in the kitchen. Was a monster burning his mother? The combination of visuals would be enough to screw up any kid scared to death over the abduction of his mother."

"Doesn't take a psychologist to know he thought a monster

was burning his mother in the cellar and the cops didn't care," Sutton said.

"He had to be petrified," Moe sighed.

"About an hour ago we learned Jack had inadvertently rearranged the order of some events. Mesmer said repression is only one way to escape pain. Another is *obscure confusion*."

"Mess up the order of things to avoid the path to a painful truth," Moe said.

"Yes. Do you recall Jack talking about a UFO? He said a shadow from that UFO left a box at the end of his driveway?"

"Of course, I remember," Moe said.

"Under hypnosis, that story changed. Jack saw what really happened. Instead of a shadow from the UFO leaving a box at the end of the driveway, Jack saw a shadow come out the cellar carrying a box. That shadow met another shadow at the gates. The two positioned the box."

"Two people. What was Jack's UFO?"

"He said it was a gray 1960 Cadillac Coup de Ville."

"The growling thing, a Cadillac idling. The headlights, popping on and off in the fog, turned into a flying saucer in young Jack's imagination."

"He did not see one man take his mother from the house to the car, Moe. He saw two men carry her, in a rolled-up rug, to the car July 14. He saw them carry her back to the cellar the night of July 15. Later that night the two shadows met at the gates and positioned the box that was brought from the cellar of the Burcher mansion."

"She was down here all the time," Moe said.

"We've been all over this property many years. I can't believe we did not find this root cellar." Shuck touched the belly of the furnace. "It never dawned on us this thing could be used to cremate people. We didn't smell it because they burned body parts in the middle of the night."

"What kind of evil kills and dismembers its victims in the victims' home?"

"And what keeps a monster killing for decades?"

Pierce entered the room from the tunnel/hallway. He slid his Glock into its holster and waited for heads to turn. "You need to see this."

The three followed Pierce into the tunnel and turned into the first room.

Can this nightmare get any more chilling, Shuck wondered? He took a deep breath and led the way inside. At the back of the fifteen-foot square room, Casper stood next to an opened coffin sitting atop a closed coffin. Shuck looked inside. "Holy Mother of Mary—"

Bullitt and Sutton eased up on each side and froze. Sutton's lips did not move. He spoke through gritted teeth. "Pierce. Assign one man to each room, two to the large room, four to the cellar, and two on each floor. Put my perimeter on high alert.

"Nobody gets on this property until Shuck and Bullitt tell us what will be done here."

"Sir?" Casper said.

"What," Sutton growled.

"The other two rooms, sir. There's more—"

"Anything alive? Anything represent immediate danger, lieutenant?"

"No sir. Bizarre—"

"Bizarre we can handle on our time. Now move, son."

"Yes, sir." Casper ran out of the room.

"Was this man missing?" Sutton asked.

"No. I saw him at the funeral today."

Bullitt pulled out his cell. "I've got to call this in, Paul."

"I know," he breathed. "But I don't want anyone out here. We need radio silence."

"Are you thinking we set a trap?" Moe asked.

"Yes. We leave everything as is," he whispered. The FBI controlled the scene.

Moe pressed his cell to his ear. "Gompers. We have two bodies—Tate Worthington and David Burcher. I need CSI on standby. Radio silence. No one comes onto the Burcher estate. I repeat. No one comes onto the Burcher estate. We have an active crime scene. A killer nearby."

"Got it." Gompers waved at dispatch. "Is Dr. Burcher with you?"

"No. And he does not know his brother is dead? I need you to call Dr. William Janice. Jack Burcher is at their clinic, Bayshore Gardens. Jack's in a private session with a Dr. Mesmer. Janice and Mesmer are partners. Tell Dr. Janice we found David Burcher dead in the root cellar at the Burcher estate. Janice will know how to pass this devastating information to Jack. Janice is a psychiatrist and friend of the family.

"We cannot allow Jack Burcher to come here. Send officers to the clinic to detain him until Interim Chief Bullitt releases him. Notify Dr. Quin—Assistant M.E. We need her on standby. For now, we are not moving the bodies."

"Anything else?"

"Find Melissa, Jack Burcher's sister. She is in immediate danger, Raymond. This thing's escalating. The Burcher family killer has taken two family members in one week. There are only three family members left—Jack, Melissa, and the grandmother, Emily. Someone go to Sun Bay and guard her room, even though I doubt they will try Sun Bay a second time."

"Any suggestions on where to start looking for Melissa Burcher?"

"Bird Island. At the funeral she said she would be going out there to deal with a weather-related bird crisis."

Sutton and Pierce met in the tunnel. "Take over team coordination, Pierce. I need to look around this place. My gut tells me the sick bastard's still around somewhere. That body's warm. I bet we're sitting on top of a damn ant farm."

"Yes, sir."

Bullitt pocketed his cell and returned back to the coffin and Shuck. "We're set." He leaned over. "I'm no forensic guy, but David hasn't been dead long."

Shuck felt the neck. "I'd guess less than six hours."

"That'd put it close to the end of the funeral."

"I saw him leave early. He told me he was opening the house for a small reception. Said Melissa would not make it because of the bird thing, and Jack had cases waiting at the morgue." Shuck wiped his eyes. "David said they had a lot of *gifted food* to get rid of. His words." Shuck dropped his head. "He didn't want any of this."

"I know. It's tough. We've been working on this forever. Gotten close to everyone."

"We are starting to get somewhere at a terrible price."

"The bastard probably clobbered David at the back door," Moe said. "Knocked him out. Dragged him down here and killed him. I wonder what's with the blanket over his legs."

It covered David from the waist down. "Looks like he tucked David in after he killed him. I'm sure it means something."

"You think there's another body in the box under David?"

"It is possible, but we can't look. We can't touch anything. Not now. When we're ready, we will get a forensic sweep. Right now, I want to leave everything the way we found it."

"What do you make of the crescent-shaped stain on David's shirt? You think he cut out David's heart?"

"The shirt had to be removed prior to the six-inch chest wound. If not, it would be torn and bloodstained. There's only the arc stain—serum. I think it is drainage from a surgical incision. Not a stab wound. He put the shirt back on David after the procedure, and after the body had been cleaned. Postmortem seepage. David is as white as a sheet. He lost a lot of blood. I do not see a lot of blood anywhere down here."

Bullitt pulled out his pen and notepad. "There's gotta be a drain somewhere."

"Our killer is moving faster," Shuck muttered. *I need to get everyone out of here—*

"You need to come with me!" The six words rolled into the room and knocked the pen out of Bullitt's hand and Shuck against the wall.

Sutton's titanic hulk filled the entry. Light from the lame lightbulb in the room found Sutton's hard face and cold eyes. No more words were necessary. They followed.

Minutes after Tate had died and David Burcher's warm corpse had been found, Paul realized he had one chance to catch the monster. Another grisly discovery would shake him to his bones. The Burcher nightmare intensified. The monster had taken control.

THIRTY

East Bank – March 13, 2005 – 22:00

F ew Hillsborough County residents knew the Alafia River had a second branch. North of Gibsonton, the primary tributary feeds a major shipping channel in the bay. The meager branch of the Alafia snakes through some very private land and pours hazardous waste into the bay.

Gibsontonians could only scratch their heads and watch the local fishing business fail. Then, in 1993, the Alafia Audubon Society noticed a significant decline in bird populations on Bird Island and on the east banks. Three years later, they discovered a drop in marine life in the same area and tracked it to the mouth of the meager branch of the Alafia. Another year later they tracked the problem to the back door of the Meriam Corporation. The global phosphorus-mining company had been illegally disposing of toxic waste for several decades.

Hillsborough County filed their lawsuit against Meriam in 1997. Five years later the $2 billion settlement seemed fair, but no amount of money could save all the spoiled land on the east bank. The county fenced it off and designate it as permanent-closure areas—no trespassing. Restoration of the marine life would take a decade following the cleanup operation. Recovery of the delicate bird sanctuaries would take longer.

The county mourned the loss of Gibsonton's local fishing businesses. The absence of fishermen on the east bank would be a sad reminder of a terrible tragedy. But there was one who reveled in the moment. For him the EPA catastrophe only validated his twisted mission. He did not need eyes on the east bank or boats in the water. He needed at least one place on the bay where he could hide and launch his unregistered boat. For him the permanent-closure areas and the poison branch of the Alafia River were wonderful.

His stealth voyages were always on a schedule. He only floated under a sliver moon—enough light to see but not enough to be seen. He navigated the robust shipping traffic, wild Bull Shark breeding cycles, changing tides, and an armada of bay-area security forces looking for drugs and illegal entries. By the time he set the fires on Bird Island, he had mastered it all. Now, with the total abandonment of a large section of the east banks of Hillsborough Bay, continuation of his night voyages would be less risky.

On March 13, 2005, he got to his boat at 22:00. He had less than twenty minutes to push the old Scout into the water and turn it's bow on the narrow sandbar. The water was rising. Waist deep he could reorient the boat with his hands alone. It was the only way for one person to handle the old Scout. And the sliver moon was the only way to navigate the very tight tributary without damaging the hull on the sharp rocks.

His launch sand bar would return in twelve hours—low tide. But this time it did not matter. He would not return to Gibsonton to hide the boat. This time he would land on Bird

Island, terminate all witnesses, and take Melissa Burcher dead or alive to the Ballast Point Pier, on the opposite side of the bay. While in route he would alert the Hillsborough County Sheriff's Office to the dreadful tragedy awaiting them on Bird Island. That multiple-homicide crime scene would capture all the hearts and minds of Tampa law enforcement, the medical examiner's office, FBI, and news media. The blood bath on Bird Island would provide the diversion he needed. His plans were always well thought out.

He did not like mooring the Scout at the Ballast Point Pier. Too conspicuous. But he had a few loose ends to attend to, and it was the most expeditious way to move Melissa from Bird Island into the Burcher root cellar. The house would be empty. If there were visitors, he knew how to enter without detection. He had done it often for many years.

THIRTY-ONE

Burcher Estate – 23:00

Shuck and Bullitt followed Sutton into the next light. It reached out of the next room onto the floor of the tunnel. Sutton stayed outside. With sweat dripping from his forehead, Shuck took a deep breath, held it, and went inside.

He saw another dust-covered bulb on another rotting electrical cord hanging from more of the patchwork ceiling of old wood and empty webs. "My God. A trophy room—"

Bullitt entered next. "We need more light," he grumbled as he looked at the floor.

"No. We need to get out of the root cellar."

"He's coming back, isn't he?"

"Yes. He's not done with this... thing."

It sat on four fat-legged stools waist high. The seven-foot long, black metal box had crumbling-rust corners and a dirt-dusted plexiglass lid with crumbling-rust hinges.

"I don't need to tell you. Touch nothing. Especially the lid." He breathed through his mouth as he leaned closer.

"I see 'em. Fingerprints. This thing's been opened recently. I mean like hours. You can see fresh smudges here and here. There's a dozen good prints."

"I now understand David's blanket," Shuck muttered.

"Are those his legs on this thing?" Bullitt groaned.

The naked, hairy, pink-skinned legs—from the knees down —still oozed blood along the stitch line. "They appear to be the newest additions," Shuck said through a cupped hand. "He's been creating an *aggregate trophy* by connecting body parts from each victim going back to—"

"—Leonard Burcher? You think?"

"I do. Some parts are mummified—treated with a preservative. Some parts are relatively new in comparison. Everything is decaying. Look at the fungus. Probably sprays it."

"Frankenstein," Sutton seethed through his gritted teeth.

The bloated abomination beneath the Plexiglas filled the metal box. The zombie-like, disfigured female head with long straw-like hair did not fit the large shoulders of the male torso. The high cheekbones, small nose, small ears, small mouth, and narrow eyebrows belonged to a woman. The oversized eyes forced into blood-encrusted sockets were of different shapes and colors. And they were decomposing on different timelines.

The mottled skin of the head and neck had been sewn onto the decaying torso covered in fuzzy mold and a gangrene roadmap of blood clots and vessels that revealed an extensive bacterial feast. Some of the dark, leathery skin oozed at injection sites—a feeble attempt to inject preservatives. The two arms did not match. One was male, the other female, both covered in bruises and contusions and fungus. The same extremes appeared with the thighs. The abdomen was as big as a watermelon. The below-the-knee legs matched perfectly. They were new. They had belonged to David Burcher just hours before.

There was a 24 inch by 12 inch rectangular flap of leathery skin on the chest. Sewn at the top, and with a zipper at the bottom, it provided convenient access to the thoracic and abdominal cavities. "I suspect the flap allowed him to drop in various organs," Shuck said. "I assume there is some sick, symbolic collection inside."

"I know those words—thoracic and abdominal," Bullitt muttered. "Maybe we'll find some of Rose Burcher's and Ronan Burcher' organs in there."

"It's time," Sutton said. "What do you want to do? We are exposed here. We are either in this or not."

Shuck gently guided Bullitt away from the horrific creation. "We need to get out of here. Remember. He's coming back. We've got a lot to do."

"How can you be so sure he's coming back?" Bullitt muttered in a trance-like state.

"No feet, Moe."

"Shit. Left something for Melissa."

"I suspect he wants her feet and Jack's brain. Just guessing."

"You think the head's empty?"

"I do," Shuck muttered. "This guy's work is almost done. This thing has some symbolic meaning. Melissa, Jack, and maybe Grandma Em finish the twisted masterpiece."

"Lord help us," Bullitt sighed.

Shuck nudged Bullitt toward the doorway. "None of our people are coming down here tonight. I want everyone gone. Now. I'm staying. Alone."

"I'm not leaving," Sutton said from the hallway.

"Yes. You are Mack. This belongs to the FBI. You have no rights. And I know you want to do what's best for the operation. What's best is for everyone to leave. This guy is smart. It will be hard enough for just one person to hide and wait. It would be impossible for more than one. We cannot afford a single mistake. I've got one shot. I cannot miss this opportunity."

Sutton nodded with a grimace. He would execute the order regardless of his feelings.

"Detective Bullitt. You must keep this off the radio. No transmissions. I am one-hundred percent certain this bastard listens to police bands. One comment can get someone killed or we could lose him. Do you understand?"

"Like the Sergeant, I don't like you being here alone, but I understand the logic. I will make sure nothing gets out on this."

"I also leave the TPD with the task of securing Melissa Burcher's safety."

"Quick update on that. We sent people to Bird Island. They should be there soon. They have not checked back yet."

Shuck turned to Sutton. "I need you to tell Novak to get all forensic and CSI people off Ballast Point. Remind them radio silence. No talk offline on this operation or anything to do with the Burcher family case."

Sutton nodded and touched his throat mic. Instantly his orders were transmitted to his people. They closed on the CSI and forensic personnel outside the gates.

Bullitt pocketed his cell. "We asked the Bay Patrol to land on Bird Island, stealth mode. They have. They're not responding."

"What does that mean?"

"It could mean a lot of things, Paul."

"Give me most likely, Moe," Shuck pushed.

"They're closing in on something and can't talk."

"Or they have a problem on Bird Island," Shuck countered.

"That's another possibility. We sent three of our best—"

"Only three?"

"Give it time, Paul. I could hear back at any moment."

"Has anyone tried Melissa's cell?"

"Of course. No answer." Moe looked at his phone. "Wait. I'm getting a text."

"Please be good news," Shuck muttered as Sutton rounded-up his men.

"Not good news," Bullitt looked up. "Jack Burcher climbed out a bathroom window at Mesmer's clinic. No one knows where he—"

"Does Jack know about his brother?" Shuck asked.

"Yes. He did not take it well, as could be expected. And, we just found someone sleeping in the boathouse."

"Again? Just now? What the hell," Shuck exploded. "We need to get control of—"

"It is Buford Penland," Sutton said.

"The groundskeeper," Bullitt laughed. "That's hilarious. He's an old guy."

"How did your men miss him, Mack?" Shuck asked.

"He was under a pile on a bunk. Sleeping under clothes, towels, and life vests tossed on the bunk. Basic boathouse crap. The man is out cold. Found hugging a half-empty whiskey bottle."

"Wonderful." Shuck rubbed his forehead. "Okay. I don't think he's a risk. Just leave him there. Don't wake him. Let him sleep it off. Hell. Probably more normal for him to be out there than not. Will help the optics."

Bullitt leaned in. "I agree. He's not our serial killer."

"Jack told me today Penland's been with them over fifty years."

Sutton turned off his head mic. "Everyone's left Ballast Point. We're the only ones here except my man with Penland. He's on his way out of here now."

"What about the cellar doors! We took one side off its hinges. We need to—"

"Already been put back the way it was," Bullitt said. "And I removed the blanket from Tate. He's where he dropped."

"It's terrible to leave him there, but I think he would want to be part of setting the trap for this bastard. I need you guys to go, now. Leave the root-cellar door like we found it—ajar."

Sutton handed Shuck his Glock. "I know you have your own. Do me a favor. Put this somewhere as backup. You never know."

"I don't like it, but I think you're right. If we're lucky I will confront a killing machine."

"One with a lot of experience and knowledge of this room."

Bullitt patted Shuck on his back. "Don't forget, Jack may show up. Try not to shoot him."

Paul chuckled. "Thanks for the reminder, Moe."

"When I get to the station, I'll pull the cars off him. We don't need a bunch of cops crawlin' all over Ballast Point messing up our trap."

"Go, gentlemen."

Bullitt and Sutton disappeared. Shuck checked his gun a last time and unscrewed the bulb over the table. He hid the Glock and turned out the lights.

Shuck crawled under the long table and pulled the disgusting pail of coagulated blood and guts to its original position. They left the root-cellar door ajar.

Paul hunkered down for a chilling wait. He hung his head in an awkward position to avoid the underside of the butcher's table. Decades of dried blood and tissue hung from between the cracks like brittle strings of spaghetti.

Let this be my time, Paul prayed. He blinked several times to adjust to the pitch black, but it did not help. *Please return to your sick den of death, the secret place where you do your work and laugh at the broken family above. What kind of monster are you? I don't ask much. If you have Melissa, please bring her here alive.*

THIRTY-TWO

Bayshore Gardens — March 13, 2005 – 21:30

T he ocean-blue metallic Chevrolet parked in the darkest corner of the lot at the Bayshore Fitness Center. She turned off the car and looked at her text message again. She was in the right place.

When the gym parking lot settled down, a shadow left nearby bushes. He slid into the car on the passenger side, closed the door, and sunk in the seat. Seconds after the interior lights went out, another police car crawled down Isabella Avenue.

"Wait." He watched the squad car disappear. "Okay. Go, now."

The Chevy lights popped on. "What's this all about?" She started the car, rolled to the gym entrance, and paused.

"In a minute." He squinted. "Okay, take a right and another right on Santiago. Just drive, please." He looked over his shoulder, and then checked his watch.

The blue Chevy merged into light traffic onto Isabella. "I don't like this—"

"I need to get out of Bayshore Gardens. They'll be in Ballast Point, too. I gotta go there. Okay? Take Granada to Grady. Then you will make a left—southbound—and then another left into Virginia Park. I know it's a lot of side roads, but we will be going in the right direction. I need time to think. Does anyone know you're—"

"—breaking my boyfriend out of the Bayshore Gardens Psychiatric Clinic? No. Remember, I live alone with a cat.

"I don't know what's going on, Jack. But I do have an important deposition in the morning. One I cannot miss. A new law firm for me. I don't know why some people think Asians can't transcribe as well as you Caucasians."

"Tell me about it," Jack said as he scanned the parallel streets for police cruisers. "I won't keep you long. You'll make your court date."

"I thought the Mesmer thing was voluntary," Kayda said. "You were looking forward to it. What happened. Am I breaking laws by helping you escape? Why are police looking for you? I mean I'll help, but I like knowing the laws I'm breaking so I can plan my prison life." She chuckled.

"He killed my brother, Kayda."

She pulled to the side and hit the brakes. "Oh my God, Jack. David is—"

"What are you doing," Jack yelled as cars honked and went around them flashing their lights and middle fingers. "Right now, I need you to drive me, Kayda. Please. I need to blend."

She pulled back onto the road and drove south. "Tell me. What happened to David?"

"The monster that has been killing my family killed my brother today." Jack dropped his head, his whole body trembled. I can't do this anymore. It ends tonight."

Kayda reached for him and rubbed the back of his neck as she watched the road. "I'm sorry, Jack. This is terrible. I don't understand why they would kill David."

Jack rubbed his eyes clear. "It must stop." He blinked away the pain and anguish.

"Is it possible your information is wrong? Is it possible David is—"

"—alive? No. David is dead. The TPD sent a small army to the clinic to keep me there. They knew I'd go berserk. I gotta give 'em that.

"Nothing Janice said to me helped. I could hardly breathe. All I saw was red. They didn't want to tell me anything. They just wanted to sedate me like my father 35 years ago. I would not allow it. From the bathroom I heard 'em talking in the next room. David was killed in our house. Idiots. They never should have left me alone in the bathroom. I handled the second floor drop easy. Landed in thick bushes, thank God. I was leaving that place one way or the other."

"I don't think you should do anything. Not now. Not when you're like this."

"I buried Patricia this morning," he seethed. "This afternoon the monster kills David. He's no longer playing by rules—following the deaths of Manhattan Project elites. He's tying-up loose ends. Or, he's gone rogue. All the elites are dead now. All of 'em. Hans Bethe was the last one. David, Melissa, and me, we are the loose ends. He wants to finish it. Exterminate the Burcher family from the planet as if we never—

"—park over there." Jack boomed. He pointed to an apartment complex. "Park in the middle of all the cars. Turn everything off."

Jack looked at Kayda. He saw her for the first time since he got in the car. He watched her push down the clutch, her shapely, tan thigh hardened. He watched her long black hair fall forward and arms flex as she downshifted. Kayda was beautiful, but he did not really know her.

Her hair flew over her shoulder. It revealed her high cheekbones and big eyes. Even while drowning in his heart-wrenching pain, he was drawn to her. She was the place he went to escape his dark world. But now, after hypnosis, his eyes were opened all the way. Dr. Mesmer gave Jack access to all the missing pieces to the puzzle. Now, his forensic expertise and adult intellect made it possible to reconstruct all of his observations, impressions, and memories.

Kayda parked. "There. We are invisible, for the moment." She turned off the car and turned a smile to Jack. Another police car went by. "That's the seventh I've seen tonight. You think they're looking for you or this killer."

She slid over. They wrapped arms around each other. Jack stared at the sliver moon and Kayda smelled his hair. "I'm sorry. David should not have died today."

Not died, today? Jack thought. *That's an odd way to say it. Maybe it's a Japanese thing.* His phone vibrated. "A text, Dr. Quin."

"Why would she—?"

"She probably doesn't know '*not to talk to me*'. I bet she's on standby. Being kept in the dark. They know her loyalty."

"Or, they could be using her to find you," Kayda said. "You know they can track your cellphone. You need to turn it off. They could have coordinates on you now."

"I will. But first I need to see what she's trying to tell me." He opened messages. "She's been turned away from my brother's death scene. I wonder why they would do that."

"Death scene," Kayda said. "You mean your house, right?"

"Yes. At the clinic I heard root cellar."

"Root cellar," Kayda gasped. "Are you sure they found David in the root cellar?"

"Why are you reacting like that?" *Do you know something I don't know?*

Kayda looked away. "I just did not expect to hear such a thing. I'm sorry."

"No. I'm sorry. I snapped. Of course, it's shocking. The killer had to be hiding in the house. He got David after the funeral. David left early to get things ready for the—"

Kayda still looked away. "I wanted to be there. I wanted to support you, but it I felt it would be inappropriate. Me being at your ex-wife's funeral. Now I wish I had gone. Maybe I would have been with David. Maybe if both of us went to the house together it would have made a difference."

You would have been killed, too, Jack thought. "There was nothing any of us could have done. David had to be next on the kill list." He pulled Kayda close. They embraced. They kissed hard and got lost in each other's eyes. He held her. He loved her. The parking lot light spilled into the moonroof and washed over the backseat. Jack saw fresh dirt on the seat—potting soil.

"Was anyone else hurt?" she asked.

He blinked away his wild thought. "Tate Worthington is dead."

"The private investigator? How?"

"I heard he was shot in the head, in my cellar. All I know."

Another squad car sped by. "Jack. You need to turn off your phone."

"Quin said they found our groundskeeper. Drunk. Sleeping in the boathouse."

"Jack. Please. Turn off your phone. They will find you." The next squad car crawled by the parking lot. "I think they're—"

"Buford never goes in the boathouse," Jack muttered. "He

has a phobia—a fear of water and closed-in places. The boathouse is double-trouble. There's no way he'd go in that boathouse on his own. He can't even swim. And he does not drink alcohol. Something's not right. I've known Buford as long as I can remember. I have never seen him drink alcohol."

Kayda removed Jack's cellphone from his hand. "I'm going to turn this off for you." She watched it power down and flicker off. Then she slid it back into his hand. "Did you say your groundskeeper's name is Buford?"

Jack blinked back into the car and smiled at Kayda. "We need to get to South Manhattan Road. We gotta go now, Kayda. Please. Drive. We can talk on the way."

She started the car. "Okay."

"I need to get inside my house tonight."

"I'm pretty sure Ballast Point will be crawling with police, Jack. You think maybe we should wait until things settle down some?"

"I have a plan. Please, just do what I say. You can drop me. Go home and keep your deposition appointment. I don't want you implicated."

"I can't just drop you off, Jack. The police are looking for you because they're trying to protect you. Someone dangerous is out there looking for—"

"—Melissa. Not looking for me." Jack gently squeezed her knee—always his way of saying he loved her without words or eyes. "I know what I'm doing for the first time in my life. I promise I will be okay. I'm not a target. Not yet." *And I will use that to my advantage.*

She pulled out of the lot. "What does that mean—you're not the target, yet."

Jack looks around. Streets are quiet. "It means I will be the last Burcher to face this killer—"

On his terms, Jack thought. *I need to face him on my terms.* "Right now, the killer is focused on Melissa.

He's saving me for last, Jack thought. *Paul Shuck knows this, too. The FBI and TPD are protecting my sister tonight. I'm sure they did not want me to get in their way, something I've done a lot of for a very long time. Mesmer opened my eyes. It's all very clear, now. I know exactly what I must do...*

"How did the hypnotism go?" She asked.

Jack studied the lady he loved as she watched the road. "I wish I had done it a long time ago. Everything's coming together, Kayda. *I must get into the root cellar,* Jack thought. *I will find the rest of the pieces to this horrific puzzle.*

A squad car came up behind them. Jack gripped her leg and sunk in his seat. The police passed. "Tell me more about the groundskeeper," Kayda said. "How old is this man, Buford?"

"Turn here."

She turned onto South Manhattan. "He's seventy something. He's been taking care of our place for a very long time."

"How long?"

"Take a right on Gandy. Blend. Buford's been taking care of our place since I was a kid. I'd say fifty-plus years. Buford is the first black man I ever knew. We was my first friend."

"My God. Is Buford's last name Penland?"

"Yes. How would you know—?"

"I remember my uncle talking about a Buford Penland a very long time ago."

"You're uncle?" Jack squinted at the next street sign. "Take a right on MacDill."

Kayda turned. "I was a child. My mother died from cancer when I was eight. My father and uncle moved me from Pasadena, California to Tampa in 1968. A year after we moved, my father died of cancer. I was raised by my uncle and the very small downtown Asian community."

"You never told me."

"Because I ran away from that life. Although I am thankful for the people who watched out for me, I was still alone. I hurt. Missed my mother and father. I wanted more in life. I think that's what saved me. I worked hard and went after every opportunity to break free."

"You're even more incredible than I thought," Jack whispered. "No wonder I fell in love with you." He gently squeezed her knee again and scanned the area. "Tell me more about your uncle and Buford. Were they friends or acquaintances."

"I remember my uncle met with him one night. I never saw a black man before, not in our poor Asian neighborhood. They were friends. They talked about starting a landscape business."

"Okay. I remember Buford started a landscape business. He presented his business plan to my father. Ronan gave him money. Helped him get started."

"Your father helped Buford Penland?"

"Oh yes. He helped a lot of people. I remember Buford ran out of money many times and my father helped him many times. At some point my father did say no more."

"Turned him away?"

"Not really. Just tried to get Buford to change his approach. He already had a job for as long as he wanted it. Made good money. Flexible hours. My father even guided him on building a business. He told Buford it would take time to do it right. Said save your money. Build the landscape business one customer at a time, like every other business. My father tried to teach him the importance of managing his cashflow—

"Turn onto Interbay. We will exit on Lykes. We're going to Jules Vern Park, on the bay."

"Mr. Penland came to our apartment one night in 1970. He talked to my uncle in the alley. It was late. Dark that night. I sat on the fire escape above them. My private place."

"1970? Do you remember the month?" *My world changed on July 14th that year.*

"I do. The month and the day. It happened to be my uncle's birthday. Mamaru Sato turned twenty-four, July 12, 1970."

Two days before my mother— Jack's heart pounded in his chest. "Mamaru Sato," he breathed."

"He had a good first-half year. Got a job with a tree-trimming company. I remember he was tired all the time. But he made money. Then he started working weekends with Mr. Penland. Every weekend in May or June that year. His road to the *prime real estate* on the peninsula."

"Funny. Buford named his business Prime Landscape," Jack sighed. "You had me going a little. Your story is interesting, but I don't think Mamaru's friendship with Buford amounted to anything—"

"—significant?" She said. "I'm not through. That night in the alley they talked about making a lot of money together, Jack."

"Well, they don't mow lawns and trim hedges for free, Kayda. It's a normal goal."

"I heard Mr. Penland say *one-million* dollars. Is that a normal goal for mowing lawns?"

"One-million dollars! Are you sure about that number?"

"I am. When I heard it, I really started to listen. Even at that age I knew that was a lot of money. I couldn't hear much. But I heard some words that now could be important."

"Like what words?"

"You mentioned a *root cellar* at your house, one you did not know about. People don't have root cellars in Tampa, Florida. They don't even have cellars."

"I did say root cellar."

"Mr. Penland talked about a root cellar. But he called it a *secret root cellar.*"

"Okay. That is not good. What else?"

"I heard the word *ransom*, Jack."

"Jesus Christ, Kayda. You didn't think it important to tell someone?"

"No. I didn't. I was a kid, Jack. And I did not know the meanings of every English word. Not until tonight did I know Mamaru knew Buford, a black man connected to your family."

"The IJRG—Imperial Japanese radical splinter group—you told me about a year ago, did you learn about them from your uncle, Kayda?"

"Yes. Him and a couple of his friends. They talked about atomic bombs, Hiroshima and Nagasaki. They were angry back then, like a lot of other Japanese people. The IJRG was made up of the really angry ones. They wished death upon all who made the atomic bomb possible."

"I had heard about the IJRG, too. I thought it ended after the war like radical groups on the American side. The extremists are never a true reflection of most people in the world. We all hurt because of that terrible war. Most people feel bad about it and want to move forward."

"Many lost their families and heritage—their genetic footprint, as you say. It was a terrible time. Many angry. And yes, most sad. Never want war. We blame the Imperial Japanese government. They brought the wrath of your country down upon the Japanese people...

"I lost my family, Jack. Both my parents died here after the war—cancer from the atomic bomb radiation exposure. That kept killing us for many years. And as you said, most Japanese people had nothing to do with that terrible war."

"Please park off the road under that tree," he said as he mulled over the new information.

"Please don't be mad at me, Jack. I told you all I knew about the IJRG a year ago. There are still some very angry people in the world. I thought they could be targeting your family because of your losses and I knew they were in Tampa.

"When you told me no one in your family had been involved in World War II, I was relieved. We both dismissed an IJRG threat. Tonight, you talk about Buford Penland for the first time. The name, it triggered—"

"—all of this. I know. I am sorry I snapped at you. For God's sake, I had to be hypnotized to remember things at that age. You're right. We did eliminate the IJRG as a possibility a year ago. Now, things are different, Kayda."

"What do you mean?"

"I have new information that connects my family to the Manhattan Project."

"The people who created the atomic bomb?"

"Yes. I recently learned my grandfather—Otto Burcher—was the twin brother of Hans Bethe, one of the members of the Manhattan Project team."

"No! Are you sure?"

"The FBI gave me some information a few months ago. I doubted it. Dragged my heals. Then I confirmed the family's *dirty little secret* today. I pressed Grandma Emily at the funeral. She' Otto's wife. Ninety-three. Em told me everything. Uncle Otto was not the man I thought. When he found out who he was, he buried it to keep his kidnapping father from going to jail."

"I don't understand. Kidnapping?" Kayda asked.

"Otto's mother—my great grandmother—Edwina was unable to have children. She suffered from deep depression. Attempted suicide. My great grandfather—Wilhelm—could not allow her to take her life. He decided to kidnap a baby boy in 1906. Took him from the hospital in the middle of the night. The real parents—the Bethes—gave birth to twins that day. Guess my great grandfather didn't think they'd mind giving up one. If he had taken Hans instead Otto, maybe the atomic bomb would have never happened. There's a thought to screw up the mind."

"I'm so sorry, Jack. This is not good for your family."

"The great grands and the grands kept the lid on this for a hundred years."

"But then it should be a secret from the world," Kayda said. "The IJRG would not know about this."

"That would have been nice. Unfortunately, the family secret got out to them. After the war, Otto was invited to a dinner with Hans Bethe in Washington DC. Otto would never tell Hans he was his kidnapped brother, but Otto had to meet him one time before he died.

"Otto donated an enormous sum of money to the US Military R&D effort. Being an anti-war advocate before it was cool, he believed advancement of military technology would be the most practical way to eliminate future wars—peace through strength. Otto was one of the first *doves* to advocate deterrence through technology."

"How did the Otto-Hans connection go public?" Kayda asked.

"A picture in the New York Times. Arms around each other and wine glasses raised. The picture was picked up by the Associated Press. Found its way onto the front pages of every newspaper in the country. At the time, Americans were still celebrating a major victory. Nothing like a picture of a war hero hugging a big military donor to sell newspapers.

"Instantly, the whole country saw the two together with big —identical—smiles. I think the only people not to see the resemblance were members of the Burcher family. Grandma Em carried the clipping in her purse."

"I don't know what to say," Kayda sighed. "Like Hans Bethe, the Burcher family would be targets of the IJRG. They would not go after the Manhattan Project team directly. That would get too much attention. It would immediately launch a nation-wide investigation. I believe it is why the IJRG targets a less notable segment of people, those who made the Manhattan Project possible. The Japanese people are very patient."

"I know now the IJRG has been methodically eliminating my family since 1948. I have direct evidence. Evidence I have been blocking. My session with Dr. Mesmer opened my eyes. Many of the pieces of the horrific puzzle now fit together."

Kayda turned off the car under a tree on Lykes Lane. The lights reached across the park into Hillsborough Bay. She turned them off and turned to the man she loves. "You say evidence you have blocked. You cannot leave me there, Jack."

"Richard Tolman was an elite member of the Manhattan Project team. Tolman died in Pasadena on September 5th, 1948. My uncle—Leonard Burcher—died the next day. Automobile accident. The FBI has confirmed Leonard did not die from injuries received in the accident. He was dead before his car landed upside down at the bottom of a ravine."

"That's terrible. Still, it could be something else. Is that all you've got?"

"Leonard was killed shortly after Otto and Hans were in the newspapers."

"I understand the timing but—"

"My mother was taken on July 14, 1970. Lieutenant Lesley Groves, another elite member of the Manhattan Project team, died on July 13, 1970, one day before."

"Oh my God," Kayda breathed as she turned away.

"My aunt—Caroline Lawton, on my mother's side. She

died on June 28, 1975. They ruled it a suicide. Caroline was poisoned."

"Was it a homicide?"

"Yes. Geoffrey Ingram Taylor died on June 27, 1975. One day before Caroline took her own life. Mr. Taylor was an elite member of the Manhattan Project team. Upon closer examination, we no longer accept Caroline committed suicide. She had no reason to—"

"I don't know what to say."

"On February 11, 1978, James Bryant Conant died. He was another elite member of the Manhattan Project team, Kayda. My uncle Harold Lawton died the next day—cold case today.

"Patricia was killed on March 7. Hans Bethe died on March 6."

"God. Otto's twin brother. It is the IJRG. But David? Who preceded David?"

"No one. Our executioner is working off script, now. All of the elite members of the Manhattan Project team are dead now, Kayda. Gone. I think our killer is finishing his work. Taking care of loose ends. The complete annihilation of the Burcher family. On his own clock, now. He will not stop until he kills Melissa, Grandma Em, and me."

"If the IJRG assigned someone to execute the Burcher family, that could mean—"

"—there are other families in their crosshairs. I bet those poor souls have no idea what is happening to their family, just like me up until now.

"Dr. Mesmer helped me put it together. I got in the way of the investigation because of a childhood psychosis." He stared at the bay. "The frightened ten-year-old boy inside me clung to the only thing he had left in the world—the hunt for his mother's killer. I could not let that ever end. I would be alone again."

Kayda reached over and touched his face. "I'm so sorry, Jack."

"Hypnosis gave me the strength to return to the most terrifying nights in my life. I opened my eyes and saw what really happened. I understand, now...

"Where to find Mamaru Sato?"

"I don't know. I have not seen him since the alley and Mr. Penland on July 12, 1970."

"He left that night. You've never had contact since?"

"Never. He abandoned me. I moved from one poor Japanese family to another for many years. Then I lived on my own. Twenty-one is when I changed my name to *Webster*. There was a dictionary in the room when I filled out my application. I wanted more. I never looked back."

Jack would commandeer a skiff. Paddle a large arc to avoid detection. Land north of the estate. He remembered a childhood trail through the foliage on the east edge of his property. It opened at the boathouse behind an old shed. He had always wondered why that shed had a lock. Maybe it was a way into the secret root cellar. Jack knew where his father kept the key.

"I need to go." He reached for the door handle. "If I don't make it—"

"Don't even say. You will make it. You must."

"Kayda. Please. This information must get to Paul Shuck. Everything we know about the IJRG and linkage of my family deaths to the Manhattan Project. My nightmare is only one piece of a much larger nightmare that must be stopped. You must tell—"

"We will tell Paul Shuck together," she whispered.

Jack smiled. "There is more to this. There is something I must do."

She touched his lips with one finger. "I know. Go."

She watched him run beneath the sliver moon and disappear into the trees. Seconds later another TPD cruiser turned onto Lykes Lane and shined a spotlight into the park. She watched as she dug to the bottom of her purse and pulled out a neatly-folded newspaper clipping, the one she had carried since September 10, 2003.

A cellphone had caught a killer sitting on a cinderblock wall behind the Calypso Sports Bar. Blood-spattered pantlegs filled the foreground. They were the legs of a dead man— Michael Brule'. In the dark background, a man sat on a wall. *There you are, Mamaru,* she thought. The second picture was a closeup—the face of a man with a bloody letter C and equal sign—the mark of the atomic bomb. *You put that there, the stupid tattoo over your heart. Do you think you are invincible? You have lost your mind.*

Kayda touched the only words she had underlined—Legacy Arms Muso Bowie Knife. *I remember that knife. It belonged to my family.*

From the glovebox, she removed a sterling silver letter opener with the Sato family crest. She touched the tip of the five-inch, razor-sharp, double-edged blade. Then she dropped it into her purse. Kayda looked at her eyes in the tilted rearview mirror. *Mamaru. It hurts me...*

THIRTY-THREE

Burcher Estate — March 13, 2005 – 23:30

Although he navigated a wide arc, he could see the Scout
moored at the end of the Ballast Point Pier. Leaving a
boat there overnight broke a slew of ordinances. Although
violations were rare, Jack remembered the one other time he
saw a boat. It was the night Ronan disappeared. Jack returned
home late. He saw it bobbing at the end of the pier—a Scout.

Thirty minutes after Jules Verne Park, he tied the skiff to a
slimy post offshore. It poked out of the water in a line with a
half-dozen other pairs—the remnants of a private dock lost to a
storm. Most homeowners rebuilt. Jack's neighbor did not. Every
night Jack would sit on his back patio with a scotch and count
the geometric eyesore. But this night would be different. Jack
would smile at the slimy posts as he tethered his borrowed skiff
—unseen.

He walked in waist-deep water to the northeast edge of the
property. There he went ashore, climbed their rock wall, and
found his childhood path through the field of gnarled briars,

spike-stickers, and giant junipers. In this instance, natures barrier had provided the Burcher estate with better protection than coiled barbed wire and armed guards. And the little-known trail gave Jack stealth access to the darkest—and ideal—corner of the property.

At the end of the path the boathouse and shed loomed. His plan was simple: break into boathouse, find the key to shed, and find the passageway into the secret root cellar. Although he was unsure the shed would provide him with access to the root cellar, he was sure the odds were good. Why else would a useless, old shed be padlocked and never talked about his whole life? But if the shed proved to be a dead end, Jack would go through the house, a less desired option. It would expose him. He could run into the TPD, the FBI, or the killer.

When he rounded the boathouse, he saw the door ajar. He inched it open and froze. Labored breathing flowed from lower bunkbed. *Is that Buford?* He wondered. *But why would Paul leave him here? Is he part of an elaborate trap?* With gun in hand, Jack eased up to the edge of the bed. The moonlight fell through the only window onto the black face of the old man he knew well.

"Buford," he whispered. "What're you doing here?"

He stirred. Jack passed his penlight over his eyes. Buford's pupils contracted. "You're not drunk," Jack whispered. "But you're not well. What's going on with you?" He shook him. "Wake up. Talk to me. It's Dr. Jack."

The old man gasped for air. He rubbed his eyes and smacked his lips. "Where am I?" Buford squinted into the moonlight at the shadow. "Who're you?" He reached for Jack's face.

"It's me, Dr. Jack. What's going on with you? What're you doing here, the boathouse? You hate this place."

Buford's eyes widened. He struggled to sit up. Then he

leaned over the side and vomited. Jack rubbed his back and scanned the cluttered room. Long ago the boathouse had been transformed into a rarely visited storage place—mostly boating things.

Jack spotted a row of oleander plants—a dozen seedlings in small pots on the windowsill. Then he saw the white powder. Like spilled flour, it dusted the small table next to the bunkbeds. Then he saw the half-empty whisky bottle.

"Gin? What are you doing with booze? You don't drink."

Buford wiped his mouth and propped himself on elbows. "Don't remember. Don't know what I'm doin' here, Dr. Jack. I feel bad." He dropped back down and closed his eyes.

Jack felt for a pulse. *Heart's racing. You're not hyperventilating. You're on something, but what?* "What'd you take, Buford?" Jack pushed. "What's this white powder? Are you doing drugs out here? You're seventy for God's sake. You should not do—"

"—drugs." He opened an eye. "They're killin' me, Dr. Jack. They got no more use for this old black man. Hell, ain't never did. Don't know why they let me live long as—"

"Who's killing you, Buford? And how are they killing you?"

He opened his other eye and grabbed Jack's shirt. "I'm sorry, Dr. Jack. I can't die with everythin' hangin' over me. All them secrets. I never meant for it to—"

"Slow down." Jack leaned into his face. "First, I need to get you help. You're in medical trouble, Buford. I think you overdosed. You could die." He pulled out his cell phone.

Buford put his trembling hand over it and forced it down. "No. It's too late for me. I remember things, now. I took a lot of white powder this afternoon. After David—"

"After David what?" Jack growled.

"I can't be here anymore. Not after David. Powder takes time, but it'll kill—"

"You're not making sense, old man. What are you trying to tell me?"

"It's poison, Dr. Jack. It comes from them oleander plants. They grow 'em everywhere around here. They like them baby plants—most deadly."

"Oleander poison?"

"They extract the poison. Send it to their people everywhere. They use a lot. Know how much to give somebody, and how long it takes to kill 'em: big, small, young, old."

"Did someone make you take oleander poison—this white powder?"

"Yup. I took it. They said they were done with me for good this time, Dr. Jack. Said I could die easy or I could die hard, but I was gonna die today—

"I didn't want 'em to cut me with a knife. Didn't want to be hung or held under water. And I sure didn't want to be gator bait. I took the poison with that gin there. He watched me. He said if I did, they'd leave me alone, let me die in this bed tonight."

"My God, Buford," Jack sighed. "What did you do, old man?"

"I gots little time, Dr. Jack. I already started hallucinatin'. Thought you were a big dog." He chuckled, and then grabbed his throat. "It's burnin' bad. Lungs gonna stop workin' soon. I'll be dead in a little while. Nothin' can stop it. It got's hold of me, Dr. Jack."

"Why would someone want to kill you, Buford? What did you do? If you're dying, you need to tell me now. Is it about my family? Did you have something to do with my mother and father and David? Talk to me now, old man."

He looked away. "I needed money, Dr. Jack. I really needed money bad. I did somethin' stupid a long time ago. Something wrong. I never said nothin'. I'm sorry."

Jack looked out the door of the boathouse. They were alone. "Talk to me," he whispered.

"We were gonna take Miss Rose. Hold her a while, that's all. We were gonna get one-million dollars, and then put her in a boat and send her back home. That was our plan."

"Who is we?" *Don't overreact. Let him talk—but he doesn't have not much time.*

"Me and my friend. An Asian kid at the time. A long time ago—1970. Mamaru Sato. We both needed money. I was startin' my business. Mamaru just bought him a fancy Cadillac Coup De Ville. It was ten years old, but it real nice. Cost way more money than Mamaru would ever see. I told 'em to get rid of it, but he didn't listen. Missed some payments. They were gonna take it back. That's when Mamaru got desperate. Came up with the kidnappin' idea. Nobody was gonna get hurt. I came up with the million dollars. It was nothin' to Dr. Ronan. He had so much money. And it sure would change our life. I made Mamaru promise Miss Rose never gets hurt."

"Keep talking, Buford." Jack's eyes narrowed. He swallowed hard and hid his fist.

"I got Miss Rose the night Dr. Ronan went out of town. I was real careful not to hurt her. Miss Rose never saw me. I got her tied up and blindfolded. Mamaru met me. We drove around with Miss Rose rolled up in a rug on the back seat of that 1960 Cadillac. It had a real big back seat. She was comfortable. I made sure.

"But then we didn't know what to do, just drivin' around. We hadn't thought things out. We didn't know where to go. So, we came back to the house. Nobody knew about the root cellar. I thought we'd just go down there for a while."

"Where is the root cellar? Why didn't we know about it and you did?"

"I found a key in the boathouse. It fit the lock on that shed.

One day I got to pokin' around in that old shed. Started to clean up the place. Tried to move the bookcase. It opened like a door, Dr. Jack. There is a tunnel. I guess I found Mr. Otto's secret root cellar. I didn't say nothing 'bout it."

"You took my mother into that root cellar on the first night?"

"Yes, Dr. Jack." The old man propped up on his elbows and looked out the only window in the boathouse. "I mean to tell you just minutes after we got down there the police showed up at the house. They were everywhere. It was a good thing Mamaru put his car in his hidin' place. They never found it. Kept it behind Evan's Garage off the Parkway."

"Enough on the car. Back to the house. The police arrived."

"They were all in the kitchen right above us. We were scared, Dr. Jack. Couldn't make a move without takin' a chance on gettin' caught. I told Mamaru we needed to do somethin' to get the police to leave. We needed to forget about gettin' any money. We needed them gone and we needed to put Miss Rose in a boat so we could fix this mess. We made a real big mistake."

"Why didn't you go through with your revised plan, Buford?" Jack seethed.

"Mamaru said the only way we get the police to leave is to make 'em think Miss Rose is dead and there wasn't gonna be no ransom. You don't get money if you kill the hostage."

"What did you do?"

"He said we needed to get hold of a fresh heart. We needed to put it in a box with a note and put it at the end of the driveway. The police would find it and leave the house. We would put Miss Rose on the back patio and go. That was the new plan. We gave up on the money piece."

"Who got the heart, Buford?"

"I drove around a while. I thought a funeral home might

have a dead body. I could get me a fresh heart there. Ain't nobody gonna notice.

"I brought it back that same night. I went through the shed. Nobody saw me. Since I got the heart, deal was Mamaru was gonna put it in the box with the note and take it out front to the gates the next night. That was the deal."

"Was my mother still alive, when you left the first night?"

"I think so. I didn't go back in them rooms. He had her in one. I stayed away. I didn't want her to know I was there. You know, like smell me or somethin'—"

"You didn't want my mother to know you were involved," Jack moaned.

"On the second night, I knew someone killed—"

"—my mother. How did you know, Buford? Just tell me the truth. Please."

"Mamaru put her heart in my hand, Dr. Jack. He said he had a boss, now. Said his boss killed Miss Rose because she got loose and attacked him. I never knew about him havin' a boss. I was in shock, holdin' that heart. I was scared and sad.

"Mamaru and his boss put the box in the driveway the second night. He told me my only job was to take Miss Rose's heart and put it where I got the other heart. Mamaru said I had to, or we'd get caught—kidnappin' and murder. He said the FBI would look for stolen hearts. If I didn't put it back right now, we'd be put to death in an electric chair—"

"That had to be the third night. How could you not go to the police, Buford? You didn't kill my mother. Mamaru's boss killed her. You took her, but I know you would not hurt her."

"I was gonna go to the police, Dr. Jack. But Mamaru knew it before I knew it. I got back from replacin' the heart later on that third night—I didn't want to run into his boss. But Mamaru knocked me out right then. He tied me to a table, in the root cellar. Tortured me, Dr. Jack. Cut off four of my toes. It broke me. I forgot how to talk for a while. He said if I ever went to the police, his boss would kill your whole family. I was scared. I tried to forget."

Jack dropped his head and rubbed his eyes. Buford coughed and fell back. His bloated head sunk deep into the pillow. Foam and blood bubbled from the corners of his mouth. His eyes had been reduced to slits on his swollen face.

"Mamaru told me his boss was watchin' how he handled himself. Said Miss Rose was a test. Now I think the whole thing was his boss's idea, the kidnappin' and killin' and all. I don't think Mamaru wanted anything but that Cadillac."

"Where did this *boss* come from, Buford? Do you know anything about him? Did Mamaru ever talk about him? Did you meet the man?"

"I never saw him. Mamaru said he was gonna pay him a lotta money to kill bad people. Mamaru was gonna be a professional. He said assassin.

"I didn't want any part of it. I wanted my old life back. Mamaru said I could have it back if I promised him two things. One, I never go into that root cellar again. And two, I forget about Miss Rose. He said if I did them two things, he'd let me live and would pay me every month to remember our deal. I never cared 'bout no money. I gave it away every month."

"This boss was going to pay Mamaru to kill *bad people?*"

"People that needed to die for crimes they got away with, is what he said."

"What crimes?"

"Murder. Said they were murderers walkin' free—I just didn't want to know. I couldn't bring Miss Rose back, but my silence might could keep 'em from killin' the family. And then they go and kill Mr. David right after Miss Patricia was put in the ground."

Jack watched the old black man shrink and weep. *You*

really don't have the ability to connect the deaths of Ronan and Patricia and the others to Mamaru and this boss. But you do blame them for David. It must be the senility and lifelong guilt and fear that has crippled you?

"Is Mamaru Sato here, Buford?"

"Yes. He made me drink the poison today. He came back tonight. I didn't move nothin'. I heard him on his phone. He said I would be dead in an hour. He just left me alone."

"Do you know who he was talking to?"

"I think his boss. He calls him a different names. I heard some before. I went to the library for one. Did my research. Then I knew."

"Who is the boss, Buford? Who does Mamaru talk to?"

"Bard—," he gasped as he contracted into a fetal position holding his stomach.

"Who? Give me the full name." Buford coughed up blood. Jack ripped off his shirtsleeve and wiped the old man's mouth and face. "Tell me. Don't die. I need your help, Buford."

"Bard," he whispered a second time with all the air he could find. He opened one eye and struggled to shape a word. Buford pulled Jack close and whispered something.

Jack checked for a pulse. He passed his penlight over each eye—nothing. Buford Penland died in the boathouse he feared all his life.

"I need to forgive you," Jack whispered as he closed Buford's frozen eyes and cleaned the blood off his face. "You had a moment of terrible weakness and fell into a dark world; one you could not comprehend. It defined the rest of your life."

Jack found a scrap of paper. "I know you would never hurt Rose. And now, I know who did." Jack scribbled a note. *I need to somehow get this to Paul...*

He felt the ledge above the only window in the boathouse. When he found the dust-covered key, he was not surprised.

When he found the fish-scaling knife, he was. The memories poured in from almost forty years ago. Ronan had taken that knife from him. I can see you right now talking to me. *"I don't care if you sneak out and sit in the wildflowers all night, son, but these damn fishing knives are too dangerous to be messin' around with."*

Jack returned to the end of the bunk and Buford. As he digested the new information, Mamaru's boss, he moved his light over the edge of the six-inch blade. *Still razor-sharp*, he thought. Then he read the worn letters pressed into the cracked wood handle—*Made in Japan*. "How apropos," he breathed.

For the first time in his life, Jack knew what he had to do.

THIRTY-FOUR

Burcher Estate — March 14, 2005 – 07:30

I t was the biggest true-crime story in the state of Florida since the execution of Aileen Wuornos. They had the Burcher family serial killer, and no one was talking—yet.

At sunrise, roadblocks on West Euclid and Selmon Expressway sealed off the southern half of the Interbay Peninsula. From the iron gates to the old house, CSI/ME vans, the SWAT Command Center Coach, a dozen TPD squad cars, and black SUVs lined the driveway. On the manicured lawns in front of the house, ambulance-and-firetruck engines churned with lights flashing. On the other side of the wildflower field and yellow tape, cameras on tripods with telephoto-lenses were locked on guarded front doors. Rumors flowed. A horrific parade of bodies could begin at any moment.

Police helicopters crisscrossed the skies above Ballast Point north to Bayshore Gardens, south to Jules Verne Park, and east a mile into Hillsborough Bay. Armed ground forces and canine squads moved from estate to estate in the elite neighborhoods.

They combed the countryside, in a one mile radius—Dr. Jack Burcher was missing.

Like piranha, the news media swarmed in schools behind the police tape. Cables ran from satellite trucks and network vans to cameras and half-dressed talking heads. But the pregame horror show could only cover backstory. The police were not talking. The world watched and waited and stayed close to their radios and TVs because they wanted more. The growing angst flowed down Crescent Drive from the Interbay Boulevard to the cordoned-off cul de sac in front of the Burcher estate. From there the FBI ground operations kept a tight lid on everything.

* * *

"How are you feeling now," Deron asked with veiled annoyance. The retired Chief of Police knew more than he would say. His presence was inappropriate and unnerving but still uncontested. No one would take the bull by the horns. Deron had been the boss for decades.

The Burcher house and grounds were a beehive of controlled activity. Few were allowed in the root cellar. Two officers carried Deron and his wheelchair down as Deron ordered—there was no way he would stay away on his own. Bullitt bit his tongue. He would choose the battle. It was his responsibility now. This time did not feel right, but he was getting close.

"I don't know how he got me," Shuck moaned as he rubbed his head. "Had not moved out from under the table for, seemed hours. I had to stretch. Got a cramp. First, I was certain the place was empty. I really don't know how he got so damn close without me knowing."

"The guy's known for his stealth ways, Paul," Bullitt said.

The medic handed Shuck an ice bag. "Since I can't get you to take a ride to the hospital with me, at least keep this on your head. It'll help with the swelling—

"Other than the large egg, you appear to be in good shape. Vitals are stable. No signs of other trauma except the rope burns, of course."

"What about needle sticks?" Bullitt reminded.

"No injection sites. As asked, we went over him with a magnifying glass to be certain. I recommend he get to a doctor today to check his head injury. Need to be sure it's not—"

"—serious," Shuck said. "I've got a hard head. Been knocked out before. I'll survive."

"You're lucky he didn't gut you like the rest," Deron scoffed. Heads turned to the dead man twenty feet away.

The Asian man laid on his left side, in a puddle of blood. Quin had just completed her preliminary examination. The medical photographer was finishing up. The body would be moved when the FBI said. For now, Paul wanted it right where it was. He needed time to think.

Quin approached the group, her eyes in her notebook and pen moving. She reached the long wood table where Shuck sat with his legs hanging and a bag of ice on his head. The others backed to open a path. They all awaited Shuck's medical clearance so they could push forward with the crime-scene investigation.

"Surprisingly, our dead serial killer *suspect* had a driver's license in his wallet," Quin sighed. "That's gotta be a first." She passed it to Bullitt. He scanned and passed it to Shuck.

"The fifty-nine-year-old, eastern Asian male, name *Mamaru Sato*, resides in Gibsonton on the other side of the bay. He drives a 1960 Cadillac Coup de Ville." She passed the insurance card to Bullitt. "A real classic."

"Dr. Burcher's UFO," Novak said under his breath. "You

remember. The long gray growling thing in the cal de sac. Big fins, black windows."

Bullitt nodded. "The car we have on video at Sun Bay the night Ronan disappeared."

"He's gotta be the Burcher family serial killer," Novak said. Shuck stared at Quinn.

"What about COD, Doctor?" Novak nudged Quinn. "You already have my—"

"—preliminary assessment," she said with an approving smile. "Yes. Mr. Novak. I do. I concur. Mamaru Sato's killer knew what he-or-she was doing."

"What the hell does that mean?" Deron barked.

With a busy pen, Quin let it pass and stayed with the three: Shuck, Bullitt, and Novak. "The knife was inserted from behind and between C-3 and C-4 vertebrae. This point of penetration is unique. It delivers the maximum damage with minimal force, and it renders the victim defenseless almost immediately—therefore, a male or female perpetrator possible.

"From my external examination, I am confident disruption of the spinal cord was enough to produce instant paralysis of the extremities—freeze arms and lock legs. At the C-3 C-4 level in the neck, the common carotid artery would be severed at the internal/external bifurcation. That would produce the most controlled rate of blood loss. Faster blood flow than severing just one carotid, and slower blood flow than severing the nearby jugular."

"And that's relevant because what?" Deron seethed.

"It suggests Mamaru Sato's killer wanted to talk to him before he died."

"Explain, please," Shuck said.

"Severing the jugular vein would have been easiest, but death would have been rapid. Mr. Sato would have spent his final moments choking on his blood and gasping for air. That would not be conducive to carrying on a conversation."

"Would you say Sato's killer is someone with advanced knowledge of human anatomy? Knows the best way to compromise and kill? Deron asked. "Someone like a forensic—"

"Jack Burcher did not do this," Shuck barked. "Don't even go there, Frank."

"We don't know that," Deron countered. "And we all must admit Dr. Quin's information could point to a forensic pathologist, someone who knows how—"

"—to kill people. Really! We haven't even found his body and you're already accusing him of committing a homicide," Shuck huffed.

"I'm only saying what needs to be said. Jack Burcher is missing. That could mean many things including he could be on the run. Jack had the motive to kill Sato, and we know Jack came here last night. He had opportunity. Now, we know Jack possesses the specialized education that fits this complex kill methodology."

"I'm not so sure this kill methodology is so rare, Francis." Bullitt said. "Anyone experienced in our field could do this. We all know about the C-3 C-4 thing."

"Jack could be dead or in desperate straits somewhere, for all we know," Shuck said. "Sato could have done something to him before he even got here. Sato could have put Jack somewhere dead or alive—like in Gibsonton. I think it makes more sense Sato came back to the Burcher estate to finish his work on David and his twisted creation.

"To suggest right out the shoot Jack Burcher—our Chief Medical Examiner and the primary victim of all this crap—is a murderer after all he has been through is appalling, Deron."

Shuck and Bullitt watched the retired chief's furtive eyes

jump around the root cellar and face twitch. "You alright, Francis? Maybe you shouldn't be down here," Bullitt suggested.

"I'm fine. I'm not sure Mr. Shuck should be here. I think he may be compromised. Clearly, you took great offense when I pointed to an obvious suspect."

"I'm going to pretend you didn't say that," Shuck fumed. "If you get in my way one more time, you will be removed, Frank. This is an FBI matter. You are a guest at best."

"I would be careful, Director," Deron said. "I may be a retired cripple, but I still got relationships in this state. Your problem's not me. There are more unanswered questions and dead bodies today than ever before in the history of this case. All under your watch...

"Mamaru Sato, David Burcher, Tate Worthington, Buford Penland, and some kind of decaying Frankenstein monster in a box—all your failures. This root cellar's another FBI failure. I suggest you drop the sensitivity bullcrap and listen to the people around you."

"I almost forgot about Penland in the boathouse," Bullitt said. "Yes, five bodies in 24 hours and Jack Burcher missing is a problem. But the good news is Sato is dead and Melissa Burcher is safe. I gotta agree with Paul. Everything we have points to Mamaru Sato being the Burcher family serial killer. More needs to be done, but the killing should stop."

"Will it? Seems to me it's accelerating," Deron huffed.

"The game plan may have changed at the end," Bullitt said. "But Sato is dead now."

"We still need more answers. Everyone's looking for Jack," Shuck said. "I'm hopeful we will find him. Let's just pray we're not too late."

"If he's not alive, I expect to find his body nearby," Bullitt said. "We know he left Bayshore upset. And we know he came here."

"We've got a hundred people searching Ballast Point and the bay," Shuck said.

Deron wheeled over to the body, his back to the group. Bullitt winked at Shuck—here comes another dig. "Let's talk about you in all of this, Mr. Shuck," Deron said. "How'd you get all tied up and put on that table. Wonder why Sato didn't kill you. And how'd you find time to call Mr. Bullitt's cell?"

"What are you saying?" Shuck seethed. Bullitt kept him from leaving the table.

"Was it you that had the last few words with this Asian guy, Mr. Shuck?" Deron pushed. "Or do you want us to believe he just suddenly appeared out of thin air, knocked you out, and then someone suddenly showed up and killed him before he—"

"Excuse me," Quin interrupted the rant. "Before you go there Director Shuck, we do need to start moving bodies to the morgue. I am ordering removal of Tate Worthington and David Burcher now."

"That's fine with me," Paul said. "I want to be present for the autopsies. If you would, have someone call when you ready."

"Agreed. Detective Bullitt. I assume you will want to attend."

"Yes," Bullitt said as he watched Deron—a man in his own world—lean over Sato. *What's with you, Francis? You broke the rules at Bayshore. Now you're being a horses-ass.*

"Good." Quin motioned Novak. "I'm leaving transport operations to Mr. Novak. If there are any issues, please go to him. He will stay on scene with full authority to make decisions for the ME office. Until Dr. Burcher returns, I will be managing these cases along with other county matters. I would appreciate you keeping me in the loop. I will do the same."

"When can we get a look inside the box under *Frankenstein?*" Shuck asked.

"After CSI finishes their work in that room. I have authorized removal of the composite-corpse. I want it left untouched in its box. It can be held in this room until ready for transport to the morgue. That will free up they mystery box. I will return. We will open it, together. We cannot afford to lose any forensic evidence."

"Good for me," Bullitt said. "Probably be another hour before CSI can—"

"What about Buford Penland?" Novak asked. "He's still in the boathouse. CSI is done out there. Have you completed your examination of that body, Doctor?"

"I am done with Mr. Penland. CSI collected trace samples of the oleander poison on the bedstand, in Mr. Penland's hair, and on his clothing. I believe he ingested a fair amount several hours before. That's what killed him." Quin closed her notebook. "You may move him. Transport all bodies in crash bags. Let's protect the physical evidence, gentlemen."

"Also helps me," Shuck said. "This is an active investigation. I don't want pictures of dead people in the newspapers. This place is crawling with the media. They are flying overhead.

"While we are on the topic, I will confirm the FBI will be the only interface with the news media. No one takes interviews. All names will be held until we decide to release them. I will take my first interview in about an hour from now. At that time, I will let them know Jack Burcher is missing. We share no info on the suspected serial killer. We have a lot of work to do. Are we all good?"

Each nodded. Quin left the root cellar. Novak followed. He stopped and turned back to the group. "The bodies will be removed through the kitchen. I will have transport vans park on the north side of the house. We have a ten foot gap between the back kitchen door and the tail of a van. You can plan on that shot making the news. They will count crash bags."

Quin waited for Novak by the cellar stairs. She pulled him close and whispered, "Keep me up on what's said down there. I'm worried about Jack. He's either hiding for a good reason, or he's in trouble—"

"He's okay. I feel it," Novak said. "He will contact us, when he can."

"I hope soon. I expect he will first contact Kayda Webster."

"I don't know if you heard. The police picked up Kayda this morning. She was at Jules Verne Park last night. They watched and waited after she left the park to see if she reconnected with Jack. Bullitt said they lost her for three hours after the park."

"That's bizarre. Do we know if she had an explanation?"

"She admitted to dropping Dr. Burcher at the park, but claims she went home and remained in her apartment until the knock at her door. She's not being truthful."

"Maybe she helped Jack and is not going to tell the police," Quin said.

"That is one possibility," Novak whispered. "A skiff was taken from the Yacht Club by the park. They found it moored at Dr. Burcher's neighbor's. Detective Bullitt believes the skiff is how Dr. Burcher got from Jules Verne to his place."

"Would make sense. Jack would know not to travel on land —they'd be watching for him. A water route sounds like his thinking.

"But that puts Jack here," Quin muttered. "I hope Deron's wild speculations do not turn out to be true. God knows Jack had good reason to kill that monster."

"I cannot see Dr. Burcher killing anyone," Novak said brushing the arms of his coat. "He can get angry, but he cannot hurt anyone."

"I would like to believe that. He did just learn his younger brother was killed."

Quin turned to leave. Novak grabbed her elbow. "The real mystery is where was Kayda Webster for three hours after dropping Dr. Burcher at the park?"

"That answer may answer all our questions, Hugo."

THIRTY-FIVE

Burcher Estate — March 14, 2005 – 08:30

He watched CSI sift through the ashes. Rubber-gloved fingers pinched a charred jawbone over an open evidence bag. Shuck nodded. The CSI technician dropped it into the bag and turned back to sift more ashes in the bowels of the old furnace.

Ashes to ashes. How many stories do you want to tell me? Shuck thought.

"Which way were you looking when you got hit on the noggin?" Bullitt asked.

"I was facing this way. The coal furnace," Shuck said.

"Sato had to come from the rooms—"

"Paul!" His name rolled into the room. "We found another way in here," Crabtree huffed as he ran from the tunnel into the main room of the root cellar. "Room number three. The last one. Thought it was just broken furniture with an old, rickety bookcase: empty jelly jars and sacks of rotten potatoes. Well, turns out that bookcase is a door. Opens into a primitive tunnel, a lot tighter than this one. It's got cement walls and a boarded ceiling full of damn spider webs."

"Where does it go, Milton?"

"To that shed behind the boathouse. To another bookcase loaded with crap—rusted tools, empty oil cans, parts of an outboard motor, fishing gear. Stuff like that. That bookcase is on a set of rusty hinges, too. And it was ajar when we got to it. Someone used it recently. Webs broken."

"Gotta be how Sato got in here behind you, Paul," Bullitt said.

"He didn't use the door in the cellar," Shuck muttered. "I never thought for a minute—"

"Wait. There's more." Crabtree handed Shuck a paper TPD evidence bag. "We found something in the tunnel. A bloody sleeve torn off a shirt."

Paul shined a light into the bag and passed it to Novak. "I wonder what that's about."

Novak examined the contents of the bag. "Dr. Burcher's shirt sleeve. I recognize it. The buttons on the cuff. The pinstripes. He only wears three-button cuffs. Real particular. Dr. Burcher wore this shirt yesterday. I know. I worked two cases with him before Bayshore."

Deron wheeled over and grabbed the bag from Novak. He peered inside. "If that blood belongs to Sato, you've got your man—Jack Burcher."

Shuck removed the bag from Deron's tight grip. "I think it would be best for you to leave now, Francis. You're tired, and I'm not in the mood for—"

"—facing the truth." Two officers approached Deron. "No need to get physical. I'm ready to leave this damn mess. Maybe your right, Mr. Shuck. I am tired. I am tired of the incompetence. Someone get me up the cellar stairs and I will be on my way."

"Remember, Francis. Do not talk to the news media." Crabtree wheeled Deron out followed by two burley officers. The room waited until the grousing faded away.

"Something's in his craw," Bullitt said. "Never seen him quite this ornery."

"Getting rid of him was easier than I expected," Shuck said with a curious stare.

Homicide Investigator Jake Jenkins had to bend down to enter the root cellar door. The basketball-tall, skinny, rookie detective, in a suit with a narrow tie, had held his new position less than a week. Although he had four years as a patrolman, and tested highest on the detective exam, Jenkins would be the proverbial deer-in-the-headlights for many months. Bullitt, his direct supervisor, had raised a few in the past. This one was the book smart and sensitive type. From experience, Bullitt planned to ease him into the chilling world of homicide.

"Mr. Jenkins. What is it?" Bullitt asked. "I did not expect to see you down here."

Jenkins eyed the body and swallowed hard. "Well sir, I know I should be focused on my assignment, organizing cold-case files, and I know I am stepping outside protocol in a number of ways—"

"You mean by being here, or by disobeying an order?" Bullitt winked at Shuck.

"Ah, those too, sir."

"Keep talking," Bullitt said with growing curiosity.

"Yes, sir. Me bringing a witness to an active crime scene is outside protocol. I had to make a judgement call, sir. I knew you would be unavailable for an indefinite period of time, and I knew the information this person had could be important to you now. So, I made a decision to risk—"

"—making a slew of procedural errors," Bullitt muttered.

Novak and Shuck turned away to hide their smiles. The

light moment was welcomed. Bullitt turned back to the young homicide detective. "Let's forget protocol and procedure for a moment, Jenkins."

"Yes, sir."

"Let's forget all those pesky, troubling things a young man worries about the first week on the job. Why don't you just spit it out, son. Let's put this one down as a learning experience. How's that, Mr. Jenkins?"

"Well, sir. I have someone in my car—Miss Kayda Webster."

Eyes widened. All heads turned to the young detective.

"Miss Webster possesses information she must give Mr. Shuck directly. She said it is information she obtained last night from Dr. Jack Burcher, sometime after he left the Bayshore Gardens Clinic and when she dropped him off at Jules Verne Park."

"I thought Webster was being held," Shuck gasped.

"No sir," Jenkins corrected. "Miss Webster was released an hour ago."

"She would not talk," Bullitt said. "Had a lawyer hinting harassment. Continue, son."

"Yes, sir. Miss Webster approached me in the parking lot. She seemed sincere. She told me things. They sounded important. Relevant to this investigation, sir. I thought it best I bring her here. You told me rule number one; time is always important when doing good police work."

The morgue clerk zipped Mamaru Sato into a crash bag. Heads turned to watch them load the body onto the gurney. "You did the right thing, Mr. Jenkins," Bullitt said. "Mr. Shuck, we have a witness waiting. How would you like to proceed?"

"Yes. Well. We cannot meet down here. And I want you and Novak present." Paul shook Jenkins hand. "Good to meet you, young man. Welcome to the force. You made the right decision. Can you navigate the news media and get Miss Webster to the house?"

"She's here, sir. I parked behind the carport in the bushes. Miss Webster is in my back seat under a blanket. I think I could bring her in through the back patio. I will need to wait for the helicopter to pass over. They are on three-minute sweeps. I timed it."

Bullitt smiled at Shuck. "Well. She's here," he gloated. "Good work, Detective."

"Moe, will you meet them at the patio doors? We do not need any interference—this place's crawlin' with people lookin' for things out of place. Hugo, I need you to secure the den for a private meeting. Let's plan on all sitting down with our guest in ten minutes."

* * *

The shades were pulled, curtains drawn, French doors in the main hallway into the den were closed. Paul entered room last. Kayda Webster sat in Jack's favorite chair by the fireplace. The beautiful lady exuded class and confidence. Paul could see why she had Jack's heart. Bullitt, Novak, and Jenkins sat on the sofa. Shuck took the chair across from Webster.

"I understand Jack Burcher wanted you to talk with me," Shuck opened.

"Yes. He said time was of the essence."

"I see. So, here we are."

"Jack wanted you to know every Burcher family member's death occurs one day after the natural death of an elite member of the Manhattan Project team."

"The development of the atomic bomb. Yes. We suspected a connection for some time, but only recently confirmed viable linkage to the Burcher family."

STEVE BRADSHAW

"Otto Burcher. The twin brother of Hans Bethe."

"You say all deaths of the Burcher family may be linked—"

"Not may be linked. Are linked. And this is not my information. It is Jack's."

"I understand. You are delivering a message from him."

"Jack said after his session with Dr. Mesmer last night, many things came into focus for him. Things he had blocked were unblocked. Jack's ability to process the new information with what he knew allowed for the eye-opening connection. He now sees the whole picture."

"What did you come here to tell me, Miss Webster?" Shuck leaned closer. He studied her every move. Her breathing. Her hands. Her eyes.

"Richard Tolman died on September 5, 1948 in Pasadena. Leonard Burcher died—"

"—on September 6, 1948," Shuck snapped. "Yes. I remember the date. I assume Mr. Tolman is one of the elite members of the secret government project."

"The Manhattan Project. Your assumption is correct," Kayda said. "An elite. On July 13, 1970 Lieutenant Colonel Leslie Groves died in Washington DC."

"Rose Burcher was taken July 14," Shuck muttered. "The next day."

Kayda did not pause. "Geoffrey Ingram Taylor died on June 27, 1975."

"Caroline Lawton, Rose's sister, died June 28, 1975," Shuck said. Bullitt stopped writing. He lowered his small leather notebook and stared at Webster. They were so close.

"James Bryant Conant died February 11, 1978," she said.

"Harold Lawton died February 12, 1978," Shuck muttered. "Tell me. What elite member of the Manhattan Project team died the day before Ronan Burcher was taken? We know he died September 10, 2003?"

"Edward Teller, Mr. Shuck. He died on September 9, 2003."

"Our assumptions were correct. I'm not surprised. We were—"

"—at Ballast Point Tavern. But you were too late. Patricia was killed and Jack was attacked. He could have been killed. You made the connections that night."

"We did," Shuck sighed. "March 7. The day after Hans Bethe died of natural causes in Ithaca, New York. Yes. We were all too late."

"We believe the Imperial Japanese Radical Group, the IJRG, is doing this," Kayda said. "Jack is now certain. We talked about it last night."

"So, you were with Jack?"

"Yes."

"Miss Webster, nothing you say now will be used against you. What is important is we find Jack. There is a good possibility he is being held somewhere nearby. He may have a limited time to live. We have a lot of people are looking for him. Do you have anything to help?"

"I don't know."

"You picked up Jack in Bayshore Gardens last night."

"I did."

"Then what?"

"I dropped him at Jules Verne Park around ten."

"We know Jack commandeered a skiff from the Yacht Club," Bullitt said. "We found it moored, a neighbor to the northeast. We can assume he got to his house. What we do not know is if Jack encountered the serial killer—" Bullitt paused and looked at Shuck.

"Go ahead, Moe. We need to be open with Miss Webster. Maybe pooling our information can help us find Jack before it's too late."

Moe nodded. "He had no way of knowing the serial killer would be at his house. There's a chance he ran into him and was overpowered. If Jack survived, he could be held somewhere."

"Why the optimism?" Webster asked.

"Hopeful is a better word," Shuck said. "Although even that is waning as we speak. Up until David Burcher's execution, there was a termination order and process. We believed Jack would be saved for last. The family patriarch. No sooner do we decipher the kill plan and it is modified. Back to square one. Nothing is predictable."

"What do you mean, modified?" She asked.

"Yesterday, after the funeral, there was a rush to kill David. Unlike all the others his death was not linked to an elite member of the Manhattan Project team. Last night there was an attempt to abduct Melissa Burcher from Bird Island."

"It failed?" Webster asked.

"Yes," Bullitt said. "The serial killer left Bird Island empty handed. The old Scout moored at the Ballast Point Pier last night belongs to the serial killer."

"How can you be sure a boat belongs—"

"The Scout was seen leaving Bird Island last night," Bullitt said. "We lost it on the bay. We found it tied to the Ballast Point Pier."

"He returned to the Burcher estate to complete his work on David," Shuck said.

"Complete? What work are you talking about? I thought David was dead."

Shuck took a deep breath. "It would serve no useful purpose to go into detail, Miss Webster. Suffice it to say this sick person returned to his secret lair."

"The root cellar! Jack heard it mentioned at Bayshore. He

knew nothing about a root cellar. So, you believe the serial killer collided with Jack in this root cellar."

"Yes. We believe it is very possible," Shuck said. "They were both here last night."

"How can you be sure the serial killer was here?" She challenged.

"We need to tell her, Paul," Bullitt said. "It's gonna get out sooner or later."

"We lost a private detective last night—Dr. Tate Worthington. He walked into a trap in the cellar. A rifle mounted. Motion detection. He died instantly. Head shot. After the horrific incident we found the root cellar. Inside we found David's body. We decided to leave everything as we found it. I would wait for the serial killer to return."

"And he did just that—returned," Bullitt said.

"Except for your head injury, you obviously survived the ordeal. Did you capture this serial killer? Seems to me you would have all the answers to your questions."

"I was knocked out and tied up. I'm sure he had some special plans for me. Fortunately for me, he never got the chance to carry them out."

"So, you think Jack ran into him sometime after you were knocked out and tied up?"

"That scenario seems to make the most sense," Shuck said.

"And since you are alive looking for Jack, you concluded the serial killer left with him."

"Close, but not exactly," Shuck said.

"Tell her, Paul," Moe pushed.

"Tell me what?"

"We have the serial killer, Miss Webster. He is down in the root cellar. He is dead."

"Dead! Oh my God! That explains your urgency to find

Jack. You think this monster did something to Jack. Put him somewhere before you killed—"

"We did not kill him, Miss Webster."

"Who did?"

"We don't know."

"God. You think Jack killed him."

"That is one of the possibilities," Bullitt said.

"He had motive, opportunity, and means. This monster killed his family over thirty-five years, Miss Webster. Such agonizing pain can make people do things," Shuck said.

"And the way he died does not help," Bullitt said. "It was surgically accomplished."

"My God." Kayda lowered her head with eyes closed. "You should know Jack called me this morning, minutes before the police came to my apartment."

"What time?" Shuck asked. *We can check police records.*

"Around five this morning."

"He's alive," Shuck said.

"And he did not kill anybody," Kayda said.

"How can you be so sure?"

She walked to the fireplace. She touched Jack's face, a family picture on the mantle: his mother, father, sister and brother—a happier time. "You should know him by now."

"I'm sorry but we—"

"You seem to have missed why Jack wanted me to come see you." She turned and leveled her eyes on Paul Shuck. "He is not worried about himself. He is worried about people he did not know.

"Jack is desperate for the FBI to know an Imperial Japanese Radical Group is active. They are responsible for his family's deaths. They are on a mission to terminate everyone in this country connected to the creation of the atomic bomb, the Manhattan Project...

"That serial killer, lying dead in the root cellar, is one of many soldiers in the IJRG's stealth army. They have been deployed across the country and maybe the world."

"I heard you, Miss Webster," Shuck said. *I never said Sato was in the root cellar.*

"Did you hear me say the Burcher family is not the only target? Do you understand after Bayshore, Jack Burcher's mission is to save lives of perfect strangers?"

"Yes. I understand." *You are Japanese. The IJRG is Japanese. You haven't asked if the dead serial killer is Japanese. A relatively small community in Tampa. It is possible you know of Mamaru Sato, or the Sato family, yet you do not ask. The absence of natural curiosity is—*

"As we speak other families are going through their own nightmares. They have no idea what is happening to them. Mr. Shuck, you must tell the world. You must mobilize the FBI, the federal government. All unexplained traumatic deaths on or around the death dates of the atomic bomb elites could be the work of the IJRG."

"I understand, Miss Webster," Shuck said as he joined her at the fireplace. "I intend to alert the FBI the moment our meeting concludes." He studied the alluring Japanese woman under a new light. *Tell the world? Does that play into the IJRG's hand. Do they want us to bring to the attention of the world a 60-year-old cause? Remind and terrify a nation, could that be a goal?*

"We're losing time," Bullitt said. "If Jack is in danger, we need to find him fast."

"When did you say you dropped Jack at Jules Verne Park?"

"Around ten o'clock."

"Then what did you do, Miss Webster?"

"I went home. He called me around five o'clock that morning."

"Where did you go after you dropped Jack Burcher off?" Shuck asked again. "I want you to think very carefully before you answer this time."

Her eyes widened. Bullitt's pen stopped moving. "Okay. I went for a drive. I was worried about Jack. I could not sleep. I didn't want to sit in my apartment."

"You drove around until four o'clock in the morning?"

"Were you watching me?" she asked.

"Yes. We were, Miss Webster. We thought Jack would reunite with you. We can confirm Jack called you at 5:03 a.m. You returned to your apartment at 4:09 a.m."

"If you say so," she sighed. "I don't know the exact time—"

"We do, Miss Webster. It would be best for all of us if you would tell us everything. This time try not to leave anything out."

She returned to her chair. Shuck followed her. "I drove around. I went downtown. I got a bottle of wine. Ended up at the Ballast Point Pier. I fell asleep—"

"—we watched your car," Bullitt said. "You left it."

"I know. I didn't do anything wrong. I went for a walk on the beach by the Yacht Club. I thought maybe Jack would return. Maybe he would need me. I drank wine. Fell asleep on the edge of the sand and the grass. When I woke up, I went home. Went to bed. My phone got me up. It was Jack."

"Tell us about that call, Miss Webster. In detail. Something you say may help us find Jack. Let's start with where he called from."

"He didn't say."

"Holding back could get him killed," Shuck pushed. "We are trying to save him, not capture him, Miss Webster. We know for a fact Jack was here last night. We have physical evidence that puts him close to the serial killer. Did Jack tell you he confronted the—"

"—serial killer? No. He did not." She swallowed hard. "But he sounded exhausted. Out of breath. Nervous. Cautious. Maybe injured. I don't know." She took a deep breath. "I think he was outdoors, when he called. I heard the wind. Cicadas, too. I just don't—"

"Okay. That's good. Helpful. Tell me what he said to you? Why did he call?"

"He wanted me to know he was all right. Jack knew I had an important deposition scheduled this morning. A new law firm for me. Thank God they cancelled on their own. They will never know I was going to miss the appointment. Unreliability is a death sentence in my business—"

"Miss Webster," Shuck barked. "What did Jack say to you?"

"I'm sorry. I'm nervous. Jack knew I would worry." She looked around the room as if the walls were closing in on her. "It was a short phone call—maybe a minute or two. I could tell right away something was on his mind. He did not tell me what he had done or was about to do, but I know he had something important, something he really wanted to tell me but wasn't ready." She smiled. "Jack does that. He's such a brilliant man. Sensitive. I've learned to wait."

"I know, Miss Webster," Shuck muttered as he realized he was drilling a dry hole. Bullitt and Novak stopped writing in their small notebooks. Jenkins tried to minimize his presence.

"So," Shuck said. "Jack phoned to let you know he was okay. Is that just about it?"

Kayda sat up with a rigid back. "I don't know if the man I love is dead or alive, Mr. Shuck. I am worried to death about him. Yes, he wanted me to know he was alive. But the main reason he called was to get me to promise I would see you as soon as possible about—"

"—the IJRG. And you've done that, Miss Webster." Shuck

could not hold her. If she was hiding anything, they had no way of getting to it.

"Yes. I have done that." She gripped her purse. "And now it's time for me to go."

An awkward silence that followed. Everyone stood and looked at their shoes. Was Kayda Webster doing Jack's work, or was she somehow involved in the Burcher family mystery? If yes, in what ways? What could be the *less-obvious purpose* of the information she dutifully provided to the FBI?

Detective Jenkins opened the sliding doors into the dark hall and went ahead to prepare the way for Kayda's stealth exit. Bullitt and Novak nodded as she and Shuck left the den. Just beyond the sliding doors they stopped.

"I hope my questioning was not too offensive, Miss Webster," Shuck said. "My job is to thoroughly examine everyone and everything in the search for truth. Sometimes it can be a bit harsh and misconstrued by the innocent. For that I am sorry."

She nodded with a slight smile.

"I do appreciate you involving yourself in something outside of your world. I know there are things you do not feel you can discuss with me now. I'm sure you believe you are protecting the man you love. I understand but want to help Jack. If you have second thoughts about anything, please call me direct." He passed his card.

Kayda dropped it into her purse and pulled him by his elbow deeper into the dark, empty hall. "Jack was here, Mr. Shuck," she whispered. "He made sure you were okay."

Shuck's eyes widened.

"He left something with you. After I depart, I suggest you check your pockets."

Shuck nodded, his mind racing.

"Jack told me something I did not share in there. Something

I do want to share now, because he is right. Jack said you are a good man, like him. You can be trusted." She leaned in, kissed his cheek, and smiled.

Kayda left to join a waiting Detective Jenkins, who stood by the patio doors at the far end of the dark hall. Paul felt his pockets as he watched the alluring Japanese lady leave the Burcher mansion. He found the square lump in his back pocket and inched out the folded piece of scrap paper. He opened it in a sliver of light, with his back to the den. He could see the blood stains and the scrawled words—written by Jack's hand.

Detective Bullitt approached from behind like a giant moth to a candle. When the sliver of light broke, Paul slid the note into his pocket. His querying eyes stayed on the patio doors, Jenkins, and Webster. "An interesting lady. I see why Jack's world has changed so much."

Bullitt's furtive eyes stayed on Paul. "Yes. Interesting—" He left his words hanging. Paul had more to share. He needed subtle encouragement.

The FBI man ignored the delicate probe by the man he had come to know well. *Probably saw the peck,* Paul surmised. *Probably saw me pat my pockets. You're too damn smart for me to lie to, but I want to keep this to myself a while.* "So, what do you think, Moe?"

Bullitt turned from Shuck to the patio doors. Together they watched through the windowpanes—a tall, lanky Jenkins guided a beautiful lady onto the lawn. They disappeared behind thick bushes. Bullitt squeezed his time-worn notebook full of observations, puzzles, and theories. He leaned into Shuck. "What do I think? I think we need to talk about the note Jack gave you last night, when you were unconscious on that butcher's table."

TWENTY-ONE DAYS LATER

Tampa Bay Sentinel

84/91°F Sunny

County Chief M.E. Jack Burcher M.D. DEAD:
Demolition of Ballast Point mansion Scheduled

Tampa – April 4, 2005: Today the FBI announced the end of a statewide search for missing Hillsborough County Chief Medical Examiner—Dr. Jackson Burcher—citing new evidence confirms his death. Dr. Burcher, the acting county medical examiner since 1995, was last seen alive at the Janice/Mesmer Clinic, in Bayshore Gardens, on March 14. That night four homicides at the Ballast Point Burcher estate were reported. These homicides are under investigation and believed to be connected to Dr. Burcher's disappearance and subsequent death.

FBI Director Paul Shuck said today, "We now have incontrovertible evidence that confirms Dr. Jack Burcher is deceased. Cause and manner of death are under investigation." When Director Shuck was asked for more information, he said, "Dr. Burcher's disappearance and death may be related to the multiple-homicides at the Burcher estate three weeks ago. It is our policy not to comment on active investigations."

On the heels of this devastating news about Dr. Burcher, Melissa Burcher, the surviving sibling and sole heir to the Burcher fortune, thanked the FBI, TPD, and citizens of Tampa for their enduring support of the family over the years. Miss Burcher shared heartfelt feelings and talked about the loss of her mother, father, and brothers—David and Jack—that has left her an orphan and alone.

"I have tried to cope with a lifetime of horrible tragedies and have come to realize there are no good memories at our home on Ballast Point. To the contrary, there are only bad memories. The time has come to do something about it. In honor of my family, and to benefit the Interbay Peninsula community, the Burcher estate will be the new site of the Ballast Point Ornithology Research/Education Center. The mansion and all structures on the grounds will be taken down and the land cleared. We will construct a world-renowned ornithological research facility, educational center, and rare bird sanctuary." **Demolition of the Burcher mansion is scheduled to begin the morning of April 7.**

County Chief M.E. Jack Burcher M.D. DEAD: Cont...

When asked, the Interim Chief of Police Moe Bullitt would not discuss the FBI findings or decision to end the search for Jack Burcher. "The TPD is saddened by the loss of Dr. Burcher," Bullitt said. "A respected Tampa citizen, an outstanding forensic medical examiner, and my friend. We will continue to work with the FBI on this and all other matters of mutual importance."

The *Sentinel* asked retired Chief of Police Francis Deron to comment on the FBI evidence confirming Burcher's death. Deron worked on the Burcher family cases for more than thirty years, in his role as a Homicide Investigator and later Chief of Police. "Evidence? I don't have a clue what Director Shuck's talkin' about," Deron said. "Seems to me you gotta have a body if you're gonna say someone's dead. I have not been in that loop. FBI's not talking to me anymore."

The Burcher family nightmare began on July 14, 1970. Rose Lawton Burcher was abducted from their Ballast Point estate. Only her heart was recovered; delivered to the house the next day. No one has been charged for Rose Burcher's abduction or death. On September 10, 2003, Ronan Burcher, retired Hillsborough County Medical Examiner, was taken from the Sun Bay Rehabilitation Center. Only his brain was recovered; delivered to the Burcher estate the next day. No one has been charged. On March 7, 2005, Patricia Burcher, ex-wife of Dr. Jack Burcher, was killed at the Burcher estate by an unknown assailant. Seven days later, on the day of Patricia Burcher's funeral, David Burcher was killed at the Burcher house. Also, dead was a suspected serial killer (unnamed), private investigator Tate Worthington, and long-time groundskeeper Buford Penland. These March 14 deaths are thought to be connected to Jack Burcher's death. All deaths are under investigation by the TPD, FBI, and County ME Office.

Anyone with information on any of these cases is asked to contact Detective Jake Jenkins at the Tampa Police Department, Homicide Division. The TPD will protect your anonymity, and all information will be treated as confidential. A $100,000 reward will be paid for information that leads to a prosecution.

THIRTY-SIX

Burcher Estate — April 6, 2005 – 23:00

I t felt like any other spring night on Ballast Point, but it was not. In one more day, the Burcher estate would not exist—and that mattered to someone.

On this night, a sliver moon hung over the live oak trees and wildflower fields as it had before men walked and lands had names. The cicadas screamed and fireflies flickered in the salt-laced breeze that left the bay and caressed the peninsula. On this night, the manicured shrubs would hug the nested Burcher mansion one last time—Melissa had decided the time had come for the house with the painful memories to go away forever.

In one day, the mansion would be demolished by the wrecking ball. All structures on the grounds would be crushed and carried away, and the labyrinth of cellars and tunnels beneath the mansion would be filled with dirt and plowed over leaving a barren scar in a field at the end of a gravel driveway to nowhere.

Jack had studied the family archives. At the end he wondered why Otto Burcher carved out the hidden root cellar and secret passages. He also wondered why Otto built such imposing stone walls in the Floridian paradise. Why the massive iron gates that could stop a tank? Over his last days he had to wonder, when did Otto know his secret would trigger the multi-generational extermination of his family? What had Jack missed? Was the diabolical plan the work of just one deranged Japanese activist? Was the serial killer a soldier of the IJRG, or was he something else? How could one man hold the anger and keep the focus, organization, and funding for more than five decades? How was the multi-generational killing spree even possible?

The FBI held a rare and unusual, high-profile news conference on April 4th. They announced the end of the search for Dr. Jack Burcher. They said they possessed *incontrovertible evidence* that confirmed his death—evidence they would not share. Could it be Mamaru Sato had Jack's blood on his hands? Would that alone be enough? Was there really enough to conclude the family nightmare was over? Melissa and Grandma Em—the last two—were safe? And why would Melissa attend an FBI news conference? Why announce her plans, the demolition of the Burcher mansion? It could have been done on the society page. Most did not think a thing of it, but for one her *wrecking-ball* words ignited smoldering coals of hate and desperation.

It was very late. Now, from the shadows of the stone wall, a monster watched the house for an hour. The place appeared abandoned. No cars in the driveway. No lights in the windows. No shadows moved. Only branches lifted and junipers swayed, and cicadas screamed, and fireflies flashed. A foghorn moaned on the bay.

Everyone was accounted for. Jack Burcher was dead.

Insider information confirmed his body had already arrived in Orlando. Moe Bullitt and Paul Shuck were busy, too. They were transporting the corpse of Mamaru Sato to Orlando. They would spend the night and most of the next day observing the impartial, Orange County Medical Examiner conduct two autopsies. His insider information confirmed their plans. The killer had always been a savvy and patient man. This was the night he had to make his move. Time was tight. The window of opportunity was open. He could not have set it up any better himself.

This killer had always had luck on his side. Even Dr. Quin's hands were full. The interim Hillsborough County Chief Medical Examiner had delayed the autopsies of Tate Worthington, David Burcher, and Buford Penland. She was fully engaged in the FBI priority: the methodical dissection of the *Frankenstein creation* found in the root cellar. Quin had already identified six of the seven victims—their selected organs and limbs—and three unidentified victims. So far, the composite-corpse did not include Jack Burcher. The forensic psychologists would fail on their attempt to understand. They had just begun their assessments of the aberrant mental process behind the horrid reconstruction project. What drove such behavior? Was it some odd ritual?

They will never know, the killer thought as he moved across the manicured lawns like a panther in the night. He jumped from shadow to shadow and only stopped long enough to scan his new surroundings for prey. *One can never be too cautious,* he thought. *I certainly don't need Melissa showing up for a last goodbye. Then again if she did it would be the cherry on top—*

Between March 14 and April 5, the Burcher estate crawled with people. *If it wasn't the forensic team it was bumbling Bullitt and slow Shuck or their pushy people pokin' and lookin' for somethin' to explain the carnage. Poor bastards—you had thirty-five years to get it right. Then come the packers and the movers, and little rich-bitch Melissa to decide the future of every bauble, gewgaw, whim-wham, and whatnot. Some, she just had to keep. Most went to Goodwill—you're welcome.* Now the house's empty. Demolition equipment to arrive in the morning. *If not for that, I could have waited a month or even a year.* But now, time is of the essence.

The shed behind the boathouse had a shiny, new padlock, compliments TPD. He would be forced to break into the house to gain access to the root cellar. He could be in and out in no time if all went well. The doors were locked, all but one—the patio. *Thank you, irresponsible person—you know who you are.* He avoided the squeaky floorboards. He knew them well. He eased down the cellar stairs and hid behind them. He always took time to vet his surroundings. Patience is a strength.

They never said how Jack died, he mused. *Did you do it, Mamaru? If you did, you broke two of my rules—timing and order. I should have fixed you in 2003. You were losin' it after Ronan. Got sloppy. Didn't need to kill Mai. I don't care what you were thinkin'. She worked for me, not you. Got to admit, I never thought she'd get into Sun Bay. One smart gal. And I never worried about her talkin'. A devout believer in Seppuku. Hara-kiri. Always carried her kaiken with her. I'm surprised she didn't put that double-edged dagger in your eye. And why leave her body in the dumpster? FBI almost tracked her to your family.*

And Patricia. I told you (Mamaru) Jack was gettin' too close. We agreed, Patricia goes down a day late. Early morning hours, as always—low risk. But you did not adhere to my instructions. Jack almost—

A sound—like a drawer opening—broke the silence. It came from somewhere in the cellar. He froze. *Am I imagining things?* Then another sound. His eyes moved to a cellar window. It was closed. Another juniper limb scratched the glass. He relaxed but would not leave his hiding place until it felt right.

I wouldn't be here if you had left David alone. He was outside the program—all the elites were dead. Supposed to leave the siblings for the next contract. New parameters—

"And your timing could not have been worse," he whispered. "Not on the very day Jack Burcher gets hypnotized." *If he's gonna remember somethin' new from that damn field in 1970, the Feds would be crawlin' all over this place.* "And he did, and they did, Mamaru!" *Worthington gets a bullet in the head. They find a damn rifle that led them to the root cellar. Did you have the idea for a rifle? What the hell could you be thinking?*

"I lost control of you, Mamaru Sato," he muttered. *You've become a wild animal bred to kill on command. Couldn't call you off.* He checked his watch. *Thank God you're dead. I can fix this. I will recover when I get my hands on—*

Another noise. With his chin on the back of a riser, he listened and sniffed the dank basement. *Is that just the wind?*

I bet you tossed him into the bay. That's why they're not talkin' about Jack. I know you, Bullitt. You pulled a bloated corpse outta the water and are runnin' your DNA. Takes a while. Probably doesn't even have a face. Missin' limbs—water and feeders are hell. Autopsy in Orlando may not answer questions on cause of death. They'd know if it was a bullet or knife early. They'd say. Probably not. Sato likes it close and personal—strangle or creative knife work. Nice touch, Mamaru. You did something right.

Another sound. This time he pinpointed origin. It came from behind the stone wall. *Is someone in my root cellar?* He sunk behind the stairs and melded into the shadows. *Unlikely, but possible. Who could it be?* He waited. Nothing. *Maybe a bay rat.*

"I can't wait here all night," he breathed as he left his hiding place.

He knew how to open the secret door without making a sound. Through the inch he saw light, but it was quiet. He pulled more. He could see someone at the table. Back to the door. *You're reading something.*

He pulled out his knife—it would be fast. He must get what he came for, what he had to have. If it meant one more had to die, so be it. He stepped into the root cellar like a spider on a web, his knife ready to slice open another throat. They were very alone.

"You can walk," Jack said without turning.

"I can. And you're not dead," Deron said frozen in his tracks.

Jack turned. Deron slid his knife into the back of his belt. "What are you doing here?"

"Curiosity. What about you?" Deron asked.

"I've been waiting for someone," he said as he turned back to the papers spread on the *kill table.* "I knew someone would not let Melissa tear down this place without one last visit."

Deron eased to the end of the table confident he could cover the five feet in a fraction of a second and put his knife into Jack's throat at any time of his choosing. They were alone. Jack did not like guns—he would not touch one to save his life. Deron knew Jack since childhood. The man could not kill a fly. If he tried, the fly had the advantage.

"Sounds like you know some things," Deron said.

"I do. But I have more questions than—"

"—answers. Of course, you do. Typical forensic guy," Deron leaned against the table and squinted at the strewn papers. Too little light to read the print. *More archives,* he thought.

"Where have you been all this time, Jack? FBI thinks you're dead. Your body is supposed to be in Orlando."

Jack smiled and laid another page onto the table, farther away from Deron. "You know the FBI, Francis. They find a body in the bay and overthink everything before the DNA."

"Okay. I can buy that. But you didn't answer my first question."

Jack pivoted in his chair. "Let's make a deal. I answer your questions. You answer mine. Then you do what you came here to do. And I do what I came here to do."

I guess it doesn't matter, now, Deron thought as he scrutinized the empty root cellar. *I get what I came for and tuck Jack in for a long dirt nap. Let the plow bury him tomorrow. Nice and tidy. Can't miss someone already dead.* "Okay. Me first. Where have you been the last 23 days?"

"On my boat. Pretty much avoiding everyone."

"Your boat?"

"Yes. Been sailing around the bay, Francis. Needed some private think time. I stayed on Bird Island for a while. Then I poked around Gibsonton."

"Why Gibsonton?"

"Come on now. You know I wanted to learn more about Mamaru Sato. He lived in Gibsonton. He kept his old Scout moored in one of those permanent-closure areas, the place people avoid thanks to the Marian Corporation."

"Oh yeah. Right." *What you know, Shuck might know,* Deron thought. *I will keep you talking so I can prepare for damage control with the Feds. You're not leaving here—*

"My turn," Jack said. "Why did you decide to kill Rose? Why didn't you just make some money and let us have her back?"

"You're already going there? Some big assumptions on your

part, Doctor." Deron pulled out his Bowie knife and looked at the razor-sharp blade.

Jack smiled. "It's only you and me, Francis. I know all about you. And I also know I'm at a disadvantage. I did not expect this meeting, not until I read your manifesto. It didn't dawn on me until you were standing behind me that you would not want to lose this document."

Deron leaned closer. His eyes narrowed. "Where did you find it?"

"Don't worry. You're hiding place was undisturbed. The forensic team is good, but they'd have no reason to look for a secret drawer on this, what I call the kill table."

"I see. So, what made *you* look?"

"Something I found at Mr. Sato's residence. The man was good with his hands in more ways than one. He made furniture, when he was not killing a Burcher. I came across a sketch of his. A long table with a hidden drawer. I was reminded of this table. Boom. Found it."

"Is it all there?" Deron squinted at the closest page.

"I don't know. I counted seventeen pages with your dated initials. The last one had your signature—Francis Austin Deron. Is that blood or red ink?"

"Blood, actually," he smirked.

"Can I assume Mamaru Sato worked for you?" Jack asked. "You his boss?"

"You know it." He held up his Bowie. "Don't forget you're at a disadvantage."

"Honestly, I really don't care anymore, Francis. You have been thorough. My family's pretty much gone. Melissa is busy with her life, and hypnosis has made me even more miserable. I'm tired of this life. I'm tired of the relentless pain. I just want to understand it before—"

"—you go. I assume you remembered everything at Bayshore Gardens."

"I remembered a lot. Filled more blanks."

"Dr. Mesmer opened your eyes," Deron said.

"I saw you come out of my basement, Francis."

"July 15, 1970. A kid sitting in a field in the middle of the damn night. Who woulda' thought? If you had been in bed like other kids, you would have had a normal life."

"I watched you carry the box to the end of the driveway. You met Mamaru Sato at the gates. He drove a 1960 Cadillac Coup de Ville. I never saw a car like that before. I thought it was a UFO—a long, gray tube with big fins floating in the night fog."

"I hated that damn car," Deron scoffed. "He never could afford it. Over his head day one. Kept the car to this day. I never knew anyone to buy just one car—damn idiot."

"You met him at the gates that night. Did you cut out my mother's heart, Francis?"

"No. I would not do that. Penland got it from a funeral home. But you know that."

"Why do any of that?"

"Penland got cold feet. He was giving Sato problems. He wanted to back out of his deal. I couldn't let that happen. Up until then I was a silent participant." He lowered the knife. "I should have taken care of the problem myself, right then. But I didn't. I thought I might need that big black man later. Access to the secret root cellar and insider information, the family."

"I guess a fresh heart and a personal note, would take the stopwatch off the case." Jack said. "Would move you guys out of the house."

"I needed a good reason to move the TPD and FBI. We were sitting on top of a problem. I should have gotten rid of Sato and Penland the next day. Mistakes I would pay for later."

"Did Buford work for you?"

"Hell no. He worked for Sato. Penland only wanted money. He didn't figure the rest out until later. A very stupid man. Sato managed the idiot. Sato kept Penland from talking and away from the root cellar—Sato's little workshop. I got involved when Penland started squawking."

"Like I said, I saw you carry the box from our cellar and meet Sato at the gates. You were more than just involved. You were running the whole thing."

"I did. Sato was not reliable. I positioned the box. Had to add to the mystique. Measured everything. I planned ahead. There'd be more boxes. And we planted the oleanders."

"Why oleanders?"

"The IJRG I contracted with required oleanders be associated with each kill. That made them official. They only paid on official kills."

"But still, why oleanders?"

"The official flower of Hiroshima. It was the first flower to bloom after your diabolical breed created and used the atomic bomb to execute 200,000 innocent people."

"Oleanders," Jack breathed. *The connection to the Manhattan Project—Hiroshima.*

"A beautiful and hardy plant. Also, one of the most poisonous on the planet. Leonard Burcher and the Lawtons were poisoned first. Then they were positioned to look like accidents or suicides. Rose, Ronan, and Patricia—oleanders were present, too. Made 'em official kills."

"Did you kill my mother?"

"Yes. Someone had to restart things around here. Leslie Groves died. Sato was new."

"You put three silver stars in her heart. Was that another requirement or ritual?"

"Ritual. The IJRG killed Groves memory many times the

day after he bit the dust. The man had a heart attack. Was a three star lieutenant general. That's why the heart and stars."

So, this is a part of a larger program. "Did you kill my father, too?"

"I did. Edward Teller—stroke. Presidential Medal of Freedom put in Ronan's brain. Mamaru did the surgery. He liked it. What kind of people honor monsters for their creation of the most horrific tool of death on earth—the atomic damn bomb?"

"Who killed Leonard Burcher in 1948?"

"Richard Tolman died before my time. Masako Sato—Mamaru's uncle—did the honors. A pioneer with the IJRG. He is why I recruited Mamaru, a boy with a history of anger. And a boy who needed money. He was teachable. Had no fear. That would work against him later."

"Who did Mamaru kill?"

"The Lawtons and Patricia—Taylor, Conant, and Bethe died. See how it works?"

"No Manhattan Project elite died on March 14. David's death did not fit—"

"—the guidelines of the Sakurakai. Very good, Dr. Jack Burcher."

"That secret society still exists?" Jack probed.

"I don't know. Maybe a permutation. Patricia/Bethe was supposed to be my end game. You, David, and Melissa, and future offspring fell to the next—"

"—monster," Jack fumed.

"I was going to say campaign," Deron chided. "You killed Mamaru. That surprised me. You're so into nonviolence and second chances."

"What makes you think I killed him?" Jack said under his breath.

"A surgical strike. Timing. Don't tell me you're in denial.

It's okay to kill bad people, Jack. You're so screwed up. It only took nine bodies to set you free."

Jack turned back to the table and scattered papers.

"I'm not a bad person," Deron said. "You are not capable of grasping the powerful concept of retribution. When the wrong is great enough, time is no factor. Retribution is honorable and right—an eye for an eye."

"It's not about grasping anything, Francis. Sane people reject your twisted logic."

Deron reached for his knife. "You don't understand why I chose—"

"—to kill my family. You are right." Jack pushed out his chair. Deron adjusted his stance and knife for a strike.

"That feeling you have right now. You want to kill me for what I did to your family. That is retribution, Jack. It is a basic instinct. We all have it. You deny what is natural and right."

"Do you think your mother would be proud of you, Francis *Austin* Deron?"

"Yes. I'm sure she would be proud of me." He grinned from ear to ear.

Jack rested a hand on the table and leaned closer. "Ralph *Austin* Bard, a Chicago financier, served our nation from 1941 to 1944 as the Assistant Secretary of the Navy. Then he served as the Under Secretary in 1945."

Deron's smile melted. His brow dipped and nostrils flared. He squeezed his Bowie knife.

"Ralph Austin Bard wrote the infamous memorandum to the Secretary of War, Henry L. Stimson, in June 1945," Jack bellowed. "His recommendation went to Harry S. Truman. You know all about this, don't you, Francis Austin Deron? It is why we're in this horrid place, now."

Deron did not move. Beads of perspiration grew on his forehead. His lower lip quivered.

"Ralph Austin Bard is the only man in history to formally dissent from the use of the atomic bomb on Hiroshima and Nagasaki. He dissented to the President of the United States."

"So, what," Deron sneered. He raised his knife and pointed the tip of the blade at Jack's face. "You know what you can do with your sanctimonious tone. You can take it with you to your grave and join the rest of your disgusting breed." He took a step closer.

"Your mother was Ralph Austin Bard's only daughter. I bet she worshipped her father, the only Navy officer that got it wrong. The only Navy officer in the United States that did not know how to end World War II and save millions of lives worldwide. Your mother poisoned you, Francis. She poisoned you from birth. No. Not me. It is you who is the demented one. You have been mentally crippled your whole life. No wonder you buy into twisted logic."

"She raised me to reject the tyranny that kills innocent people," Deron breathed.

"No one wanted to use the atomic bomb, Francis. We didn't even want to be in the war. Pearl Harbor brought us in. The Imperial Japanese attacked us. They killed thousands of innocent people. They forced our hand."

"That does not justify the killing of every living creature in two cities!"

"40 million people died in World War I—a four year war. 80 million died in World War II—an eight year war. My math says that is an average of 10 million war deaths a year, Francis. World War II ended five days after the bomb fell on Nagasaki. Yes, 200,000 people did die. But more than 9 million lives a year were saved. Most of the lives saved were Asian. As terrible as war is, bring it to an end with a fraction of the carnage is the only reason the a-bomb was used.

"Still, one cannot justify killing anyone at any time. Not

then and not now. The Burcher family is not at war. We did not participate in any war. Francis, your logic is flawed just like you are flawed. You are opposed to innocent people being killed by monsters, yet you are the monster killing innocent people—my mother, my father, my brother, and my wife."

"Retribution is part of war," Deron huffed. "This war is not over until—"

"You have been brainwashed by your mother. You are blindly committed to the IJRG and cannot see the irony, the insanity. Your live for what you claim to detest...

"You can end this, now."

"I know. I will. It is your turn to die, Jack."

"Not today," Shuck barked. He and Bullitt stepped from the shadows of the tunnel. Deron froze, except for his hand with the knife. It moved behind his back.

"Put the knife down, Frank," Bullitt said. "Come on, now. This is over. Let's talk."

Deron slid the Bowie into his back belt and smiled. He pulled his gun from his back belt and swung it around. He put it to Jack's head. "I always have a backup plan, fellows."

"Don't do this, Frank." Shuck and Bullitt held their guns on Deron. "You don't need to kill anyone tonight. You said yourself the Manhattan Project elites are gone. Your assignment was over with Hans Bethe. Let it be over. You're not getting out of here. You know that."

With his arm around Jack's neck and muzzle pressed to Jack's temple, Deron pulled him from the chair to his feet. They backed from the table. "I will kill your prize Medical Examiner," he said. "You know I've got nothin' left to lose—just like the song says. Why don't you guys do the right thing? Let me leave unencumbered. This will be over only if I get out of here."

"I can't let that happen, Frank." Shuck eased to the far side of the long table. Bullitt moved to opposite side of the room. They had two clean shots.

"You're a smart guy, Frank, you know how this works. We've got you in a crossfire. You can't get out of this alive unless you drop your weapon and raise your hands."

"That whole press conference thing was for me, wasn't it?" Deron asked.

"Yes. It was for you, Frank."

"You wanted me to think this place would be empty tonight. All of you out of town."

"Yes. We did. And it worked didn't it, Frank?"

"Mighty fine police work. Gotta give credit where credits due. Jack Burcher's not dead, you guys are not out of town, and plans to take down this place are just more lies."

"Not lies, Frank. Plans change. Nothing's definite anymore. You know that."

"I'm a cripple. How'd you know I'd come pokin' around?"

"We knew you could walk for some time, Frank. We just didn't know why you kept up with the wheelchair. Then we knew you'd come back here sooner or later. You've never thought that highly of forensic people. I know you thought your secret was safe."

"That's right. Damn nerdy scientist types. No clue how the world works."

"Those nerdy scientist types found your manifesto, Frank. We thought you might want it back before the place got plowed under."

"So, Jack lied to me, too. He didn't find my contract. Your boys found it." Deron backed up to the door in wall to the cellar. He dragged Jack by the neck and pushed the door open with a firm back kick. The two stood in the dark opening. The pitch-black cellar, now the only way to freedom for the real monster. Just one foot away.

"I'm gonna need to go, now," Deron said. "You're right about a few things. I know how this works. I know you won't shoot me. Can't risk hitting Burcher or me pullin' the trigger and blowing his brains out before I drop. And yes, I know you know Jack's gonna die somewhere between here and where I'm going. But a cop can't be thinkin' about a negative reality.

"It's gotta be frustratin' to every police officer. You want to stop me, but you just can't risk speedin' up the death sentence for the helpless hostage. You boys gotta be accountable. I don't." Deron pressed the muzzle to Jack's head and pulled back the hammer. "I'm cocked with a hair trigger," he growled. "There's no way to keep this man from dyin'—" On Deron's last word his eyes widened, and his grin melted away. No one moved.

Deron's arm loosened around Jack's neck. *That's odd,* Jack thought. Then the pressure of the muzzle on his temple lessened. The gun began to slide down his sideburn. *Are you taunting me? You are right—Shuck and Bullitt won't do anything. It's gotta be me.* Jack reached up and moved the tip of the barrel from his head. No resistance. *Why are you letting me? Are you rethinking things?*

It happened in less than a second. Jack grabbed the barrel, pulled the gun out of Deron's limp grip and broke loose. He turned back to counter Deron's reaction, but there was none. He just stood there. His cold eyes locked on Shuck. Jack backed up to the furnace. *This is not over yet. You still have your Bowie—*

Deron moved. He reached for his back. "Don't go for the knife, Frank," Bullitt yelled.

Deron turned his head to Jack. He opened his mouth, but words did not come out. Instead, thick streams of blood ran from his mouth onto his shirt. Deron took one step forward. His eyes rolled into his head and he dropped like a dead tree. When his face slammed on the floor, they could all see the Bowie knife—the handle stuck out of the center of his back.

Melissa's blond hair caught the soft light first. She stood in the opening to the dark cellar. Then the rest of her appeared. Her eyes were wide and face full of terror. Her hands trembled. "I... I wanted to visit before—then I heard—" She gasped for air.

"You're okay, honey," Jack called out to her as he stepped over Deron, his arms outstretched. Melissa's eyes found her big brother. She was swallowed by his embrace.

EIGHTY-NINE DAYS LATER

EPILOGUE

Burcher Estate — July 4, 2005 – 15:00

Again, cars lined the gravel driveway from the iron gates
to the mansion, but this time it was for a good reason.

Cars filled the cut wildflower fields on the Burcher estate.
Invited guests included the Tampa Police, the County Medical
Examiner's Office, the Sheriff's Office, FBI, city first
responders, the Janice/Mesmer Clinic, and Ballast Point
friends and neighbors. Each guest received an embossed
invitation. The festivities would begin at three, fireworks on the
bay at seven. It was the small print that explained the massive
turn out:

*Melissa and I want to thank you for your support of our
family in thoughts, words, and deeds over our most difficult and
challenging times. We sincerely value your friendship and invite
you and your family to be our honored guests this Fourth of July.
We look forward to celebrating the birth of our nation, and the
rebirth of our futures in this wonderful land.*

Sincerely,

Melissa Rose Burcher & Jack Ronan Burcher, M.D.

After a month of therapy, Melissa took full responsibility for the arrangements: circus tents with carnival attractions, a giant Ferris Wheel, bumper cars, pony rides, face painting, a petting zoo, and twenty food trucks—unlimited food and drink compliments of the Burcher family. Melissa even rented the barge anchored a hundred yards off their east banks. It held $200,000 in fireworks ready to light up the skies after sundown. The three-hundred-plus guests enjoyed bands playing country, jazz, and classic rock. Following the fireworks their special guest, Jimmy Buffett, would perform—*Come Monday* and *Margaritaville.*

"Where's the boathouse?" Shuck asked as he walked onto the expanded, covered dock. Closest to the water, at one of the ten tables, sat Jack Burcher, Moe Bullitt, Hugo Novak, and Deborah Quin, all dressed casually and holding drinks. The other nine tables were empty. Two worked the outside bar, on the fringe of the carnival-like festivities.

Jack shook Paul's hand and pointed to the empty chair across from him. "Sit. Enjoy a view of the bay for a change. The boathouse—we decided to get rid of it. Built this thing. I gave in to Melissa and her plans for the place. She's moving back. She has it in her head we will be entertaining more. A place on the water seemed appropriate."

"I've gotta agree," Paul said. A waiter set a vodka gimlet in front of him. "Wow. Nice touch. Thank you." The waiter left. "How'd he know I like vodka—"

"—gimlets? Because I filled out a questionnaire, Paul. The service has pictures of our most valued guests. And they know what you like, provided I know."

"Vodka kept in the freezer?"

"Of course. And fresh-squeezed lime juice and sugar syrup."

"Nice touch." Shuck reached over for Dr. Quin's hand. He nodded at Moe and Hugo. "Good to see you taking a break, Deborah." *You look really great,* he thought. *I guess I never allowed myself to notice before, the relentless nightmare and all.*

"Even medical examiner's celebrate the fourth, Paul." Quin winked.

"This is a big deal," Shuck said. "Place is buzzing. Can anyone get a table out here?"

Jack smiled and sipped his scotch. "Anybody can go anywhere they want, including the house. These people are special, Mr. Shuck. One way or another they were there for me and my family, even when I lost my way. It's time to celebrate *them.*"

"Slight correction, sir," Hugo said over his beer mug. "They are not permitted to journey into the cellar, or the infamous root cellar. Those particularly horrid places are behind locked doors, sir. Like archeologists, we shall be sifting through the dirt and ashes for some time—excavating and analyzing the gory artifacts and remains of—"

"Think that's quite enough, Sir Novak," Jack said. "Let's not spoil the moment, old boy."

"I doubt many will break away from the fun and free food to sit on the dock with two Medical Examiners, the FBI, CSI, and an opprobrious homicide detective," Moe said.

"I would define you more as vituperative, Moe." The table chuckled. "On my way here, I saw the lines—circus tents, a carousel, Ferris Wheel, food trucks, and I do believe horse rides."

"Ponies, Mr. Shuck," Moe said. "For the little people."

"Well then. I shall stay right here. The best seat for the fireworks. I do read my mail."

"It's been a while," Jack said. "I've left you all alone." He held up his glass. The table followed. They touched and sipped. "Paul, has the FBI made progress on the national picture—the IJRG contracts?"

He leaned back in his chair and panned the area. "I can say yes. But first. The IJRG acronym stands for *Imperial Japanese Retribution Guard.*"

"Not Radical Group. That would have been good to know a while back."

"We know of 12 contracts. All were entered into between 1965 and 1969. To date we have identified 81 cold cases connected to the Manhattan Project. We've tracked the money. It's been a slow and arduous process. The money trail ends in the Caymans. We've backtracked through England, Germany, Bolivia, and India to a moving target in the Pacific Rim. We may never find the originating source. They move around a lot."

"What kind of money are we talking about?" Jack asked.

"Estimates around $700 billion over thirty-five years. A significant stealth endeavor."

"Good lord," Bullitt gasped. "I guess crime does pay for some."

"Do we have any idea how the IJRG paid for services rendered?"

Paul lit a cigarette. "Four categories. An official, qualified kill paid $10 million. An associated kill—like Tate Worthington, Mr. Brule', Buford Penland—paid $3 million. Collateral damage—like a man walking a dog in the wrong place—paid nothing. The IJRG also had an unsanctioned-kill category. David's death was rogue. Outside their program. It was not part of the Manhattan Project approved target list. His death resulted in a $5 million penalty."

Another scotch and vodka gimlet arrived at the quiet table. When they were alone again, Shuck leaned in. "Deron held the Tampa contract with the IJRG since 1968."

"How did it work for him?" Jack asked.

"He earned an estimated $49 million. We know he paid Mamaru Sato $100,000 a year. And we now know Sato paid Penland $10,000 a year. A reminder to keep quiet. Mr. Penland was not a Deron expense, according to accounting in the margins of the manifesto, or contract."

"Where did Deron park his money?" Jack asked. "He had $45 million and did not reveal it in Hillsborough County."

"Has substantial property in Tortola—the British Virgin Islands, and Matanzas—Cuba. He has three accounts in the Caymans under aliases: Francis Bard, Marion Bard, and Frank Austin."

"Tell me. Why the Michael Brule' kill?" Moe asked. "Seemed a departure from—"

"Was sending a message to Jack," Paul said. "The blood mark on the friends face. It was noted in a margin of Deron's manifesto. Brule' was classified as an associated kill."

"We just got confirmation on the knife," Moe said. "The Legacy Arms Musso Bowie. Very old. Belonged to the Sato family."

"I'm surprised he left a family heirloom behind," Jack muttered. "Seems sloppy for a sophisticated killer with a long-term mission."

"The Bowie knife belonged to Masako Sato, Mamaru's uncle," Paul said. "We now believe Masako killed Leonard Burcher in 1948."

"And the Belford Box Company that closed in 1985, What's that all about?"

"Purchased by Frank Bard with his fake San Francisco address and fake ID on the closing documents. Frank Bard bought a $300,000 dollar business for $2 million, provided no questions asked. He wanted his own boxes. We all know why."

"We solve a lot of murder cases with packaging," Moe muttered.

"We have not located the prior owners—two guys. They conveniently disappeared. We noticed a new entry in Frank's books. A windfall of $1.9 million. He got his money back."

"Those box people could be a part of our composite-corpse," Quin said. "I still have a few unidentified organs and body parts."

"What do we know so far about the contributors?" Jack asked.

"Are you asking about body parts by donor?" Quin asked.

"Yes. Briefs would be nice. It's okay. I need to know."

"Rose's arms and hands. Ronan's torso, one ear, and one eye. Caroline Lawton's head without eyes or ears or brain. Harold Lawton's eye and ear. Patricia's kidneys and uterus. David's lower legs. The rest, unidentified donors."

"Mamaru Sato worked a lot with his hands," Jack muttered.

"Woodworking," Moe said.

"He made the kill table. His twisted butchering had to be an extension of his hobby. The psychopath could not just dispose of the bodies in the coal furnace. He had to create a trophy, something he could laud over. His great accomplishment."

"There is nothing about a composite-trophy in Deron's manifesto," Paul said. "It does talk about the three silver stars and the Presidential Medal of Freedom."

"I'm sorry, Jack," Quin touched his hand. "I know you want details, but these hurt."

"Thank you, Deborah. I know. I'm okay." Jack smiled and lit a cigarette. The music and the sounds of kids playing flowed from the wildflower fields. "I do wish Mamaru Sato had killed Francis Deron that day in my conference room. Patricia and David might be alive today."

"You don't wish death on anyone," Jack. "Even if you knew, you would have done all you could to save the man's life."

"Maybe. To get him later on my terms," Jack fumed into his glass.

"No, sir, Novak said. "I know you very well. It is precisely what separates us from evil."

"I do think he tried to kill me that day, Jack" Shuck said.

"Mamaru Sato? What makes you say that?"

"I was getting close. I don't believe he was aiming at the medallion. He could care less about that symbol. He wanted me out. Probably Deron's order."

"He missed you and hit Francis."

"Maybe after the first shot he stopped looking and just kept squeezing. Deron had to know about it. He got in the way. Or yes, maybe Sato was gunning for him, too."

"I don't know. They did break into your offices and take the medallion," Moe said.

"And got a look at our classified Burcher files. Deron wanted to know what I was not telling him. The medallion was Sato's thing—eye candy. Probably wanted it for his trophy."

"Hang around its neck," Moe scoffed. *But we never found the thing,* he thought.

"Deron's fake paralysis act made me even more suspicious," Paul said. "Trouble was I could not figure out how or why he would be involved."

"I had my suspicions, too," Jack said. "I thought it odd, when he attempted to remove the *Presidential Medal of Freedom* I had just taken out of my father's brain. Francis tried to treat it as a joke—unacceptable taunting on his watch. He did not want us to give it any of our time. He would have taken it out of the chain-of-evidence if we had not stopped him."

"Maybe he thought Sato was going too far with clues. Deron felt exposed."

"The morning after Patricia was killed, Deron fled from

Jack's hospital room the second he heard we had arrested an Asian man found in the Burcher's boathouse."

"He feared Sato had been caught. Would talk. Give him up," Bullitt said.

Jack took a long drag from a short cigarette. "He seemed paranoid after he got shot."

"Bet he thought Sato tried to kill him," Bullitt said.

"There are dated notations in the margins of the manifesto," Paul said. "The day Deron got out of the hospital an expense moved from $8,300 to $10,000 a month."

"Mamaru got a 20% raise," Moe said. "Buying his loyalty."

The waiter removed empty glasses and delivered fresh drinks as the group sat in silence taking in the magnificent bay.

A gentle summer breeze lifted Jack's hair. "Even after all this, something still feels off," he muttered.

"I wish I could say it's over," Paul said.

"What does that mean?" Moe barked. All heads turned to the FBI Director.

Shit, shit, shit! Why did I say that...? Paul mused looking into his glass.

"Sato's dead," Moe said. "Frank Deron's lyin' in the county morgue. The FBI's got the IJRG international terrorist group on the run. It's gotta be over for the Burcher family."

"What are you saying, Paul?" Jack asked.

"I shouldn't have said anything."

"Well, you did."

"I really don't think we should go there, now. Let's just enjoy the rest of this day."

"Too late, my friend. We are there and after all we've been through you owe us."

"You know anything you say stays here," Bullitt said. "We are family."

"Now, only after you talk can we begin to enjoy the rest of this day," Quinn said.

Shuck rolled his eyes and set down his glass. Moe was right. They were more than partners and victims. They lived everything together.

"Okay. I meant we do not have all the bad guys, yet. That's all."

"Are you saying Melissa is still in danger?"

"I'm saying you all are in danger, Jack. This thing is not over."

"Good start. Keep going."

Paul looked at Quinn, then Bullitt, Novak, and then stopped on Jack. "What I am about to say is extremely confidential. It must stay with the people at this table. Do you all understand?"

Heads nodded. Everyone leaned closer.

"We have been monitoring a thread of encrypted IJRG communications into their Tampa operation. We learned Frank Deron's contract was terminated the day David was killed."

"Released. March 13," Bullitt muttered. Then why—"

"His IJRG contract cancelled, but Deron was not having it. To our surprise, a new IJRG thread into Tampa appeared—a second communication stream. We learned an unknown entity close to the Tampa operation was contracted."

"Deron's successor," Jack muttered. *Jesus. They're relentless...*

"This new thread between the IJRG and the unknown entity came alive minutes after David's time of death, and hours before we found his body."

"A lot happened that day," Moe said. "Patricia Burcher's funeral, Jack's hypnosis in Bayshore Gardens, the Tate Worthington shooting, and the discovery of the secret root cellar filled with all the grisly surprises, and Sato's death—"

"You said two threads the day David died," Jack said.

"One thread itemized Deron's failures, the reasons for his termination: the unauthorized execution of David, Deron's inability to derail your hypnosis session, the high risk execution of Patricia, and Deron's inability to control Mamaru Sato's wild behavior."

"Yes. That's one thread," Bullitt said. "What about the second thread? Tell us more."

"Right. The *new* thread. We only recently deciphered that one."

"It took the FBI from March to July to decipher?" Quin scoffed.

"Yes. Codification changes. They did not want Deron reading the new thread—"

"—because the IJRG planned on eliminating him," Jack said. "It makes perfect sense for them to change things up."

Paul looked around and leaned closer. "The new thread is meant only for Frank Deron's replacement. It talks about a plan to reveal the root cellar by mounting a rifle in the ceiling and setting up motion-detection in the main cellar area."

"They wanted to create an incident so we would tear the place apart."

"And they talked about leaving ajar the secret door into the root cellar. It also talked about their plan to terminate Mamaru Sato on March 14—the new, unknown entity."

"Bastards have been leading us around by our noses," Moe scoffed.

"They knew on March 13 the FBI would hide and wait for the serial killer," Paul said. "They knew once we found the root cellar, we'd have one shot at catchin' the guy we've been hunting for decades. They even talked about leaving one FBI Agent alive on the kill-table."

"To find the bloody manifesto and set the trap for Mr. Deron," Novak said.

"They were giving us Sato and Deron," Jack muttered. "Cleaning house."

"They gave us Sato on March 14—dead," Paul said. "We trapped Deron on April 6, where he met his end—thank you Melissa. We were led to believe the manifesto was important to the IJRG, Deron's only leverage. In retrospect, that was a bad assumption on our part."

"The second thread just deciphered, can you identify origin and destination?" Jack asked.

"Origin, to a degree. It came from the IJRG command center in the Pacific Rim."

"What about destination, the recipient?"

"We track the first thread to Deron's home. The new thread is to Deron's replacement—"

"—the *unknown entity* now targeting us," Jack fumed. "I get it. The new leader of the Tampa operation here to exterminate the rest of my family."

"Or be stopped," Paul said. "I just can't talk about that with you, today."

"I did not kill Mamaru Sato," Jack said. "I know your people think I did. You know me. I didn't kill that man, nor did Francis Deron. It should be clear to everyone Mamaru was killed by the new IJRG Tampa entity. They orchestrated everything after David's termination."

"There are some in the FBI still not on board with that, Jack."

"You know the IJRG wanted that secret root cellar discovered, Paul."

"But why? How would that help the IJRG?"

"They knew under hypnosis I would put my mother's abductors in our cellar both nights in July 1970. The same time the TPD and FBI were crawling all over the place. They knew my hypnotic revelations would send the FBI back to my cellar for yet a closer look."

"They did classify Jack's hypnosis as a Deron failure," Bullitt added.

"You ask why. Well, Deron's replacement turned a failure into an advantage. They made sure we found the root cellar. They set a trap—the rifle and motion detection. I have been in that cellar hundreds of times moving boxes around. That boobytrap was new."

"There are other explanations," Paul said.

"Neither Deron nor Sato would set a trap to keep us out of the root cellar. We never found it in thirty-five years. The new IJRG entity did not want it anymore. They could use it to get rid of Sato and Deron and trophies. It would be the centerpiece of their master plan. If we still could not find the root cellar after the boobytrap, they made sure the secret door in the wall was left ajar."

"What if," Paul said, "they did. Why the root cellar?"

"David's warm body would be there. Sato would return with Melissa. The manifesto is in a drawer of the kill table. It would lure Deron. They created the perfect storm, Paul."

"You know he's right," Moe said. Quin and Novak nodded.

"This new Tampa IJRG entity is smart," Jack said. "Melissa, Grandma Em, and me are just loose ends. Deron's replacement is not messin' around."

"They call Deron's replacement little dragon," Paul muttered swirling ice in his glass.

"Little dragon!" Jack breathed. His heartbeat climb into his throat.

"I got a text a little bit ago. We intercepted another transmission, on the new thread."

"Sounds like *little dragon's* workin' today," Bullitt breathed.

"It was received here," Paul said.

"Are you saying the transmission was accepted on estate grounds?" Jack whispered.

"Yes. I am. Someone here is not your friend, Jack. Don't worry. Our people are here. You won't see 'em. We're monitoring every square inch. Lookin' for the slightest anomalies—"

On Paul's last word, Jack's eyes moved above his shoulder and squinted. Paul watched Jack's face change from confused to something else. Bullitt, Novak, and Quin moved eyes to Paul as he leaned back and sipped his gimlet. They were processing, too.

Paul studied Jack in the eerie silence. It swept over the table. He saw that face before. September 12, 2003. One o'clock PM. Hillsborough County Morgue. Jack just walked into the long conference room to recount the events of the night before—the night Ronan Burcher's brain was delivered to the gates. That day Paul saw Jack's face change the moment his eyes found the attractive stenographer, Kayda Webster.

"Come on old people." Melissa's words rolled off the sprawling lawns onto the new dock like a cold gust of unwanted wind. "You guys can't hide out here all day and drink booze," she teased. Melissa desperately tried to hide her true feelings, those that would follow her the rest of her life. She had killed a man. She stabbed Francis Deron in the back.

"Come on now, ya 'all. We're hostin' a big ole party at the Burcher estate—a first. All the little people want to rub elbows with all the big people," she teased.

The details of Deron's death had not yet been shared with the public. The Tampa Sentinel knew their beloved and retired Chief of Police died the night of April 6 at the Burcher estate. But that was all they knew. The Sentinel learned long ago all information related to the Burcher family mystery flowed slow.

Knowing their Chief Medical Examiner was alive, and knowing the serial killer was dead, gave them plenty to write about for now. Although they dissected Mamaru Sato's life, no one knew the FBI was hunting bigger fish—the IJRG.

Jack's smile followed Kayda and Melissa onto the dock to the table. The two separated. Melissa moved to stand above Paul Shuck. She would face the magnificent bay and her newest family. Kayda took another path. She went around the table to Jack, her back to the bay.

On her way, their eyes met. Kayda's lingered a long second, and then jumped to the sparkling bay—no one would see everything but Jack. *Did the events of the last six months reawaken your nightmare—the loss of your family?* he wondered as his life's pain again washed over him, the horrific deaths of Rose and Ronan, and now Patricia and David. Each loss stabbed his heart each time the memory visited. *Your family was taken from you, too. I cannot begin to comprehend the pain from the day a bomb decimated Hiroshima and stole—*

Jack could not see Kayda's soft smile. And he could not watch her mysterious eyes leave the bay as she eased up behind him. Melissa orchestrated the festive banter. She held captive the hearts and minds of the other four at the table. But Jack could only feel Kayda's hand on his hair. At that moment he felt they were two, alone. But he could not see her big green eyes count the oleanders, on the tables that surrounded them— there were six.

Then Jack felt her gentle touch on the back of his neck— the touch that always sent chills through him and made him forget his pain. *Are we the only ones that share this misery and love? Like so many innocent victims, we have done nothing to anyone except fall in love.*

Jack saw Paul's scrutinizing eyes. *Do you know Kayda*

means little dragon? You are a smart man—Jack smiled. Kayda bent down and kissed the top of his head.

Paul dropped a hand under the table. His glass pressed against his lips. *Is it possible you've emerged from your family nightmare, found a paradise? Or is this just a moment, like the eye of a horrific hurricane determined to kill all in its path?*

Kayda's hand slid under Jack's collar and moved between his shoulder blades. The table talk and laughter grew louder, and the sounds of the Fourth of July festivities bounced across the estate grounds and fell off Ballast Point into the sparkling water of Hillsborough Bay. Paul's eyes studied. He smiled at Kayda. His hand found his gun.

We face an even greater risk together—hunted by all sides. Do we want to do this? Do we want to put our fate in each other's hands? Is our shared innocence strong enough? Jack reached back and squeezed Kayda's knee like the first time saying—*I love you.*

She pressed her fingernails into his back like the first time saying—*I love you more.*

FORENSIC MYSTERY/THRILLER

STEVE BRADSHAW

Forensic Mystery/Thriller Author

Steve Bradshaw draws on his experience as the youngest forensic investigator in Texas history, with over 3,000 unexplained-death investigations, and as an innovative biotech entrepreneur and founder-president/CEO of a leading-edge medical device company.

Now, dedicated to writing his unique brand of forensic mystery/thrillers, Steve takes his audiences into the fascinating worlds of fringe science, modern forensics, and the hunt for real monsters. His novels are available where books are sold in softcovers and eBooks. Several of his novels are now available the in audiobook format—Amazon Audible.

We invite you to stop by Steve's website and join his member/guest family to receive insider information, special offers, and to connect with the author.

Steve Bradshaw travels the country talking and signing books with book clubs, groups, organizations, and companies. To schedule Steve, visit his website and send your request.

Website: stevebradshawBOOKS.com

Email: steve@stevebradshawBOOKS.com

Facebook: facebook.com/steve.bradshaw.9400

Twitter: twitter.com/sbauthor

LinkedIn: Linkedin.com/pub/steve-bradshaw/18/246/660